# The Reluctant Queen

ALSO BY SARAH BETH DURST

*The Queen of Blood*

# The Reluctant Queen

## Book Two of the Queens of Renthia

### Sarah Beth Durst

HARPER Voyager
An Imprint of HarperCollins Publishers

THE RELUCTANT QUEEN. Copyright © 2017 by Sarah Beth Durst. All rights reserved. Printed in the United States of America. No part of this book may be used or reproduced in any manner whatsoever without written permission except in the case of brief quotations embodied in critical articles and reviews. For information, address HarperCollins Publishers, 195 Broadway, New York, NY 10007.

HarperCollins books may be purchased for educational, business, or sales promotional use. For information, please email the Special Markets Department at SPsales@harpercollins.com.

Harper Voyager and design are trademarks of HarperCollins Publishers LLC.

FIRST EDITION

*Designed by Paula Russell Szafranski*
*Map illustration by Ashley P. Halsey*

Library of Congress Cataloging-in-Publication Data

Names: Durst, Sarah Beth, author.
Title: The reluctant queen / Sarah Beth Durst.
Description: First edition. | New York, NY : Harper Voyager, an imprint of
    HarperCollins Publishers, [2017] | Series: The queens of Renthia ; Book 2
Identifiers: LCCN 2016038530| ISBN 9780062413352 (hardcover) | ISBN
    9780062413376 (ebook)
Subjects: | GSAFD: Fantasy fiction.
Classification: LCC PS3604.U7578 R45 2017 | DDC 813/.6—dc23 LC record
    available at https://lccn.loc.gov/2016038530

17 18 19 20 21  LSC  10 9 8 7 6 5 4 3 2 1

For my husband, Adam,
with love
always and forever

Everything has a spirit: the willow tree with leaves that kiss the pond, the stream that feeds the river, the wind that exhales fresh snow . . .

And those spirits want to kill you.

It's the first lesson that every Renthian learns.

At age five, Daleina saw her uncle torn apart by a tree spirit for plucking an apple from his own orchard. At age ten, she witnessed the destruction of her home village by rogue spirits. At age fifteen, she entered the renowned Northeast Academy, and at age nineteen, she was chosen by a champion to train as his candidate. She became heir that same year and was crowned shortly after, Queen Daleina of the Forests of Aratay, the sole survivor of the Coronation Massacre. She'd heard at least a half-dozen songs about her history, each more earsplitting than the last. She particularly hated the shrill ballads about her coronation, a day she wished she could forget. Instead she had it hammered into her skull by a soprano with overly enthusiastic lungs.

Six months after her coronation, now that the funerals—and so many of her friends' graves—weren't so fresh, all of Aratay wanted to celebrate their new queen, and she was swept along with them. For her part, she planned to demonstrate her sovereignty by healing one of the barren patches created during the massacre and replacing it with a new village tree.

*It is*, she thought, *one of the worst ideas I've had in weeks.*

At dawn, Daleina lay awake in bed and wished she'd chosen to celebrate with a parade instead. Parades were nice. Everybody liked parades. Or she could have simply declared today a holiday and sent everyone back to bed. *But no, I had to be dramatic and queenly.*

She wrapped her silk robe around her bare shoulders and walked toward the balcony. She'd chosen chambers within the branches of one of the eastern trees, rather than occupying the former queen's rooms. It felt wrong to sleep in a bed owned by the woman she'd helped kill.

Leaning against the smooth wood of the archway, she peeked out. Her loose hair, with its streaks of red, gold, orange, and brown, fell into her face, and she shoved it back. Outside, the lemon-yellow sunlight poked between the leaves, and the bark glowed warm where the light touched it. She saw hints of sky, pale morning blue, but only when the wind blew hard enough to disturb the canopy of leaves overhead. The trees were thick in this part of the forest, with branches that curled around one another and leaves that blocked most of the sky above and all of the earth below. People were already perched in the branches, camped out early for the best view. Of *her.* Sighing, she retreated. *You knew you'd have an audience,* she told herself. *Stop acting so surprised.*

An amused voice behind her said, "They're no longer calling you the Queen of Blood. Now they call you Queen Daleina the Fearless."

Daleina snorted. "The only fearless people I've ever met were frightfully stupid." Turning, she faced Captain Alet, her devoted guard and friend. Alet always seemed to have an unnatural sense of when Daleina was awake. She'd entered soundlessly and now stood in front of the ornate door. She wore her leather armor and had knives strapped to her arms and legs. Her thick black hair with the white stripe was wound up and pinned in place, and she'd tucked at least two more knives into her curls.

"It's supposed to be a compliment, milady, but if you'd like me to discourage it, I could always stab a few of the worst offenders."

"You're too kind. Bloodthirsty, but kind." Squaring her shoulders, Daleina crossed to her wardrobe. She opened the doors to reveal her celebration dress, a confection of lace that shimmered in the morning light. She touched the fabric lightly. Seventeen seamstresses had worked on it, painstakingly adding hundreds of glass beads so she would look as if she'd been sprayed with sparkling dew. The dress would catch the light even in near darkness. It was far and away the loveliest–and most impractical– thing she'd ever seen.

"You'll have many more songs written about you after today," Alet said.

"Especially if I die."

"Especially then," Alet agreed.

Daleina arched her eyebrows. "You're supposed to say that of course I will succeed. That I'm the finest queen that Aratay has ever seen, the best of the best, the jewel of the forest, the scourge of the spirits that spill our blood, and so forth." All the courtiers were fond of those phrases, and Daleina was certain they were recycling them from when they'd used them for her predecessor, Queen Fara. Daleina knew full well she'd never been the best of the best.

She'd merely been the only one left.

Alet was silent, and then she said, "You can still call it off." Her expression was blank, hiding her thoughts expertly. Daleina had practiced that expression in the mirror, but it never quite worked for her. A twitch of her lips or her eyebrows always gave her away.

"You know I can't."

"You *can*," Alet corrected. "You *won't*."

Daleina studied her friend. Alet had a fresh scar above her eyebrow. It was puckered and red, but whoever had struck her had missed her eye. She'd chosen to wear her war armor today, instead of ceremonial. The leather still had the royal crest, but it was painted gold and green, rather than encrusted with ornaments that could snag on a branch or a weapon. *Why had she*– Suddenly, Daleina understood. "You can't follow me. I must do this alone. That's what's upsetting you."

Alet made a face. "You'll be vulnerable to arrows, spears, any kind of thrown implement. This isn't like the trials, where you're separated from the populace. You'll be exposed to everyone and, while all your people love you deeply, a few of them also want to kill you."

"Human enemies don't concern me," Daleina said. "The spirits will protect me."

"You know you can't trust them."

"In this, I can."

Alet shook her head. The knives in her hair did not move. One stray curl slipped out of its pins to touch her forehead, though. Daleina was surprised Alet allowed even that much out of her control. "The spirits want you dead," Alet said flatly.

"They want to kill me. Slight difference. If they allow a human archer to pierce my heart with his or her arrow, then they're denied the pleasure of skinning me alive." Daleina lifted the beautiful dress out of the wardrobe and carried it to her bed. "Help me change?"

Sighing, Alet left her post by the door and crossed to the bed. "You should call one of the palace caretakers to assist you. This ridiculous dress has at least a thousand buttons."

Daleina slid her robe off her shoulders, and it fell into a puddle of silk at her feet. "It has thirty-seven buttons, and I don't want any caretakers with me today. I want my friend."

She saw a muscle in Alet's cheek twitch, nearly a smile, and Daleina smiled back. She held up her arms, and Alet dropped the dress over Daleina's head. She felt as if she were wrapped in a cloud. The layers of skirts fluttered around her. Presenting her back to Alet, she faced the mirror while Alet buttoned her.

She'd need a touch of powder under her eyes to hide the signs of sleeplessness. She couldn't let anyone suspect that she was at less than her full strength. In that, Queen Fara had been correct: the people didn't want to think they had a weak queen. Perhaps add a bit of pink to her cheeks. She looked pale, sheathed in the shimmering white and gold. "Regal or sickly?" Daleina asked.

Stepping back, Alet surveyed her. "You look ethereal."

Daleina rolled her eyes. She'd never been described as "ethereal" in her life. "Just tell me if I need paint or powder."

"Neither. You're lovely, and the people should see your loveliness."

"You're in the oddest mood today, Alet." Daleina faced the mirror again and frowned. The sight of the queen on her first celebratory appearance should comfort the people and set the correct tone for the rest of the celebration. She shouldn't have allowed the dressmakers to add so many layers of skirt or to leave her arms bare. She felt both exposed and confined. Spinning in a slow circle, she watched herself in the mirror.

Quietly, Alet asked, "Have you blacked out again, Your Majesty, since the last time?"

She halted. Yes, she had, alone in her bath last night. "Not once," she lied. "It must have been a fluke. But Master Hamon will find answers. He has my complete confidence—and six vials of my blood, which should be more than enough to run every test he can think of."

"You could postpone this until—"

"Enough, Alet. If you're trying to shake my confidence, you're doing a very good job of it." Leaving the mirror, Daleina crossed to her jewelry box. She selected a simple necklace, delicate leaves carved out of wood and strung on a ribbon of silk. It had been a gift from her family, after she'd been crowned. Her mother had whittled the leaves, and her sister had woven the ribbon. Coming behind her, Alet took the necklace.

Holding her hair up, Daleina let Alet clasp it around her throat. Alet then took a brush and brushed Daleina's hair until it cascaded smoothly over her shoulders and back. Neither of them spoke, until a bell chimed outside.

"Be strong, milady," Alet said. "Half your chancellors think you're foolish to interact with spirits without an heir ready. But then again, half your chancellors are too afraid to venture beyond their chambers."

"And the other half?"

"Already in the trees, ready to cheer your victory."

Daleina turned to face Alet. "And where will you be?"

Alet's expression didn't alter. "Right here, waiting for you to return."

Embracing her, Daleina pressed her cheek to Alet's cheek. The hilt of one of Alet's knives dug into her ribs, but Daleina ignored it. It felt good to have a friend again, as if the friends she'd lost—Linna, Revi, Mari, Zie, Iondra—were all still with her somehow, carried on by Alet. "If I were sentimental, I'd say you were sent to comfort me."

"If you were sentimental, I wouldn't like you half as much."

Releasing her, Daleina laughed.

"Go," Alet said. "Show them all what it truly means to be queen."

QUEEN DALEINA OF ARATAY SWEPT ONTO THE BALCONY. HIDDEN in her hair were pins to help keep her crown firmly on her head, and hidden in her bodice was Champion Ven's knife to help keep her head firmly on her neck. As she emerged, she heard the cheers from her people, who filled every available branch in all directions. Their voices blended into the wind and blew into her. She felt as if she were breathing in their love, or at least their enthusiasm. Raising one hand, she smiled at them, and they cheered louder.

*Very nice*, she thought. *Now go away.*

Carefully and deliberately, she blocked them out—the sight of them, the sound of them—and she breathed, filling her lungs and then emptying them completely. She narrowed her focus to only that, her breath. Swallowing the wind, she tasted the air, sharp with pine. And then she walked forward, three steps to the lip of the balcony.

Collectively, the crowd fell silent. She felt their silence as a change in the wind, a shift of breath. Grown from the tree itself, the balcony jutted out far above the forest floor. It had no rail, only a delicate braid of living vines to decorate the edge.

*Catch me.* She sent the order flying like an arrow out of her mind and into the world. The moment the words left her, she flinched, even though she'd braced herself. It felt as if a strip of skin had been ripped from her body. Before the coronation, she hadn't had the power to issue a command that broad and expect to be obeyed. She'd had to trick, redirect, and coax the spirits as if they were uncooperative toddlers, but now she was expected to use the power the spirits had given her. She didn't like it, but she wasn't about to let anyone see that.

She stepped onto the air.

The wind shrieked in her ears as she plummeted. She closed her eyes, stretched her arms wide, and focused on the feel of the air slapping her. *Catch me!* She put all the force of her mind into the command, devoid of doubt, of fear, of any emotion. She would be obeyed. *Now!*

Shrieking like the wind, the air spirits whipped around her. Opening her eyes, she saw their faces, translucent with empty eye sockets and pointed teeth. They reached for her with pale multi-jointed fingers, and they caught her dress, each layer spread out until she looked like a glittering cloud.

*Lift me,* she ordered.

She felt their hands on her back, rotating her until she stood upright on the backs of one of them. Rising up, she tilted her face toward the canopy of leaves above and did not think about how close to the forest floor she'd come. The people in the branches were cheering again, and the air spirits snarled and swiped at them.

*Do not hurt them.*

Hissing, the spirits retracted their claws. A few dug their claws into the fabric of her dress, and she felt the tips on her flesh, but they did not pierce her hard enough to bleed.

*Higher.*

The spirits drove her upward, through the branches. Leaves slapped her face. Tiny branches stung her arms. The white lace dress wore flecks of blood between the glass beads, but it still sparkled as she burst through the canopy of leaves into the sky above the forest.

Daleina filled her lungs with the air from above. It tasted as clean and sharp as water from a mountain stream. Few ever breathed this air. Below her lay the forests of Aratay, a vast sea of green that stretched from the true sea in the south to the mountains in the north and to the untamed lands in the west. Soaring, she stretched her hands out and felt the leaves brush against her palms. She felt like a bird, riding free on the wind, until one of the spirits leered at her, its teeth bared and its tongue darting in and out. Glancing down, she checked to be certain she was high enough, and then she changed from a command to a question: *Play?* She sent the question spiraling out across the clouds—and she felt it answered.

Undulating through the clouds, an air spirit flew toward her. It had the sinewy body of an ermine and the wings of a bat. Flying beneath her, it lifted her higher in the sky. *Race?* she asked it. She pictured a map in her head, of the forests from above, and, with her mind, pinpointed the place she wanted to go.

The ermine spirit trilled a challenge to the others. They bugled and chirped their answers, and then the race was on. Daleina wrapped her arms around the spirit's neck, squeezed with her thighs, and held on as it shot forward into the clouds. Droplets pelted her face, and then she burst out above the clouds into the sunlight. Other spirits zoomed alongside them, dipping and soaring between one another.

Slowing, the spirits dove toward an opening in the canopy. She heard their chittering laughter, like the sound of breaking glass, and she suppressed a shudder. Several feet from the bare ground, they halted and released her. She landed in a crouch and then stood.

Out of the corner of her eye, she saw they weren't alone. Seven men and women stood shoulder to shoulder in a semicircle on the edge of the barren patch, but Daleina didn't acknowledge them yet. Instead, she bowed to the air spirits. "You have honored me with the beauty of your world. I thank you."

Momentarily, the air spirits quit snarling. One of them placed its hands together, its long fingers touching one another. She saw specks of red at the tips of its nails and wondered if that was her blood or another's. The spirit bowed to her, and then all the air spirits spiraled together up and up into the circle of blue sky above the grove. She wondered what the masters at the academy would think of her approach and then decided she didn't care, not today.

Straightening, Daleina turned to face the representatives

of the local village. There were four women and three men, all dressed in ceremonial robes. In unison, they bowed low to her. She bit back a shout at them to go home. She didn't want or need an audience for this. The spirits were capricious, and she'd need to summon many for this task. But these women and men knew that and had come anyway. *Spare me from curious fools*, she thought but didn't say. It would be unqueenly behavior to insult the very people she'd come to help. *And I'm the queen.*

She had to keep reminding herself of that.

The eldest hobbled toward her. Her face was sunken in so many wrinkles that her eyes were barely visible. Her lips were cracked and pale, and she licked them before she spoke. "On behalf of all, we thank you."

*Thank me when it's done*, she wanted to say, but again bit her tongue. A queen didn't show doubt or weakness, and this ritual was as much about appearance as it was about results. In a formal voice that carried across the grove, she asked, "Do you have the seed?"

Trembling, the woman held out her hand, fingers curled shut. Daleina waited while the woman turned her fist over and then opened her fingers. An acorn lay on the palm of her hand.

Daleina cupped her own hands, and the woman poured the acorn onto them. "Thank you for this gift." The words of this ritual were simple, even if the action that followed was not. Dropping the formal tone, she pleaded, "Please, would you return to your village? For your own safety." *Go, you trusting fools.*

The woman shook her head. "We will stay, Your Majesty. You will keep us safe."

Daleina tried again. "I can't promise that. You should leave."

But the woman only smiled. "We trust your power. And we trust you." Behind her, all of them bobbed their heads. "You ended the Coronation Massacre."

She wanted to argue more, but she couldn't spare the time or the energy, and she most certainly didn't wish to talk about Coronation Day, a day that had gone from beautiful ritual to nightmare fodder when, rather than choosing whom to crown queen, the spirits had killed all the other heirs—her friends—and nearly killed her. She closed her eyes briefly to blink away that memory, and opened them up to look at the elders.

Pure trust shone from the villagers' eyes, the way babies gaze at their mothers. Telling herself to let their faith fuel her, Daleina knelt, laid the acorn on her lap, and dug her fingers into the soft earth. *Come to me*, she called. She felt the earth shift and rumble, as if it trembled from an earthquake. *Gently, softly, come to me.*

The earth buckled under her, and she saw the men and women topple to their knees. *Idiots*, she thought, and then she didn't spare them another thought. This required all her concentration. *Gently, softly, come to me*, she repeated.

A mud-covered hand burst out of the ground. Moss peeled away as if it were the peel of an orange, and a small manlike creature pulled himself halfway out of the ground. His voice was the crunch of rock, but she didn't understand the words. She guessed he was insulting her. She showed him the acorn. *Prepare the earth*, she told him.

His face stretched into a toothless smile. Several tongues flicked out. She followed his gaze and saw he was ogling the villagers. This was the most critical time: after a spirit was summoned, when its hatred of humans was freshest.

Again, she pushed her will firmly at him: *Dig, now.*

With a scowl, he dove back into the earth. She stood, knees braced, as the ground rolled beneath her like the sea. He and his kin would soften it beneath, prepare it for the roots that would come. Next, she needed tree spirits. Lots of them. *Come*, she called to the trees, the bushes, the grasses, the thorns, the flowers. Stepping back, she dropped the acorn into the hole that the earth spirit had left behind. *Make it grow, tall and strong.*

Laughing, the tree spirits separated themselves from the shadows of the forest. Tall, lithe, and translucent green, they danced through the grove. Flowers flowed from their hair. Moss flourished in their footprints. Daleina spread her arms wide, welcoming them. She pushed her mind toward them, sharing an image of the acorn, sprouting. The spirits flowed to her, pressed close, and then swirled around the hole.

*Yes! That's right!*

Her vision split, and she saw through their eyes as they poured their energy into the acorn. The nut split open, and a tendril of green burst from its brown shell. It unfurled. Still laughing, the tree spirits danced faster, a whirl around her. She felt the sprout thicken and grow. More leaves poked out of it, and she felt as if the leaves were poking out of her flesh. Below, the earth spirit softened the soil, and the acorn's roots shot through the ground, thickening and hardening. The tree shot toward the sky, higher and higher, growing thicker and thicker. Branches stabbed out from it.

*Shape it*, she ordered the spirits. She pictured the trunk opening wide to form houses within. The branches were to be stairs, rooms were to be formed and shaped as if carved out of the soft inner wood. She pressed this image out toward the spirits, and they howled—they wanted the tree to be wild and free; she wanted it to be a new home for the villagers who lived on the forest floor, a safe home, above the dangers of the wolves and bears and countless creatures who hunted at night.

She pressed harder and harder, bearing down on the spirits, filling their minds, and they in turn forced the tree to grow in the shape she pictured. *Grow higher, wider, like this . . .* She added more rooms and more. This tree would house many. Above, the branches spread into a canopy, blotting out the sun.

And then, without warning, her mind went dark.

Sightless, she heard the spirits shrieking and then heard the men and women screaming—for her, for themselves—as she toppled onto the churned dirt.

## CHAPTER 2

She woke to blood: on the dirt, on the trees, on her skin. It even seemed to stain the sky, until her mind woke enough to realize that she was seeing her white skirts, billowing in the wind, not the clouds overhead. Around her, she heard shrieking, shrill, mixed with laughter that was as wild as a tornado. The spirits were creating the wind as they swirled through the grove.

Suddenly, pain shot through her leg, sharp and fast, and she screamed, loud and high. Jerking forward, she clutched at her thigh, and a tree spirit skittered away from her on all fours. Leering, it wiped her blood from its mouth.

"No!" she shouted. "Stop!"

There was blood, as if it had been flung from a bucket, in every direction. Her mind took an extra second to understand what she was seeing: the spirits had torn the men and women to pieces and thrown their body parts around the grove. That, there—it wasn't a root; it was a leg. And that was a torso, cracked open like a shellfish and then shredded. Daleina balled up every bit of her mind that wasn't screaming and threw it at the spirits. *Stop! I am your queen, and I command you, stop now!*

All stilled.

The spirits hung in the air. All of them stared at her with their blank, translucent eyes. One held the head of a woman. Blood pooled on the ground below and sank into the moss, staining it a deep russet red.

*You will obey me.*

One of them laughed, shrill, and then fell instantly silent as Daleina, forcing away the pain, pushed herself up to sitting and then slowly stood. She felt the blood run down her leg, warm and wet, and her knees shook. But she stayed upright. She reached with her mind toward the one who had laughed.

*Burn*, she commanded.

It twisted and writhed, screamed and cried, but she held her order firmly in her mind. The spirit began to fade, growing more and more faint, and she knew elsewhere in the forest, a great tree burned, wreathed in fire spirits. She'd learned this since she'd become queen: kill a wood spirit and a tree dies, but kill the right tree and a spirit dies. Reaching farther, she called to the water spirits.

*Do not let the fire spread*, she told them.

She watched the fading tree spirit. It continued to contort itself, its face now more childlike. It wept tears of polished amber. In only seconds, the spirit vanished, and all that remained was a pile of yellow jewels.

Across the forest, the fire died with the tree. Daleina half felt and half saw the water spirits douse the embers, seeing it distorted through their eyes. At last, the ashes were cold, and the spirits danced as if oblivious to the death of their kin.

She turned then to the others, who held themselves still and silent.

*Build.*

She felt their relief and joy as they flew up toward the branches and wanted to rip that feeling from them. . . . *No, I can't hurt them.* Clamping down on her feelings, she let the spirits build, and the tree began to grow again, shaped into the village she had planned. She pivoted slowly, painfully, to face the bodies of the villagers who had come to watch.

They were all dead.

Except no, the old woman still breathed. She lay on the ground, unmarked except for a dark wet patch on her stomach. Daleina took a step toward her, and her leg crumpled under her. Gritting her teeth, she crawled the rest of the way. She lay beside the old woman.

The woman opened her tiny eyes.

"I'm sorry," Daleina said. *It's my fault. They're dead, and it's my fault. I was supposed to protect them. They trusted me, and I failed....*

"Kill me," the woman whispered.

"I'll fetch healers..." She should have told Hamon to meet her here, or at least let Bayn join her. The wolf could have held some of the spirits off, or also been killed. *I should have made them leave. I shouldn't have come at all.*

"Won't heal." The woman moved her gnarled hand to shift the fabric of her shirt. The wound was through her stomach, her organs pierced. A fatal wound. She'd die slowly, painfully, inevitably, poisoned from within.

"I can't kill you," Daleina said, unable to take her eyes off the wound.

The woman made a sound that could have been a laugh or a cough. "You already have, Your Majesty. Show me the queen's mercy." Each word was a forced whisper.

Daleina held her gaze for a long moment, until the old woman closed her eyes. "I'm sorry," Daleina said again, but she knew the words weren't enough to make this right, and she didn't deserve forgiveness. *Another massacre, and this time it's all my fault.* Sorrow, guilt, hate, rage ... all of those emotions rose into Daleina's throat, and she forced them down into a tight knot deep inside.

Drawing Ven's knife from her bodice, Daleina pressed it to the woman's throat. With one quick hard stroke, she severed her jugular. Bright arterial blood sprayed onto Daleina, covering her hand and arm.

She turned her head to look at the tree spirits. They'd done her bidding, built the tree village as tall and strong as she might have wished.

*Go,* she told them.

They fled into the forest.

She wanted to call them back, cause them all to burn, but she knew she shouldn't. If she destroyed every spirit for following its own nature, she'd destroy her home. The spirits were tied to the land, and the land to them. She could not have one without the other. Revenge against the spirits was pointless; it would hurt the land and not bring these people back. But it was so very, very difficult to hold that truth in her mind.

She pushed her thoughts toward the earth, summoning the earth spirits. *Bury them.* Obeying, the earth spirits widened the ground beneath the torn bodies of the villagers. She made herself watch, to feel the responsibility for these deaths, as the ground closed over them. When they finished, she sent the earth spirits back into the ground and called the spirits of water and air, together.

At her command, rain fell on what was once an open grove and was now a shaded grave. The blood ran into streams and into the earth, washed away. She let the rain fall on her, soaking through her bloody dress, washing her own wound. Pain throbbed in her leg. But she ignored it until the rain had done its work.

When the spirits were again gone, she tore one of the layers of her skirt and bound her thigh tightly. The tree spirit had merely begun to feast on her flesh. It hadn't sliced deeper, and for that, she was grateful. Still, she felt weak and dizzy, though she didn't know if that was from blood loss, shock, or whatever had caused her to black out so completely that her commands were broken.

*This shouldn't have happened,* she thought. She'd been crowned; the spirits shouldn't have been able to revert to wildness, even with her unconscious. This wasn't the way it worked. Revi, Linna, Zie . . . they'd lost their lives, but she'd been crowned and that should have kept everyone else safe. The deaths should have ended on that day. *I'd promised myself: no more innocents will die.* Six months into her reign, she'd broken her promise.

She looked around the former grove. At least when the other villagers came, they would not find their new home stained with blood. They could begin anew here. Minus their loved ones. Hobbling to the tree, she took out her knife again and carved seven lines, one for each death, so that the villagers would know their kin's fate.

Keeping a tight rein on her emotions, Daleina summoned the air spirits. *Carry me home.* They lifted her into the air and flew her fast over the top of the green. She focused on the horizon ahead, determined to not lose consciousness again. When they burst through the canopy, she heard the cheers of the people in the trees . . . only to hear the cheers die as they saw her, her dress limp and pink with the watery blood.

The air spirits delivered her to her balcony. She forced herself to stand, and she released the spirits. Spiraling upward, they fled. Leaves and branches shook in their wake.

Queen Daleina looked out at the trees, at her people. She pitched her voice so it would carry. "Seven are dead. But the tree is grown, and the village will thrive. It is done." She then pivoted and walked into her chambers without waiting to hear their response.

Out of sight of the crowd, she fell as her leg gave out. She was caught by familiar arms, and this time, when darkness came, she welcomed it.

WHEN SHE OPENED HER EYES, THERE WAS NO BLOOD. THERE were no bodies. Only Alet, who sat on one side of her, and Hamon, who sat on the other in his blue Royal Healer robes—he must have been summoned when she collapsed in her room. Daleina lay in her own bed, swaddled in silken sheets and nestled among many pillows. Her wound was dressed in bandages, and she wore a nightgown. She wished she hadn't woken up, at least not yet, so she wouldn't have to remember why she lay there. It was too late now, though. Her leg throbbed, but her head was clear.

"Your Majesty?" Alet asked, a dozen questions in her voice.

Not ready to speak yet, Daleina gazed up at the colorful lace canopy above her, intricately embroidered with images of the forest at peace: deer drinking from a stream, bluebells blossoming between the trees, leaves dancing in the wind, and she wanted to tear the canopy apart. *It lies. The forest is never at peace.*

"Tell us what happened, Your Majesty," Hamon said, his voice deep and soothing. He'd practiced that voice, she knew. She also knew he wasn't as calm as he sounded. He didn't possess Alet's skill at looking expressionless. He always felt things so deeply that it bubbled up and overflowed—it helped make him such a great healer. Besides, Daleina had known him since she was a candidate. She knew his face better than she knew her own—his spring-green eyes, his midnight-black skin, his sharp chin, his soft mouth, and now the crease in his forehead between his eyebrows that said he was worried. Fleetingly, she wondered if he missed kissing her with those soft lips, and then she pushed that thought to the back of her mind, lumping it with all the guilt and anger and regret that she couldn't afford to feel right now.

"You already know," Daleina told him. Her voice came out as a croak. Alet pressed a cup of water into her hands, and with Hamon and Alet's help, she was propped up on pillows. She drank and then tried to speak again. "The world went dark, and I lost control of the spirits."

"They could have killed you," Hamon said flatly, and Daleina knew he was fighting back more than worry. There was fear in his eyes. For her? For their people? Both? He'd seen her bloody before. He'd been with her during her training, sewed her skin back together more than once, stanched her wounds, nursed her damaged eyes until they healed.

"Why didn't they?" Alet asked.

Daleina saw Hamon shoot her a dark look. But it was a valid question. "I don't know." The spirits might not think like humans, but they *did* think. Killing the queen would have set them all free, and the bloodbath would have spread beyond the grove to the entire forest. That was what the spirits had tried to achieve after the last queen had died, on Coronation Day, when they'd murdered all the other heirs. "Maybe they didn't kill me because I wasn't running away. Or they wanted to save me for dessert." Or maybe they didn't want to destroy Aratay. As much as the spirits hated having a queen, they needed one to keep them in balance. To keep them from tearing Aratay apart in their bloodlust.

"But if they'd killed you without an heir . . ." Alet began.

"I know," Daleina cut her off. She knew better than anyone. Closing her eyes, she wished she could stop picturing the blood on the moss and on the spirits' teeth. She wished she could stop seeing the broken bodies from Coronation Day, her friends with the light gone from their eyes and the breath ripped from their lungs.

SARAH BETH DURST

"You shouldn't have taken the risk," Alet insisted.

"I had to. I had to buy time." She opened her eyes, wishing she could will them to understand, the way she could force her will on the spirits.

Alet was scowling. "Time for what?"

"Time to cure me." Daleina touched Alet's arm, knowing she didn't want to hear this, but it was pointless to hide it anymore, at least from her. The blackouts had started three weeks earlier and were becoming more frequent. "It's getting worse, Alet. The blackouts. I can't predict them. I can't control them. More will die if this sickness . . . or whatever is wrong with me . . . isn't stopped. I had to make a grand gesture while I still could." Shifting on her pillows, she fixed her gaze on Hamon. "You've had my blood for days now. Tell me what you have discovered."

Hamon shifted his eyes toward Alet, as if he wanted to ask her to leave.

Daleina felt her insides clench. *It's bad. I know it.* He wouldn't hesitate if it wasn't serious. She imagined building a wall around her heart. *Whatever the news, it won't break me.*

"You should rest first," Hamon said, "and then we'll talk."

Alet's fingers curled around Daleina's hand, but Daleina shook her away and straightened, sitting upright against the gold headboard. She would be strong on her own. "Don't worry about Alet, Hamon. Tell me. This is not a request."

He took Daleina's other hand and held it tight, so she would not pull away. "I have run every test twice. Some even more. Every answer has been the same. I'd run them a dozen more, if I thought it would change, if there was a shred of doubt—"

"Quit dithering, Hamon," Daleina cut him off. Her heart felt as if it were beating doubly loud, and she thought she heard a roaring in her ears. Placing her other hand on his, she pried his fingers off of hers. She laid both hands freely, calmly on her lap. She wouldn't let Hamon or Alet see what she felt. "I'm dying, aren't I?"

"No!" Alet wailed.

"Stop it, Alet," Daleina said, calm. "Hysterics won't help. And it isn't your style anyway. You're a fighter."

Kneeling on the side of the bed, Alet pledged, "Then I will fight this—"

"It can't be fought, not with knives or words or any tool or herb or potion known," Hamon said wearily. "You have the False Death."

Daleina nodded, as if she had expected it all along. Inside, she felt as if she were crumbling, but outwardly, she merely clasped her hands tightly together. It *did* explain what had happened in the grove. "That's why the spirits broke my command. And that's why they didn't kill me. They thought I was already dead."

"You *were* dead," he said. "For a moment."

That's what the False Death was: moments that mimicked death, gradually leading to a true death. Daleina swallowed, but her throat felt dry. "How long do I have?" She was surprised that her voice sounded so steady.

He reached out as if to take her hand again, and then stopped. "I have an herb, glory vine, that will help slow the symptoms. In the meantime, I will search for a cure. Simply because one doesn't exist yet doesn't mean—"

"How *long*, Hamon?"

He sighed. "Three months. Maybe more, but maybe less. And the false deaths will become more frequent and last for longer as time passes."

"Can we predict them, the false deaths?" If she could predict them, she could avoid the spirits at those times and avoid disasters like what happened at the new village tree. As long as no spirits witnessed her collapse and as long as she wasn't actively connected to any of them . . .

He shook his head. "In most cases, no. But there is evidence that suggests that using power may trigger a false death—that is most likely what happened to you earlier. You should resist commanding the spirits as much as possible."

She could do that, couldn't she?

"But even if you avoid using your power entirely, that will only slow the disease. The false deaths will still come, and eventually . . ." He didn't finish his sentence. He didn't have to.

Daleina saw the grief in his face and in Alet's. She looked up at the lace canopy instead of into their eyes. She wanted to rage and cry and scream, shout that he had to be wrong, that this couldn't be happening, that it wasn't true. But she didn't, and she couldn't. Not yet. *Hold it together. You're a queen. Behave like one.* "Summon my champions."

"Now?" Alet said.

At the same time, Hamon said, "You should rest—"

"Call them quickly and quietly," Daleina ordered. "Do not alarm anyone in the palace." She fixed her gaze first on one, then the other. "We cannot afford a panic. Do you understand? What I have to tell the champions is for their ears alone. Alet, gather them now, as many as you can, and brook no argument. Hamon, fetch me a painkiller, one that will allow me to walk to the champions' chamber without anyone suspecting my wounds. I must be seen as strong, for as long as that is possible." She held out her arm so that he could help her stand. She swung her legs out of bed and placed both feet on the floor—pain swept through her body, and she hissed. She forced herself to breathe evenly and straighten. *I will not panic*, she thought. *I will not break.*

"What will you tell the champions, Your Majesty?" Alet asked.

"The truth," Daleina said, her voice steady, even though she felt like screaming inside. "That they must find me an heir before I die."

## CHAPTER 3

C arved into the top of the palace tree, the Chamber of the Queen's Champions was known far and wide as a marvel. It was said to have been created by one hundred tree spirits, working together under the command of a long-ago queen, in a mere instant. It was enclosed by arches of curled wood—living wood with leaves that whispered together when the wind blew. Sunlight poured into the center of the chamber, illuminating the queen's throne in a perfect star pattern. The champions' chairs circled it, each chair alive, budded from the tree. Higher than the surrounding trees, the only way to reach the chamber without using spirits was to climb the stairs that spiraled up from the palace on the outside of the tree's vast trunk.

It was indisputably impressive, but today Queen Daleina hated it. She also hated the nameless long-ago queen who'd thought it was a grand idea to construct so many stairs.

Hitching her skirt up, she climbed higher. *Halfway there.* She could summon an air spirit to fly her to the top, but if she blacked out . . . Eyes were watching her, from the branches, both human and spirit. Chin held high, she kept her expression blank and continued step after painful step.

*Of course, if I black out from the pain walking these stairs . . .*

Hamon had offered to walk with her. Alet had insisted. Daleina had overridden them both. She also hadn't taken the painkiller, not yet. She hadn't wanted it to dull her mind. She'd need her wits to face the champions. Not all of them were fond of her—seeing her as queen was a constant reminder that their chosen candidates had died. She wondered how many would be secretly glad she was dying, and then she banished the thought as quickly as it bloomed. *It doesn't matter what they feel; it only matters what they do.*

As for what she felt . . . that didn't matter either. She couldn't allow herself to feel. She must be as heartless as the stone, as unfeeling as the lake, and as steady as the tree. In that, the pain helped. She couldn't dwell on her emotions when she had to focus on not yelling out curses like a forest-floor woodsman with every step.

By the time she reached the champions' chamber, sweat ran in a trickle down her spine and her cheeks felt flushed. Leg throbbing, she sank into the wooden throne. She allowed herself one moment to breathe, and then she straightened her back, blanked her face, clasped her hands on her lap, and waited.

One by one, her champions came.

Sevrin, from the northern forests, his beard black and eyes blacker, with an ax strapped to his back and a sword at his side. He'd been champion to Berra, an heir that Daleina had met only once before she'd died.

Piriandra, from the east near the mountains, her face scarred from a fight with wood spirits—a fight she'd won, despite her own lack of magic. The tales said she'd fought them with bare hands, sharp stones, and a clever mind. But all her strength hadn't helped when her candidate, Linna, one of Daleina's dearest friends, was in the coronation grove.

Havtru, from one of the outer villages, who had been a berry picker until his wife was killed by an earth spirit. He was new to their number, but not new to loss.

Ambir. Tilden. Gura. And more, until the chamber was full of warriors. Many of them reminding Daleina of her lost friends. She noted that several chairs were empty, though. One of the missing champions had been wounded in a skirmish with bandits by the Semoian border. Three others were too far away to be summoned, absorbed in training their new candidates out in the forest—word would have to be sent to them. The last ... As she wondered where he was, the final champion walked into the chamber: Ven, her champion, the one who had chosen her as his candidate, the one who had believed in her and trained her and never once failed her, even after she quit believing in herself. Looking at him, she felt a lump in her throat. Her news would hit him hardest of all. They'd survived so much, to lose now to an unfightable illness ...

*No*, she commanded herself. She would not crumble in self-pity. She would do what had to be done, as she always did, as queens of Renthia always did.

Still, Daleina watched him as he crossed the chamber floor, his boots silent on the wood. He wore hunter's green and brown, designed to blend into the trees, and he had a bow and arrow slung across his back, as well as a sword at his waist. She remembered when she'd first seen him, when she was ten. He'd leapt from branch to branch, like a hero from a tale, trying to save her doomed village.

Laying his bow and quiver against the side of his chair, Ven sat. He stretched his legs in front of him and crossed his feet at his ankles. He didn't so much as glance at the other champions; he looked only at her. She wondered what he read in her face: sorrow in her eyes, or regret, or anger, or if she merely looked tired? *I wish I could shield him from this.* He regarded her steadily, his pale blue eyes unwavering. When she'd told Alet to summon the champions, when she'd climbed up here to share the news, she knew this was going to be tough.

But she hadn't thought about how difficult it would be to tell this to *him*.

"Your Majesty, what does the Crown require of us?" Piriandra asked. Her voice was clipped, as if she didn't want to waste the time it took to say the words. Champion Piriandra, she knew, was one who had never forgiven her for becoming queen. She'd rejected Daleina on her search for a candidate, labeling her not good enough, and had believed Linna would be a better queen. It would be easier to take if Daleina hadn't agreed with her—Linna should have been queen, or Iondra or Zie or *any* of them. Anyone but Daleina.

Belatedly, Daleina realized the champions had been waiting patiently for her to speak while she'd been lost in thought. She felt herself start to blush and struggled to keep her expression under control. She was queen, for as long as she lived. She must look and act it, even when she felt like a schoolgirl playing dress-up in stolen clothes. "Word of what I am about to say must not leave this chamber. I will have your pledge on this. Unless the need outweighs the cost, you must be silent. I trust you to weigh that need appropriately."

She heard shifting as the champions straightened in their chairs. She had their attention, certainly. Queen Daleina fixed her gaze on each of them, deliberately silent now, to let the weight of her seriousness fall onto each of them.

"Have you taken precautions?" Ven asked.

Her gaze shifted to him. It was a teacher's question, and she had been an excellent student. "Of course," she said. There were no spirits anywhere near the chamber. She was certain of it. They were in the trees below, out of hearing—she'd always been good at sensing spirits, even before she had the power of a queen. She could sense them without commanding them, without risking triggering another false death. She also knew Alet was positioned at the base of the stairs, to prevent any human listeners from creeping too close.

He nodded approval.

It was amazing how much that gave her strength. She still would do anything for that approval. He had been harder on her than any teacher she'd ever had in her training school, testing her daily, forcing her to fend off spirits while she ate, slept, and traveled. He'd trained her body and mind. *I'm sorry, Ven.* She owed him better than this. She was supposed to have a long reign, to keep their people safe for decades. She felt as if she was betraying him.

His lips shifted into a frown, and she knew he'd seen something in her face that he didn't like, something she'd not meant to show. Her hands trembled. She'd faced hordes of spirits, controlled the wills of hundreds, but controlling herself in this room was harder.

As she fought to stay strong and calm, Ven stood and crossed to her. He knelt in front of her throne and took her hands in his. His scarred, strong hands engulfed hers, hiding her trembling. Whereas Hamon and Alet's touch was full of pity, his gave her strength. "You have orders for us, milady," he said. "We will obey. We are yours to command."

Following his lead, all of the other champions—some quickly and some slowly—rose from their chairs and then knelt. Thanks to Ven's melodrama, he had effectively communicated that this was no ordinary meeting and reminded them she was queen, not a candidate or an heir, while at the same time distracting them from her discomfort. She owed him thanks, yet again.

Raising her voice so all the champions could hear, Queen Daleina said, "Your orders are this and only this: find me an heir."

She saw them exchange glances.

"Your Majesty." Sevrin spoke, his voice smooth and urbane as always. "Many of us have chosen candidates already. Indeed, we began our searches the day after the massacre. But cultivating a suitable candidate takes time, and given the severity of—"

Daleina shook her head. "Ready an heir. Not in your own time. In mine. You have three months."

Ven's hands tightened on hers as the other champions broke into talking, overlapping one another so they sounded like birds startled from their roosts. She waited, letting the words tumble out of them, until she heard them repeating themselves. She stared into Ven's water-pale eyes and let them soothe her, like looking across the tops of the trees, Aratay's green sea.

At last, the champions fell silent.

"I have the False Death," Queen Daleina said. Saying it out loud hurt, each word like a hammer in her heart. The words tasted like poison in her mouth, and for the first time, it felt real. She did not let her expression change.

The silence deepened.

Releasing her, Ven stood.

She looked up at him. The sun was behind him, and his face was in shadows. "You must train your heirs before three months end," she told him.

"Impossible!" Sevrin said. Others cried out, echoing him.

"There is no doubt," Daleina said, eyes on Ven. "I have experienced the blackness multiple times now. My blood has been tested. The diagnosis is certain." His jaw was clenched, and she saw the muscles in his cheek twitch. His entire body was tense, as if he wanted to punch something or someone. It was, she thought, an entirely appropriate response. If she could punch this sickness out of her body, she would. "Champion Ven, take your seat."

He obeyed.

One of the champions, Ambir, had tears rolling down his weathered cheeks. He was the eldest of them, and Daleina knew he'd hoped to retire before ever facing another trial. He'd lost his candidate, Mari, in Greytree, and it had broken his spirit as thoroughly as the spirits had broken Mari's bones. Across the chamber, Champion Piriandra was tossing one of her knives from hand to hand, a nervous habit.

"My healer is working on a cure," Daleina said. As the champions began to speak, she held up one hand to silence them. "But as there is none known yet, we must proceed as if he will fail. If you do not already have a candidate, you must choose one as quickly as possible. If you do have a candidate, you must accelerate their lessons. All of you will present your choices to me in two weeks' time. That's fourteen days, understood? Once I have approved your candidates, you will have one month to train them, and then we will begin the trials to determine which of them have the skills to be an heir." Standard was: training first, then an audience with her, but this reversal would push them faster.

Another champion, Havtru, spoke. "You said three months."

"I will weaken sooner than that," she pointed out. "It would be a shame if I weakened too much to help your candidates because of your slowness."

"There are no candidates advanced enough," Sevrin objected. "One month is impossible!"

Daleina and her friends had had only a few months to train

with their champions when Queen Fara had called for the trials. Of course, they had all had years in the academy first. She suspected most of the new candidates had far less experience. But what choice did any of them have? "This is the time we have. It is what *I* have. Consider yourself lucky to have any warning at all." She felt herself growing angry. *Good. Be angry.* Anger would fuel her. She seized the emotion and rose to her feet, pushing aside the pain in her leg. "My champions, Aratay needs you, and I am calling on you to answer that need. You have proven yourself before. You must do so again. For if you fail, all our people fail with you."

Ven leaned forward. "We will not fail you, my queen."

Sevrin began, "But we must discuss—"

Daleina cut him off. "The discussion is over. There is nothing more to say. Your queen is dying without an heir. It is your sworn duty to ready an heir. You must do it quickly. I strongly suggest you begin now."

Ven was on his feet instantly, as were the other champions. As one, they bowed and stayed bowed as Queen Daleina swept past them toward the stairs. She did not look back. Keeping her chin high and back straight, she walked down, her hand on the trunk. The bark scraped her fingertips. Pain from her leg radiated through her body, and her head began to throb. *Keep walking. Don't collapse. You can do this.*

Where the stairs curved into the heart of the palace, Alet waited for her. Coming inside, out of the sight of the watchers, Daleina leaned on her friend. Drawing out a handkerchief, Alet wiped away the sweat from the queen's forehead. "How did they take the news, Your Majesty?"

"Not as heroically as one might hope." Daleina looked back at the stairs, which wound around the tree, out of sight, as if it were swallowed by the green. "They're afraid."

"But they'll find you an heir?" Alet asked.

She heard the hope in Alet's voice, but she didn't have the strength left to lie. "They'll try."

AFTER SHE REACHED THE PRIVACY OF HER CHAMBERS, QUEEN Daleina peeled the bandages away from her leg. The wound had reopened, and blood had soaked the gauze. She'd need to re-dress it. But first, she had to rest, only for a moment. Leaning back, she closed her eyes and breathed in and out, trying to keep her mind clear and calm.

She heard a hiss.

Opening her eyes, she saw a wood spirit perched on the back of a chair.

"I didn't summon you," Daleina said. Its eyes were bright, as if the sun reflected off the sunken eye sockets, but it was entirely in the shade. She could see the shape of her wardrobe through the spirit's translucent body.

This spirit was small and gnarled, with arms and legs that looked like twigs. It was covered in leaves, as if that were its fur. Daleina thought it could be a child, but that didn't make her trust it.

It pointed one twig-like finger at the blood on her leg.

"Have you come to watch me bleed?" she asked, keeping her voice even, calm.

It giggled, a shrill sound like wind through a narrow hole. She hadn't had a spirit visit her chambers before. Usually they kept their distance, afraid of being compelled to obey another order. "I have come to watch you die," it said.

The words felt like claws in her skin. It was rare that the spirits spoke directly to her, especially uninvited. For an instant, it was hard to breathe. She wanted to send it away—force it away—but she didn't dare use her power. "How do you know?"

"Whispers through the woods."

She nodded. She should have expected as much. The spirits could communicate with one another the same way she could communicate with them. She'd been lucky that she'd woken in the grove before word of her supposed death had spread any farther. "I will not let you hurt my people," she informed the spirit.

Suddenly, the tree spirit was beside her, so fast that she hadn't seen it move. It smelled like rotting wood, split apart in the rain. It smiled with its sharklike teeth, and it stroked her cheek with one finger, lightly, even tenderly. "We will not hurt them . . . while you live."

"And when I die?" She didn't mean to ask the question. She knew the answer. But it came out of her all the same.

The wood spirit didn't answer. It only laughed again, and then it sprinted for the window and was outside the same instant a knock sounded on her chamber door. She stared at the open window, at the green outside.

Another knock.

Reaching for a blanket, she tossed it over her leg, hiding the wound. She winced as the fabric touched her. "Captain Alet, who is it?"

"Healer Hamon is here to see you." It was another guard who answered, not Captain Alet. She recognized his voice, though couldn't remember his name.

"Let him in," Daleina commanded. "And please spread the word that Healer Hamon should always be allowed in." The last thing she needed was any delay in her healer reaching her. She wondered where Alet was.

Hamon entered and closed the door behind him. Relaxing, she removed the blanket. Cool air touched the raw flesh. Wordless, he crossed to her with a basin of water and a washcloth. She flinched as he began to clean the wound again.

Not looking at her, he said, "I will find a cure."

"There is no cure, Hamon." She knew her voice sounded tired, but she didn't bother to try to change it. Not with Hamon. He'd seen her at her worst and come back—she didn't have to pretend with him. "What we need is a way to predict when I will experience the false deaths. If spirits are near when it happens, or worse, linked to me, if they know I'm"—she couldn't bring herself to say "dead"—"out, then more people will die. We need to minimize the deaths until an heir is found. Buy as much time as we can."

"And find a cure."

"Don't lie to me, Hamon," she said gently. "It's only you and me here. No one has ever recovered from the False Death. We don't even know what causes it!" She knew it had to be tearing him up inside, that he couldn't fix her. He was a healer because he had a need to fix the broken. She treasured that about him. Studying his face, the set of his shoulders, the steadiness of his hands as he rebandaged her leg, she thought that wasn't entirely accurate. She treasured *him*, and she had never told him. She only pushed him away and let him push her away after Queen Fara died. They hadn't found their way back to each other. If her time was precious, she would make sure those other things that were precious to her weren't neglected anymore.

His face was earnest. "I would never lie to you, my queen."

"You lie to me every day, and I to you." She ever so gently pressed her lips to his. His eyes widened in surprise. She'd been the one to say things would change, after they killed Queen Fara, and she'd been right. But maybe it was time for things to change again. "Make me remember that I'm still alive?"

"Yes, Your Majesty." He gently wrapped his arms around her, and this time, when she kissed him, he kissed her back. She tasted his tears on her lips.

## CHAPTER 4

As the other champions filed out of the chamber, Ven laid his hand on the queen's throne. Like the chairs, the wood was alive. Living leaves curled over the top, and branches were woven into patterns on the back. He had been so very proud of her in the moment she'd broken the news that broke their hearts. She had held herself like a true queen. He had no doubt she'd summoned them within minutes of learning the news herself. Before she'd allowed herself to grieve, she'd considered her people first and what her death would mean to them.

*Her death* . . . such an ugly phrase. On any day, at any hour of her training, Daleina could have fallen, killed by the spirits she sought to control, but he'd never let himself believe it would happen. After Sata's death, she was his bright hope for the future. And now . . . "How is she?" he asked out loud.

"Not well," a woman's voice said—Captain Alet, the queen's guard. She'd entered quietly, but Ven had heard her. "Seven men and women died during the ritual. She lost control of the spirits."

Hearing that made him feel as if he'd aged a decade in one day. With Queen Fara, he'd been afraid she was losing control and then discovered the truth was worse. Daleina had sworn no deaths of innocents during her reign—their deaths must have torn her up inside. "She didn't speak of that."

Alet didn't reply.

"Is she in pain?"

"One of the spirits was chewing on her leg when she woke. And then she climbed those ludicrous stairs without any consideration for her wounds. So I would say yes, she is in pain, but she will deny it until she can't. You taught her well."

He wondered if he should go to her. She'd given an order, but there were plenty of other champions who could find an heir, and she might need him with her.

On the other hand, what could he do? *She doesn't need pity; she needs action. And an impossible cure.* Ven lifted his hand from the throne. "When you see the queen—"

"You'll need to find someone else to send your message," Alet interrupted. "I'm coming with you. You're the best champion that Aratay has; you're the most likely to find the next heir."

"I work alone."

"To be ready, your candidate will need to be trained faster than any ever before her, and having a second trainer will help." She added, "You know I can best you in a fight."

"You have a responsibility to Queen Daleina," Ven objected. "And you could not best me." It was more an automatic response, since he wasn't one hundred percent certain that was true—he'd seen Alet in the practice circle. She was fast and skilled and also at least two decades younger than he was. He *should* be able to hold his own, but he wouldn't bet on it.

Not that it changed his mind.

"Any of the guard can watch her door," Alet said as if reading his doubt. "You know as well as I do that Aratay needs a decent heir as quickly as possible. Queens don't lead safe lives, with or without any sickness."

Studying her, he considered it. Last time, with Daleina, he'd taken a healer with him to train her—Healer Hamon—but he'd never considered taking another warrior. He'd meant what he said: he worked alone. But Alet was one of the finest fighters he'd ever seen, and that could be invaluable. He'd met her while he was hunting the spirits who'd killed his former candidate, the heir Sata. She'd been the one who'd revealed Queen Fara's treachery. Later, Ven had found Alet in ceremonial armor, standing guard in an inconsequential portrait room, and she'd informed him that her skills were being wasted. He'd spoken with her commander, who had said she was there as punishment—she'd bested several of the old-timers in a practice bout and hadn't had the courtesy to salute them. Ven had told the commander precisely what he thought of that—adding a few colorful bruises in as punctuation—and the next day, Alet had been assigned to active duty. When Queen Daleina took up residence in the palace, she selected Alet to guard her and had her promoted to the rank of captain.

And yet now she wanted to leave that very post.

"Why do you want to do this?"

"Queen Daleina wants an heir."

"And?" Ven waited.

"And I don't want to watch her die." Alet didn't meet his eyes. Her gaze was fixed on the empty throne. "Call it cowardly if you want, but it's the truth."

But he would never say that. How could he call it cowardly when he felt the same way? He made the decision in an instant. "Very well. Our first step is to select a candidate."

"Do you have one in mind?"

"I thought I'd start with Northeast Academy. It's where I found Daleina." *And where Queen Fara trained as well.*

"Sounds promising. Lead on."

He strode to the stairs. Behind him, Alet followed, her feet as silent on the steps as a cat's paws. Now that he was taking action, he felt better. Dwelling on the capriciousness of fate wouldn't help Daleina. His queen was facing death without an heir. He couldn't fix the first part, but he could fix the second—and he would.

Halfway down the stairs, he jumped from the steps onto the nearest tree. He landed on a branch, and it bowed under his weight. Balancing himself, he ran over the branch. Beside him, Alet leaped from a thicker branch and landed on a narrower one, running lightly across it, ahead of Ven. Heavier, Ven chose one of the ropes and swung past her. She sped up, jumping from limb to limb, and so did he. For those brief moments, Ven felt the wind on his face and allowed his mind to empty of all thoughts.

At last, they reached their destination. With a powerful leap,

Ven hurled his body toward the top of the school, where the bells hung to call the students to class. He caught himself on a limb.

Six old trees wound together to comprise the training school, their bark fused into a tower. They'd been grown as a fortress to defend against air spirits and had evolved into a school for those gifted with mastery over more than one kind of spirit, one of several such schools in Aratay. Far below, within the circle of wood, on the forest floor, the practice circle was shielded by layers of leaves. A few figures darted up and down the spiral stairs.

This was where he'd found Daleina.

This was where he'd find his new candidate. He hoped.

He'd only visited a few times since Daleina had been crowned. He'd meant to be more involved, but he'd become absorbed in overseeing security at the palace, as well as recruiting and training a new champion. With his Daleina on the throne, he hadn't wanted to think about candidates or trials or heirs yet. *Shortsighted and stupid*, he thought. But he'd rectify that.

"Shall we, or would you prefer to brood for longer?" Alet asked. Without waiting for an answer, she scampered from branch to branch like a squirrel, down the interior of the tree. He took the stairs, watching Alet as she swung and twisted and leaped and flipped her way down to the forest floor. Reaching the bottom, he felt a twinge in his knees after so many stairs, while Alet looked unwinded and fresh. She didn't comment on this, though from the twinkle in her eye, he was certain she'd noticed. *This might have been a mistake.* Together, they strode into the practice circle.

Many of the students and teachers were there, and he was pleased to see the headmistress was present as well. Headmistress Hanna was an older woman with startlingly white hair and impeccable posture who had governed this school for as long as Ven could remember. She chose every teacher, determined every schedule, and supervised every student with the attention of a general to an army. He bowed to her as he reached her.

"Ah, Champion Ven! We did not expect you." She clasped his hands and kissed his cheeks, right, then left. She was smiling, a rarity, and the bruise-like circles that used to be under her eyes had faded.

"You look well, headmistress," he said. "May I present Captain Alet, member of the royal guard?"

Alet bowed, and the headmistress inclined her head before turning back to Ven. "You haven't been to visit in a while." It was a motherly reproach, and he winced appropriately. "What brings you here today?"

He didn't mince words, not with her. "I came to choose a candidate."

She studied his face for a moment. Last time, when Sata had died, he'd only chosen a candidate because the headmistress had pressured him, but that had been a different time, when he was in disgrace with the reigning queen. He tried to keep his face neutral and hoped she didn't guess the real reason he was here. He respected her, but after Fara's death, he didn't trust her. She'd do what she thought was right for Aratay, damn the consequences. "Our girls were about to practice their control. You can watch them." Hooking her arm through Ven's, she guided him toward the students. "Of course, none are up to the caliber of dear Daleina, but I think you'll be pleased at how nicely they're coming along. I am certain that whomever you choose will blossom under your tutelage." He couldn't detect any sarcasm in her voice, even though Daleina had been far from the best student. She'd aced all of her academic classes but had floundered in summoning—the one area that really mattered here. But maybe her words weren't for his benefit—she was rewriting the narrative of Daleina's history for the benefit of her academy. He let her.

With Alet, he positioned himself at the edge of the practice circle. There were twenty-four students, all in soft leather uniforms, with their hair tied back and faces smudged with dirt and sweat—he'd interrupted the middle of practice. *So few?* he wondered.

At the headmistress's command, each student took a turn summoning one of the smaller, weaker spirits that lived in the mosses and fountains and breezes. They attempted to set it on a task, such as fetching a leaf or stirring the wind. When they failed, a teacher would step in and banish the spirits.

"Ven, they're children." Alet's voice was a whisper.

Looking at them, really looking at them, he felt his heart lurch. *She's right*, he thought. Nearly all of them were first and second years, no more than sixteen years old. All of these girls had been sent here by their families because they'd displayed mastery over more than one spirit. Girls who could only influence one spirit stayed at home and were apprenticed to local hedgewitches—they would grow to be valuable to their community—but the hope was that *these* girls would grow to be valuable to the realm. The problem was, they weren't done growing.

*It's more than just a problem*, Ven realized. *It's a disaster.*

"Headmistress Hanna, where are the older students?"

"Already chosen, or gone," came the answer. "After the coronation, we had an influx of champions looking for new candidates, and an exodus of students who wanted a less dangerous life. These are the students who remain."

The afternoon wore on, until each of the girls had demonstrated her so-called skills more than once with a variety of spirits. Ven's heart sank further and further.

At last, the headmistress approached him. "You don't look pleased, Champion Ven."

"That's his normal expression," Alet said.

The headmistress flashed her a brief smile. "I am aware of our favorite champion's temperament, guardswoman. Come, Champion Ven, what did you expect after the coronation took our best and brightest?" Her voice held an edge, and Ven briefly wondered if she blamed him, but then he dismissed the thought. No one could have predicted what had happened on Coronation Day, when the spirits turned on the heirs instead of crowning one. He still didn't know how Daleina had triumphed that day. She never spoke of it.

Quietly, he asked, "Do any have ability with all the spirits?"

"Of course, Champion Ven, they all do, or will. Anyone who fails their level's basic aptitude tests is immediately sent home. None of the current students have reached mastery levels yet, but they are hard workers, and I believe you will see their potential."

He turned back to the practice circle without replying. A young girl was knocked flat on her back by an earth spirit no larger than a mole. It launched itself at her ankle, biting her before one of the teachers stepped in.

*I can't do it.* He'd be leading them to slaughter. At least Daleina and the other young women had all been fully trained by the time the trials began.

He turned his attention to the teachers, hoping against hope to see the right spark of power there. These women were older, experienced, but none had mastery of all the spirits, or even the potential for it. Most were only adept with one, which was why there were so many masters on the field. One (or more) for each kind of spirit: air, earth, water, wood, ice, and fire. They took turns teaching and protecting the students, and their training was rigorous but effective—this school had produced several queens over the years, including Queen Daleina and the current queen of Semo, in the northern mountains, who had switched countries in the middle of her training. Reports indicated she was well suited for Semo, since her greatest affinity was to earth spirits, and the mountains housed as many of those as Aratay had wood spirits. But the potential for greatness didn't solve his immediate problem.

"Who are you going to choose?" Alet asked. "The redheaded one shows promise." She pointed to a wiry girl who was practicing a sword pattern in one corner of the training field.

Ven grunted. The girl couldn't have been more than fifteen. She was all gangly bones and new muscle. Her lips were pressed into a determined line. "She has focus," he admitted. But was that enough? He'd chosen Daleina because of her determination. He'd known from the instant he met her that she would make a good queen. No, a great queen.

*And she would have,* he thought. *She would have been one of our greatest. If she'd had time.* His fists were clenched. Consciously, he loosened them and shook his hands out. That was, indeed, the problem: *time.* There wasn't enough time to grow any of these girls into the woman that the land needed.

Abruptly, he turned and stalked out of the practice circle, across the entrance foyer, and out of the academy. He heard Alet following him. Only when he was far enough that he couldn't hear either the girls or their teachers did he stop.

He saw a flash of gray in between the trees. Kneeling, he held his hand out, and a wolf trotted out, doglike, to sniff his fingers. He rubbed behind the wolf's ears. Bayn didn't like the capital, and Ven didn't blame him. "I don't suppose you have any power over spirits," he said to Alet without turning around.

She barked a humorless laugh. "Me? None. Hence developing the intense fighting skills."

No one knew why some were born with power and some weren't. No one knew why it was only women, and no one knew why some had more power than others. Sometimes it was passed down, mother to daughter, and sometimes it wasn't. Sometimes the power manifested early, and sometimes it didn't. But every generation had at least a few women who had enough power to control the spirits and enough strength of mind to become queen. The problem was finding one. "We won't find her here," Ven said.

Bayn was watching him steadily. He was an uncanny beast, so intelligent and aware that sometimes Ven forgot he was just an animal. Ven found himself looking at Bayn as if expecting him to think of the perfect solution, as if the wolf could even know what the problem was.

"Give them a chance," Alet said. "You don't need to rush your choice. You have fourteen days—milady knew you'd need time. She's sensible, even when others aren't."

He heard the admiration in her voice and shared it. Daleina was extraordinary. This shouldn't be happening to her. Balling his hand into a fist, he struck a tree. Bark flew away from his knuckles. He heard a growl behind him, and it wasn't the wolf. *Let them come*, he thought savagely. He could use a fight.

Alet caught his arm as he pulled back for another punch. "You're angering the spirits."

"They anger *me*." He could fight them, if he had to. Spirits were difficult to injure, but they hurt and they died, like all else, with enough effort. Still, it would be stupid to risk injury because of a temper tantrum, and the headmistress wouldn't be happy if he caused a tree near the academy to die. He suppressed the urge to pummel the tree and instead climbed it. Alet followed him.

Below, the spirit he'd woken with his punch stalked around the base of the tree. Roots thickened beneath its feet, and ferns unfurled. It snarled but didn't pursue them. Bayn faded back into the underbrush.

Out of the corner of his eye, Ven saw Alet speed up so that she climbed beside him, grabbing branches at the same time he did and hoisting herself higher. Soon, they had a rhythm—the boughs bent beneath them and then flung them upward as they leapt. "Ven, you have to choose a candidate. I know you don't want to. I know it means admitting what we don't want to be true, but you must. The queen needs you. She's counting on you. *You*, Ven. You're the one who found her. You're the one she expects to find her heir."

"I'm not saying I'm not going to find one. I'm just not going to find her heir at an academy." Standing on the top branch, he straightened until his shoulders and head were above the canopy. He looked out across the green sea, the top of the forests of Aratay.

Climbing up, Alet stood beside him. "You don't know that. One of the other academies—"

"They will all be the same. Children, all of them." There was no reason to think another academy would be any different. Northeast Academy was the finest. He'd be wasting his time. *Daleina's time*, he corrected. "If I choose a child, she will die, and Aratay with her." Ven shook his head as if that would clear his mind of the images of those children, torn apart by spirits. "It's been a century or more since Aratay was heirless. And so I believe we must find our heir the old-fashioned way. Not through an academy."

Alet's fists were on her hips as her feet straddled two branches. Wind slapped against her, shaking the tree, but she remained motionless, glaring at him. "You're telling me you want to head blindly out into the forest, in search of a miracle?"

"Yes," he said.

## CHAPTER 5

The forests of Aratay were as vast and deep as an ocean. There were dark paths that hadn't seen sunlight in a century, as well as quiet groves of new saplings with trunks only as thick as a child's finger. A few roads, glorified animal tracks, ran on the ground between the trees, and the wire paths ran through the upper canopy, but most towns were nestled in the branches, midforest level, and connected by bridges. Other towns and villages were within the trunks. A few others thrived on the forest floor, and a rare few men and women, primarily the canopy singers, lived in the top level, nearest the sun. Naelin and her family lived midforest in a loose collection of homes that counted as a village. When Naelin first moved there, the village hadn't even been large enough to warrant a name, but now it was called East Everdale, as if tying it to the larger town of Everdale would lend it legitimacy. She liked it just as much with or without a name. It was home.

Naelin loved the forest, all the layers and shades of green, so many shades that there weren't words to describe them all—a spectrum of green, from the hopeful green of new leaves to the contemplative moss green on the forest floor, so dark it was nearly black. She wished she were a poet to capture in words the way the forest changed as the light changed. She had to content herself with just drinking the colors in as she stole a few precious moments alone before her husband came home for dinner. She settled into the crook of a branch above the roof of her home, a torn shirt on her lap and a needle with thread in her hand.

Below her, inside the house, she heard the voices of her children: Erian and Llor. As they clomped inside, Llor was bragging about how many squirrels he'd shot with his new bow. Erian praised him and then told him to skin the squirrels himself, because Mama would be so impressed if he did. Naelin smiled. She'd done right there. She heard her own voice echoed in her daughter's. Naelin listened as Erian patiently coached Llor through the steps for preparing the meat. He squealed and eww-ed, and soon both children were laughing. Picking up the torn shirt, Naelin added a few more stitches, and then she froze.

She sniffed the air.

The forest smelled stronger, as if it had recently rained.

With her foot, she thumped on the roof of their house. "Erian, did your father put out the fresh charms for the spirits?" she called.

"Yes, he said he did . . ."

*He says a lot of things*, Naelin thought. *Some of them are even true.* "Would you check, please?" She kept her voice light and pleasant. "Look on the shelf and see if they're still there."

Naelin heard rustling, as if Erian were sorting through the herb shelf. Familiar prickles walked up and down her skin—she was being watched by flat eyes, spirit eyes. Multiple sets of them. They weren't close enough to see yet, but she could sense them.

"Erian?"

He hadn't done it. Naelin was certain.

"Erian, I won't be angry. Tell me the truth, baby. When were the charms last laid?"

Erian's voice was a wail, rising through the roof. "I don't know! Father said he did today's and yesterday's. . . . But the basket is still here, and the herbs are dry. I'll take it now—"

Naelin jumped to her feet, dumping the half-mended shirt off her. "No! Stay inside, both of you. Close the shutters, lock the doors, and hide yourselves. You know where. Not a peep."

She heard Llor begin to cry. She hadn't meant to scare them, except that yes, she did. They should be scared. Scared children hid, and she needed them to hide right now.

The cities and towns had organized protection, but on the outskirts, everyone looked after their own—they'd lived through enough queens to know you couldn't always depend on their protection, no matter what the songs and tales gleefully promised. Songs were written by canopy dwellers and tales by city folk. The spirits out here were bolder. Despite this, she'd always done fine. She had a knack for making the charms that repelled the spirits. There hadn't been a problem since before the children were born.

But something about today felt very, very wrong.

Crouching, Naelin scanned the forest. From the scent, she thought there were at least two tree spirits nearby, drawing closer, past where her husband usually hung the charms. She inhaled deeply. And maybe . . . yes, an earth spirit as well. Her breath caught in her throat. Two kinds of spirits at once.

The forest was not merciful today.

Reaching into her pockets, she clutched the bundle of herbs she'd prepared for herself. The herb charm was meant to discourage spirits, to fool them into thinking that she was just a part of the forest—benign, rather than one of the humans they hated. It wasn't strong enough to force them away once they'd taken an interest in her.

Silently, she cursed her husband. And she cursed herself. She should have taken care of the charms herself. But the last time she'd tried, he'd taken it as a grave insult, accusing her of sabotaging their marriage, of playing the martyr, of not allowing him a role in protecting their family. Wives make the charms; husbands lay them out—that's how it was always done in Everdale, never mind that it was different in other villages and never mind that she had done it herself for years after her parents died and before she married Renet.

*I am a fool.*

The smell was growing stronger. She saw a branch twitch, and then another. Naelin pivoted, trying to watch all the branches at once. Below, through the leaves, she saw an earth spirit sniff around the base of their tree. It was covered in fur and had a face like a squeezed walnut. It raised its face to look at her, and she shuddered. Its teeth were exposed, and it ran a black tongue over its fangs. "You cannot touch us," she told it. "I will not let you."

Reaching for the knife at her belt, she realized she wasn't armed except with a sewing needle. She hadn't expected to need to defend herself on the roof of her own home. But even if she'd had her knife, she was skilled with chopping up herbs, not fighting multiple spirits.

"Go away!" she yelled. "Leave us alone!"

*Stupid*, she told herself. Damn his pride. She should have known better. But lately, he'd been trying so hard to be a better husband, and the kids hated it when they fought. . . .

One of the branches bowed only a few feet in front of her. A tree spirit clung to it. The spirit leered at her. It was in the shape of a monkey with pale green fur, but it had a child's face.

She filled her lungs and shouted, "Help! Someone, help!"

But no one was going to come. No one *could* come. There wasn't anyone close enough, and even if there had been, they'd run in the opposite direction to save their own skin. She wouldn't even blame them. Better one die than many, as the saying went.

Below her, she heard the door rattle. Looking down, she saw a larger spirit—a tree spirit with long arms like sticks and hair of grass, shaking the door. "No! Stay out!" She lunged forward toward the lip of the roof, and the monkeylike spirit dropped in front of her.

She froze.

Cackling, the spirit dragged its nails along her skin, lightly without breaking the flesh. She couldn't make her voice work. Her throat felt clogged. *Stop!* she wanted to scream, throwing the thought out of her as if it were a shout.

The spirit frowned and withdrew an inch, its nails hovering just above the surface of her flesh. Below, the rattling ceased.

Horror squeezed her heart. They had heard her.

She wanted to draw back the thought. She licked her lips. "I didn't . . . You couldn't . . . I'm not . . ." *Oh, what have I done?* She knew full well how it worked: use your power, and more will come. Use your power again, and even more will follow. And then more and more, until at last they number more than you can control. And then they kill all they find. It had happened to her mother. Hidden beneath the floor of her childhood home, Naelin had been the sole survivor. She'd heard it all: her mother trying to stop them, to defend herself, to protect them all. She'd heard her father die, and her brother and sisters. She'd been the only one to make it to the hiding place, and she'd stayed there long after the spirits had gone.

No one had come to help. No one had come to see if anyone was left alive.

She'd buried what remained of her family alone, and she'd locked the house behind her. She'd been nine years old, the same age as Erian was now. She'd had a little brother the same age as Llor was: six, and she'd had twin baby sisters.

She'd sworn to never make the same mistake that her mother had made. Never let the spirits hear her. Never give them reason to notice her family. Stay silent, stay secret, and stay safe. It had kept them well for all these years. But now . . . There had to be another way to repel them.

The monkeylike tree spirit watched her as she leaned forward to see down her family's tree. Around the base, three earth spirits circled the roots and sniffed at the bark. She looked up and saw more eyes in the trees.

*There is no other way*, she thought dully. *They will kill you now, or you will stop them now and they will kill you later. That is the choice. What do you choose?* She stared into the empty, emotionless eyes of the monkeylike tree spirit. The forest was silent. No birds. No wind. It felt as if everything were holding its breath—as if the spirits were waiting for her to choose.

Naelin felt tears on her cheeks. She took a deep breath and focused all her fear, all her determination, all her love for her children into words that she forced silently outward into the forest:

*You will not hurt us.*

*You will leave.*

She felt the words exit her like arrows from a bow, and her hands flew over her mouth, as if she were keeping the rest of her inside, as her lungs and heart and stomach wanted to follow the words into the air. Her head began to pound, but she repeated the thought, stronger and louder: *You will not hurt us!*

*You will LEAVE!*

With cries and calls, the spirits fled. The branches shook, leaves quivered as they leapt and soared and vanished in between the trees. The scent of forest receded, and the pressure inside her head lessened. She sagged backward against the curve of the trunk.

She'd done it.

She should feel triumphant, but she didn't. Closing her eyes, she pictured again her parents and siblings in the moments before the spirits attacked, heard the sounds as her mother was overwhelmed, heard the delighted shrieks of the spirits as they tore Naelin's world apart. Rocking forward, Naelin buried her face in her hands. "What have I done?"

"You saved them!" a familiar voice crowed from below.

She jumped to her feet.

Below, on the forest floor, was her husband, Renet. "I saw it! You were magnificent! They fled from you like . . . like . . . You did it! I knew you could! I knew you had it in you!"

Lowering herself to the front of her house, Naelin didn't trust herself to speak. She didn't want praise, not for this, never for this. Her hands were trembling as she unlatched the door. "Erian? Llor? It's safe now. You can come out."

For a brief, terrible instant, she thought she'd failed—that the spirits had broken in, found them, while she dithered over whether to use her power or not—but then Erian flung open the trapdoor in the floor. Her daughter helped Llor climb out.

Dropping to her knees, Naelin gathered up her children in her arms and held them close. They threw their arms around her neck and clung to her as if they were both still toddlers, afraid of the dark. "They're gone," she whispered into Erian's hair. She breathed in the scent of her children, felt the warmth of their bodies.

Behind her, she heard Renet climb the ladder and burst into the house.

"I knew you could do it," he repeated.

Slowly, Naelin lifted her face from her children to look at her husband. "What," she said carefully, not yelling, no anger in her voice, but calm careful words, "do you mean you 'knew'?"

"I didn't *know*, but I suspected." He dropped to his knees beside them, his face alight with excitement. "And it's true. You have power!"

She stared at him and tried very hard not to let her entire body clench. "Tell me you are not saying you wanted this to happen. Tell me you didn't 'forget' the charms on purpose. Tell me—" She stopped herself. Llor was sobbing into her shirt, and her brave Erian was shaking as if she was crying as well. She hugged her children tighter and tried to think calmly, rationally. The spirits knew what she could do now. They'd come again. How soon? And how many?

Belatedly, she realized Renet was talking again. "... the champion will be in Everdale as soon as tomorrow!"

"Is that why you did this?" she demanded. "You think a champion—"

"—is looking for you! Yes! Or he will be, once he knows that you have the power. I heard he's searching for a candidate, village to village, the way they used to a hundred years ago. Oh, Naelin, don't you see? This is our chance!"

"Chance? Chance for what—to be the target of every spirit in the forest?" She tried to keep down the anger, her children a reminder that she did love this man. But ...

"No, no, a million times no! Renet, promise you won't tell the champion about me. I don't want to be a candidate. I refuse to be." Just thinking about it made her squeeze her children tighter. If this champion chose her, he'd take her away from them, from Renet, from her home, from her life. Leaving Erian and Llor would be like leaving her soul behind.

Burying her face in her children's hair, she breathed in and out, trying to calm herself enough to think. They'd have a little time before the spirits dared return. She'd make as many charms as she could. She'd cover the house with them, not just the nearby trees; she'd shove them in between the shingles and around the windows and in the fireplace. They'd all take precautions. She'd make herb packets for them all to carry. She'd refresh the charms herself and double-check them, in case Renet had any more reckless ideas to "test" her.

Eventually, if they were careful, if she didn't use her powers again, if they didn't give the spirits cause to come to them, the spirits would forget and move on. And then Erian and Llor would be safe again. And she would have her home and life back.

So long as her husband promised not to tell.

Calmly, or as calmly as she could, she asked, "Renet, do you love me?"

"Of course! But—"

"If you love me—if you *ever* loved me—then promise me when the champion comes to Everdale, do not tell him. Do not tell anyone.

"Ever."

## CHAPTER 6

For four days, Ven and Alet traveled the outer forests: racing along the wire paths through the canopy, then descending to the comfortable towns that sprawled through midforest, and then ferreting out the tucked-away towns on the forest floor, where people lived between the roots of great trees behind barriers of stone and wood. Every town and village had its own hedgewitch, and Ven insisted they see them all. He judged them abruptly and, he knew, unfairly, but he was looking for something very specific: potential. Not undeveloped potential. There was plenty of that at the training schools. What he wanted was something else entirely. Missed potential.

So far, he hadn't found it.

Alet pointed to a squirrel that was racing up a nearby tree. "There's dinner."

Smoothly, Ven drew an arrow, fit it into his bow, and aimed. The squirrel scampered down a narrowing branch. He'd reach the end in three . . . two . . . one . . . As the squirrel leaped, Ven shot. The arrow pierced the squirrel cleanly through the eye, and the squirrel plummeted. Alet raced to catch it, diving from branch to branch, and then snatching it out of the air by its tail before it hit the dirt.

By the time he met her on the forest floor, she had already started a small cooking fire between two rocks. "Getting slow, old man."

He was forty-one, not decrepit. "I'm neither old nor slow."

Laying the squirrel on a rock, she began to skin it. "Everything's relative."

"You may be half my age, but I have twice your skill."

Pausing, she arched her eyebrows at him.

"Quarter more your skill," he amended.

She said nothing.

"Would you settle for 'more experience and wisdom'?" Ven laid the protective charms in a circle around them. He was sure Alet had been careful to pick only dead wood for the fire, but there was no sense in risking angering any spirits.

"They say the mind decays rapidly as one's age advances." She skewered the squirrel with a stick and then wiped her hands on a fallen leaf. "Did you hear what they were saying at that last town? You started a trend. A few other champions are searching the villages too, even ones who already have a candidate."

He hadn't heard, but he was pleased. *It can't be that stupid an idea if others are imitating me.* "There are many women who don't appreciate their own power or recognize their importance." Taking the stick with the squirrel meat, he held it over the flame. "Not every gifted child is sent to a training school."

"Only the good ones."

"Or the ones whose parents notice their powers."

"Everyone who has powers knows it," Alet objected.

He twisted the stick. "But not everyone who has power wants to be queen."

Alet fed more sticks to the fire, and the flames shot up, dancing with the smoke. "Why would you want anyone who didn't want to be queen?"

He didn't have an answer to that so he changed the subject. "We'll visit Everdale next. You spread word of our search, and I'll talk to the local hedgewitch."

"Word has already spread. I swear village gossip spreads faster than the wind."

"This time, stress that we're not looking for children. We're looking for women who missed their chance. We're looking for the overlooked."

"Maybe they were overlooked for a reason." Flames licked the squirrel meat, singeing it. "Remember the one in North Blye? She could talk to spirits all right, but she also talked to dead twigs, empty puddles, and random piles of dirt. And how about the one you were so enthused about in Cohn? She fainted at the sight of a spirit, not-so-conveniently after she'd summoned a boatload of them. You were lucky you weren't eaten alive."

"You were lucky too," he pointed out.

"That was skill." Alet shrugged. "Point is, everyone with significant enough power is at an academy already, so that's where we should be. This is a fool's quest."

She wasn't wrong, especially about that woman from Cohn. But he was also convinced of the futility of choosing a too-young student. The conventional route wasn't going to work with their time limit.

*Daleina's time limit*, he amended.

He wondered how she was. She'd had four days now with the diagnosis. He was certain that Hamon would be with her, ensuring she was comfortable, and he was equally certain she was ignoring all the healer's good advice and pushing herself as hard as she could for as long as she could—that's what he would do, and he'd trained her.

After they ate, Ven and Alet took turns sleeping until the shadows in the forest lightened to pale gray and the birds began to chirp. It wasn't dawn yet, but it was close enough to navigate and that was all they needed. *Ten days left—no time to waste.* They packed their camp fast, rolling their bedrolls and stomping out the fire. Scooping up his charms, Ven climbed up into the trees. Alet was close behind him.

In the predawn light, the journey to Everdale was swift, and they swung into the heart of town as morning light filtered through the leaves. The center of Everdale was a large platform suspended between several tree trunks. Shops were built against the trunks, and merchants were scurrying around, setting up stands and tents for the day's market.

Sighing, Alet trudged toward the market. "I'll spread the word that we're here."

Adjusting the quiver on his back, Ven headed for a shop with a sign boasting of the best protective charms north of the river. He tried the door, expecting it to be locked, but it swung open easily. In some towns, he'd had to nearly batter down the door in order to talk to the hedgewitch this early. He didn't have time to wait for niceties like market hours. "Good morning?"

"We're not open yet, but come in and welcome!" He heard a woman's voice, but he didn't see anyone. The shop was dim and cluttered, with displays of candles on barrels and shelves stuffed with herbs and charms. Wind chimes hung from the ceiling, and he ducked under them—they jingled as he passed. A middle-aged woman with uncombed hair and a stained apron bustled in through a back door. She was carrying a lantern, which she hung on a hook to brighten the room. The shop didn't look any less cluttered in the light. Layers of dust lay over the charms, and cobwebs filled the rafters. Seeing him, she gasped, and then plastered a smile on her face. "What can I interest you in, good sir? Charms, I presume? We have a wide variety, suitable for every kind of spirit. Even one known to ward off an earth kraken."

He suppressed a sigh. He could tell already that this woman was more shopkeeper than candidate. He guessed her power was mild, perhaps only extending to skill with crafting charms. "Which spirits do you have mastery over?"

"Wood, though I'd call it more affinity than mastery." She gave a high-pitched, self-conscious laugh. He wondered what was making her nervous. Him? That had happened before. He was oversized for these tiny shops. He felt like if he breathed too heavily, all the pottery would shatter and the rafters would shake. "You look like a well-traveled woodsman. Let me see what I have that will suit you for journeying . . ." She bustled toward the overladen shelves.

He stopped her. "I am looking for a woman with mastery over more than one kind of spirit, a woman that the recruiters overlooked."

The hedgewitch froze like a deer in range of his bow. "No one like that here," she said hurriedly. "I'm the only one with any spirit affinity nearby."

Ven frowned. "Are you certain—"

The front door swung open, and a man poked his head inside. "Corinda, word is that the champion— He's here! You're him! You must be!" Trembling, the man stepped into the shop. He looked like a typical woodsman: a serviceable ax was strapped to his back and charms hung from his belt. His beard was unevenly trimmed, and he was clutching his hat so tightly that the brim curled. "Corinda, you said you'd tell me when he came."

The hedgewitch pivoted to face the man. "First off, he just got here. Second off, I lied, Renet, to protect you from making the worst mistake of your life. Go home, apologize to your wife, and hope she doesn't throw you out on your sorry behind."

"It's not a mistake! It's an opportunity—"

The woman took a step toward him. "Renet, one more word, and she will never, ever forgive you. And you will regret it for always."

He shrank back. "But she doesn't understand—"

"She knows full well what's best, and she won't want you blabbing—"

Ven interrupted. "Am I right in assuming we're talking about a woman with powers?"

The man Renet bobbed his head so hard that it looked as if it was about to fall off. "My wife, great sir! She pretends she's an ordinary woodswoman, just good with charms, but she's more! I've seen proof with my own eyes. When I heard you were coming to Everdale—"

The shopkeeper plopped herself between Ven and Renet. "Stop there, Renet." To Ven, she said, "Sir, this man likes to exaggerate. He's always looking for a way to get rich quick. He wants the easy way out, instead of working hard for his family and himself. This is just his newest scheme, trying to sell off his wife to the capital—"

"It's no scheme!" Renet said. "She commanded wood spirits *and* earth spirits only yesterday. Saved my children from them!"

"He's wasting your time, great sir," the shopkeeper said.

"It's my time to waste," Ven said, though it wasn't true. It was Queen Daleina's time. But he kept his voice placid and firm. It wasn't so much the man's insistence that caught Ven's attention; it was the hedgewitch's resistance. She was too nervous, too vehement. He focused on her. "Why are you protecting her?"

"Because he isn't!" She flapped her arms as if she wanted to whale on him but didn't dare with Ven present—and it was pretty clear from the way the man flinched, she would have. "You're supposed to be her husband! You're supposed to care about her, what she needs and wants. Instead, all you think about is you, you, you. You want to be rich. You want to be safe. But at what cost? What happens to Naelin? What happens to your children if this man takes Naelin away? You think about that? Well, you best think about it and shut your trap. Those children need their mother, not their feckless father."

Ven held up his hand before the man could reply. "I'd like to meet your wife."

Renet exhaled in a puff, and his face broke into a wide grin. "Of course, great sir!"

NAELIN POUNDED THE HERBS WITH THE PESTLE. SHE TRIED NOT to imagine the herbs were Renet's face. She told herself she didn't actually wish him harm. He was more like a puppy, exuberant and irresponsible . . . and needing to be on a leash.

"Mama, are you and Father going to fight again tonight?" Llor asked.

She sighed. Their home was too tiny to hide things, and she'd been yelling too loudly. "No, sweetheart, he'll come home with fresh flowers as he always does, and everything will be all right."

"Until you need to yell at him again," Erian pointed out. She carried a pitcher of water to the table. To Llor, she said, "Sometimes Father needs yelling at."

Naelin's mouth quirked into a smile. It was true. But she wished she didn't feel like yelling at him so often. He meant well, usually, and he certainly hadn't meant for any harm to come to Erian and Llor. *It could have, though*, she thought. They could have been killed. Her smile faded, and shivers ran up and down her spine again. She redoubled her efforts in mashing the herbs. Extra protection charms. That would help. And she'd string up garlic and onion, make the place smell so noxious that no spirit would want to come near it.

She heard the ladder creak outside.

"Father's home!" Llor cried. He ran to the window and threw open the shutters.

Dropping the pestle, Naelin rushed to the window and pulled her son back. "Ask first." She tried not to let fear into her voice. Windows weren't safe right now, not until she was sure the spirits had lost interest in her. She closed the shutters and latched them.

"He's early," Erian observed. "Do you think something's wrong?"

With Renet, it could be anything: a spirit attack, a forgotten lunch, or he simply didn't feel like working today. That had happened before. Sometimes it was nice, like when he'd sweep the whole family away on an impromptu picnic, and sometimes it wasn't, like when he'd come home furious about some imaginary slight that was obviously her fault. Regardless, she wasn't in the mood for his whims today. "Renet, is that you?" she called.

"Yes!" he called back. He sounded cheerful.

She wasn't certain if that made her relieved or annoyed. *Both*, she decided.

"I've brought guests!"

This time, she was the one to open the shutters and lean out the window. Looking down, she saw only her husband on the ladder. And then she felt eyes on her. Skin prickling, she looked up sharply, expecting to see more spirits, but instead two people, a man and a woman, were perched on branches directly opposite their house.

These were not her husband's usual friends. Not only had she never seen them before, but they didn't look like *anyone* she'd ever seen. The man was tall, very tall, with a salt-and-pepper beard, hard blue eyes, and an old scar on his forehead. He had a bow and quiver on his back, as well as a travel sack, and wore green leathers that looked as if they'd seen a lot of tree bark. He was the kind of dangerous handsome that the women from town liked to whisper about. Staring at him, Naelin had to force herself to tear her eyes away in order to examine his companion, a lithe woman with bare, muscled arms, curls pinned back from her face, and knives strapped to her calves. She was watching Naelin as if Naelin were a squirrel, a tasty, plump squirrel that the woman was considering for dinner. Naelin wanted to close the shutters and tell Renet to take his "friends" back where they came from. But these didn't look like the kind of people you were rude to, at least not safely.

*Champions*, her mind whispered, but then she pushed that thought away. It couldn't be. Renet had promised. Besides, wouldn't champions look more regal? These two looked like wild hunters, the kind of people who roamed the forest without a permanent home.

Before she could decide what to do, Llor was tugging at the door, and Erian was undoing the locks. Llor tumbled backward as the door swung open. Reversing direction, he launched himself forward and hugged Renet's leg. "Father! Don't worry. Mother's not still mad. She said she wouldn't yell at you anymore."

Renet glanced at her, his expression like a toddler with chocolate on his face who expects to be smacked but doesn't regret the chocolate. *Please*, she thought. *Please, tell me these aren't champions. Please say you didn't do it.* He'd done something, though—that much was clear.

When had their marriage become like this? At the start, they'd been so happy. He'd made her laugh like no one else ever could. He'd taught her to dance, and she'd taught him to read, at least a little—he hadn't been a very good student, and she hadn't been a strict teacher. They used to spend moonlit nights on the roof, catching glimpses of the stars through the leaves. They used to skinny-dip in the forest pools. But that was years ago. Now she couldn't remember the last time they'd laughed together, or even seemed to be having the same conversation. Somewhere along the way, they stopped being able to talk without shouting, and their easy friendship had slipped away, argument by argument. "Who are your friends?" she asked as the man and woman came through the door.

He turned to them and bowed slightly. "May I present my wife, Naelin."

"And me!" Llor tugged on his father's shirt. "Present me next." He said the word "present" carefully, copying his father.

Renet ruffled his hair. "This is my son, Llor, and my daughter, Erian."

Erian curtseyed and then drifted closer to Naelin. Automatically, Naelin put her arm around her daughter's shoulders. She didn't blame Erian for being wary of these newcomers. She certainly was. They seemed to fill the house just with their presence.

Llor hopped over to the man. "Is that a longbow? Can I see it? Is it hard to pull?"

"Llor, don't pester him," Erian said.

Naelin squeezed Erian's shoulders before letting her go and stepping forward. "Welcome to our home. I'm sorry, but Renet didn't say your names. . . ."

The man ducked to fit under one of the rafters. Drying herbs brushed his hair. "I am Ven, Queen's Champion. And my companion is Captain Alet, a member of the royal guard."

She felt as if all the air had been siphoned out of the room. It was harder to breathe. She sucked in more air, aware she was gasping, unable to stop. This was at the same time the worst and most wonderful thing she could have imagined. A champion, here. Queen Daleina's own champion, in her home!

"Wow," Llor said, his eyes as wide as an owl's, "you're a *hero*."

"What's the queen like?" Erian asked breathlessly at the same time. To the woman, she asked, "Are you her personal guard? Do you know her? Is she as beautiful as they say?"

"More beautiful," the guardswoman said gravely.

"Did she really defeat a hundred spirits by herself?" Erian asked.

"I heard they flee when they see her!" Llor jumped in. "She just has to look at them, and they run. I heard she tore one apart with just a word! And she destroys them too and sets their trees on fire from miles and miles and miles away!"

"She can do all that," the royal guard said.

Llor's mouth opened in a silent "wow." He was staring at the champion and the guard as if they'd descended from the sky above the forest. Naelin understood—she'd told tales about Queen

Daleina and her champion to Llor (and Erian, who claimed she was too old for bedtime stories, but always listened in). Queen Daleina was the one who kept them all safe. She was Aratay's protective charm, the woman who battled fear and *won*. And this was the man who'd taught her.

And now they were here . . .

"They wanted to meet you, Naelin," Renet said, his voice trembling. "Please, I know you're angry, but please listen to them, Naelin. They've been looking for you."

She took a step backward, and the heels of her feet hit the hearth. *Oh, no. He'd promised!* He'd kissed her and promised, and she'd believed him.

"According to your husband, you controlled tree spirits and earth spirits yesterday, to protect your family," the champion said.

All wonder at their presence drained out of her. It didn't matter how legendary they were; what mattered was why they were here. "He lied," Naelin said flatly.

"I know what I saw!" Renet cried. "You were surrounded, and you sent them away. How, if you didn't control them? Admit it! You have powers."

She shook her head, hard. *I have to convince them.* "Renet, what have you done? You lied to these good people, these important people, interrupted their day, took their time. I'm sure they have much more important things to be doing than visiting us."

"Oh, please stay and visit!" Llor cried. He grabbed on to the wrist of the champion and hung there, dangling his full weight. The champion's arm muscles tightened, supporting the child's weight, but he didn't shake him off or even look at him. The champion's eyes bored into Naelin, as if he could see all her thoughts and all her secrets. Naelin looked away, at the woman, but the guardswoman's eyes were no more comforting—in fact, they were almost hostile.

"I'm a simple woodswoman," Naelin explained. "I make charms for my family and for sale. Over the years, I've gotten adept at it. As soon as the spirits came close enough to sense the charms, they fled. There was no power involved. No commands.

I'm afraid my husband, in his enthusiasm, was mistaken." *Please, believe me*, she thought.

The champion continued to study her, and she felt her face flush red. She wished she were a bird and could fly out the window. Her daughter pressed closer to her again, and Naelin put an arm around her, unsure which of them was comforting the other.

Kneeling in front of Llor, the champion asked, "Did your mother scare away the monsters?"

Llor shot a glance at her, and Naelin shook her head. "No," Llor said.

*Good boy*, Naelin thought.

"We hid under there." Llor pointed at the rug that covered the trap door. "When we came out, the monsters were gone, and Mama yelled at Father for a while. He let the spirits come, because he isn't very smart."

The guardswoman made a noise that nearly sounded like a laugh.

"Why do you say 'he let the spirits come'? Why blame him?" The champion's voice was gentle, and Naelin suddenly wondered if he had children. She'd never thought of champions as good with children.

"Because he didn't put the new charms out, on purpose. Mama thought that was mean. And I think it was mean too."

Renet's face flushed red, then purple. "I only wanted to test—"

The champion held up a hand, cutting him off. "I'm speaking to your son right now. I've already talked to you. As I'm hearing it, you intentionally removed protections around your children and didn't warn your wife." Deliberately, he turned his back to Renet.

Renet shrank back, like a little kid who knew he was in trouble but couldn't imagine what he'd done wrong, and Naelin wanted to shake him for not understanding. She'd explain, again, tonight why she hid her powers, why her parents had warned her about champions, why she'd never gone to any training school. Only the strongest used their powers against the spirits and survived. And she was not the strongest. She wouldn't survive. No matter how wealthy it would make her family if she went to the capital, she believed her children were better off poor than motherless. It wasn't such a hard concept to understand.

"Tell me about your mother," the champion said to Llor.

"She smells nice," Llor said.

"Good. What else?"

"She tells me stories at night, so I can sleep," Llor said. "I have bad dreams sometimes." Quickly, he added, "But I don't cry. I'm not a baby."

"You're not," the champion said seriously.

"Mama thinks I am. She doesn't even let me walk to school by myself. All the other kids get to, but Mama—"

"That's enough, Llor," Naelin said crisply. She fixed her gaze on the champion. "I protect my family by being careful. Extra careful, perhaps, but we aren't like you. People like us can't afford to be fearless."

He rose, and Naelin shrank back, again reminded of how tall he was. He was like a tree, with arm muscles as solid-looking as a trunk. "You think we are fearless?"

"You can fight spirits," Naelin said. "We have to make do the best we can."

"It sounds like you 'make do' well," the guardswoman said.

Naelin inclined her head. "Thank you." She began to hope that meant they believed her. She had practice in lying about her power, but never to people like these. She felt naked in front of them and was aware of every flaw, from her bony elbows to her too-thin eyebrows to her hair that had recently begun to show a few strands of gray. *People like this shouldn't be talking to people like me. They're like roses, and I'm like . . . like dirt. Practical, ordinary dirt that never does anything extraordinary or even unexpected.* She patted her hair, then forced her hand down. "Again, I'm sorry your visit was for nothing, but I'm not anyone the likes of you would ever be interested in."

The champion executed a bow—to her, a bow! Flustered, she tried to curtsy and knocked into Erian. The champion seemed not to notice, or pretended not to. "We thank you for your time." He turned toward the door, and the guardswoman followed him.

"Naelin!" Renet said, his voice a strangled cry. He hurried

across the room, gripped her arm so hard that she flinched, and whispered in her ear. "You can't just let them leave. This is our chance. Don't be a coward! You could change our lives, right here and right now. These people have the power to offer us every-thing we've always wanted: safety, security, wealth."

She pried his fingers off her arm and pushed his hand away. In a low whisper, barely a breath, she said, "And death." He flinched.

She thought she saw the champion pause . . . but no, he was only turning to descend the ladder. Llor and Erian rushed to the door to watch them. Leaning out the door, Erian gasped, and Llor squealed in delight. Leaving Renet, Naelin hurried to join her children. Arm around each of them, she looked outside.

The champion and the guard had left the ladder and were leaping from tree to tree, higher and higher. In their wake, leaves shook and trembled.

"They're leaving!" Renet cried.

"Good," Naelin said firmly.

Naelin and her children watched until they disappeared from view. She told herself she was grateful that was over and glad they were gone, but still she continued to stare out at the trees long after the leaves stilled. It wasn't every day one met heroes.

CHAPTER 7

High above the tiny house in the woods, Ven perched with Alet. "She's lying." He watched the woodswoman emerge from the front, check in all directions, and then climb onto the roof of her house. She had a basket of charms dangling from the crook of her elbow. She began to lace the roof with them.

"You'd rather believe the idiot husband?"

"I know when people are hiding secrets."

She snorted.

"I'm not boasting," he said. "It's truth. I've had to learn." He thought of Fara—he hadn't known what the queen was hiding, but he'd known she had secrets. "It's the palace. You can't survive there unless you learn to read people. With time, you'll learn it too."

"Right, O wise and experienced one. Explain this secret, then: Why would a woman marry the kind of man who'd deliberately endanger her? If he'd been wrong, she and the children would have died horribly, and he'd be a murderer."

"But he wasn't wrong."

"Unless he was," Alet said. "You saw all the brand-new charms in that house."

He'd seen them, but he'd seen something else too, the fear in the woodswoman's eyes. She'd tried to hide it, but he was used to looking for it—you could learn a lot about an opponent by deducing what they were afraid of. *I'm right.*

"Even if it's true and she's hiding tremendous secret power, it doesn't matter. You don't want an unwilling candidate. You know firsthand how difficult the trials are, and that's for someone who *wants* to pass."

"She'd want to pass," Ven said. "She wants to survive. All those charms in the house? She's desperate to survive. And for her family to survive."

"So?" Alet said.

Ven glanced at his companion. She wasn't going to like what he was about to propose. Frankly, he didn't like it much either. "I think her desire to protect herself and the people she loves will outstrip any unwillingness. I think she'd fight for them, if she had to."

"If she *can*," Alet said. "I still say she may not have any power at all."

"Then we need to talk to the villagers, learn more about her, and if she seems suitable, we test her," Ven said. "Test both her power and her willingness." Looking down again, he watched the woodswoman venture onto one of the limbs. She was clearly an experienced climber—she'd balanced herself correctly to compensate for the thinness of the branch, which wasn't an easy or obvious maneuver. Stretching, she affixed a charm to the next tree over. There was determination in her. He could see it even from this distance.

He felt Alet glaring at him. "You want to do exactly what that husband of hers did," she accused. He heard the disgust in her voice, but he refused to let it affect him. He didn't take this job to be *nice*. "You want to trick her into using her powers, *if* she has them."

"I will get her to tell the truth, no tricks involved," Ven said. "But yes, I intend to make her use her powers. Unlike her husband, though, we'll be able to protect her if things go wrong." And then . . . *We'll see what she's really made of.*

"Things will go wrong," Alet predicted.

Ven shrugged. "They always do."

AT DAWN, NAELIN FILLED HER POCKETS WITH PROTECTIVE charms, kissed her sleepy children, and informed her husband that if he let them leave the house, she'd let the spirits tear his arms off. He only grunted at her and rolled over in bed, wrapping the blanket around him like a cocoon.

Hesitating in the doorway, she looked back inside at her comfy, snug home. Toasty warm, it was bathed in amber light from the fireplace. Her favorite chair was by the hearth, piled with quilts. A half-knit sweater lay on the tiny table next to it. Maybe it would be smarter to stay home. Surely she could cobble together a few meals—baked roots, at least. They were out of flour, though, and also eggs and sprouts. Realistically, she couldn't feed all four of them for more than a day or two without needing more, and it was safer to travel the well-worn bridges to the market than for either her or Renet to venture into the forest to hunt. After a dinner or two of baked roots, Renet would insist on heading out. *I don't want to have that argument. Or any other argument, for that matter.*

She locked the door carefully behind her and checked the ladder—all clear below. The forest felt crisp and awake, sparkling with morning dew and alive with the chirp of cheerful birds. Or territorial, amorous birds.

She climbed down the ladder and lowered herself onto the forest floor. Hurrying, she stepped over roots and around underbrush, aware of every twig that broke under her feet and every bit of dirt she disturbed, but she didn't see any spirits. Up ahead was the main road: the rope bridges that spanned the forest between Everdale and the neighboring towns. Quickly, she scurried up the ladder to the relative safety of the familiar path.

As she continued on, she began to relax. It was nice to be out of the house and away from Renet's accusations. By the end of the night, "coward" was the kindest thing he'd called her, as he ranted on and on about how she'd ruined her family's one chance at future happiness.

She wasn't a coward; she was practical. Any overlap between the two was coincidental. Renet was delusional if he thought people like the champion and the guard, whose lives were intertwined with royalty, offered safety and security. In fact, the opposite was true. Look at how many had died during the last trials and during the coronation. All but one.

You could sing all the songs and tell all the stories you wanted about it, but it didn't change the fact that most people who used their power didn't become queens. Most died.

He'd accused her of having no ambition and she wanted to shout right back, *You're right!* She was a woodswoman, and she liked being one. She didn't want to be anything else. She liked her life, except when Renet decided it would be fun to turn it upside down. She liked her home and her family and her neighbors and the forest and everything exactly as it was, thank you very much. She did not need champions and royal guards squeezing into her warm, snug home, making her children starry-eyed, and encouraging her husband's ridiculous notions.

Yes, she had power. But she didn't have *enough* power. She wouldn't be one of the few who survived; she'd be one of the many who fell, and what did that gain anyone? Was it worth her death for Renet and the children to live in a bigger house, wear nicer clothes, eat fancier spices, and collect shinier knickknacks? They had everything they needed—a roof over their heads, clothes on their bodies, and food on their table. *Why can't he be content with that? I am!*

Inhaling the fresh forest air, Naelin steadied herself. She was supposed to be calming down, not riling herself back up. The champion and his companion were gone. Renet would reconcile himself to that, eventually, and life would return to normal. She simply had to be diligent with their protections, and everything would be fine.

Up ahead, she saw the center of Everdale. Colorful tents had been pitched on the platform, and from the sound of it, the spaces between them were already packed with people. She heard voices and laughter overlapping, and she felt safer already. Spirits wouldn't dare attack a crowded marketplace. Joining the flow of shoppers, Naelin stepped onto the platform.

Men and women fell silent as she passed. Heads turned, and eyes tracked her. She heard whispers start up in her wake, and she told herself it was her imagination—they weren't talking about her. She greeted a few neighbors she knew by name as she hurried by, and they warily waved back.

Trying to ignore the stares and whispers, she chose her supplies, haggling only when the miller tried to inflate his price beyond what was reasonable. She handed him a small pile of coins, the bulk of what she'd earned selling her last batch of charms, and he accepted them with a loud moan that she was bankrupting him. She thanked him as if he weren't being ridiculous, and she tucked the sack of flour into her larger pack.

Across the market, the town hedgewitch, Corinda, waved to her. "Naelin!" Corinda hurried through the crowd, jostling people out of the way with her plump elbows. "Oh, Naelin!"

"Corinda, I'd been thinking that I should bring you more charms to sell—"

The woman embraced her. "I've been so worried for you!"

Naelin patted Corinda's back awkwardly. *All right, that's . . . nice?* She wasn't outwardly affectionate with people who weren't her children very often, and Corinda had never greeted her with a hug before. "You have? That's . . ." She searched for the right word. Sweet? Odd? Alarming? "I'm fine. We're all fine. Why would you be worried?"

Corinda leaned close enough for Naelin to smell the honeybread on her breath and faintly sour sweat on her skin. "Because of *them*. You know. I was there when Renet told them about you. I tried to shush him, but you know how he is." She hugged Naelin again. "Oh, I thought they'd take you for sure!"

Naelin wished that Corinda wouldn't talk so loud. She glanced right and left—the other shoppers were listening in, and a few didn't bother to hide it. "There's no reason for them to take me," Naelin said in a loud, steady voice. "I have no powers."

"But they think you do," Corinda said. "They've been in town, asking about you."

Naelin felt herself grow cold. *I didn't fool them*, she thought. *I should have known.* "I thought they'd left." She pulled away from her friend and glanced through the crowd, half expecting to see the champion and guard watching her. Her skin prickled with goose bumps. "I have to get home."

"Of course," Corinda said. "Go safely. But Naelin, you should know that they're talking to everyone. And people are mentioning . . . you know." She nodded significantly northward, toward the school.

*Oh, no,* Naelin thought. She'd hoped that everyone had forgotten. It had been years since anyone had mentioned it. Erian had been little, younger than Llor was now, when a rogue wood spirit had split the base of the tree that held the school. The tree had teetered, all the children trapped on the platform high above. Down below, with the other parents, Naelin had seen it all happen. She remembered knowing with absolute clarity that if she didn't do something, the tree would fall and all the children with it. And she remembered watching, with the other parents, as the spirit was forced to heal the tree, knitting the base together, strengthening the trunk with vines, holding it upright until the children could be rescued—and then Naelin had fainted, which was when the rumors began that she had done it. "No one has any proof."

"People don't need proof to spread rumors," Corinda said. "You'd better get home and lay low. The queen's own champion, well, it's the most exciting thing to happen in Everdale in ages, and everyone wants to talk to him. Pretty soon, they'll be making up stories about you just for the chance to look at the man who chose the woman who became queen."

"I'll stay home," Naelin promised. "Once they move on, people will forget. Something else will happen, and they'll talk about that."

Corinda brightened. "Ooh, you could always have an affair with someone. *That* would change the conversation. Or *I* could have an affair with someone . . ."

Naelin flashed her a smile, and hoped she didn't look as worried as she felt. "Thank you for the warning." Waving goodbye, she abandoned her plan to buy enough supplies for the week and instead hurried through the market.

As she pushed through the crowd, Naelin was acutely aware that people, her neighbors and supposed friends, were indeed staring at her and whispering about her, and she felt anger grow in the base of her stomach, right next to the fear. Those strangers had no right to come here, to her home, and muck up her life. She'd made a nice life for herself and her family. She fit in, or she thought she did. She'd worked hard to be just another woods-woman. It wasn't right that they'd torn all that open.

Reaching the rope bridges, she didn't stop. She hurried over the swaying path, glancing back over her shoulder frequently. She'd never felt unsafe in the market before. It was supposed to feel familiar and friendly and—

Rounding a corner, she halted. The champion and the guard lounged against the rail of the bridge, casually, as if they'd been waiting for her, and her anger bubbled over. "What are you still doing here?" Naelin demanded. "I told you I'm not who you need." Part of her recoiled. *I can't talk that way to a champion!* But she didn't back down. This wasn't just about her—she had to be strong for Erian and Llor.

"We like what we heard about you," the champion said.

"You heard lies." Naelin tried to hold on to the anger—it was better than feeling the fear. "Everdale is a boring little town. You're exciting. People will tell you whatever you want to hear, just so you'll stay longer."

"Except you," the guardswoman pointed out.

*Is that what gave me away?* Naelin wondered.

"I'd like to propose a test," the champion said, watching her. "We will rile up a few spirits. If you lack the power to send them away, we will leave you alone. If you don't . . . then you drop the lies and listen to what your queen and country require of you."

Naelin backed along the bridge. This was . . . *unfair*, her brain supplied. *Dangerous. Stupid. Stupidly dangerous.* "You'll get me killed."

"Not if you use your power," the guard said.

"I have children at home," Naelin pleaded, "two young, beautiful children who need their mother. Don't make me do this." She glanced back and forth between them, trying to find a shred of sympathy in their eyes. The guard's expression was colder than a mountain stream.

"They'll be well provided for, regardless of the outcome," the champion said, as if that would soothe her. "The Crown has funds for families such as yours. Your husband and children will never want for anything ever again."

"Except for their mother!" Naelin's voice was shrill. Her muscles screamed at her to *run, run, run!* But she knew she couldn't outrun two trained warriors.

The guardswoman clucked her tongue. "That's not a winning attitude. Use your power, and you'll survive."

*And then you'll take me away*, Naelin thought. She couldn't win. This was a trap. Use her power, and they'd take her away from her family, to the capital, where she'd face worse and worse tests until one finally killed her. Or don't use her power, and risk dying here and now. "You're condemning me to death. If the spirits come after me, I won't be able to stop them, and you'll be murderers."

"The queen will pardon us," the guard said cheerfully. "Good luck!"

"Use your power," the champion advised. He then grabbed on to a rope above the bridge and shimmied up. The guard ran and leaped off the bridge, landing squirrel-like on a branch several trees away.

Naelin stood frozen for a moment. What was she supposed to do? Go home, and risk whatever "test" happening there? Stay here, all alone? Or return to the market?

*Market*, she decided. The champion wouldn't dare "test" her while she was surrounded by innocent people, and her family would be safe. Spinning around, she ran back toward the platform. It wasn't far. Just around the bend.

The rope bridge shook under her, and she shot a look behind her.

Three wood spirits, laughing gleefully, were loping toward her on all fours, like gangly squirrels. Naelin ran faster, her side pinching and the bag of flour pounding on her back. Ahead, she saw the platform—"Help! Help! Spirits are coming!"

On the platform, her cry was repeated, and people scattered, screaming. She kept running, her calves burning and her breath raking her throat. A clawed hand snagged her skirt. She felt a tug and heard the fabric tear.

Swinging her bag off her back, she threw it full in the face of the nearest spirit. The flour sack burst against its face, and the white dust plumed all around them. Coughing, the spirits slowed. She scrambled forward and onto the platform.

Ahead, in the market, it was chaos, as people ran for weapons and to hide. Stands were knocked over and used as barriers. Children were snatched up by parents and hidden inside barrels and behind boxes. Someone was shouting orders, and Naelin ran into the center of the tangle of people. She'd made it! Now the champion and the guard had to come! They wouldn't let the spirits hurt innocent people, right?

"More above!" someone shouted.

Looking up, Naelin saw air spirits swooping between the branches. Leaves spun in whirlwinds in their wake. They plucked at the scarves that had served as tent covers, and the fabric swirled through the air as if this were a celebration—a terrible, terrifying celebration.

Caught up in the press of people, Naelin was swept backward toward the shops. She pulled charms out of her pockets and began handing them to everyone she could reach. "Keep these out," she commanded.

But the spirits didn't attack. They circled the crowd—air spirits above and tree spirits on the platform. Screaming, people shifted out of the way, flattening against the shops, as the spirits slinked through the market, looking in every corner and sniffing the air, as if they were searching for someone.

*For me*, Naelin thought.

She'd be found if she stayed here, out in the open. Glancing behind her, she saw a familiar shop—Corinda's! With a burst of speed, she wove through the throng of people and pushed her way to the door.

Standing in her shop doorway, the hedgewitch was busily handing out charms. "Pay me later; take it now," she was saying. Seeing Naelin, she cried, "You should be home!"

"Shh! You don't see me!" Naelin squeezed past her inside and crouched by the window. Outside, six tree spirits stalked back and forth across the platform. Six! They hissed at the crowd, and people held charms in front of them with shaking arms. *Don't attack*, she thought, but she didn't let the words escape her own mind.

With the champion and the guard out there somewhere watching, she didn't dare use her power. Naelin ran to the shelves. The flour had stunned them, and the charms repulsed them—what if she combined the two? Corinda's shop had every ingredient a hedgewitch would ever need. Naelin pulled canisters from the shelves and began dumping the contents into a bowl. She recited the recipe in her mind, multiplying the ingredients and then stirring. She felt a faint tingle on her arms, raising her arm hairs. Almost done.

Cradling the bowl in her arms, Naelin ran to the window. She peeked out. Across the platform, by the fallen stands, she saw the miller pointing a shaky finger at Corinda's shop. Silently, she cursed him and his overpriced flour.

The tallest tree spirit swung his head toward the shop, and Naelin shrank back. She hugged the bowl of herbs tighter against her chest. Her heart was beating loud, and she thought of Erian and Llor—Erian with her smile that lit her eyes and Llor with his cheerful grin. She pictured them curled up in bed, peaceful, and awake, Erian talking about her day at school and Llor tugging on her skirt, asking her to play.

Sniffing the air, the spirit stalked toward the shop. It gestured, and the others fell in behind it, fanning out. The air spirits hovered inches above the platform. Corinda backed inside. "Hide," she whispered to Naelin. "They're coming!"

Crouching beside the door, Naelin readied the bowl.

Corinda slammed the door shut.

Outside, the spirits howled. Corinda shoved a barrel in front of the door to brace it, and then she was knocked backward as the door burst open. Wood splintered in all directions. *Now!* Lunging forward, blocking her fallen friend, Naelin hurled the contents of the bowl at the spirits as they spilled through the doorway.

The spirits squealed. Scraping at their bodies, they howled. Their arms lashed out, and Naelin retreated. Grabbing Corinda's arm, she dragged her away as the spirits boiled inside, covered in herbs and shrieking as if she'd burned them.

One of the spirits charged, though, plowing into Corinda. Its claws raked her, and Corinda cried out. Naelin threw herself forward, trying to pull the spirit off her friend. The spirit slipped through her fingers and launched itself at her, sinking its fangs into her shoulder. Naelin screamed, and it bit harder. The pain blanked out all reasoning, all memory, just the desire for it to stop, stop, *STOP!*

The thought flew out of her like an arrow, and she felt the word yank at her skin as sharply as the spirit's teeth. Her blood on its fangs, the spirit reared back as if she'd hit it. Naelin clutched her shoulder, and saw the spirit had stopped.

*All* the spirits had stopped.

Cringing, they clustered just inside the shop. Holding her shoulder, Naelin pushed herself up against the wall. She glanced at Corinda. There was blood on her friend's arm, and she was moaning.

The champion and the guard strolled through the smashed doorway. Smiling, they walked past the cowed spirits. "You did it," the guardswoman said. "Congratulations!" Her voice was loud enough to echo across the platform, and Naelin saw people outside, crowded together by the door and window, listening to every word.

"The two things that a true queen needs are the instinct to survive and the instinct to protect," the champion said. "You have both. Your queen and country need you." He held out his hand and commanded, "You will come with us."

Naelin looked at his hand, at her wounded friend, and then at the spirits who were watching her with wide, hollow eyes. This champion and guard had let the spirits come here, where they'd hurt an innocent person and terrified others. The spirits could have killed Corinda. Or Naelin. Or everyone in the market. And the champion and guard would have let them, all in the belief that what the country needed was more important than ordinary people's pain, more important than their lives. *Stupidly dangerous*, she thought.

Clearly and loudly, Naelin said, "No."

The champion shook his head. "You don't understand."

She understood enough. Fixing her eyes on the spirits, she

formed a deliberate thought and threw it at them, *Help me escape. Keep them here.*

Snarling, the spirits leaped toward the champion and guard. The guard drew her knives, and the champion—Naelin didn't stay to see what he did. Clutching her bleeding shoulder, Naelin bolted past them, out the door, and across the platform.

Outside, the crowd shrank away from her, and she saw people she'd known for years—friends of her late parents, shopkeepers she'd visited weekly, woodsmen and woodswomen who had bought her charms from Corinda's shop, neighbors she'd seen daily on the forest paths and in town—staring at her as if she were as dangerous as a spirit. No one called out to her, and no one tried to stop her.

Naelin ran onto the rope bridges, toward home.

## CHAPTER 8

H ome.
Gray roof, bark-brown walls, blue shutters, with pots of pepper and tomato plants on the windowsills and a basket of herbs hung by the door, to soak in patches of sunlight—her home, that she'd bought with Renet, fixed with a hammer and nails bartered in exchange for her charms, shaped with their love and laughter and pain—Naelin had sunk her heart into this place. It had kept her and her family safe from wind, rain, wolves, bears, spirits, shielded them from both winter cold and summer heat. It had cradled them through all the important moments, the momentous moments like Erian's and Llor's births and the quieter moments like when she tucked them in at night or when they shared breakfast on a lazy morning. The kitchen floor boasted scuff marks from all the times they'd scooted their chairs closer to the table, and the bathroom still had water stains from the time Renet had tried to rig a shower. Llor had lost his first tooth in between the floorboards, and Erian had once scrawled doodles on the wall before Naelin had taken away her pencil. She hadn't planned to ever leave.

Now she had no choice.

Naelin sped toward it, up the ladder, and inside. She threw herself into the kitchen and her arms around Erian and Llor. "Pack quickly," she told them. She kissed both their foreheads. "Only what you need."

"Mommy, I don't wanna—" Llor's voice pitched into a whine. His sister shushed him. "Don't you know her serious face?"

Llor screwed his face up like a shriveled apple. His lower lip quivered, and Naelin realized she'd scared him when she burst inside. "Everything's all right, sweetie, but we have to take a trip. Just for a little while. You can bring Boo-Boo."

He brightened and scampered to fetch his stuffed squirrel, the one Erian had sewed for him out of old bedsheets and extra buttons. Its tail was an old scrub brush that she'd cleaned and dyed. With the boy on a mission, Naelin retrieved three sacks from the rafters and began to stuff them with clothes, charms, bedding, and medicines. To hers, she added a few kitchen supplies: a paring knife, a tea strainer, forks and spoons, a ladle that had been her mother's. As she packed, she tried hard not to think about anything but practicalities: there wasn't time to sift through the layered memories, to linger over the lopsided owl carving that Erian had made or the shredded baby blanket that had been Llor's or the pastel sketch of her wedding day. She still had the dried circle of roses that she'd worn in her hair, and up in the rafters, neatly packed away, was her wedding dress with the beaded embroidery on the bodice that had taken her grandmother six months of sewing every night . . . *I'll go to my home village*, she decided. Ever since the day her parents died, she hadn't gone back. She rarely even mentioned the place. No one would ever guess she'd gone there. With luck, her old house would be uninhabited, though the roof had probably caved in by now—

She heard her husband stomp his feet at the door, knocking off the debris, and she felt a lump in her throat. There was no point in keeping the dirt out, not anymore. *Stop*, she told herself firmly. She didn't know she wouldn't come back. All she had to do was find a place to lie low until this blew over, until the spirits forgot, until the neighbors moved on to other scandals, and then she could return. A month, maybe more, and then it would all return to normal.

Or mostly normal.

"You won't be coming with us, Renet." She didn't turn around. "You're leaving?" She heard the shock in his voice, as if she'd hit him with a frying pan, and all she felt was tired. He couldn't be surprised. He'd set this in motion. How did he expect it to end? Naelin blinked hard and told herself firmly that she would not cry. Over her home, yes. Over her life here, the cozy comfortable life she'd carved out for herself and her family, yes. But later, not now.

"You went too far this time, Renet. I can't forgive this." She bustled over to Llor and added a blanket to his pack, as well as warm socks. She checked Erian's pack and added her brush. Erian's eyes were overbright, trying hard to be brave. Naelin squeezed her hand and tried a smile, failing dismally. She then loaded the pack onto Erian's back. "Did everyone make a pee? Llor, do you have to pee?"

Lip still quivering, he shook his head. She watched him wiggle on a chair, and then she pointed to the bathroom door. He scooted in, and she crossed to the window over the kitchen sink, the one with a view toward town. She didn't know if the champion and the guard would come after her again, or if they'd give up on her as too much trouble. She didn't have much hope for the latter. Regardless, the spirits wouldn't forget this place so fast. *You know you have to leave,* she told herself. *Quit dithering.*

Renet was standing in the middle of the kitchen, running his hands through his hair as if he were totally blindsided by this. "Naelin, be reasonable. You're overreacting."

She faced him finally, and in a low voice she never thought she'd need to use, said, "I'm not going to do this in front of the children. I'm not going to talk badly about you in front of them, not now and not later. You can be the sweet, doting father in their memories. But you cannot come with us now. We aren't safe with you." And with that, she shepherded Llor and Erian toward the door and left Renet with his mouth hanging open, his face slack, his eyes as stunned and hurt as a shot deer.

*I won't cry now.*

Carrying their packs, they climbed down the ladder and hurried across the forest floor. Llor was whimpering. "Why can't Father come with us? Where are we going? I don't want to go. I want to go h-h-home, with Father."

Erian clutched Naelin's arm. "Mama, look."

Slowing, Naelin looked up and saw a face peering at them from within the bark—its eyes were like knots in the wood, and its face was curved with the folds of the bark. "Keep moving," Naelin whispered. It would lose interest once she had some distance.

But it didn't.

And even more came.

An earth spirit, with a body like a badger and a face like a wrinkled man, crawled out of a hole between two roots. Three air spirits, no larger than Naelin's palm, flitted between leaves, pacing them, above. She caught a glimpse of a fire spirit, bobbing in the distance, just at the edge of her sight so that she wasn't certain if it was a trick of her eyes. Her skin prickled, and the air felt like it crackled, as if the entire forest were watching them pick their way toward the ladder that led to the bridges. Naelin helped Llor over a root. He was puffing from the exertion—his little legs weren't going to keep up if they needed speed. She could carry him, she thought, for a little while, but not also the packs, and they'd need them, if they were to camp—

*Who are you fooling?* she asked herself. They couldn't camp, not with so many spirits watching them. She'd been naïve to think she could walk away from this mess and nothing would notice or follow her.

"Mama?" Erian whispered, her voice tight.

"I know. I see them."

"What do we do?"

That was the question. They could return home, seal the house with as many charms as she had, and try to wait it out. They could flee faster and hope the spirits lost interest, but there were more now than before, and the spirits would keep following them.

Naelin forced herself to stop.

Stop her legs from striding forward faster than Llor could follow.

Stop her thoughts from tumbling in knots faster than she could untangle.

*It's too late.* She'd used her power, and the spirits had noticed her. The fact that they hadn't attacked yet was luck, and she couldn't trust her children's safety to luck. She needed to get the spirits to stop noticing her, and she had no idea how to do that. But she did know two people who were experts on spirits . . . though she doubted they'd want to help her after she'd turned the spirits against them. *They caused this mess*, she thought. *They have to fix it.* "We're going to visit Aunt Corinda," she said at last.

Llor brightened. "Will she let me play with Master Wuggles?"

Naelin stared at him for a moment. "What?"

"The cat," Erian said.

"She named it Master Wuggles?"

"Yes!" Llor trotted happily forward now. "I said she should name him Lord Mouser the Third, because she's always saying he acts like he's ruler of the house, plus he catches mice."

She shouldered Erian's pack along with her own, after it snagged on a bush. A glitter of yellow eyes flashed from within the bushes—*a wolf*, she guessed, *much too close*. Naelin kept her voice deliberately light. "Was there a Lord Mouser the First and Second?"

"No."

She took Llor's pack as well, hurrying them toward the ladder to town. She shot glances at the bushes, watching for the wolf. "Then why would he be the third?"

"Because he's not the fourth," he said, as if she were the stupidest person in the world.

"Ahh. Of course."

"Mama," Erian whispered. "There's an animal in the bushes."

"Just keep moving," Naelin said.

"Mama, I think it's a wolf!" Fear shook her voice.

Just what she needed. Fate must have been very angry with her. "Shoulders back, chin up, look like a predator, not prey. Let's make it a game. Be a bear."

Tears were leaking out of the corners of Erian's eyes, but she nodded and held her back straight and chin up, trying to look brave. Llor stomped and growled, "I'm a bear! Grrrr!"

"That's it. More noise!" Naelin growled too. "Roar!" She

stretched her arms up and crashed her feet deliberately on the loudest twigs and driest leaves. At least this might scare off the wolf. She had no hope for it scaring the spirits.

They reached the ladder, and she shooed them up, climbing up behind them. Below, earth spirits prowled around the base of the ladder. She felt like a target, dangling in the air, with both hands occupied on the rungs, but she focused on climbing rung after rung until they reached the bridge.

She shepherded Erian and Llor ahead of her, feeling the sway of the bridge beneath them, wondering at what moment the spirits would attack. It might not even be a direct attack. She'd heard of perfectly sound bridges suddenly fraying, ropes snapping and wood rotting beneath the feet of woodsmen who had angered the spirits. Soon, she saw the marketplace ahead of them, the bright canopies, torn and fluttering in the wind. A few people scurried between them, but most doors were shut and windows barred. She headed directly for the hedgewitch's shop. "Stay behind me," she told Erian and Llor, "and don't enter until I say it's safe."

Ducking into the shadows, she squinted, trying to force her eyes to adjust quickly—there were figures across the shop, behind the counters. Corinda was huddled in one corner, her face buried in her arms, squeezing herself as small as possible beside a barrel. The two strangers, Champion Ven and Captain Alet, were plastered against the wall, visible as blurred figures through the translucent bodies of the spirits.

They were still here. *Good*, she thought.

Now she had to convince them to help, after she'd just refused them. And trapped them.

The air spirits were amorphous and had spread like jellyfish into one undulating mass, with eyes and mouths that floated in the top nodules of their bodies, and appendages that wrapped into one another. Both the champion and captain had swords drawn, aimed toward the center of the gelatinous bodies, and were speaking to each other in low voices.

"Mama, what are they doing?"

She felt every muscle tense, ready to hurl herself between danger and her child. "Llor, I asked you to wait outside."

Erian jumped in. "Sorry, Mama! I tried—"

"Are the spirits going to hurt them?"

She walked forward, just a step, watching the spirits. Their bodies continued to flow into one another, but they didn't seem to be moving closer to the two. They'd made themselves into a wall, keeping them there, like she'd told them to. She hadn't imagined her command would last so long. "I don't think so."

"Are they going to hurt to the spirits?"

Same answer. "I don't think so." Naelin had no doubt they could kill the spirits if they wanted to. She also knew what would happen if they did—their deaths would destroy a part of the forest, perhaps even the village tree itself.

"Shush, Llor, you aren't supposed to kill spirits," Erian said. "Bad luck."

"Bad things happen when you do," the champion agreed, calmly, his sword steady. "I've seen a spirit die and a tree crumble to dust, the moisture sucked from the air, the land barren. We try to avoid killing them."

"I am sorry about this . . ." Naelin began, and then she stopped. She wasn't sorry—this wouldn't have happened if they hadn't called the spirits down on her. Maybe at least now she had the upper hand. "I'd like to offer you a bargain. You teach me to how to keep the spirits away from my family, and I will order the spirits to set you free." She felt Erian slide her hand into hers. Llor was clinging to her leg. She wrapped her free arm around his shoulders.

"You tried to run and they followed you," the champion guessed.

"They noticed me because of you. Now I want you to fix this. I want my life and my family back the way it was." *Minus Renet*, she thought with a pang. She couldn't trust him anymore, especially now that she'd seen how precarious their safety was.

"You can't change what happened," the champion said, "and you can't deny who you are."

Naelin held her children closer and kept a very tight rein on her thoughts. She wanted to leave the smug, self-righteous bastard to the spirits, but he was the one with the knowledge she

needed. "Who I am is a mother, a woodswoman, a charm maker."
She didn't add wife. "It is my right to define me, not yours."

The guardswoman snorted. "I like her."

"I don't care," Naelin shot back. "I don't need your approval,
and I don't care if I fit your image of what a woman with power
should be. Find yourself a little girl to brainwash. Just help me fix
what you broke."

"Aratay needs you," the champion said.

"My family needs me more."

He shook his head. "Are you truly this selfish?" Through the
oozy bodies of the spirits, he seemed to blur and bobble.

Llor piped up. "Don't call my mama selfish! I don't care if you
are a hero. You are *not* a nice man. I hope the spirits eat you!"

Kneeling, Naelin gathered Llor and Erian closer, their warm
bodies as comforting as blankets. Llor was vibrating in anger, his
pudgy fists curled up. Erian looked pale, her lips pursed, as if
she were concentrating hard to understand what was happening.
Naelin didn't tell Llor to apologize or take his words back—she felt
the same way. Trying to bargain was a mistake. But she couldn't
think of any other options. No one in Everdale could help her.

The guardswoman sighed heavily. "Tell her."

Champion Ven objected, "Queen Daleina wouldn't—"

"Not *that*. About her power."

Naelin's eyes narrowed. She trusted them about as far as she
could throw them, which was not at all, given how many muscles
they both had. It was clear they had secrets, and she was one hundred percent certain she wouldn't like them. "What about my
power?" She hated using the word "my." She never asked to have
power, and she would *not* let it leave her children motherless. "I
don't want it. Never wanted it."

The champion pinned her with his pale blue eyes. She didn't
know how they could look so clear through the blur of the spirits'
bodies, but they were sharp and bright. "You're strong."

"Ludicrously strong," the guard put in. She poked one of the
spirits with the tip of her sword. "These spirits refuse to budge.
We hurt them, and they still stayed."

"I told them to hold you here," Naelin said.

"Yeah, a while ago, and then you left," the guard said. "Your command should have faded, but look"—another poke—"freakily obedient. I've never seen anything like it, at least in someone who's not a queen. Or even trained."

"She's right," the champion said. "You have more raw power than I've ever seen, and if I know that, you can be certain the spirits do too. They aren't going to leave you alone, no matter where you run."

Naelin clutched Erian and Llor harder, until Llor squawked. She forced herself to loosen her grip. "And if I order them to leave me alone? If I'm so very powerful, they'll obey, right?"

"Or they'll leave the entire village, and no plants will grow, no fires will start, and you'll destroy your home," the champion said. From the corner, Corinda chirped, a half moan half cry. "You're untrained. That makes you dangerous."

Naelin's mouth felt dry. She swallowed and tried to form words.

"I have a bargain for you, Mistress Naelin," he said. "Come with me to Mittriel. Meet the queen. Talk to her. And I will teach you to control your power."

Suddenly, Erian gripped her arm. "Mama, he wants you to be an heir?"

He smiled. "That's right. Your mother can be a hero."

Both Erian and Llor burst into tears. "No! Mama, no!" Llor wailed. Erian clung to her and cried, "No, Mama, the heirs died! They all died! I don't want you to die!" Kneeling, Naelin wrapped her arms around them both and held them.

"Nicely done," the guard said.

The champion swore. "I never claimed to be a people person."

Naelin murmured into their hair. "Queen Daleina didn't die, did she? They want to teach me how not to die. They want to show me how to keep you safe. I won't let them make me an heir. I won't let them take me from you."

They cried as if their hearts were breaking, and she felt her own heart twisting. All she wanted to do was kiss their damp cheeks and heal what this day had shredded inside them. She wanted to knit their lives back together, take them home, pretend none of this had happened, erase it from their memories. "Don't go, don't go, don't go!" they cried.

*I don't want to!*

From the corner, Corinda, with her voice quivering, said, "You have to go with them, Naelin. Renet can—"

"I've left him," Naelin said firmly. Speaking the words out loud made it official. As she said the words, she felt her body shudder once and then she felt calm. At least there was one decision she was certain about.

"Witnessed, and gladly," Corinda said. "Leave Erian and Llor with me. I'll watch them as if they were my own—"

"No, Mama, we aren't leaving you!" Erian shouted, with Llor echoing her.

Naelin fixed her eyes on the champion. Every fiber of her body screamed, *Don't leave them.* "Will they be safe here, with Corinda?"

The champion hesitated—she saw the moment of hesitation. "Yes."

She narrowed her eyes, the way she looked at Llor when he claimed to have brushed his teeth but still had bits of his dinner stuck to them. "You're lying."

He shrugged—at least he respected her enough to be called out on the lie. "It's possible the spirits will realize they're yours. Some are . . . vengeful. But I can promise they will be as safe here as anyplace in Aratay, and safer than they would be with you. In fact, the less contact you have with them, the safer they'll be."

"You really are horrible with people," the guard said to the champion.

He glared at her. "You can do better?"

Naelin wanted to turn and walk out of the shop. No, she wanted to run. Far and fast, beyond Aratay if she had to, she'd take her children as far as necessary to keep them safe. "You are asking me to give up my children? On the chance they *might* be safer? But you can't promise their safety."

"No one can promise safety, except the queen," the guard said. It was a saying that Renthians often repeated, usually when people were about to begin a journey. She said it like rote, but the familiar words sank into Naelin. "Life is unsafe," the guard continued. "That's why we need you. You have the power—"

"I want the queen to promise their safety," Naelin interrupted. Everyone fell silent.

"I will come, I will train, but the queen will protect Erian and Llor." She felt Erian stop crying, her shoulders stilling and her body pressing against her, trusting Naelin. "You want me? That's what it will take."

Champion Ven studied her, and Naelin held herself still, steady, and strong under the force of his gaze. "Done," he said. "Now tell the spirits to release us."

*Release them*, she thought at the spirits. As easy as turning a faucet, they flowed away from the champion and guardswoman. Solidifying again, they spread wings and flew out the door and up toward the sky.

Llor broke away from her and ran to the door, watching them leave. "You did it, Mama!"

*Yes, I did*, she thought.

"Come, take your pack" was all she said. She held out Llor's pack to him. Beside her, Erian shrugged on her own pack. "We have a journey to make."

## CHAPTER 9

T know five songs about the False Death."
      Daleina cracked one eye open and rolled onto her side to
look at Hamon. "Tell me there's one with a happy ending." She
watched him, mortar and pestle on his lap, as he mashed the petals of a glory vine. Its overly sweet scent hung in the air of her
chambers, suffocating the fresh air from the open window.

"I thought there was one about a dying lover who drinks a
miracle cure procured after completing seven quests. But then I
realized that's the ballad of Tyne, about the farm boy from Chell
who was dying from the bite of a jewel snake—the antidote was so
rare that only a single recluse had it, and she demanded that his
lover, a sheepherder's daughter—"

"Hamon?" she said his name gently. He didn't babble often,
but he hadn't slept much in the past few days, or left her side.
She'd had to encourage the rumor that they were lovers again,
in order to explain why a healer was constantly in her chambers.
If he'd ever stop working, she'd happily make it not just a rumor,
erase his worries and any thoughts of this illness she had. In the
sliver of moonlight, he looked sweetly handsome.

"Oh, sorry, what I meant to say is that all the songs about the
False Death describe the same symptoms: shortness of breath,
heart palpitations, organ failures . . . Obviously, they use more
poetic language, the stilling of the heart, the slowing of the wind,
but what strikes me is that you did not have any of the warning

signs and still don't. You began with the false deaths and have few other symptoms, aside from tiredness, which could be due to simple stress."

She closed her eyes and then opened them again. Her lids felt heavy, and she wondered what time it was. Very late. Or very early. She didn't want to think about her sickness—it felt unreal, as if it were happening to someone else. "Do you think that's good or bad?"

He was silent.

"Bad," she guessed.

"It means rapid onset, which is unusual." He chose his words carefully. "I don't know of any cases like this."

"My father always said I was special."

He carried his mixture over to her and held it up to her lips. She propped herself up on her elbow, took the bowl from him, and drank without help. She winced—the glory vine tasted like dirt and moldy berries, with an aftertaste of chalky salt. "All right?"

She licked her lips. "Delicious."

He nearly smiled. "You are a bad liar."

"Let's hope I'm not." She stayed propped up, watching him as he carried the bowl back and carefully washed it out. "If people guess I'm sick, there will be panic. I want at least a few candidates approved and in training before word gets out. It would be even better if I could have at least one actual heir in place." She wondered why she could talk about it so calmly. It was as if the knowledge of what was happening had separated from how she felt—she felt fine, therefore she would always be fine. *I suppose I'm an optimist*, she thought. *A pragmatic optimist.*

"You're going to need help, someone you trust. Early onset could mean you will worsen faster than we thought, and I can't be with you all the time if I'm going to be researching a cure."

"I trust Ven, but he's searching for a candidate with Captain Alet." She closed her eyes. She didn't want to think about this. It was bad enough that she had the False Death, but early onset? A kind that Hamon didn't even recognize? *I don't think this is precisely what Daddy meant when he said "special."* "Sing me one of the songs, about the False Death. I want to hear how someone made this pretty."

He began to sing, his soothing voice rolling over her,

*"Soon but soon, little dove, I'll be here by your side,*
*to drink the wine, taste your tears,*
*don't cry, little dove, I'll be here by your side,*
*when darkness comes, I will not feel,*
*but when day returns, I'll be here by your side,*
*by your side, little dove, for death is not goodbye."*

"Very pretty," she murmured. Her limbs felt as if they were stuffed with wood. She wanted to ask, *Is this normal?* but she felt too tired to form the words. Tomorrow she'd cry again. Tomorrow it would feel real, and she would face whatever needed facing. But for now, her pillows were soft, and she felt her thoughts drift apart, disintegrating as she reached for them.

"Will you think about it? Someone you trust? Who do you trust?"

"My sister," Daleina said, either out loud or only in her head. "I miss my sister."

HAMON WATCHED DALEINA DRIFT BACK TO SLEEP AND TRIED TO convince himself it was normal sleepiness. He didn't make a habit of lying to himself, though, not about medical matters. She'd had another blackout only this morning–not a complete "false death," but she'd lost consciousness for seven seconds. The nearby spirits hadn't reacted, which meant she hadn't died either in a false or true sense, but her heart rate had slowed, and she had gasped for air when she woke. It wasn't surprising it was wearing her down.

He knew precious little about cases of early onset. Ordinary cases were rare enough. It cropped up in families, but often skipped generations, and it tended to strike the elderly, whose bodies were already failing. His former teacher, Master Popol, had waxed on about it once–said it was a mistake in the brain, an interruption between mind and body, a failure of communication, and the fact of its existence had bothered the loquacious healer so much that he took it as a personal affront. Communication between body and mind shouldn't fail, any more than communication between healer and patient, and then his teacher had moved on to discussing how best to cultivate trust between healer and patient. Calmness helped, and Hamon was trying his best to stay calm. Honesty was important, and he hadn't lied to Daleina about her sickness, but equally important was knowledge. A healer, Popol was fond of saying, should be a fountain of facts, and Hamon wasn't, at least not with regard to this illness.

*I can fix that,* he thought.

Seating himself by the window, he lit a firemoss lantern, squeezing the moss to wake its light and adjusting the shutters on the lantern so its light fell only on him, not on his sleeping queen. He then pulled a stack of blank paper from his pack and began to write. He'd say he was conducting research, in attempt to apply for admittance to the university. He'd claim he wanted to transition from healer to scientist, and his chosen topic was the False Death, but first he wanted to glean the accumulated wisdom of his illustrious future colleagues—yes, praise them, make them feel special, flatter their wisdom and knowledge. He could play the humble scholar. Seeking out more parchment, he decided he wouldn't limit himself to the healers and scholars of Aratay. He'd reach out to those in Semo and Chell, even as far away as Belene and Elhim. Someone, somewhere, may have a scrap of information that would help Daleina. He addressed each letter just as carefully, sealed them with his own personal seal, and tied each with a ribbon of healer blue.

As the dawn bells rung, he summoned a caretaker to the queen's door and handed the stack of letters to him with strict instructions to send them with utmost speed. While he waited for replies, he'd delve into the hospital's library—there could be case studies that were relevant—and talk to everyone with any scrap of knowledge . . .

*Everyone?* he asked himself.

"You're doing it again," Daleina said. She'd gotten out of bed and was washing her face in a basin. She met his eyes in the mirror. She looked like her usual beautiful self, albeit with a bruise-like darkness under her eyes and a crease on her cheek from the folds of her pillow.

"Doing what?"

"Worrying so much that you're nearly vibrating. It won't matter how good a liar I am if anyone can read my condition off you without even knowing you." She sounded so calm and reasonable. He didn't know how she did it. Except that he used to be able to do it with every patient he ever had—detach himself, see the symptoms as separate from the person, project an air of soothing calmness. He'd worked hard to develop that air. *It's harder when the patient is Daleina*, he thought.

"Did I ever tell you why I became a healer?" he asked.

"Your father died, and you couldn't save him," Daleina said immediately.

He blinked, surprised she remembered that story. He'd only told her once, and she'd never repeated it or asked any questions. It had been a highly edited version of the truth—he'd said his father had been ill, and he hadn't been able to heal him. "Yes. And it was my mother who killed him." That wasn't a detail he mentioned often to anyone. Or ever.

He saw Daleina flinch—he'd shocked her. He'd known he would. Compassion welled up in her eyes, her beautiful eyes, and he looked away and forced himself to continue: "She slipped bloodwood into his dinners—he always had a roast pork sandwich, and she cured it with salt and bloodwood. Never let me have any and only ate a little herself, though in retrospect I think she must have regurgitated it afterward to avoid any symptoms. When I asked her about it, later, she said she was merely helping nature along. He'd been complaining of pains in his legs, she said. That's it. Just pains, the ordinary stiffness that you'd develop from a life of high-altitude tree cutting, the kind that could be eased with a soak in hot water. She had no other reason, even claimed to love him, though I doubt she has the ability to love anyone."

Daleina was quiet for a moment. "How old were you?"

"Eight."

"And that's when you left?"

He heard the sympathy in her voice and wished he could wrap it around him like a cloak, but he didn't deserve it. "No, that's when she accelerated my lessons, teaching me about plants and herbs and poisons. I left when I was twelve, after she used me to kill our neighbor, an elderly man whose snoring kept my mother awake at night."

Glancing at Daleina, he expected to see sympathy mutate into revulsion in her eyes—he'd confessed to murdering a helpless old man—but instead there was only more pity, which wasn't better. He looked away from her at the tapestries that filled her walls with rich greens, golds, and blues. "Hamon?" Her voice was gentle. "Why are you telling me this?"

"That's how I knew about glory vines . . . and about nightend berries," he said. Daleina flinched at the mention of the berries that had ended her predecessor's life. "She knew—knows—about all sorts of obscure plants and their uses, mainly because she doesn't feel bound by any ethics when it comes to experimentation. She may—and this is very much only a dim possibility—have some shred of knowledge that could help you."

Suddenly, Daleina's eyes widened, and he knew she had leaped to guess where his thoughts had taken him. "You want to ask her about the False Death."

"I *don't*. Because if I reach out to her, she will know where I am, and she will come to see me." For years, he'd kept himself away from her, mostly by traveling, first with Healer Popol and then with Champion Ven, staying in the outer villages and away from cities, but if he contacted her, he'd have to tell her where he was, if only so her response could find him. He knew her well enough to know she wouldn't merely send word. She'd come here, whether or not she could—or would—help. "But if I don't . . ."

"You're asking my permission to invite this . . . your mother here?" Her words were careful. She'd become more careful with her words and her tone since she'd been crowned. If he hadn't known her, he would have thought she was measuring the decision of what to ask the cook to prepare for dinner.

"You misunderstand me. I am not asking. I *am* going to invite her. If there's a chance there's knowledge she has that could help you, then I must. I am telling you as a warning: if"–*when*–"she comes, she is as likely to want to kill you as to heal you. You must not trust her. Ever."

"I have to say this sounds somewhat like a bad idea."

He studied her, the warmth of the morning sun filtering through her hair, making it glow like a halo around her face. Her eyes were bright, awake, healthy, and beautiful. She had a way of looking at you that made you feel as if you mattered, that she would do anything she could to keep you safe, that she was devoted to you. He knew she looked at everyone that way, that she felt personally responsible for their safety, but it still warmed him and made him want to work that much harder to keep her alive and well. "You dying is a bad idea, and I'm not going to let it happen." If that meant reaching out to the demons of his childhood, then he would. "I'd walk through fire for you."

She looked on the verge of saying at least a half-dozen things, considering, then discarding them. At last, she only said, "I'll keep a bucket of water handy."

He loved her more in that moment than he ever had.

## CHAPTER 10

It wasn't that Ven disliked young children.

On the whole, he had no strong feelings about them one way or another, except when they were dead, which was sad, wasteful, and made him want to bash things. Live children . . . he hadn't spent much time with them since he was one. He was impressed with their ability to annoy one another.

"Mama, he's doing it again," the older one—the girl, Erian—said.

"Am not." The younger one was . . . oh, what was his name? F-something? B? Ven watched the boy deliberately slide a stick behind him and poke his sister, lightly, in the side. She swatted at him, but he was quicker, dropping the stick and spreading his hands to show his innocence. "I'm all the way over here, Mama. I can't even reach her. Must have been a spirit."

Their mother, Naelin, was sewing a fresh charm onto the boy's jacket. She didn't look up from her neat, even stitches. "Llor, we don't joke about spirits."

*Llor.* He'd been that close to remembering.

*Well . . . not really.*

"You may joke about rabid squirrels," Naelin added, "like the one behind you."

Both children whipped around so fast they nearly toppled off the branch. There were no squirrels behind them, rabid or otherwise. Just a blackbird, who cocked its head at them, then cawed before flying off its branch. "Mama," Erian said, with a note of profound disapproval in her voice.

Ven saw the corner of Naelin's mouth twitch into an almost smile. He liked that she had a sense of humor. Boded well for her ability to survive what was to come. "Say good night to Champion Ven and Captain Alet," she told them.

In unison, the children said, "Good night, Champion Ven. Good night, Captain Alet."

Putting down her sewing, Naelin helped secure both her children into the netting that Ven had strung up between the branches. She wrapped blankets around them and kissed them both on the cheek. "Sweet dreams, my loves."

It was a simple act, but so full of absolute love that it made something ache inside Ven's rib cage. He rubbed his chest as if it were indigestion.

"I don't want to dream," Llor told her.

"Why not?" Naelin asked. "Dreams can be nice. You might have one about a friendly bear who carries you for a ride through the wood. Or a dancing bear, who performs on high wires."

Llor giggled. "In a dance dress?"

"With ribbons in his fur."

He stopped giggling. "What if I have a nightmare?"

His sister answered, "Then I'll hug you until you fall back asleep."

"What if *you* have a nightmare?" he asked her.

"Then I'll tell Mama, and she'll tell me silly stories until it goes away," Erian said.

"Tell me a silly story now," Llor demanded.

Naelin kissed them both again, on the foreheads this time. "Now it's time for sleep. You've had a very full day." Ven flinched as she said that, though she hadn't looked at him. He'd kept forgetting the children didn't have long legs. They'd needed to rest frequently, drink water, and poke at each other. He hadn't crossed half the miles he normally would have. Still, she managed to make him feel guilty with that one statement, as if it had been his idea to bring children on a training journey.

Speaking of which . . . *I have to start training her*, he thought.

*Tonight.* He'd neglected it in the interest of traveling as far from her home village as possible, to minimize the risk of her changing her mind, but now they were sufficiently far away and also not near anyone else, so he wouldn't have to worry about endangering any innocents.

He waited while she told the children a story—apparently they had finagled one out of their mother—about a snail who wanted to climb a tree to see the sunrise. The snail was swallowed whole by a bird, excreted over the ocean ("Poop!" Llor shouted with glee), and then washed ashore on an island known for its beautiful sunrises on the beach—but the snail never saw a single sunrise because he was so tired from his three-year adventure that he slept late every morning thereafter. Ven supposed the story had some sort of moral, possibly linked to a *go to sleep right now* message, but he couldn't get past the idea of the snail surviving all that.

"You're staring at her again," Alet said in a low voice as she dropped onto the branch beside him.

"I was not—"

"I get it. She's a mama bear. Even I admire that. I never had that. It was just my sister and me growing up—our mother left shortly after I was born, and our father worked all the time, until he got too sick to take care of himself, much less anyone else. We'd have loved someone to kiss our boo-boos and tell us bedtime stories. I'm guessing you had a less-than-ideal childhood as well? Not that I want to discuss it, because I don't."

Watching Naelin did not make him think about his childhood. In fact, it woke very different thoughts, but that was not a matter he even wanted to consider. He had a job to do. "We aren't discussing anything; we're training a candidate. Starting now." He unwrapped the charms from the hilt of his knife and then buried the blade in the flesh of the tree. Wriggling it back and forth and twisting it, he felt the blade cut into the soft pulp and watched Naelin. She'd left Erian and Llor in their hammocks and returned to the fireside, resuming her needlework with the new charm.

After a second, her head shot up. "There's a spirit nearby."

"You're the one with the power," Ven said, watching her as he deliberately bored the knife deeper into the wood. "Send it away."

"You're the one with the knife; *you* send it away," she countered, and then stopped. "What are you doing?"

"Starting your training." He plucked the knife from the tree and used it to point at a branch behind Naelin. "Be alert."

She flung herself to the side, stretching her arms wide, to block the branch between the spirit and her children. She then grabbed the charm she'd been working on, ripped it from her son's jacket, and held it ready to throw. Reaching over, Ven plucked it out of her hand and tossed it off the branch. It fluttered down, hitting branches as it fell, until it was out of sight. "What are you doing?" she whispered—he noticed that even scared she kept her voice low so as not to wake and alarm her children.

"Use your power."

"It will draw more."

"Then you'll use more power. You will use it until you understand it." He twirled his knife in the air. "I know many ways to anger spirits, and I will keep doing it until—"

She didn't wait for him to finish his pronouncement. Instead, she scooped Llor into her arms and shook Erian awake. "Come on, loves, let's climb a little, all right? Just a little climb, down to the forest floor."

Erian rubbed her eyes. "Mama, what's wrong?"

Llor wrapped his arms around her neck and burrowed his face into her hair. His legs clung around her waist like a baby monkey. Ven was pleased to see Naelin was strong—she appeared to be planning to climb while carrying the child. Physical strength wasn't essential for an heir, but it helped.

But what exactly was she doing? She wasn't *leaving*, was she?

Yes, she was.

"Champion Ven is not making good choices," Naelin told her daughter, "so we are going to give him a little time by himself to think about what he's done."

"Oooh," Erian said to him, "you're in trouble. Once Mama locked Father out of the house for a whole night, even though it was raining. He got very wet before she threw him a tent."

"Champion Ven can handle his own messes," Naelin said crisply, "as can your father. It's important to understand that actions have consequences." She was already climbing down, positioning her body to block Erian from the spirits, while carrying Llor—she'd clearly done this before, climbed defensively. *Mama bear*, he thought.

Behind him, Alet murmured, "You're just going to let them go?"

He tried, and failed, to keep the amusement—and admiration—out of his voice. "I believe I'm supposed to stay here and think about what I've done." Above, he spotted a rustle of leaves, and an angular face poked through—its features were twisted bark, its eyes were embers, and its hands were covered in thorns. It hissed at him, displaying rows of teeth. Instantly, he felt less amused. Naelin was supposed to use her power to protect all of them. Instead, she was rapidly fleeing the area, and the spirits had correctly decided he was the one who'd damaged their beloved tree. Behind him, Alet sighed. He heard her draw her sword.

NAELIN HEARD THE FIGHTING OVERHEAD, AND IT WAS QUIETER than she'd have imagined: the scuffling of feet on bark, the hollow ring of steel as it hit flesh, a grunt, a hiss. She climbed faster. Erian and Llor stuck to her as if glued and didn't speak.

She jammed her feet into the crevasses of the bark, feeling her way down. Llor clung to one side of her—he'd wrapped her belt around his waist as they'd practiced. Erian was in front of her, climbing within the curve of Naelin's arms. She felt her daughter's movements as she brushed against her, and heard the breathing of both her children. Away from the camp, darkness closed around them like a blanket, and Naelin listened as hard as she could, hoping the spirits didn't notice them.

Eventually, her foot landed in dirt—the forest floor. She peered into the darkness around them. They'd come down between the curves of the roots. "Hide here," she whispered, and herded Erian and Llor into the folds of the massive roots. They clustered together, roots on three sides of them, snug in the embrace of the tree. Naelin gathered her children close and wished they hadn't left home. She didn't belong out here, risking her family, trusting a man who didn't understand that some risks weren't acceptable. She thought of Renet and wondered if she'd traded one man with bad judgment for another, but she couldn't bring herself to miss him. At least Champion Ven had never lied to her. "Sleep," she whispered into her children's hair.

"I can't," Erian whispered back.

"I know. But pretend, and maybe you'll fool yourself and actually fall asleep."

Llor snuggled closer, and she breathed in his sweet little-boy scent. It didn't seem to matter how many mud puddles he fell into, he exuded a smell that was better than baking. "Mama, I'm scared."

"That's good. Fear can be your friend. It tells you when to run and when to hide. The trick is that after you've run and hid, you have to tell your fear thank you very much, you're fine now, come back later."

"Will Champion Ven and Captain Alet be okay?" Erian asked, her voice small. Naelin held her tighter. It was easy to forget that Erian was still a child too. She was growing up so fast and wanted so badly to be an adult already.

"Yes," Naelin started to answer and then stopped as she saw a shadow move within the other shadows, a shift of gray. "Shhh."

They obediently quieted, knowing better than to ask why.

It didn't *feel* like a spirit. She couldn't sense any crinkling in the air, but she heard the nearest bushes rustle, and then Erian let out a tiny gasp and squeezed tighter. *An animal?* It sounded larger than a squirrel. Raccoon? Badger?

Naelin saw a shape move again and heard a low rumble, a growl. *Predator.* She held still, feeling as if every muscle had locked. They'd tucked themselves into the crook of branches for safety, but now it felt more like a trap.

And she knew in that instant she'd use her power again. But not as a first resort. Not the way Champion Ven wanted. If she did this, she did it on her own terms.

Resolute, she held her children in the crook of the tree until their breathing slowed, becoming even, and their bodies relaxed, limp against her. Awake, she stared into the darkness.

Night was never just blackness in the woods. It was layers of colorlessness, shapelessness, and silence. Here, the silence was buoyed by the crickets, whose song melded into a steady hum in all directions.

She didn't intend to sleep at all, but somehow, despite the fear, despite her swirling thoughts, despite whatever lurked out there in the shadows, exhaustion overwhelmed her and she drifted into sleep, curled up with her children.

SHE WOKE AT DAWN, AS LIGHT FILTERED, GRAY AND DIM, TO THE forest floor. Seated in front of her, back to her as if he were on guard, was a massive wolf. Naelin tensed, squeezing her children tighter, and she felt Erian and Llor shift, waking. She loosened her grip on them, wiggling one arm free. Her kitchen knife was in her pack . . . which she'd left up with the champion, of course. She cast around for anything that could be used as a weapon—a stout branch, a sharp rock.

Champion Ven spoke. "His name is Bayn."

She swallowed, not trusting herself to speak. He was here, and he knew the wolf. That was . . . good? Champion Ven was leaning against the trunk of the tree, arms crossed, face in shadows. A streak of blood stained the sleeve of his armor. In the dim dawn light, it looked like rust. He looked like he'd walked directly out of a heroic ballad, and she felt instantly safer. Not safe, but safer. Her heart kept thudding fast, though. "He seems to have taken a liking to you," he said.

In her arms, Erian woke and tried to stifle a scream—it came out as a shrill *meep!* The wolf turned his head to look at them. His yellow eyes fixed on Naelin. She didn't move.

"Doggie?" Llor said, his voice mushy with sleep.

"He's . . . tame?" Naelin's voice only cracked a little. She licked her lips and tried again. *Show no fear.* "He won't hurt us?"

"Why don't you ask him?"

*Because he's a wolf,* Naelin thought. "Don't mock me."

"Never."

She thought she detected a twinkle in his eye, but perhaps that was her imagination. Surely he didn't have a sense of humor.

Erian took the champion literally and addressed the wolf, "Hello, Mr. Wolf, are you planning to eat us?"

As if her question were beneath his dignity, the wolf looked away, scanning the forest once more. Around them, leaves rustled, and above birds chattered at one another, calling as they flew unseen from branch to branch. The forest was awakening as dawn filtered through the leaves.

"Nice doggie," Llor murmured, and then yawned, as if it were perfectly normal to wake up next to a wolf.

After a few more minutes of no one being savaged by any wild animals, Naelin extradited herself from Erian and Llor and stood. Her muscles twinged, and her back ached. She hadn't slept outside in years, and never as unprotected as this. She stretched her back and tried to shake out her foot, which tingled from being tucked underneath a not-so-small child for so long. At Champion Ven's feet, nestled against the tree, were their packs—all the supplies that Naelin had left behind when she'd climbed with the children in the night. She didn't see Captain Alet and felt a rush of alarm. "Is the captain all right?" Naelin asked.

"She's fine, but you left us in danger. That's not behavior appropriate for an heir."

She considered for a moment how to reply to that. She knew he expected her to be abashed, or at least apologetic that she'd fled, but after searching her feelings, she decided she didn't feel sorry at all. She settled on, "I'm glad that neither of you were hurt." *There, that was true.*

"You agreed to be trained," he said. "If you're to survive the trials, you *must* be trained."

"You agreed to keep my children safe," she shot back. "If you want me to train, then tell me what you plan. No surprises. No assumptions. I will not be your performing monkey, dancing to your tunes without questions." *There. Let him respond to that.*

"Mama likes explanations," Erian spoke up. "If you tell her why you want to do something and show you've thought it through, she'll consider it." She was parroting something Naelin told them all the time. If they acted mature, she'd treat them as mature. She nodded approvingly at Erian. *Nice to know she'd been listening.*

Champion Ven sighed and ran his fingers through his hair. "Perhaps you're right. I am used to candidates who need to be taught about spirits in the wild—they've spent years within the academy, learning to use their power within a highly controlled environment, and it's my responsibility to throw them into the real world and teach them to adapt and bend, so that they don't break. You, though, you already know about the dangers and unpredictability of the world. Perhaps what you need *is* the structure."

Naelin blinked at him, unsure if that was an apology, an insult, or a compliment. She thought . . . maybe the latter? "Exactly what do you mean?"

"Tell me what you already know, and we'll devise a lesson plan."

He was trying very hard to be both nice and reasonable, which was impressive given how she had abandoned him to the spirits last night. "I won't agree to any plan that endangers Erian or Llor."

"You've made that clear." She thought she heard a hint of amusement in his voice. He was laughing at her, or at least near her. "And Bayn apparently agrees with you. He's been on guard all night."

She looked at the wolf again. "Thank you."

The wolf inclined his head as if he understood.

"If we're in agreement . . . ?" the champion asked.

Naelin nodded, cautiously, still watching the wolf. She wasn't certain she trusted this conciliatory mood of Ven's. It felt like it should be some kind of trap, except he was agreeing with her. *What's the catch? Oh, right . . .*

"I still haven't agreed to become an heir."

"It doesn't matter. You still need to be trained."

She stared at him. He stared back. And for the first time, she felt like she was with someone who saw who she was, all her strengths with all her faults, and . . . approved? "All right then."

"All right. We begin today. Now."

## CHAPTER 11

Naelin saw Ven exhale, as if he'd been worried she'd refuse. Granted, she *was* still refusing to become an heir, but he must have been worried she'd refuse to train at all, after the stunt he'd pulled last night. Truthfully, she'd considered it. If he'd been a little less honest, a little less kind . . .

He settled himself on a root. "Have you ever summoned a spirit?"

"Never. And I won't, not out here, not around Erian and Llor." She used her this-is-not-open-to-debate voice. It worked well with her children; she wasn't certain it would work at all with a champion.

"But you've sent spirits away? You've commanded them."

She saw where this was going, and she didn't like it. "Only when Renet forced me. Only what you saw. I'll send them away again if I have to, but only if it's necessary, and I won't summon them. Not here, with us all alone and not enough charms."

"I know you can sense spirits. Describe that to me."

It felt like a change of subject—she'd been expecting an argument instead. She didn't hesitate, though, and answered promptly, feeling like a schoolgirl. "It's like a crackle in the air, like lightning about to strike."

"Good. You should also be able tell their proximity, their size and strength, and their general intent, whether they plan to tear you to bits that instant or generically just want to kill you. Can you do that?"

Behind her, Naelin heard Erian gasp-yelp at the word "kill" and saw the champion wince. He clearly wasn't used to watching his words. She wondered if that had gotten him into trouble before. Not everyone appreciated honesty. She did, though. Minutely, she relaxed—he didn't *seem* like he was trying to trick her into anything. "I don't think so. Or at least, I've never tried." *I'm not stupid, or reckless.* She'd spent so much time pretending she didn't have power, acting as if she were normal. She'd never wanted to jeopardize what she had by experimenting.

"Then that's where we'll start." He held up his hand to stop her question before she asked it. "Don't worry. We won't summon anything. This exercise won't endanger anyone." He looked at her, sincerity clear in his eyes. And also respect—that was a look she hadn't seen in Renet's eyes in a long time. Ven was treating her as if he valued what she thought and felt. "If this is going to work, you're going to have to trust my word."

Reaching behind her, Naelin squeezed Erian's shoulder, as much to reassure the young girl as herself. She kept her eyes on Ven, particularly watching his hands to be sure he didn't stab the trees again. She knew she shouldn't trust him after last night . . . yet she wanted to, especially when he looked at her like that. "I'm listening."

"When you are with your children, your awareness grows, doesn't it?" He pointed to Erian and Llor with his knife, and then appeared to think better of it and tossed and caught the knife so that he was pointing at them with the hilt instead of the tip. Llor whistled, obviously impressed. If Naelin weren't careful, the boy was going to develop a serious case of hero worship. Ven seemed oblivious to it, which was another point in his favor. He was confident without being arrogant. She'd met plenty of people who were the reverse, as well plenty who were far less worthy of adoration. "You expand your sense of what's 'you' to envelop them, the same way you're aware of a knife in your hand as an extension of you."

"Yes, precisely." She was surprised to hear him describe it so exactly.

"I've been a bodyguard. It's similar to parenthood. Except

with moderately more bloodshed." He actually smiled at that, and it was all she could do to not smile back. She *wanted* to be angry at him, but there was something about him that made that impossible. Maybe his earnestness. Or his determination. He was just so blasted *sincere*. He radiated heroism, even when he wasn't doing or saying anything particularly heroic. *If I'm not careful,* she thought, *I'll be the one with the case of hero worship.* Shaking herself, she tried to focus on his words. He continued. "What I want you to do is expand your awareness as far as you can. Consider the forest around you as part of your body and reach your mind out to touch your new 'limbs.'" He sheathed his knife.

Erian crawled up beside her. "Can I try?"

Champion Ven looked at her sharply. "Does your daughter have any affinity for spirits?"

"No," Naelin began, and then stopped. "We don't know." They'd never experimented with it, and she wasn't about to start. "Erian, I need to work with Champion Ven for a while. Why don't you . . ." She trailed off, unsure what to suggest she do. She didn't want Erian to stray far, but she couldn't expect her to huddle in the roots for however long this took.

The guardswoman dropped from a branch onto one of the roots. She wore no sign of last night's battle—her face was scrubbed clean, her hair tied slickly back, her leather armor stiff and spotless. She twirled a knife in one hand and then tucked it into a sheath. Crouching, she studied Erian. "I can teach her a few things. Defensive moves. How to break a hold."

That sounded . . .

"Yes!" Erian sprang to her feet.

. . . perfect.

As Captain Alet guided Erian to a patch of soft moss and demonstrated a defensive stance, Naelin began to revise her opinion of her. She was a kinder teacher than Naelin would have expected, not barking at Erian or scolding her for her lack of knowledge. She positioned the girl's limbs, even gave her an encouraging smile.

Both Naelin and Ven watched them for a moment.

"Mama, may I play with the doggie?" Llor asked. He'd crawled closer to the wolf and was holding his hand out, palm up, for the wolf to sniff. The wolf declined to sniff.

"Only if he wants," Naelin said, damping down her natural instinct, which was to scoop up Llor and run as far and fast away from the predator as she could. So far, the wolf had done nothing but protect them. "His name is Bayn. Don't pull his tail."

"I wouldn't!" Llor cried with all the dignity of an insulted six-year-old.

A ghost of a smile crossed the champion's face. "There, your children have babysitters, at least for the next few minutes. Now will you focus on your training?"

*Unusual babysitters*, she thought, but he was right. Erian and Llor were both nearby and as safe as she could hope them to be, given the circumstances. She didn't have any more excuses. "Sensing the spirits won't summon them?"

"Not in my experience, which is considerable."

He was trying hard to sound soothing, she could tell, and that impressed her. She didn't know why he wanted her as his student so badly, especially when she refused to become an heir, but sensing spirits did sound both harmless and useful. "All right, I'll try it."

Crossing her legs, she sat on one of the roots. She felt the bark dig into her thighs, through the fabric of her skirts. She felt the damp morning chill in the air and breathed in the heavy, wet, mossy taste of the forest floor. Birds were chirping in the trees above, and a few bushes rustled nearby, most likely squirrels. Concentrating, she tried to do as he said—imagine that she was part of the woods around her, that her arms extended into the trees, that her thighs poured into the earth, that her lungs expanded to breathe in all the air.

Half of her kept listening for Erian and Llor—she heard the captain giving Erian instructions, and Erian answering with questions about how to hold her arms and her shoulders, adjusting her foot position in the crumbled old leaves and pine needles. In between the roots, Llor was babbling happily to the wolf, telling him all about his collections back home: he liked to collect rocks, feathers, and interesting sticks, but Mama didn't let him bring the best sticks into the house because they were too pointy, which was endlessly disappointing. Mama was fine with rocks, he confided, as long as they weren't too big, and fine with feathers, as long as he found them himself and didn't try to pluck them from any birds. He even had an eagle feather that was as long as his arm, but he'd had to leave it behind when they left. He promised to show the wolf when they went back sometime.

She shook her head. "I can't do it. My children—"

"Don't block them out," Ven advised. "Embrace them, and then stretch farther. Pretend you're listening to them and making charms at the same time. You've done that, right?"

*That* she could do. She was used to splitting her attention between her own tasks and her children. It was how she went about every day. She'd never tried to reach beyond, but she supposed that the champion was right—in theory, it shouldn't be too different. She stretched her mind, and felt the quivering of nearby spirits. It was so simple and easy that she gasped. *I can feel them.*

There! A wood spirit, above, skittering along a branch.

To the east, an air spirit flitted through the trees, rustling the leaves, drawing a breeze behind it.

Below, an earth spirit burrowed.

She could feel their size and their mood, the same way she could feel an itch on her arm. It was shockingly easy, a parlor trick, a matter of concentrating on the "crinkling" in the air and bringing it into focus. She wondered, traitorously, why she'd been resisting so hard. If she'd known this . . . If her mother had known, when the spirits came for her . . .

"You'll practice this every day, until it becomes second nature."

Naelin nodded. She disliked the way they seemed to crawl on her skin, even though they weren't nearby, but that was a slight sacrifice for the boon of knowing where they were. She rubbed her arms, feeling the gooseflesh, and pulled her awareness back to their camp.

"With practice, you'll be able to expand your range," he said. "A queen is aware of every spirit in her country. She's granted that awareness in the coronation ceremony. In the ceremony, she links herself to all the spirits in Aratay and can awaken that link whenever she chooses. It helps if you have practice beforehand, so the sensation doesn't overwhelm you." Shaking her head, she opened her mouth to say that she was never going to be queen so this was a moot point, but then he said, "Daleina was always skilled at sensing spirits, even before Coronation Day."

He'd been there, at the massacre, she remembered. She could see the memory of it in the way he looked out at the forest, as if he were seeing that moment and looking at another set of trees. She had the urge to reach out to touch his arm, to comfort him, but she didn't.

She didn't argue when he told her to practice more. She kept at it for nearly an hour, until Llor began to clamor that he was hungry and she realized so was she. After breakfast, they continued to travel, and she continued to practice.

Naelin caught the champion shooting her glances every few minutes, as if she were a puzzle that he wanted to solve. If she hadn't been so busy helping Erian and Llor keep up and "feeling" out the spirits around them, she would have asked him what he found so fascinating. She didn't consider herself fascinating at all. *Don't read too much into it,* she cautioned herself. At some point, he'd realize she was too difficult a student and came with too much baggage, and he'd go find himself a child to train, one who wanted this. Until then, though, she'd absorb any trick that would keep them safe.

And she'd find a way to safely leave.

THE NEXT MORNING, NAELIN DECLARED THE CHILDREN HAD TO BE washed. She found a stream near their camp, with a willow tree that draped over the water. Every time the wind blew, tendrils of leaves stroked the water, creating ripples that spread toward the pebbled shore. Naelin kept an eye on the ripples, her senses open, watching and listening for spirits. Two were perched in the branches of a tree to the north, and a water spirit lurked around the next bend, catching fish as they swam between the rocks and then bashing them against the closest rock.

Close by her, Llor splashed in the shallows while Erian

scrubbed her face. When she finished, she handed the cloth to Llor, who promptly tossed it onto the shore. "Not dirty," he proclaimed.

"Very dirty," Naelin informed him. She dunked the cloth into the water, caught his arm, and began to scrub his neck. He twisted and squirmed, kicking at the water until it splashed his sister, who screeched. "No screaming, Erian. You know better than to make loud noises in the forest. And Llor, don't splash your sister, and don't fidget. Hold still, and it will be over faster."

With zero warning, Erian burst into tears. "It's not my fault! He splashed me."

"And that's why I told him no splashing. Erian, we don't cry about nothing."

Erian sucked back a sob. Her lower lip quivered. "Father would understand."

The words felt like a stab. Naelin wanted to say she was sorry, but she wasn't the one who'd forced her to use her power. She wasn't the one who'd brought a champion into their home. She wasn't the one who'd changed their lives. She was trying to do her best . . . She sucked in air and tried to stay calm. It would only escalate things if she showed she was upset too. "Cry if you need to then. I know this is difficult, and I can't promise it will get easier. I *can* promise I'll keep you safe as best as I can."

"Safe isn't enough," Erian sobbed. "I want to go home."

"I want to go home too," Llor said, and then he started to cry as well.

Wishing Renet were here to scream at, Naelin opened her arms, and both of them piled onto her, their wet clothes soaking hers as they sobbed onto her shoulders. *I'm sorry. I'm so sorry.* She stroked their hair as they cried and felt like crying as well, but she didn't let herself. She couldn't afford to break down, not when there was no one here to help put her back together.

She heard a soft clink and looked up. Captain Alet was crouched on one of the rocks. She had her knife drawn and was focused on a shape in the water.

The water spirit.

It was sliding toward them, like a serpent through the ripples.

Leaping from the rock, Alet landed in the water and stabbed her knife down. The spirit squealed, dove under, and sped rapidly away. "You can't lose focus," she said, "no matter what else occurs."

"I never wanted this," Naelin said. "I wanted an ordinary life: house, husband, children, an honest living. A few herb plants. Neighbors I didn't hate. A quiet life."

"We rarely get what we want."

"What did you want?" Still cradling her children, Naelin watched the guardswoman clean her blade and then splash water on her face and neck. Patches of dirt turned into mud that dripped over her shoulders.

She shrugged. "Not that life. Far too boring."

"Peaceful isn't boring."

"I wanted to matter. For my life to matter. So many people die and no one knows they ever existed. They're ripples in a stream, disappearing when the wind blows."

Erian was beginning to quiet. Llor was still sniffling. He'd most likely forgotten why he was crying. He just knew he was supposed to be crying. Naelin let them rest against her. "You've lost people?"

"Plenty." Her voice was distant, and her eyes fixed downstream. All trace of the water spirit had disappeared. Casting her mind out, Naelin felt it, hunkered down in the rapids, a ways downstream. It seemed to have forgotten them. "All, in fact. Except my sister. I'd do anything for her, anything to make her proud of me."

Naelin cast around for something else to say. "Sounds like you found important work, being the queen's guard, working with Ven. I'm sure she's proud of you."

Still looking downstream, Alet nodded.

"What's the queen like?" Naelin asked. She wanted to ask more: Will she listen? Will she understand? Will she help? Will she keep my children safe?

"Noble," Alet said. "Serious. Driven."

"Have you known her for long?"

"Long enough to know she's a good queen," Alet said, and

there was a look on her face that Naelin couldn't quite name—it was a little like longing. "She wants to protect her people, and she's willing to give her life for that. She understands duty and sacrifice."

Holding Erian and Llor close, Naelin wondered if she was being insulted. "Are you suggesting I don't? I'd give my life for my children." She felt her children shift in her arms, squeezing her tighter. "But I'd far rather give them a mother than a martyr."

A brief smile crossed the captain's face. "Before you, I thought all women of power wanted to be queen. Refusing seemed inconceivable. Your lack of ambition is . . . strangely admirable. You are deeply committed to living a forgettable life."

"Forgettable is fine. I don't want fame; I want happy." She pressed her lips to Erian's hair. "But I'll settle for content. I don't think that's so strange."

Alet studied her, as if weighing the truth of her words, and finally said, "I'll help you, as much as I can."

Naelin's eyes widened. She hadn't expected to find an ally in the stern guardswoman. If her arms hadn't been full of children, she would have hugged her. As it was, she could only nod her thanks. "I appreciate that. We all do."

"You must be able to say no to the queen," Alet said. "It won't be easy. She's intense, and she *is* the queen. In the glory of the palace, you'll want to say anything to please her. You'll want her to look on you with approval. It can be hard to remember who you are and what you must do." She had a look in her eye—that odd kind of sad longing again, regret maybe—as if she'd tried to refuse the queen and failed.

"I have two reminders," Naelin said. "The palace won't intimidate me."

"I hope not. For their sake." Alet held out her hand toward Erian and Llor. "Come, children, and I'll show you the proper way to stab a water spirit."

Tears dry, they went with her willingly.

## CHAPTER 12

*A*rin had decided at age four that her sister, Daleina, would be queen, but oddly at no point during her calculations had she imagined herself visiting the palace. She'd also never thought she'd need to have her eyebrows plucked to see her sister, but the caretaker who had hustled her away after her arrival had gasped in shock at what apparently looked like two woolly caterpillars who had laid down for naps about Arin's eyes. Arin thought her eyebrows were fine, and furthermore that Daleina wouldn't care, unless being queen had changed her that dramatically. Usually Daleina only cared that Arin had all her limbs still attached and functional. But the caretaker looked as if she were having heart palpitations at the very thought of Arin and her woolly eyebrows intruding on the sanctity of the palace, and so Arin submitted to the ministrations without protest.

Besides, it was nice being taken care of.

One caretaker, dressed in an embroidered gold robe and boasting a painted image of a bird on his neck, was scrubbing at the calluses on Arin's hands, while another, who had leaves painted on her arms, knelt in front of a velvet cushioned stool and was trimming Arin's toenails. A third was whirling around the room, selecting far more clothing than Arin thought could be worn by a single person without falling over. She pictured her sister weighed down by twenty elaborate robes and suppressed a giggle.

The room she was in looked as elaborate as the people with their painted skin. It was decorated with peacocks and songbirds and streaks of sunset colors. The walls were inlaid with mosaics of different-colored wood, honey and mahogany and cherry, in patterns that made her head feel like she was hanging upside down if she looked at them for too long. The ceiling was laced with strands of firemoss that looked like lit cotton candy, and the floors were blanketed in carpets on top of carpets that looked so plush that Arin hoped they let her stay barefoot after they were done decorating her toes—she had no idea why Daleina would even notice what her sister's toes looked like, much less care.

At last, they finished, pronounced her acceptable, and stripped off the linen robe they'd given her and dressed her in a soft, satiny blue dress that pooled around her ankles. Her feet were encased in the softest leather she'd ever felt. She wiggled her toes inside it and thought they were absurd for any real work. She'd have them scuffed in less than an hour. Just one climb onto the roof to fix a tile would destroy them, and never mind a trip into town. The forest floor would shred them. She'd heard that the palace courtiers seldom went outside, but she hadn't believed it.

"May I see my sister now, please?" Arin asked, in as polite and meek a voice as she could, the voice that usually got her what she wanted. Arin liked to be nice to people. It usually resulted in side benefits. Unfortunately, these people seemed to not be interested in hearing a word she said. They chattered to one another, debating the merits of one rouge over another, as if it were of utmost importance. *All right, maybe I should just find her myself.* Getting out of her chair, Arin began to walk toward a door. "This way?"

One of the courtiers scurried in front of her and bowed. "Only when you're called for, esteemed mistress. Many apologies for the inconvenience, but perhaps you would like a walk through the rose gardens? Or a tour of the palace treasures? We have many delightful sights and pleasantly appointed rooms."

"My sister asked me to come." More like commanded, really, though Mother and Daddy had said, somewhat doubtfully, that she might not have had a hand in the wording. Arin planned to talk to Daleina about that, nicely of course. *Just because she's queen does not mean I'm at her beck and call.* Family should be exempt from royal bossiness. "Does she know that I'm here?"

The courtier dodged the question. "She has many demands on her time—"

A soft, firm voice interrupted, "I will take her from here."

Arin recognized the man who'd entered the room—he'd visited with Daleina before the trials and had examined her broken leg. She smiled at him with relief. "Healer Hamon! Very good to see you."

He wrinkled his nose for a brief second—he must have gotten a whiff of all the dueling scents—and then smoothed his face into a pleasant smile. "I see the courtiers have welcomed you."

Laughing, she held out her arms, the sleeves draping in voluminous waves, and turned in a circle. "They've made me presentable."

He kept his smile on. "Well then. We shouldn't let their hard work go to waste. Let's present you." With a bow to the caretakers, he guided Arin out of the room and into a hallway with polished black walls that wound to the left and then rose up in a series of white steps. Hamon's hand was on the small of her back, and at first Arin thought he was guiding her, as if she weren't capable of responding to simple left-right commands, but then she realized he was, in a way, claiming her as his approved guest. The courtiers and guards they passed looked at her, looked at Hamon, and moved to the side, allowing them to pass without challenge.

"All of these people—they're to protect Daleina?"

"She's the most important person in Aratay," Hamon said, his voice low but calm and pleasant as always, "especially while we have no heirs. No one wants to take a chance with her, when it comes to her protection."

She couldn't imagine living surrounded by this many guards, to have this many people aware of your every movement, to be essentially imprisoned inside this palace. She wondered if Daleina saw it this way, as a pretty cage. *Maybe she does.* Daleina had never viewed being queen as a pleasure, merely as her duty. Arin felt a tiny stab of guilt and quickly buried it. The pleadings of a little girl could not be blamed for a lifetime of choices. Daleina had chosen to stay at the academy, to train with her champion, to take the trials, to claim the crown. Thinking of the Coronation Massacre, Arin felt her throat dry. "It *is* safe here, isn't it?"

Hamon swung open a door without answering, and Arin blinked as sunlight flooded into her. She raised one fabric-draped arm to block the bright light and peered into the room.

The Queen's Chamber was the most beautiful room she'd seen so far. Everything was ivory and gold and gleamed in the sunlight that poured in from the balcony. Stepping forward, she saw that the trees outside had been grown bowed to leave a gap for the light. She also saw a silhouette of a woman—the queen, her sister—standing on the balcony.

Behind her, Hamon said, "I will be available to you when you have questions."

She turned to ask what he meant—when she had questions? What kind of questions did he expect her to have?—but he was already closing the solid, carved doors.

"Daleina?"

She expected Daleina to smother her in a hug like she usually did, as if she were still a little kid whom she could pick up and swing around, but her sister stayed on the balcony, motionless, looking out over the trees. She could have been a statue. Arin approached her slowly, aware of the carpet compressing beneath the thin soles of her fancy shoes and of the swoosh of her satiny dress behind her. She felt like a cat who had been dressed up and wanted to claw at the fabric until she felt like herself again. Stepping onto the balcony, Arin stood beside her sister. "So . . . what are we looking at?"

"Anything but you," Daleina said. "If I look at you, I'll cry."

"My eyebrows aren't that bad."

Her sister's lips quirked and then wobbled. Arin watched her take a deep breath in and realized that Daleina wasn't joking—something was very, very wrong. "It was Hamon's idea to bring you, though he claims I was the one who named you," Daleina said. "I don't remember. I was half asleep at the time. Maybe I did, but I shouldn't have. You should be home."

"Not exactly the welcome I expected. You sure know how to make me feel wanted." She tried to keep her voice light.

"I should have told them to send you home. Made up an excuse that wouldn't hurt your feelings, but once Hamon said you were here . . . Forgive my selfishness."

"Of course. And I also forgive your crypticness." Arin laid a hand on Daleina's arm. *Come on, talk to me. Look at me!* "Do you want to talk about what's going on, or would you rather skirt around it until you feel ready? I could tell you about Daddy's ridiculous new project. He wants to build a birdhouse that's a replica of the library in the Southern Citadel, complete with bird-size fake books on the shelves. He'd been trying to convince Mother to whittle the books for him for the past two weeks. He thinks there might be a market with extremely wealthy collectors."

"People collect birdhouses?"

"Oh yes, Daddy has been gossiping with some of the other woodsmen—he wouldn't call it gossiping, of course. 'Sharing trade information.' Gossiping, I say. Anyway, apparently there's a man on the forest floor who carves life-size statues of bears and raccoons with hollowed-out stomachs to use as cupboards, bookshelves, or baby cribs. Daddy has decided his niche will be bird—"

"I'm dying, Arin."

Arin quit talking. Daleina's words fell into her like stones into a pond, and Arin felt them ripple out from her gut, sweeping through her veins, making her feel as if she'd been submerged. "What do you mean?" she asked carefully.

"I have the False Death."

No.

No, she couldn't.

Not Daleina.

"But you're so young!"

"It's not unheard-of."

"It's rare enough. And we've never had a single case of it in our family. It's inherited, isn't it? How could you have it? On Daddy's side, Grandma died of ridiculous old age, and Grandpa fell and broke his neck. On Mother's . . . I don't remember, but not the False Death. I think there was some kind of sickness . . . Your healers must be wrong. Besides, you don't look sick." In fact, she looked lovely, her gold and red and orange hair shining like a tree in autumn. Gold flecks had been painted around her eyes, which made her eyes pop even more. Daleina had always had intense eyes. She'd always been intense about everything. Dying certainly wasn't making her any less intense. "They're wrong."

"Hamon is one of the best. The other palace healers are in awe of him."

"That's nice, but he's *wrong*."

Daleina looked at her, for the first time since Arin had come onto the balcony, and Arin felt the full weight of those very intense eyes. "You are less comforting than you're supposed to be."

"I'm not letting you die."

"You don't exactly get a say in this."

"You're going to fight this."

Daleina looked away. "It's inside me. I can't throw a knife at it."

"He's looking for a cure, isn't he? Your healer boyfriend?" She thought of how calm his voice had sounded, urbane, as always, and wasn't certain if that had been an act or not. Healers were trained to have exquisite bedside manners. She'd corner him later, find out how serious it truly was, though she'd never heard of the False Death not being serious. *This can't be happening. Not to Daleina!*

"He wanted someone I trust here with me while he looks for a cure," Daleina admitted. "That's why you were summoned. But I don't want you in danger—"

Instantly, Arin said, "Whatever you need, I'm here for you."

"He wants you to monitor my symptoms when he can't."

*Why me?* she wanted to ask. *Why not one of the palace healers?* But she didn't ask, because she didn't want to be sent away. *Daleina wanted me, whether she remembers that or not.* "You've had symptoms?"

"Seven people died."

"Oh."

Daleina clasped her hands behind her back and stared out at the green as if it held all the answers. The sun still washed over her, bathing her in light, which glistened off the sparkles on her face and in her dress so brightly that it looked as if she were exuding light.

In as deadpan a voice as she could manage, Arin said, "Most people when they get sick just sneeze a lot. You're such an overachiever."

Daleina snorted, which was almost a laugh, and then she was serious again. "If I black out, you must hide. Promise me that. Every room we go into, scout out where you'll hide if it happens, and if I collapse, you must go there. And whenever I don't need you ... at all other times, I don't want you anywhere near me."

"Daleina, I don't—"

"Promise. Or I call the guards and have them send you home."

Arin stared at her. She'd *never* used that tone with her. She sounded ... well, like a queen. Arin didn't like it. "Yes, Your Majesty."

"Say it."

"I promise."

Daleina's shoulders sagged. "I don't know what the right thing is to do. Do I warn people, so they can be prepared for the blackouts? Or do I not, so they don't panic? It would be different if I had an heir. I'd abdicate in an instant."

"You can abdicate? I thought queens—" Arin stopped. A queen *could* abdicate, yes, but she couldn't abdicate and live—the spirits would hunt her down, and she'd lack the power to defend herself. Even if she had the protection of the new queen, she'd be in constant danger. Eventually, the new queen's control would slip, or she'd die or become distracted, and the spirits would reach Daleina. It had happened before. There were songs and tales about past queens who had tried to abdicate and live out their lives in peace—all of them had failed. Every single one, dead within a year. It couldn't be done. *She's serious about this*, Arin thought. *She truly believes she's ... She's truly sick.* Suddenly, Arin felt like hitting something, and she *never* felt that way. She was kind to small children and irritating animals, as well as irritating children and small animals. She was patient with even the most exacting of customers who came into the bakery, including Mistress Millia, who requested cream-puff pastries without cream and then complained when the fluff collapsed, which of course it did when you bit into one. "You can't tell them." There would be panic, especially without an heir. But if there was an heir . . . "He'll find a cure. You can't abdicate before Hamon finds a cure."

"I've told my champions to accelerate the training process. They'll be presenting their candidates to me soon, and I will choose heirs in a month."

"Then Hamon had better work quickly," Arin said.

Daleina nodded, but it seemed more of a polite acknowledgment than actual agreement.

The sun was beginning to shift, and the leaves at the top of the canopy created shadows on the balcony. Side by side with her sister, Arin watched a spirit spiral up toward the sun and then zip along the tops of the trees. Daleina spoke again. "So, Daddy's building birdhouses?"

"Fancy ones."

"And Mother's all right with this?"

"She says there are worse hobbies he could have."

Daleina's lips quirked. "Probably true."

"Definitely true. Did I ever tell you about our neighbor, the one who knits sweaters for her pet squirrels?" Arin dove into an elaborate, mostly true account of their neighbor's antics, growing more animated in her description until at last Daleina let out a faint laugh, and Arin felt as if she'd won a victory.

For the moment, at least.

## CHAPTER 13

Mittriel, the capital city of Aratay, was teeming with people, scurrying everywhere, like squirrels preparing for
winter. Navigating a bridge that was wider than the entire market of Everdale, Naelin and her children barely fit between the
crowds. If Alet and Ven hadn't been with them, clearing a path,
she was certain they'd be at a standstill. *Or cowering in a corner somewhere*, she thought. Erian and Llor were on either side
of Naelin, clutching her hands, like burrs attached to her skirt.
They gawked at everyone and everything.

"It's all so . . ." Naelin tried to find a word that would sum it up
and failed.

"Colorful?" Ven offered.

"Yes." Every inch of every tree was carved or painted, and every branch was draped in ribbons and signs, pointing to various
shops and restaurants. Bridges crisscrossed both above and below and were clogged with men, women, and children who were
all as brilliantly decorated as the trees. Out in the villages, everyone wore brown or green to blend into the forest, but here . . . "I
didn't know it was possible to make dyes so very . . ." A woman
walked past her with a garish orange bonnet that attached to her
sleeves with multicolored beaded strands. The beads jingled together as she walked. ". . . orange."

"She's wearing a pumpkin on her head," Llor whispered as he
stared.

A few of the people stared back at them. Naelin was aware of how bedraggled they all looked after several days of travel, even though she'd scrubbed all their faces every time she found a stream that wasn't occupied by a water spirit. Her dress, which she'd sewn herself, felt like rough patchwork, compared to the elaborate outfits worn by the capital citizens.

"Mama, we aren't sparkly enough," Erian said.

Alet patted Erian on the shoulder. "You're just fine. They're the ridiculous ones."

Naelin shot her a grateful look. She appreciated Alet's kindness to all of them, especially when she felt so very small, brown, and drab, like a sparrow who fell in a mud puddle. "It is a bit intimidating," Naelin admitted. "I feel like I've been thrown into a coop of peacocks."

"Reasonably accurate," Ven said, and the smile he threw her felt like a lifeline. "You'll either get used to it or eternally hate it." He stopped and pointed. "*That*, though, is a sight that I'll never get used to and never hate." They were approaching from mid-forest, where the bridges merged together into a wide painted bridge that led into the palace gates.

"Oh, Mama, it's beautiful!" Erian gasped.

She was right: the white trees of the palace shone as delicate and ethereal as the moon. Their branches entwined, creating a lacework of smooth limbs that spread into a thin canopy of golden leaves. Six spires rose above the canopy, capped in arches. One, an observation deck known as the Queen's Tower, rose highest from the center. Another, which held the famous Chamber of Champions, bowed off to the side. Others were said to hold various throne rooms and bedchambers, each more ornate than the last. Elegant stairs wound around the trunks, and balconies adorned the higher reaches. Naelin wanted to scoop up her children and run home, to their drab, snug hut.

"Are we going to live there?" Erian asked.

"What? No. Of course not. That's the palace." She'd been foolish to think she'd have an audience with the queen herself, to think Her Majesty would care about one woodswoman's family.

"But you said the queen would protect us," Llor piped up. "I heard you! I listen!"

Erian's eyes were round. "Are we going to meet the queen?"

Before, she would have said yes. She'd had every intention of marching into the palace and demanding . . . Oh, it all sounded so ridiculous now. Who was she to demand anything of the queen? *I'm no one, nothing, not even a properly trained hedge-witch.* Just a woodswoman whose skills did not apply in a place like this. She was no one, and while her children meant the world to her, the queen was responsible for all the children in all of Aratay. There was no reason for her to take any special interest in Naelin's. Most likely, Naelin would never see her, even from a distance. *And that's fine. I don't know what to say to a queen.* "You'll stay with me, wherever I go. If it's to meet the queen, we meet the queen. If it's to meet the fourth assistant pig keeper, we meet the fourth assistant pig keeper."

"Why do they have four pig keepers?" Llor asked. "Do they have that many pigs?"

"It's the *palace*," Erian said. "They probably have hundreds of pigs!"

"Thousands?" Llor asked.

"Hundreds of thousands," Erian said, with full confidence, and then she amended, "Or they could, you know, if the queen wanted, which she probably doesn't, because they're pigs. And she probably wouldn't keep them in the palace anyway, because it's fancy."

"Pigs aren't fancy," Llor said wisely.

"Do these kinds of conversations happen often with you?" Ven asked Naelin.

Naelin smiled, feeling better. "When you have children, you find yourself uttering sentences you've never imagined anyone would need to say, such as 'You can't go to school naked' and 'Please don't put a chipmunk in your father's shoes.'" Her smile faded at the memory of that—it had been a funny moment. She and Renet had laughed for a week—Renet kept walking around with one shoe on asking where he could find his other chipmunk. They'd had good moments. *Why did he have to ruin it all?* She poked at that sadness, wondering if she missed him or just missed what could have been.

"You won't be meeting the queen yet," Ven said, interrupting her thoughts. "She will let us know when she's ready to approve the candidates."

Naelin refused to think about the word "yet." It was far more likely that she'd never be allowed near the queen. The queen of Aratay had far more important people to meet than an ordinary woodswoman.

"Until then, we're going to Northeast Academy."

"Ooh, Headmistress Hanna?" Erian jumped up and down. Naelin felt the same way—she'd heard stories about the famous headmistress. She expected her to be at least nine feet tall and glowing like the moon.

"Yes," he told Erian. "Alet, will you guide them there? I need to go ahead to let the headmistress know to expect you."

"Of course," Alet said.

Naelin tamped down an impulse to grab his arm and say don't leave. She wasn't a child, and she trusted Alet to shepherd them through the city. Still . . . she'd gotten used to traveling with him.

"She'll judge if you're ready," Ven said to Naelin. Without waiting for a response, he sprinted ahead, weaving through the crowds as if they were obstacles in a race.

That sounded every bit as stressful as meeting the queen. Watching him leave and wishing he'd stayed, Naelin murmured, "I'm *not* ready. What do I say to Headmistress Hanna? She faced the spirits at the Massacre of the Oaks. She's trained two queens."

"You managed to charm Champion Ven," Alet said. "You'll be fine."

Naelin nearly stopped walking. As it was, she caught her foot on Llor's and stumbled against Erian. Erian squawked, and Naelin had to spend several seconds checking to be sure everyone was all right—they were—before she asked, "Exactly what do you mean by that?" She thought her voice sounded steady, normal, but she couldn't help the way her heart began to thump harder.

Erian answered instead of Alet. "He admires you. It's obvious, Mama. And I like him too. He scowls a lot, but he doesn't mean it." For a second, Naelin let herself sink into that thought–her children liked him, and he was kind to them. Gentle, even.

Naelin glanced at Alet, who nodded, an amused smirk on her face. "He's not used to people standing up to him." Alet shrugged. "You've impressed him."

She hadn't wanted to impress him, much less charm anyone. Except ... *No.* "Right. Well, I'm not looking for admiration, especially if you're implying the kind of admiration I think you're implying." She thought of his pale-blue eyes, always studying her. She'd assumed he was assessing her as a potential heir, not as ... Never mind. It was ridiculous to be having these thoughts while she was on her way to meet a living legend. Alet was teasing her. *And I'm being silly, indulging in fantasies.* "Ridiculous."

"You left your husband, spoken and witnessed," Alet pointed out. "Do you plan on returning to him?" Striding purposefully forward, Alet parted the crowd. Naelin, Erian, and Llor scurried behind her.

"Well, no, but ..." She'd left him, taken the children, and announced in front of witnesses that she had no intention to return. That severed their vows, by forest law. But she hadn't paused to think through the implications, that maybe fantasies didn't have to *stay* fantasies. Instead she'd been so caught up in reacting, and then the travel ... "This isn't the time for talk like that." She had greater things to worry about than whether Ven was the kindest, most intense, most sincere man she'd ever met ... It was indulgent to even think like this when she had two children to look after in a strange, overwhelming city. Naelin looked at Erian and Llor and wondered if they'd realized that their family was shattered, permanently. She wondered if they'd ever fully understand. *I've hurt them,* she thought. Whether they knew it yet or not, whether she meant to or not, whether she had a choice or not, whether it was her fault or not, she'd uprooted their lives.

GUILT IS AN UNAVOIDABLE AND USELESS EMOTION, HEADMIStress Hanna decided, *especially after you've committed regicide.*

Still, Hanna allowed herself to wallow for a few minutes. She'd opened her window and sat on the sill. Ahead was the thick green of the forest. Far below, shrouded in bushes, was the forest floor. Birds called to one another, familiar territorial cries that sounded like beautiful insults.

She heard her office door swing open behind her. Without turning around, she said, "I don't require anything." Except a cure for the queen.

A familiar voice said, "I trust you don't intend to fall?" Champion Ven. She hadn't expected him, yet was not surprised. Healer Hamon had predicted he'd return from the forest after failing there and choose one of her students.

It was a shame none of them were ready.

More than a shame.

Out loud, she said, "It would be irresponsible of me, as well as create an unseemly pile on the academy entranceway. I couldn't ask the caretakers to clean such a mess." She didn't leave her perch, but she did shift sideways so that he could sit beside her.

He didn't sit. "Tell me you don't do this often."

"Only when my thoughts are stifling. I like the fresh air." Up this high, the wind whipped around the top of the tower. She felt it push against her feet. "We did a terrible thing for a just cause, and now it appears the universe is punishing us."

"Daleina told you?"

"Healer Hamon. He visited this morning."

"It's not a punishment."

"Hamon told me that as well, but it does not feel that way. I believe in fate, and I believe fate wants revenge for our hubris in trying to control it." Hanna sighed heavily. "Instead of protecting innocents, we have condemned them. Without a suitable heir . . . I fear we have done our country a great wrong."

He laid his hand on her shoulder. "I am sorry that the guilt is so bad that you want to jump, but I cannot allow you to do it."

Glaring at him, Hanna pushed away his hand. "I was *not* about to kill myself. I told you, I wanted fresh air." What she contemplated in the solitude of regret was her business, and she did not welcome his bald words.

"You were feeling melodramatic. But there isn't time for that. You have a job to do."

She bristled more. "I am well aware—"

"I need your help."

She stopped. *That* was a sentence she hadn't expected him to ever utter. "You?"

"I found a woman with more raw power than I've ever encountered. Problem is, she has no interest in using her power. She wants to pretend she's invisible, live someplace unmemorable with her two kids and—"

"More power than Fara?"

He flinched, as if the mention of her name felt like a blow. Hanna knew that feeling. "Yes, I believe so," he said. "But she refuses to use it. She wouldn't summon any spirits while we were out in the forest. She's afraid."

Hanna heaved herself up from the window ledge, using Champion Ven's overly muscular shoulder for leverage, and walked to her desk. She eased herself into her chair. "She's right to be afraid. You should know that the other champions are pushing their candidates hard. One candidate died this morning. She was a student at Southern Citadel Academy. A very promising one. I'd considered her the top contender."

She saw memories flicker over Ven's face and knew he was thinking of his former heir, Sata. She'd once been the best of the best, and Queen Fara had killed her for it. "All the more important that I found a strong candidate," Ven said. "She will catch up and surpass the others . . . if she agrees to try."

"Tell me all."

"She's the one," he said. Hanna listened as he told her how he'd found her, what he'd observed, and what he'd planned for her future. He painted a clear picture: a mature woman who knew her own mind but not her own power, a woman who'd settled in marriage but loved her children, a woman whose determination matched Daleina's but whose ambitions didn't extend beyond her own little sphere.

"She's a grown woman," Hanna pointed out when he finished. "What makes you think she'll act the way you want her to act?"

"Because she has a weakness: her children."

Pushing up from her desk, Hanna paced around her office. If this woman were as powerful as Ven suspected, she might be needed more badly than he even knew. Champion Ven didn't involve himself in broader politics, but Hanna stayed abreast of all the news and rumors, and she knew about the problems on the border. Queen Merecot of Semo was stretching her muscles—if she heard of Daleina's weakness, she wouldn't hesitate to strike. Hanna remembered Merecot from when she was a student at the academy and doubted the girl's ambition had dimmed. She was the type to crave power. If she sensed weakness, or worse a power vacuum . . . "Her children are not her weakness."

"Oh?"

"They are her strength. And yes, I do believe we can use that."

Inside the academy, Naelin softly closed the door to the room where both Erian and Llor had fallen fast asleep, side by side in the same cot, cuddling each other like they were both each other's blanket. She leaned her forehead against the door and wished it were possible for her to sleep. She felt bone tired from the journey here . . . all of it new and scary, and the act of staying strong and brave in front of her children was beginning to make her feel like a chunk of cheese rubbed against a grater.

"Asleep?" Alet asked, behind her.

"Like worn-out puppies." Straightening, Naelin turned to face the guardswoman. She was glad to see her again—a familiar face! Alet was dressed in crisp, fancy leather armor, with a royal crest emblazoned on her chest in green and gold, marking her as a member of the Royal Guard. Her hair was neatly coiled, with the white stripe in her black hair pinned back beneath a helmet. She was armed with multiple knives with jeweled hilts that looked as much like ornaments as weapons. "You're going to the palace?" Naelin asked.

Alet nodded. "On my way there shortly. I wanted to make sure you got dinner before I reported for duty."

Naelin felt her lips pull up into a smile, despite her tiredness.

The knots in her stomach began to unravel. "Captain Alet, are you mothering me?"

"Are you going to let me?"

She thought about it for only a split second. "Absolutely."

She let Alet lead her down the spiral staircase into a dining hall. Set within the tree, the hall was a semicircle and boasted arched ceilings and plenty of windows that overlooked the practice ring. Even the long tables were curved to match the room. Following Alet, Naelin joined a line of students, carrying trays of food. She accepted a heap of potato-like roots, a wedge of nut bread, and a slab of meat smothered in some kind of sauce, as well as a cup of gooseberries. Around them, students chattered and laughed. She was grateful when Alet picked a table apart from them and set her tray down. Joining her, Naelin studied the students. All of them were children. "Ven wants me to go back to school? This won't work."

"You don't have to befriend them," Alet said, dipping her nut bread into the meat sauce. "You just have to learn what they know. Not to put too fine a point on it, but all of them, including the scrawniest pipsqueak who will most likely wash out before the end of the week, know more about your power than you do."

"All I want to know about my power is: How do I get rid of it?" Her stomach rumbled, and she cut into the meat. She tasted a wedge of it. Not as good as a home-cooked roast from a fresh kill, but it was surprisingly decent. She nibbled on it. It was heavily salted and had spices that she didn't recognize—they tickled the tongue, but not unpleasantly, a nice peppery kick. If she could find out who the cook was and ask what kind of spice he or she used . . . She realized Alet was staring at her. "What?"

"You're in the famous Northeast Academy, about to be interviewed by Headmistress Hanna herself, and you still don't want this life?"

"I told you I didn't."

"I thought you'd change your mind once you got here. I thought maybe you were just afraid." She was looking at Naelin with . . . respect? No, not quite. It actually looked a bit like relief.

"I *am* afraid. Anyone with sense would be." Naelin waved her hand to encompass the academy, the capital, all of it. "I don't belong here, no matter what the queen said. This isn't my world or my fight." Her last words fell into silence as the entire dining hall quieted.

Everyone turned to stare at her, and then turned toward the doorway.

She twisted in her seat to see an elderly woman in a green-and-black robe, accompanied by Champion Ven. His gaze swept the dining hall, searching for someone—for her. Seeing her, he pointed and spoke to the woman.

Naelin tried to read his expression, to judge if he seemed happy to see her, relieved, resigned, any emotion at all, but his face was expressionless and professional. She tried to sort out how she felt, seeing him, and was surprised she'd missed him, though it hadn't been long. *A ridiculous reaction*, she scolded herself, and blamed Alet's words for planting such thoughts.

The woman's wrinkled eyes fixed on Naelin, and suddenly Naelin felt five years old, pinned by the glare of her grandmother, a formidable woman who'd taken no nonsense from anyone, especially when it came to interrupting her baking.

Alet handed her the wedge of bread. "Take this with you," she said in a low voice. "I'm told magic makes you hungry. Remember: if you don't want this, then keep saying no. Don't let them change your mind."

Naelin tucked the bread into her skirt. "Thanks," she whispered.

"Candidate Naelin, report for lessons," Ven barked.

All the students shifted again in their seats, and Naelin felt dozens of eyes on her as she weaved her way through the tables of children toward Ven and the older woman, whom she guessed to be Headmistress Hanna. She wondered if she was supposed to bow, salute, or shake hands. She settled on inclining her head respectfully. She glanced up at Ven, hoping for a hint of what was to come.

Naelin didn't know anything about Headmistress Hanna, except that she had featured in several of the bedtime tales that she liked to tell Erian and Llor. In those tales, Headmistress Hanna was the wise, powerful mentor—the woman who had proved herself at the Massacre of the Oaks, who had trained heirs, who had advised queens. She was the calm lake, the bedrock beneath the city, the soft soil that grew the wheat. She was a living legend as much as Champion Ven and Queen Daleina, and Naelin again felt small, insignificant, and horribly out of place. She wanted to tell them they'd made a mistake, and at the same time, she wanted this woman to never look at her with disappointment in her eyes, the way she was right now.

"I know of your objections to training, to all of this. Champion Ven has apprised me of your situation and preferences, and while I sympathize, I reject your conclusions," the headmistress said. Her voice rung clear across the dining hall. "You live in this world. Your children live in this world. Therefore, it *is* your fight. All that remains is to determine what kind of weapon you have to fight with."

Naelin opened her mouth to defend herself, to say it wasn't that simple, but the headmistress swept away before she could speak. Feeling like a chastised child, Naelin followed the headmistress and Ven out of the dining hall, all eyes still on her. Glancing back, she saw Alet leaving as well—on her way to the palace. She wished her friend could stay.

As soon as Naelin crossed the threshold out of the dining hall, she heard the students burst into chatter again, most likely about her, and she tried to tune it out, telling herself that she didn't care what a bunch of children who'd never lived in the real world thought of her.

She did wish Ven hadn't seen her publicly scolded.

*You shouldn't care about that*, she told herself. *You have other things to worry about.*

Following them down the spiral stairs, Naelin studied the headmistress—the stiff hold of her neck, the smooth sweep of her jaw, the press of her thin lips. "Headmistress Hanna, I can't—I won't—be an heir. There are others far more suited—"

The headmistress cut her off. "We shall see."

Reaching the practice ring, Naelin felt her feet sink into the mossy ground. It was bare of trees, and yet the circle of dirt and moss held fallen leaves and pine needles, as if there were once a forest here. She'd heard about the famous academy ring that changed for its lessons, from a forest to a desert to a lake, depending on what the masters required. She'd never thought she would be here. "What would you have me do?" Naelin asked.

"Summon a spirit," the headmistress said crisply.

"But I've never—"

"You can sense them," Ven said encouragingly. "It's not so different."

"Form a thought, and send it out," the headmistress said. "I recommend a simple command: Come." Her expression softened. "Do not be afraid. I will be here, and so will Champion Ven."

"Go ahead," Ven urged. "It's safe here. The academy is filled with masters whose primary role is to disperse spirits that students call."

"But I don't—"

"You have power; you must be trained," Headmistress Hanna said sharply. "You are a danger to yourself and others if you aren't. This is true whether you become an heir or not."

*I've survived this long without any training,* she thought. She'd been fine and her family safe until Ven had showed up. Until now—until Renet's idiocy—she'd never even been tempted to use her power. "I don't want my power."

"And I don't want a knee that aches in the rain," the headmistress said crisply. "It's a part of you, and you must learn to cope. Refusing is a child's act. It is hiding under the covers and hoping the monsters don't notice the lump in the bed. Summon a spirit, Mistress Naelin."

Naelin drew in a breath. "My mother was killed by spirits, for summoning them." She hadn't said the words aloud in a very long time, not since she'd shared it with Renet late one night before they'd married. She didn't like to drag the memory out into the light of day.

"Then you must not repeat her mistake," the headmistress said. "But her mistake was not in using her power; it was in using her power *poorly*. Training will give you greater control and greater safety." The words felt like slaps.

"It didn't help the heirs," Naelin said quietly. "I know the story of the Coronation Massacre." She saw Ven flinch, but she wasn't going to back down. She wasn't a child to be cowed by a stern frown—or at least that's what she told herself. "You aren't doing this for my own good or my safety. You want to use me, and I don't want to be used." She swallowed hard. It wasn't easy to say words like this to a legend. Clasping her hands behind her back, she hoped they couldn't tell that she was shaking. She was aware she wore borrowed clothes, pressed on her by the academy's caretakers, and that her children slept safe in cots above, feeling protected for the first time in days. She was, in many ways, at their mercy. "I am not ungrateful for the attention . . ."

"You see your power as a disease?" the headmistress asked. "Then think of me as the doctor performing a test to assess how sick you are. Cooperate with your healer, and we can work together for a cure. If your power is minimal, then we will find a way to distract the spirits from you. You can proceed with your life as planned, and the queen will never hear of you."

Yes! That was exactly what she wanted. Dare she hope? "Truthfully? You promise that? I summon a spirit, and then you'll help me be free of all this?"

"If you are not powerful enough, that would be best for all," the headmistress said. "If Champion Ven is wrong about you, then we will all help you with what you wish."

Naelin looked at Ven. "And you'll agree to this? You'll help me leave if Headmistress Hanna says so?" *Please agree!*

His expression was blank. Finally he said, "I will."

She studied his face and decided she believed him. He wouldn't lie to her, she felt certain of that. She had a chance to end this right now, return to her life . . . or start a new life, with her children, far away from where everything went wrong. Maybe in the west, a small outer village near the unclaimed lands, someplace no one had ever heard of her. All she had to do was show the headmistress she wasn't anything special, and then this whole nightmare would be over. She'd never have to convince the queen she wasn't worthy.

"Now, Candidate Naelin."

Taking a few more deep breaths, Naelin closed her eyes. She stretched her mind out as she'd been practicing and felt the crinkle in the air of tiny spirits: fire spirits that writhed within the lanterns, air spirits that flitted through the clouds above, tree spirits that crawled up the walls of the academy, and earth spirits that burrowed with the worms beneath her feet. She settled on the earth spirits—they felt closest—and did as the headmistress had instructed. She shaped the command in her mind and pushed it out, imagining herself calling her children home:

*Come!*

And they came.

Little spirits clawed their way through the soil, pushed aside the moss, and sniffed around the practice ring. They looked like moles, with pointed noses and soft black fur, but their eyes and hands looked human. Behind them, busting through the holes they'd made, were larger spirits. These looked like clumps of rocks, with rock faces, arms, legs, torsos. Rock grated together as they moved, creeping closer to Naelin.

Voice even and calm, the headmistress asked, "How many did you call?"

"I don't know," Naelin said, backing toward the stairs as the spirits shuffled toward her, sniffing the air and pawing the ground. "I said, 'Come.'"

More continued to pour through the holes in the ground. Reaching into the folds of her robes, the headmistress produced a silver bell. She rang it sharply. "It's customary to begin with a single spirit."

"Untrained, remember?" She hadn't meant to call so loudly. She hadn't even known there were different ways to call, or a way to call only one. There was, as Alet had pointed out, a lot she didn't know. She felt her heart sink. This wasn't the act of someone with minimal power.

"Ask them to return to the earth."

*Leave*, Naelin thought at them.

"With conviction, please," the headmistress said. Above, from the stairs, Naelin heard the pounding of footsteps, but she couldn't make herself tear her gaze from the spirits, who kept clawing their way out of the holes. She hadn't known there were so many. She'd only ever seen one or two at a time, but here . . .

She tried again. *Leave!*

A few of the smaller ones scampered back into their holes. Emboldened, she walked toward them. *Leave!* Quailing from her, the spirits retreated, pulling the moss in after them. By the time the other masters had poured into the practice ring, every spirit she'd called had vanished again, retreating into the earth. Her head buzzed. Her blood buzzed. Smiling wildly, she turned back to Ven and the headmistress—

And then it came.

Tentacles burst through the soil on either side of her, and she felt the ground shift, knocking her onto her knees. She felt the spirit beneath her, as broad as the entire practice ring, its tentacles reaching beyond. It felt hungry, a vast yearning emptiness beneath her.

The headmistress yelled, "Earth kraken!"

It flexed its tentacles, and the academy walls began to shake and splinter.

*Leave!*

*Lea—*

## CHAPTER 14

Hamon stood as straight and stiff as the guards. He was sweating beneath his healer's robes, the summer's humidity so thick in the air that it curled on his tongue, but he didn't move from the spot where he'd planted himself as he watched his mother unload herself from a basket. When the basket conveyor held out his hand for payment, his mother waved her hand, holding a kerchief, toward the palace, and launched into what looked like a monologue-style explanation. Hamon made eye contact with one of the palace caretakers and nodded, and the caretaker scurried down to the bridge to pay for his mother.

Seeing him, she beamed and waved enthusiastically.

"I regret this already," Hamon murmured.

"At least that saves time later," a cheerful voice said behind him—Daleina's sister, Arin. "With low expectations, you can't be disappointed."

"You should be with the queen."

"She sent me away. Again. She can't seem to decide whether she wants me glued to her side or shipped to the other end of Renthia, neatly stored away in a box inside a mountain on the other side of a desert."

"She loves you. She both wants you near and safe."

"Got that. In theory, it's sweet. In practice, annoying." Side by side, they watched his mother unload her trunks, bags, and boxes that held her precious microscope and special glassware.

She appeared to have brought her entire laboratory with her. He'd have to be clear that she wasn't staying one second longer than she was needed. "I take it you don't feel the same way about your mother?"

"We've had a . . . *strained* relationship."

His mother enlisted the caretaker and three guards to help her carry her luggage across the bridge toward him. She herself carried only a hat box, which—if she remained consistent with past behavior—held her most rare herbs, powders, and potions.

And poisons.

"You'd better leave," Hamon told Arin. "The fewer people she meets, the fewer she can hurt." He'd already requested guards on his mother's rooms—for her safety, he'd tell her.

"You could give her a second chance," Arin said. "People change."

"Not all people." He strode forward and took a box from one of the guards, forestalling his mother from flying at him, arms open, for an embrace. "Greetings, Mother. Thank you for coming so quickly."

"Oh my darling boy, of course I came! I have been so worried about you!"

"Let's not begin with lies."

"Whyever not? Lies are the foundation of civilized society." She clapped her hands together in apparent delight as she turned on Arin, who hadn't left. "Oh, and is this your girlfriend? She's very young, isn't she, Hamon? But I suppose you have your pick as a royal healer, and young means more childbearing years. My dear, am I embarrassing you?"

"Only yourself, Mother," Hamon said.

"Well then, I'll have to try harder."

He studied her. She matched the woman in his memory. She was still beautiful, with a smile built to charm and eyes that sparkled and a face that could turn heads. But she was also smaller, frailer, and grayer. Her skin was wrinkled around her eyes. Her hands looked shriveled and ash-gray in spots—clearly she hadn't stopped messing with dangerous materials.

"Yes, I'm older. Frail, weak, and ugly. I can see you thinking it."

"You know you're still beautiful, Mother."

"Aw, how sweet." She puckered her lips. "Come, give your darling mummy a kiss." Her lips were apple red.

Hamon did not move. "Did you paint your lips with one of your own concoctions?"

Grinning, she smacked her lips. "Secret ingredients."

"Then no." To Arin, he said, "She used to paint her lips with a sleeping powder and then kiss men. Stole from them while they dozed."

"Ah, but they had delightful dreams." She hooked her arm through Hamon's. "How about you lead me to my hopefully palatial quarters, request a feast to dine on, and then explain how you are going to compensate me for the years of pain of knowing my only child had willingly abandoned me? While you're at it, you can also explain your hubris in believing that I would now aid you, after you so cruelly rejected all of my pleas for help and love."

He led the way into the palace. "You came."

"I wanted to see my only son. Also, the palace." She waved at the shimmering walls and then toward Arin. "You'll see about that feast, won't you? That's a good girl. I've been eating travel food for days, and I am certain it's rotted out my insides. I want cake. Frosted cake, with fruit and three different sauces."

"I'll make it myself," Arin offered, and then—thankfully—veered off down another corridor. Hamon made a mental note to tell Daleina to caution Arin to stay away. She was too young and impressionable to handle a woman like Mother. In fact, he couldn't think of anyone in Renthia who wasn't too innocent for Mother.

"Good girl. I like her. You should marry her. Give me grandchildren. I'm supposed to want grandchildren, aren't I? I'd be a doting grandmother, always giving them treats and surprises."

"She's not my girlfriend. She's barely more than a child herself." *And I would never, ever let you near any grandchildren.* He felt a throbbing in his temples. Behind him, he heard one of the guards stifle a laugh and knew others would see only the flighty, funny act and not the crafty, morally void woman behind it. "You have been invited here for serious reasons, and I expect you to act accordingly."

"So exceedingly pompous, Hamon. I never taught you that."

"There's a lot you never taught me." *Such as empathy and compassion and kindness.* He'd worked hard to become the opposite of everything she was. Halfway up the main tower, he stopped outside a thick green door with iron hinges curled to look like vines and leaves. Swinging it open, he half bowed to welcome his mother to her quarters. She swept past him inside, and the guards followed with her belongings. They stacked them to the side as she examined the four-poster canopy bed, the marble washbasin, the alabaster fireplace, the lounge chairs that had been grown from the tree itself and matched its polished white look. Curtains hung over the wall as if over a window, but when his mother swept the curtains aside, she faced only a mural of red, gold, and black stones inlaid in the wood.

"A lovely prison."

"A temporary home," Hamon corrected. "I will return with samples for you to study. Please, make yourself comfortable, and"–he forced himself to say the words–"thank you for coming, Mother."

The last part seemed to genuinely startle her. She was silent as Hamon and the guards backed out of her room and shut the door. "Two guards at all times," Hamon said quietly, so his words wouldn't travel through the wood. "You don't talk to her. You don't take anything from her. You don't touch her, or let her touch you. Understood?"

The guards saluted, and Hamon left to find his queen and bleed her.

QUEEN DALEINA WATCHED THE SPIRIT PICK ITS WAY AROUND HER chambers, flitting to the top of her mirror and then scrambling over the beams to the wardrobe. It nibbled on a curtain, chewing the fringe, before it settled on a chair. "You aren't dead yet," it announced.

"I'm not."

"Why not? Thought you'd be dead by now."

"Are you here to frighten me?" She refused to let it see that it was working. The spirits were bolder, coming into her chambers. They'd noticed she was unwilling to use her powers, though she didn't know if they'd guessed why. Hamon had said using her powers could trigger more false deaths, and she believed him. She'd had one blackout after she'd encouraged a fire spirit to douse the palace lights, and of course there was the blackout at the new village tree. Luckily, no one else had died since then.

It bared its teeth and then giggled, a shrill sound that made shivers crisscross her skin. "Your fear is delicious." It skittered closer, moving so fast that it seemed to wink in and out, and less than a second later, it was beside her, close enough to lick her. Its tongue flicked in and out, and she pulled back.

"You will leave now," she told it.

"Aw, will you hurt me?"

"He will." She whistled, once, sharp and high, and with a growl, the wolf Bayn leapt through the curtains across the balcony. Jaws open, he sprang for the spirit.

Squealing, the spirit bolted out a window and disappeared with a rustle between the branches of one of the trees. Daleina scratched Bayn's neck, and the wolf leaned against her leg. "Good job," she told him. "Sorry to disturb your nap."

He padded back out to the balcony, circled twice, and then laid down. She spared him a smile, though it faded quickly. The spirits had noticed she was avoiding commanding them, and it wouldn't be long before they did more than merely mock her—this was a test, to see how she'd react. She wasn't convinced she'd passed.

A knock sounded on the door. "Yes?" Daleina called.

A familiar voice answered in crisp tones. "Captain Alet, returning to duty, Your Majesty."

Smiling, Daleina crossed the room and opened the door herself. "Alet!"

Alet began to bow, but Daleina hugged her friend instead. "Delighted you're back, and that you weren't eaten by bears or wolves—"

Bayn made a huffing noise from the balcony.

"Sorry, Bayn." Stepping back, she surveyed Alet. She looked well. No visible wounds. She'd bathed recently—her skin had that fresh-scrubbed look, and her hair was smoothed back beneath a traditional guard helmet. "Were you and Ven successful?"

Alet closed the door and didn't answer. She was frowning at Daleina. "You haven't been eating enough. Or sleeping enough."

"I take it I don't look majestically ethereal?" She'd been avoiding mirrors—she could tell she was beginning to look sickly, even if no one else had commented on it. Alet, though, would never lie to her. This was part of why Daleina had missed her so much.

Alet moved to pivot toward the door. "I'm calling for food."

Daleina stopped her with a hand on Alet's arm. "I'm fine. Well, not fine. But I'm not hungry. I'd rather hear about your journey. Did Ven find a new candidate?"

"He did."

She felt tension run out of her legs and arms like water. Her knees wobbled—she hadn't realized exactly how much she'd been counting on that answer. "And do you think she will do? Is she strong? Is she *good*?"

Alet hesitated—and in that pause, Daleina felt her newly formed hope crumble. "She is both strong and good," Alet said at last.

"But . . . ?"

The guardswoman crossed to the balcony as if checking to be sure the room was secure.

"Alet?" Daleina said. "You might think you have perfected the stoic soldier face, but those of us who know you well can read you like a book. No secrets between us, Alet. Did Ven find me an heir?"

"I'm sorry," Alet said, and when she turned, Daleina saw both pain and sorrow in her friend's eyes, "but I don't believe he did."

Daleina closed her eyes and, for a moment, let the pain of that disappointment roll over her, and then she locked the feeling away with bricks around her heart. "I see. Well, Aratay thanks you for your efforts."

"Now that I have returned, I request to resume my duties as your guard." Her tone was formal—an official request. She'd worn her palace guard armor, Daleina noticed, clearly expecting a yes.

Daleina opened her mouth to reply yes, of course, but the words stuck in her throat. She had a sudden image of Alet, fighting the spirits while Daleina was semi-dead. Dying, while Daleina was helpless to save her. "Hamon says the false deaths will become more common and last longer. Any guard near me is in danger."

"All the more reason it should be me. I am the best."

"Alet . . ." Daleina couldn't say she wanted to protect Alet because she was a friend. She shouldn't value one guard's life over another. And Alet was correct: she was the best. If anyone had a chance of surviving an onslaught of spirits, it was her. "I would be honored to be guarded by you."

"The honor is mine," Alet said, and then hesitated again. "And I am glad . . . that is . . . it's good to see you. I didn't . . . I mean, while we were gone . . ."

Daleina managed a smile. "I missed you too."

Bowing, Alet opened the door and stepped outside to resume her position as guard. Daleina heard her dismiss the other guard and then greet Hamon. As she listened, Daleina tried to think nothing and feel nothing, but the insidious thoughts kept running through her head, *Ven failed. And I'm a danger to everyone I love.*

She watched Hamon enter and close the door behind him. Not trusting herself to speak, she waited for him to tell her why he was here. She didn't ask if he'd found a cure, or even clues. She couldn't shake the horrible feeling that she'd just doomed her friend.

Stopping at a table, he unrolled a packet of medical supplies. "Your Majesty, I've come to take more samples, if you feel well enough." Selecting a syringe, he prepared it and laid out two additional tubes. "Are you feeling light-headed, weak, or dizzy?"

"Fine." She watched him for a moment, noting that he hadn't met her eyes since he began fiddling with his needles and test tubes. "Hamon, what is it?"

Crossing to her, he rolled her sleeve up and then tied a ribbon tight around her arm. "Make a fist." She obeyed and watched as he tapped her inner elbow, feeling for her vein. He inserted the needle. "My mother has arrived. I will be asking her to examine your blood. I won't be telling her who owns the blood." He drew the blood evenly, then removed the needle and pressed a piece of cotton to the pinprick. "Pressure on this, please."

She pressed down on the cotton as he stoppered and stored the tubes. He labeled each of them and secured the needle in his pack, covered with a sheath to show it had been used. Everything had its place in Hamon's pack. Everything he did was done with precision. "How do you feel, seeing her again?"

"There's no time to feel anything," Hamon said. "She's here to serve a purpose. Once she's done, she will leave. I feel nothing."

Leaning forward, she brushed her lips against his. "Nothing?"

"Nothing for her," he amended. "Everything for you." And then he was kissing her back, hard, as if he could hold her to life by the strength of his lips, his tongue, his hands.

How she wanted *this* to be the cure.

PEEKING AROUND THE DOORWAY OF THE PALACE KITCHEN, ARIN listened to the familiar sounds of pots, pans, knives thumping on cutting boards, spoons tapping on edges of bowls, and let the smells of nutmeg and cinnamon and sage roll over her. Inside was a comforting amber glow, spilling from the vast fireplaces, at least three that she could see, each manned by a boy who poked at its embers with an iron rod. Stacks of wood were next to them, waiting to be fed into the fires. A fleet of cooks buzzed around several long tables.

"You there!" a voice boomed, a deep male voice that cut beneath the chatter and clanking of the kitchen. "This is a kitchen, not a tourist spot. If you need a meal, talk to a caretaker."

Arin glanced behind her before realizing that he was addressing her. A second later, she spotted the speaker: a barrel-sized man with a full red beard that was laced with flour. He was swinging a ladle around him as if it were a conductor's baton.

"I'm Arin, the queen's sister." Sound ceased for a moment, and all eyes stared at her. Stepping into the kitchen, she smiled at them. "I'd like to bake a cake."

She was welcomed in, wrapped in an apron, and given her own

table plus three dedicated helpers. Mixing bowls and spoons appeared at her elbows, and as soon as she asked for ingredients, the helpers delivered them. She tried asking for a few obscure ingredients, and those were delivered as well. Grinning to herself, she dove in, determined to make the finest cake she'd ever made.

Soon, she was just as speckled in flour as the head chef, and the heavenly smell of baking cake wafted from the oven. She'd done five layers and was mixing the filling, pausing to taste it. Scooping a spoonful, she turned and snagged the nearest cook. "Here. Try." She pushed the spoon between his lips.

His eyes flew open and he nodded.

"More vanilla? Touch more vanilla. Right. Thought so." She turned back to her filling and saw, out of the corner of her eye, one of the helpers sliding a cake layer out of the oven. "Not yet. Puffed and golden, not curved and slightly yellow. Back in."

This. This she could do. Not comfort a queen, or even a sister. Not protect against a disease she couldn't see. But select ingredients, stir, and bake. Make food that made people smile. She could control this. Allowing the cake layers out of the oven, she let them cool while she prepared the frosting. Under her direction, the helpers smeared the filling between the layers, but she was the one who did the icing, pouring it into tubes to add rosettes and ribbons of sugar. She shaped it into petals and added vines and leaves. So absorbed in her work, she didn't notice that half the cooks in the kitchen had drawn closer and now circled her table, watching her decorate.

"You have an artist's hand," the head chef told her as she stepped back, breathed, and noticed her audience. "Is it for the queen?"

"It is for a guest of the queen." Perhaps this would sweeten the woman's attitude. She was clearly here for a reason—and knowing Hamon's devotion to her sister, Arin felt safe assuming that reason was directly related to Daleina. "Can I borrow a platter?" Better than a platter, a cake plate and lid were found, and she carefully lifted it. Two helpers scurried forward to balance it.

"Bring it to the lift." The head chef gestured to a cabinet alone in a wall. He lifted the door and revealed an empty cupboard inside—a dumbwaiter. "Place it in. How high up?"

"Clever." She'd seen lifts outside in villages, used to haul harvests up from the forest floor, but never within a tree. "Six staircases up." The cake just barely fit. The door to the dumbwaiter was about the size of a child. He showed her the crank and let her turn it—the cake rose up into the heart of the tree.

He handed her a token imprinted with an image of an oven. "This will tell the guards you have permission to handle the item and that the ingredients have been screened for poison. If it were going to the queen, you would need to call for a taster to sample it first, but for a guest, this will suffice." One of the helpers continued turning the crank, raising the cake upward.

She thanked him and the helpers, handed back the apron, attempted to shake the flour off her hair and clothes, and then headed up the stairs with the token clutched in her hand. Any envy she felt for the staff of cooks and the stocked kitchen was balanced by the thought of tasters, sampling every bit of food before it could be trusted. *They're overcautious*, she thought. Everyone loved the queen—or if they didn't, they at least acknowledged that they needed her, especially while there was no heir. This was, in a way, the safest time for Daleina. If she weren't sick.

On the sixth level, Arin handed the token to the guards and was allowed to remove the cake from the dumbwaiter. One of them helped carry it to Hamon's mother's room. Two guards were posted. Since her hands were full of cake, one of them knocked for her.

"Enter!" a voice rang out. "Especially if you are brawny and nude!"

The guard swung the door open, and Arin carried the cake inside.

"Oh, even better, that looks like food. Come, bring it here, child." Following her voice, Arin carried the cake across the bedroom and then laid it on a table beside two chairs. Hamon's mother moved a microscope so the cake could fit. "Guards, you may leave us." In a conspiratorial voice, Hamon's mother said, "I don't like to share. Come now, open it. Let's see what feast you've brought for me."

"Your cake." With a flourish, Arin lifted the lid and was rewarded with a gasp and a clap.

"Oh, you delightful child! This is magnificent!" Hamon's mother circled the cake, admiring it from all angles. "You made this for me? I'm so delighted I could kiss you."

Remembering what Hamon had said about his mother's lipstick, Arin took a step backward. Now that the cake was delivered, she should leave. She hadn't meant to be away from Daleina for so long—it was only that she'd been absorbed in the baking. For the first time since she'd come to the palace, she'd felt like herself again. She'd felt useful and appreciated, instead of the horrible, drowning helplessness she felt when she thought about her sister's illness. "Enjoy," she said, and added a curtsy.

"Tell me the truth now," his mother said. "Did you do this, or merely deliver it?"

"I'm a baker. I like to decorate."

"You have a steady hand. Useful." Circling around Arin, Hamon's mother examined her. "Yes, yes, I think you will do nicely. I am in need of an assistant. My Hamon has delivered to me an intriguing puzzle, and the work would go faster with a set of young, steady hands."

She felt as if a warning bell were chiming in the back of her mind. She knew she wasn't supposed to stay and spend time with Hamon's mother. He might be angry as it was, but she'd wanted to deliver the cake while it was still fresh. Stale cake made no friends. "I am sorry, ma'am, but I already have a position at the palace." She was supposed to be watching her sister, even though Daleina kept sending her away.

"Not one more important than this." All trace of the flighty, overblown personality had vanished, wiped clean as if with a washcloth. "Make no mistake: my son wouldn't have called me here for anything less than the gravest of emergencies. He's a fool if he thinks I haven't guessed whose blood he wants me to test, or to think that I can't read the fear in his eyes. You will help me, because it is necessary."

All excellent points, but she should check with—

Without waiting for Arin to speak any objections out loud,

Hamon's mother beamed at her and clapped her on the shoulder. "Be a good girl and borrow something sharp from one of those guards. Let's cut the cake, and then dive into work, shall we?"

She hesitated again. Bringing a weapon anywhere near Hamon's mother did not sound like the best idea.

"Do you think I am going to slit your throat and make a run for it?" The woman smiled. "I wouldn't have come if I'd wanted to run. I'm here to see how this turns out. But if you won't ask a guard, then I'll simply do it myself."

Arin tensed, but Hamon's mother picked up a plate and used it to slice a wedge out of the cake. "See? Messy but effective. Don't be so untrusting." Hamon's mother handed Arin the first slice and took a second piece for herself.

Biting into the cake, Arin watched Hamon's mother. She dived into the cake with gusto, inhaling chunks of it as if she hadn't eaten in days. Arin nibbled at her slice. It was, Arin admitted, excellent cake. The hint of nutmeg was what turned it from merely good to great, and the frosting . . . Odd that it should have a tang to it. She hadn't remembered adding that flavor. She had an excellent memory for tastes.

Arin blinked as the cake blurred in front of her for a moment.

"Are you all right, child?" Hamon's mother asked.

Shaking her head, she cleared the blurriness. Everything snapped back into focus. Looking at Hamon's mother, she realized how kind a smile she had. Anyone who smiled like that couldn't mean any harm, and of course it was important to help her. Arin felt silly for resisting. She *wanted* to help this woman. "I'm happy to help you any way I can."

"Of course you are, my child. And you won't leave me when I need you, will you?"

*She's beautiful,* Arin thought. And brilliant and kind. "Never."

Hamon's mother smiled at her, and Arin took another bite of cake.

## CHAPTER 15

The academy twisted, as if unscrewed by a giant hand, and cracks shot up the walls, splitting into a dozen more cracks. Naelin scrambled to keep her feet beneath her as the ground writhed and rolled. She caught Ven's arm, and he yanked her out of the loose, sandlike soil that filled her shoes and pulled on her ankles, and toward the stairs. They fell onto the steps as he herded the headmistress in front of them. The other masters swarmed around their headmistress, helping her to higher stairs.

"Focus," the headmistress ordered them. "Act, don't react."

Above, the students were screaming. Pressed against the windows, they clung to the sills as the tower shifted and shook. Naelin tried to see her children—*Which window?* She couldn't see them, but they must have woken, must be scared, and she wasn't there.

"Send it back, Naelin," Ven told her, gripping her arm. "You can do it."

"Erian and Llor—" She had to reach them! She had to—

"You have to do this for them!"

*Yes.* Yes, she did.

He was right.

She'd called this monster; she had to stop it. Turning, she stumbled down the steps toward the roiling earth. Acting on instinct, she knelt on the last step and thrust her hands into the shifting sand. *You will not hurt them. You will STOP.*

She felt the earth kraken shudder and recoil—its presence was overwhelming, like falling into a bottomless lake, murky water all around you, clingy mud beneath your bare feet. She felt its hostility crawling over her skin, and then she felt its curiosity.

"Fill it with yourself," Ven said behind her. "Your strength."

"Your thoughts," the headmistress added. "Your emotions. Your fear. Your love."

*Go,* she told it. Into the command, she shoved all her fear and love for her children, every shred of hope she had for them and their future, every wish for their happiness, every memory of late-night worrying while one of them lay sick beside her, every time she'd patched a scrape, every tear she'd kissed away, every tear she'd caused, saying *stop, don't do that, no!*

It withdrew. Curling its tentacles with it, it sank into the soil. The ground heaved as it departed, and Naelin kept her mind in the sand and stone beneath until the feel of the kraken vanished like a storm cloud dispersing in the wind.

Shaking, she sank against the stairs, and then she heaved herself up and pushed past the masters and the students—up to where she'd left her children. She burst into the room.

"Mama!" Launching himself across the room, Llor threw his small, quivering body at her. Erian followed. Her face was streaked with tears, and her hair was matted on her cheek. Naelin gathered them both in her arms.

"I'm sorry," she said into their hair. "I'm so sorry."

"You saved them," a voice said behind her—Ven. "You sent it away. You, alone and untrained."

Muffled, she said without looking at him, "I also called it. It was my fault." *You told me to,* she wanted to say. It was his fault too, pushing her to do what she didn't want to do, what her instincts told her was too dangerous. But she could pin her anger on him only for a moment before it turned back to herself. She was the one who had summoned more than a single, weak spirit. She'd endangered everyone.

"Think what you could accomplish with training!"

She held Erian and Llor tighter, breathed them in, felt their own breath in their warm bodies as they shook against her, silently crying, still scared. "You can't train me. I'm a danger. To them. To everyone."

"Next time, it might come on its own. Or another like it. Don't you want to know how to keep your children safe always? Don't you want to keep *all* the children safe? As a trained heir, you could do that. As queen, you could do more." The hope in his voice, the belief in her, was heady.

"You're trying to manipulate me."

"Yes. Is it working?"

She stroked her children's hair and felt as if her heart were shattering into a thousand shards. She couldn't risk them living through what she'd lived through, watching their mother draw too-powerful spirits, listening to her die. But was it already too late?

"She can't be trained here," the headmistress said.

Ven's head shot up. "But she—"

"You have to take her to the queen. She's the only one with enough power to handle things if Naelin summons spirits she can't control."

"This isn't the time—"

The headmistress cut him off. "It is precisely the time. There is, in fact, no time to waste. She needs the queen . . . and the queen needs her."

Slowly, Ven nodded.

*Yes, we need the queen*, Naelin thought. The queen could keep the kraken from ever coming back. She had power over all the spirits. *Maybe she could command them to forget me. She could order them to leave me and my children alone, forever.*

Pulling back from Erian and Llor, Naelin caressed her daughter's cheek, pushing her hair back behind her ear. She smiled at both of them, a trembly smile but the best she could do. "We're going to the palace. Isn't that exciting? You'll need to be very, very good."

"I don't want to!" Llor wailed.

"The queen will help us." She patted his back as he wrapped his arms around her neck. "She'll keep us all safe. From the spirits. From me." She took a deep breath. "I seem to be . . . more than a hedgewitch." There was no hiding from that fact. Ven was right. She knew full well that spirits like that didn't come to a weak, immature power. Whatever was in her . . . it was big, bigger perhaps than her mother's power had been. Scarier. But if the queen could convince the spirits to ignore the power they'd seen in her . . .

Llor whimpered. "Are there going to be more monsters?"

She hugged him tighter and wished with all her heart she could tell him no. "There are always monsters. But I'll always be here to scare them away."

"Will you . . . will you be safe, Mama?" Erian asked. Her lip was trembling but she wasn't crying anymore. She was trying to be brave.

"Of course," Naelin said. "Everything will be fine. You'll see. We'll all be together, and that's what matters." The queen was more powerful than anyone. She could help Naelin, if she chose to.

"Promise?" Llor said.

"Double promise," Naelin said. They linked pinkies, all three of them, while Ven and the headmistress looked on silently. Smiling, Naelin didn't let her children see a shred of fear or doubt . . . even as those feelings tried to eat away at her insides.

Soon—sooner than Naelin would have liked—they were at the palace gate. She stayed with Erian and Llor as Ven spoke with the guards. After a minute, Ven waved them forward, and Naelin shuffled toward the gate with the children clinging to her middle. They all stared at the guards, stiff-backed and armed with swords and staffs with glittering blades on the ends. All the guards stared straight ahead, motionless.

"Are they statues?" Llor reached out a pudgy finger to poke one, and she caught his wrist.

"Don't touch," Naelin cautioned.

"Can I tickle them?"

"How is that not covered by 'don't touch'?" She kept a firm grip on his wrist until they were past the guards and through the grand gate.

Inside, the palace was just as elegant as outside, with polished wood walls and glass globes lit within by either firemoss or fire spirits. Reaching out with her mind, Naelin felt the presence of dozens of spirits, flitting around the palace, more out in the capital, mostly small, harmless spirits, no larger than birds. Earth spirits worked in the garden, and a water spirit bathed in pools that Naelin couldn't see—she could sense the spirit's contentment, though, with the water that surrounded it.

Ven strode ahead of them, nodding at the guards that flanked a vast stairway, and then veered around the stairs toward a door beneath it. Naelin exhaled—she hadn't been relishing the thought of ascending those stairs, all the guards watching her. Her footfalls felt thunderously loud in the cavernous entrance hall.

"You'll have to be prepared the meet the queen," Ven said. "Don't be offended. The caretakers have firm ideas about what constitutes 'presentable.'"

Before Naelin could ask for specifics, the caretakers descended on them: three coiffed women and two men whisked them through the narrow door, away from Ven. They clucked to one another, chattering so fast that it felt as if they were speaking a different language. One yanked on Naelin's hair and then sniffed before recoiling. Naelin clutched Erian and Llor closer.

One of the caretakers bowed to her. "You will bathe now."

"Don't want to," Llor said.

"That's an excellent idea." Naelin spied steaming baths through a half-open curtain. "Go with the nice man. Mama will be right nearby." To the caretaker, she said, "Don't take him farther than I can hear. And don't listen if he screams when you wash his neck."

Llor relinquished her hand and went with the caretaker. "I'm ticklish," he warned the caretaker. "I bite when I'm tickled."

"No biting!" Naelin called after him.

Erian still clutched Naelin's hand. "Please don't make me go with them."

"They just want to clean us. Don't you want to be clean?" She knelt in front of Erian. "You'll feel better clean. Smell better too. I bet they have lovely smelling baths here."

Another caretaker bowed. "You can choose your fragrance. Pine, lilac, magnolia."

"Ooh, magnolia." Naelin faked a smile, her eyes still on Erian.

"That's a flower from a tree that only grows where it's warm, in southern Aratay. I've heard it smells sweeter than honeysuckle." Through the curtain, she heard Llor yelp and water splash and hoped her son wasn't about to bite a person who worked for the palace. They must have had young visitors before, right? "I'll be right nearby." She prayed the caretakers wouldn't make her break her promise. She was aware of the guards just outside. She couldn't let her children cause a scene here, not if she wanted them to be allowed to stay with her. "Don't you want your hair untangled? You have enough snarls that I'm sure birds are using it as a nest. They've probably already laid eggs inside." She pressed her ear against Erian's hair. "I hear chirping! The eggs are hatching!"

Erian giggled and then let the caretakers lead her into a bath. Eyes on the curtains, Naclin followed her caretakers toward her own bath. The tub looked to be stone and was cradled against the wall of wood, which glistened with beads of water from the rising steam. She shed her clothes and lowered herself into the water. It smelled sweet, like vanilla, and the bubbles hid her body from the caretakers as they efficiently scrubbed her arms, back, and hair. She told herself she'd birthed two children—she didn't care about modesty.

She let them dress her in layered golden skirts and a bodice embroidered with so many tiny beads that it felt like a pebbled floor when she ran her hand over it. They wound her hair into elaborate braids that twisted around one another so tightly that she doubted she'd ever untangle it, and they doused her skin in lotions. One plucked at hairs in her eyebrows. Through it all, she tried to shape what she planned to say to the queen.

Erian and Llor waited for her back in the polished hall. Llor wore a golden tunic and a sullen expression, while Erian was beaming, all dolled-up like an illustration out of a book. Her hair had been braided with flowers. "I smell gross," Llor proclaimed.

"Maybe the queen likes gross smells," Naelin said. "Let's go find out."

Taking her children's hands, she followed the guards that led them up the spiral staircase. Llor was huffing by the time they reached the top, and Naelin was breathing deeply as the guard handed them to a new set of guards, these in armor trimmed with silver, who led them through a curved hallway, covered in mirrors and murals and decorated with sculptures that represented Renthians from Aratay and beyond: woodsmen, courtiers, acrobats, farmers, mountaineers, islanders . . . She wished she could have lingered over each one, carved from various woods and stones and even gems, but the guards didn't slow. Up ahead, she saw Ven, dressed in his usual green armor, but cleaner with damp hair. She stopped in front of him—his eyes were drinking her in, and she felt a blush warm her cheeks. She couldn't remember the last time she'd blushed. She was *not* a blusher.

"You don't smell gross," Llor said, accusingly.

"If they'd left you unbathed, you'd have scared all the guards," Ven told him. "They aren't used to people as fierce as you."

Only slightly mollified, Llor took Ven's hand. Naelin saw Ven's eyes widen as her son slipped his hand into the champion's as if he owned it, and she stifled a smile. Ven, she was pleased to see, did not release the boy's hand. Instead, he held it gently as he led them through a doorway carved with the images of birds and woodland creatures into the throne room.

Naelin spotted Captain Alet. Standing on guard beside the throne, Alet wore jewel-encrusted green-and-gold armor, and carried a knife sheathed on each arm and each leg. Naelin met her eyes, and Alet nodded a welcome. She then winked at Erian and Llor, who giggled. Naelin felt slightly better. But only slightly.

On the throne was the queen.

She was . . . well, she was beautiful, though it was difficult to tell how much of that beauty was due to herself and how much was the richly layered fabrics and jewels. She had gold, orange, and red-streaked hair that shone in the firelight, catching the flames in her curls. Jewels were laid across her neck, sparkling like caught stars, and Naelin stared at them for a moment before she noticed a simple wooden necklace between them, three carved leaves. The queen also had an ordinary knife at her hip, with a battered hilt and a plain leather sheath. But what struck Naelin the most as she progressed forward was: *She's so young!*

Intellectually, she'd known that. Queen Daleina had only just recently completed her training at the academy when her predecessor called for the trials. She was, at most, nineteen or twenty years old. Young enough that Naelin could have been her mother, if she'd chosen to have children sooner. Encased in her royal clothes, on the throne . . . the queen looked as if she should be out in a village, starting her own shop, kissing nice young men, or setting out to find her place in the world—not ensconced here with the responsibilities of an entire nation on her lap.

"I'm sorry," Naelin said, before she thought about the words.

An expression flashed across the queen's face—so fast that Naelin couldn't tell what it was, only that it was a break in her emotion. "For what, pray tell?"

She felt Ven's eyes on her as well as Alet's, but she couldn't look away from the young queen. She shouldn't have said anything, but now that she had, she couldn't stop. "For this, Your Majesty." She waved at the throne, at the room, the chandeliers, the murals, the guards, the windowless walls, the gilded cage. "You should have had a childhood. I am sorry that Aratay has asked so much of you."

The queen continued to regard her with her deep summer-green eyes. She had intense eyes that felt as if they were staring right into your heart. Eyes that had seen too much. "It may ask this much of you as well."

"I've told Ven . . . Champion Ven, that is . . . I've said no."

Queen Daleina blinked. "No?"

"I don't want to be heir. I don't want this power."

"She said no," the queen repeated, to Ven.

"I'm aware of that," Ven said, "but she has agreed to be trained, and I believe she will change her mind about becoming heir, once she understands how much she is needed." The champion and his queen were looking at each other with expressions so fierce that Naelin was certain there was another layer of silent conversation that her ears couldn't hear. She had the same sense she did when Renet lied to her.

"A bad queen can be as dangerous as no queen," Queen Daleina said. "You know that."

"She's what we need," Ven said, firmly, calmly, and the words sunk into Naelin like a stone into a pond. *Oh no*, she thought. The incident at the academy hadn't convinced him she was unsuitable. In fact, the opposite seemed to be true.

"I'm not," Naelin tried. She glanced at Alet, who nodded encouragingly. She remembered what Alet had said once, when they were out in the forest, that it was difficult to say no to the queen. *But I have to.* "I'm a woodswoman, a mother, not a potential heir. I don't want this. Never wanted this." She took a deep breath. "Your Majesty, please . . . I want a quiet life, a peaceful life."

The queen rolled her eyes up and studied the ceiling. In a mild, too mild voice, she asked, "Champion Ven, did you force this woman to come here?"

"No!" He hesitated. "Persuaded, perhaps."

Little hands balling into fists, Llor shouted, "He promised Mama you'd keep us safe! She said she'd train if the queen keeps us safe! They made a deal!"

Naelin nudged him. "Shh." And Erian whispered, "Say 'Your Majesty'!"

Shrinking back behind Naelin, Llor added in a mumble, "Your Majesty."

"I see." The queen drummed her fingers on the armrest of her throne. Naelin noticed that her nails had been nibbled down to the nubs. *Still a child*, Naelin thought. It wasn't right. "Let me see if I am understanding this correctly: you agreed to be trained, if I would keep your children safe, but you did not agree to become an heir."

Naelin bowed again. "And now I don't even wish to be trained. I wish to be free. Please, Your Majesty, can you use your power to tell the spirits to forget me? Make it so they never noticed my power?"

Drummed her fingers more.

Naelin felt Erian's and Llor's hand dampen in hers as she sweated. This was it. "We'll find a quiet home far from anyone." Naelin was trying not to beg. "I won't ever use my power again. All I need is for you to command them to ignore me, until they forget about me."

"It is not possible to command the spirits to forget," the queen said. "And at best, a command to leave you alone would only work as long as I am alive. After my death, the spirits would come for you and rend you limb from limb, along with those you seek to protect. If you are as powerful as Ven says and if you refuse to use your power, they will treat you like a queen who lost her throne—they'll hunt you and destroy you."

Erian whimpered and clung closer. Llor began to cry.

"You're young and strong," Naelin said. "You'll outlive me. You can keep my children safe, even after I'm gone."

"You cannot be certain of that," the queen said.

"Queen Fara did not live a long life," Ven added.

The queen bowed her head.

"Please, Your Majesty." Naelin couldn't seem to make her voice louder than a whisper. Her throat felt tight. "I'm too dangerous."

"Untrained, she summoned the earth kraken," Ven told the queen, "and then banished it."

The queen's fingers halted. She held them motionless above the arm of the throne. Studying Naelin, Erian, and Llor, she didn't speak. Naelin tried to read her expression, but Queen Daleina may as well have been carved out of wood.

"It damaged the academy walls," Naelin said. "People could have been killed, because of me."

"Because you were untrained. Trained . . ." Ven turned back to the queen. "Trained, she could protect the palace, when you can't. She could train here, be here for when she's needed."

The queen's eyes shifted to bore into Ven's eyes. Silence weighed heavily on the throne room. Llor fidgeted beside Naelin, but she kept a tight grip on his hand.

The queen spoke. "If she doesn't want to be queen . . ."

Naelin jumped in. "I don't."

". . . that only proves she's saner than I. It doesn't, however, absolve her of her responsibilities to this land. You will train her quickly, Champion Ven?"

"I will."

"But . . ." *No, this wasn't the way the conversation was supposed to go!* She'd told the queen no. Surely that had to disqualify her.

"Your Majesty, while I'm flattered that Champion Ven believes I'm worth his time, the fact remains that I have prior responsibilities. My children come first, before any ambition—"

"Do you think I sit here because of ambition?" The queen rose, and her train pooled around her feet. She swept down the stairs, past Naelin, to an archway. After a moment's hesitation, Naelin joined her, herding Erian and Llor beside her. Ven and her guards, including Alet, followed at a discreet distance.

The archway opened into a vast curve of windows that overlooked the royal gardens. Roses in a riot of colors filled the garden beneath them, so much rich color that for a moment all Naelin could do was drink in the jeweled rainbow below. Then she noticed a girl, older than Erian, perhaps thirteen or fourteen, walking between the roses, randomly plucking the blossoms and laying them in a basket. Every few feet, she kicked the skirts out of her way, clearly unused to walking in such a long gown.

"My sister Arin," the queen said, and Naelin saw the tangle of emotion in her eyes: love, regret, guilt, fear. "You see, we all have someone we want to protect. You will train, Mistress Naelin, and you will train hard and well, for the sake of Aratay, my sister, and your children.

"You will protect them all."

## CHAPTER 16

H amon smoothed the wrinkles on his robe and then ran his fingers through his hair. Going to see his mother made him feel as if he were eight years old, with smudges on his cheeks and dirt under his nails. She used to spot every stray mark.

Now he felt like she could spot even deeper, and that made him nervous.

Flanking the door, the guards fixed their eyes down the corridor, politely ignoring the way he was fidgeting and delaying. He appreciated that. He made a mental note to commend them to their superior.

He schooled his expression into a neutral one, reminded himself to remain calm and professional, and then nodded to the guards. One of them opened the door, and he heard light laughter from inside—the voice of a young woman.

"You allowed her a guest?" he hissed to the guards.

The guards exchanged glances. "She insisted."

"You *spoke* with my mother?"

"Not her. The queen's sister."

Hamon barged into the room. His mother was sprawled on one of the couches, her feet bare and propped on a pillow. Daleina's sister, Arin, was twirling around the room with scarves draped over her arms. Seeing Hamon, she dropped the scarves.

"Ah, Hamon, there you are at long last! Come. Sit. Lady Arin and I were just celebrating our success." She lifted a glass of what looked like sparkling pear wine—if so, it was one of the most expensive drinks in the capital. On the side of the room were the remnants of a several-tier cake, as well as a cascade of grape stems and a half-eaten side of spiced meat. Ants crawled over the cake, and Hamon thought he saw a mouse scoot beneath the tablecloth. Blossoms from the royal gardens—blossoms from rare, specially cultivated flowers—were strewn around Mother's microscopes, test tubes, and beakers, in a very expensive celebratory wreath.

Scurrying to the side bar, Arin poured a crystal goblet of pear wine and held it out to Hamon. "Celebrate with us, and drink to your glorious mother's health!"

"No," he said. "No to all of this. Mother, what are you doing? You know I have you here for a serious purpose."

Mother waved the glass in the air until the wine spattered on the floor, the couch, and her arm. "And I have fulfilled it! Grandly and magnificently."

For a moment, he couldn't move, couldn't think, couldn't breathe. "A cure?"

She swigged the pear wine. "Don't be absurd. I am flattered at your faith in my abilities. Sincerely flattered, actually. To know you think so highly of me . . ."

"Mother, if you did not find a cure . . ."

"A *cause*, my boy," she said. "I found a cause."

That was not an excuse for celebration. That was obvious. "She has the False Death. It's genetic. The cause is in her ancestry." Every letter he'd received back from scholars across Renthia agreed with that: she'd been born to this fate. All had expressed condolences for his sick "friend" and wished him luck with his studies.

"The cause was in her wine," Mother said. "Or her cake. Or her bread. Or dusted on her pillow. Or poured into a wound."

Hamon sighed. "Clearly this was a mista—"

"She was poisoned, dear Hamon. Very cleverly poisoned."

Hamon felt his knees buckle. He thought of Queen Fara and the nightend berries. His head felt as if it were swimming. His Daleina, poisoned? "Impossible. It's False Death."

"Indeed it is. She has been given a poison that causes False

Death. Or more accurately, causes symptoms that mimic it. You have done research into other cases, yes?"

He'd researched many cases—the scientists and healers he'd contacted had sent him reams of research. He hadn't found any examples of cases with no symptoms other than the blackouts. In that, Daleina was unique. He simply hadn't known what it meant. Hamon sank onto a chair. "This would explain why she had no other symptoms, if it wasn't natural. But does such a poison exist? I've never heard of one." And neither had anyone else who had responded to his inquiries. No one had mentioned this as a possibility.

"Frankly, nor have I. But I tested the blood thoroughly. The sickness was introduced from the outside. You can check my work." She nodded to a table that ran along the back. It was filled with glass tubes and stacks of parchment.

Arin hurried over to the table and showed him a dish with a drop of blood. It was under a curved bit of glass. He slid it under the microscope and peered in.

Coming up behind him, Mother said, "I treated that sample with everberry sap. If the cells had the abnormality that causes False Death . . ."

Peering at it, he saw the cells tinged with orange dots. "They would have rejected the sap. Of course." He made a fist, wanting to pound it on the table, but restrained himself so as not to damage any of the equipment. He should have thought to test for this. But why would he have suspected a poison when one like this had never existed? "What else?"

Setting aside her wine, she led him through the various tests and experiments she'd done. It was, he admitted, impressive—she'd done at least a week's work in three days, rerunning all the tests he'd done, plus adding many of her own. Several were so clever that he thought he should take notes.

All of them gave the same clear result: it was the False Death, but it wasn't natural.

"How could this happen?" he asked. New poison or not, there were systems in place to prevent any kind of poison from touching the queen. He'd been especially careful, given Queen Fara.

"She has tasters, and I am her healer. Only the most trusted people are allowed in her rooms or near her throne."

"My boy, you know there are many ways for a poison to be delivered." She was smiling at Arin as she said it, watching the girl neaten the food display.

Hamon followed her gaze. "Mother, what did you do?"

"Do? I solved your problem."

"I mean to her."

Mother laughed. "You think I would poison my best assistant?"

Arin laughed too, a merry cascade. "Mistress Garnah would never harm me! She's the kindest soul that has ever lived. And so very wise."

Hamon shook his head. There was something not right here, but he had a more important question: "Do you know how to make the antidote?"

"Again, you flatter me. I had no idea you thought so highly of me. I admit this is quite gratifying. I am so pleased I came." She sauntered over to the food table and plucked herself a grape. "The poison dissolved in her system already. I can't separate it out. But . . . if you find an undiluted sample, I should be able to manufacture a cure."

Again, he felt unable to breathe.

"Ah, that look in your eyes! If I do find a cure . . ." She let the sentence dangle and sashayed across the room.

He followed her with his eyes, watching her like a hawk watches a squirrel . . . or perhaps more like a squirrel who has seen a hawk. Mother was no one's prey. "What do you want?"

"Respect. Yours. The country's. I want a position in the palace. Master . . . Healer?"

"You're no healer."

"Master Chemist then?"

"You're too dangerous to be allowed access to the kind of power—"

Arin scowled at him. "Mistress Garnah is not dangerous! She's enlightened and pure! She wants only what's best for you, her son. She loves you and has missed you. She told me. You were to be her apprentice—the one she would pass all her knowledge on to—but instead you ran!" Scooping a slice of cake onto a plate, she held it out to him. "Have a piece. You'll feel better."

"Fix her," Hamon said, pointing at the queen's sister, "and prepare to create an antidote. You will be well rewarded." He strode out of the chamber. "I will find the poison."

Passing the guards, he said, "Don't eat the cake."

HER BORROWED EMBROIDERED SHOES QUIET ON THE SMOOTH wood, Naelin followed Ven up a staircase into one of the many spires of the palace. He had barely spoken after he'd come to claim her for training. He'd introduced the guards who would be watching her children while they slept, and he waited while she'd grilled them on their qualifications and trustworthiness. But after that, silence.

It occurred to her that maybe he was afraid of what she was going to say. Or not "afraid," perhaps. He was a champion. But . . . wary.

It was almost funny.

If she had been younger, Naelin might have yelled at him and cursed him out. She might have hated him, blaming him the way she used to blame her parents—her mother, for being reckless with her power, and her father, for not finding a way to protect them. Or the way she still blamed Renet, who had started all this.

But she wasn't interested in lying to herself: She'd been the one to summon the kraken. It was her power, and she'd been foolish to think the queen would help her, or could help her. There was no easy fix.

"Talk to me about your training plan," Naelin said.

He was silent for a moment. She had the sense he hadn't been thinking about her or her training at all. At last, he said, "With Daleina, she had to learn how to use her power judiciously, favor the techniques that worked for her and abandon those that didn't. A handful of gravel thrown in the eyes of your enemy can be as effective as a boulder dropped on his head."

"And with me?"

"You have to learn not to drop boulders on everyone's heads."

She snorted. "How exactly do I learn that?"

"By dropping a few on my head. You draw them, and if you can't handle them, I'll stick my sword into them. Fairly straightforward. We don't have time for nuance." He was climbing the stairs as if he wanted to pound them flat with his feet. She was struggling to keep pace with him. The stairwell was lit with firemoss, and their glow wavered as she and Ven passed.

"What if I draw another kraken?"

"That's why we're climbing up instead of staying on the forest floor. Besides, even big spirits don't like being jabbed with pointy metal sticks. You surprised me back at the academy. I won't be surprised again." Reaching a landing, he halted in front of an ornate door, decorated with carvings of vines. He pulled out a key. "No one lives in this tower. Not anymore. You will be able to practice here without endangering anyone."

The door swung open, and Naelin gasped.

She thought she'd seen opulence in the throne room and the grand halls, but the rest of the palace was nothing compared to these rooms. Gold seemed to drip from every surface: the curved couch, the table with the glass surface, the mantel over the fireplace, the washbasin with the filigree pitcher. It all glittered in the light of a dozen cream-colored candles on candelabras. On a dais was a canopied bed, piled high with pillows. But it was the ceiling that stunned her the most: inlaid with tiny crystals, it sparkled like the night sky. Marveling, she walked into the center of the room. "You want me to practice *here*?"

He didn't answer, and she looked over at him. His hand was on the mantel, tracing the curves of the carving. His eyes were sad.

"Ven, whose rooms were these?"

She guessed the answer as he gave it: "Queen Fara's." He rubbed the dust from his fingertips. "No one comes here now. We can practice here uninterrupted."

Naelin walked through the rooms, afraid to touch anything, and out onto the balcony. Before her was the night forest. Lights dotted the branches, lining bridges that were obscured from sight. She felt the spirits out there, amid the branches. She heard Ven walk onto the balcony with her. "You knew Queen Fara well?"

"Very well."

"What was she like?"

"Everything you'd imagine a queen should be. Fearless. Ambitious. Determined. Utterly convinced of her own infallibility. She lacked any shred of humility, but she was so powerful that it didn't matter." Leaning on the balcony railing, he was staring into the forest as if it held answers.

"I'm nothing like that."

He didn't answer.

She'd never measure up, not to his expectations and not to his memories. *He's deluding himself if he thinks I'm queen material.* "What was Queen Daleina like before she became queen?"

"Determined, though in a different way. She didn't feel as though she was owed the crown like Fara; she felt it was her duty. She'd committed herself to this path at a young age."

"And you? Were you always destined to be a champion?"

"Yes."

Naelin resisted rolling her eyes. This was absurd. She was consorting with born-from-the-womb heroes. She wasn't worthy of this. "You must have made a choice at some point. Something set you on this path. Come on, confess. You weren't born with muscles. Or did you punch your way out of your mother's womb?"

A faint smile crossed his lips, nearly hidden within his beard. "She'd say that's exactly how it happened. She'd like you, I think. She was a mama bear too." He lapsed into silence again, lost in thought.

"You don't normally train people this way, do you?"

"Usually, trainees have to learn to turn their whisper into a shout. You, on the other hand, have to turn a shout into a whisper. If I were to train you the usual way, you'd likely cause a few natural disasters before we were done."

"You aren't comforting." And she didn't like her own thoughts. Insecurity was the shortest path to failure. "Can we just start?"

He nodded abruptly as if she'd interrupted him, and then led the way back inside the room, to the fireplace. Two candelabras flanked it, but the fireplace itself was cold. All the ash had been cleared away. Logs were stacked within, as if for decoration rather than use.

"No surprises," Naelin warned.

"No surprises," he agreed. He drew his sword and crouched, ready. "Start with a fire spirit, call it into the hearth. Concentrate on one that's already in the palace, feel it first, attract its attention, and direct your command at it. Just at it, as if you were whispering and didn't want anyone to overhear."

She widened her awareness, brushing against the tree spirits that skulked in the branches, an earth spirit that snuffled at the roots far below, an air spirit . . . there, a fire spirit, flitting around the balcony curtains, shriveling their edges with its heat. *You. Only you. Come to me.* She tried to whisper, a gentle command.

She felt the spirit pause, curious. Patches of bark blackened beneath its feet as it lingered on the balcony. She pushed again, harder. *You, come to me.*

It sped closer, a streak of light. It dived inside the room and straight into the fireplace. Flames shot up a foot, and Naelin scrambled back, but then the fire calmed, and the spirit spun inside it, dancing music-less. It was no bigger than her hand, with a body made of fire and a face of twisting flame, white at the core, a molten gold chest, orange arms, and red hands that ended in black fingers. Its eyes were ember, and its mouth held a tongue of flame that flicked in and out.

Naelin studied it. It stared back.

"Good," Ven said.

"It was the only one nearby."

"Still, good. See if you can command it."

It flickered as it moved, and Naelin realized its ember eyes were trained on her, as if waiting. "To do what?" The firelight danced, and Naelin felt as if she couldn't look away. She felt the warmth on her skin and inside her, as if the fire were inside her chest.

"Control which log burns—and which one doesn't."

She eyed one log, a thick chunk of oak. It was untouched by flame yet, waiting for one of them to toss it in. *Burn that.*

With a cackling howl, the fire spirit dove onto the log. Flames shot out of the hearth, raced across the room, and hit the bed. One of the silken pillows burst into flames. Running, Naelin grabbed a pitcher from the washbasin and hurled its contents onto the bed. Water dampened the flames, and smoke curled up to stain the canopy. Shrieking, the spirit fled, bursting out the archway to the balcony and shooting straight up to blend into the stars.

"On the plus side, you didn't destroy the palace," Ven said mildly.

Naelin stared up at the stars. "I may need more practice."

## CHAPTER 17

Lying flat on the floor, Daleina stared up at the painted ceiling. She took a breath and then another, pushing her fear deep down inside her, burying it beneath her breath. *You have to do this.* It was her duty, despite the risk. Slowly at first, she sent her awareness out. If she was careful and slow . . . maybe the False Death wouldn't come. She touched the spirits in the palace first. Present in every corner of the complex, they felt like a buzzing on her skin. She then expanded to the capital, touching the earth spirits that burrowed beneath the roots and the air spirits that flitted between the trees. There were fewer in the busier areas of the city and then more as she spread outward—

*Click.*

She heard, distantly, the door to her bedroom open and then footsteps coming closer, but her mind felt stretched like bread dough. She kept her focus on the spirits—if anyone hostile tried to enter her room, Alet would stop them. And if Alet failed, Bayn would defend Daleina. Ever since he'd returned, he had stayed by her side. He was with her as often as Alet and more than Arin. Her sister had visited her only twice since coming to the palace. *Safer that way*, Daleina told herself, and pushed that bit of hurt down with the fear. After all, she was risking another false death right now. It was better that Arin was nowhere nearby. She continued to reach out, spreading herself across the forests of Aratay.

Whoever had come into the room was waiting. She heard their breathing.

She almost had it, all of Aratay. Her skin felt slicked with sweat. She felt the rain in the east and the sun in the west as if they were hitting her skin as well. She breathed in pine and magnolia and lilac and the sweet smell of the earth.

*Stay awake*, she thought. *Stay alive.*

This was the most dangerous moment, when she was connected to all of them. If she died while she was connected to them . . .

"*Do no harm,*" she thought.

She sent the thought out to all of them, adding to all the other times she'd made that command, feeling the order burrow into the spirits.

"*Do. No. Harm.*"

She felt them resist, flailing against the reissue of the basic and most essential command, and then she felt it sink into them, like a weight inside them.

Pulling back fast, Daleina reeled her mind back into her body. She became aware of the coolness of the floor, the smell of the wood fire in the fireplace, the sound of guards walking up and down the corridors outside. She pried her eyes open. Her lids felt crusty, as if she'd been asleep for hours, and her muscles felt stiff. She exhaled—if she'd triggered another false death while she was linked to the spirits . . . but she hadn't, and the essential command had been reinforced. She'd done her duty and all had survived—this time.

"No new blackouts?" a voice asked. Hamon.

She turned her head to see him but kept lying on the floor. She knew from experience that standing up too soon would make her entire head feel as if it had been shaken. "Not today."

"You've been poisoned."

She blinked once, twice. Slowly, she peeled herself up from the floor. She sat with her head between her knees for another moment. In a light and painfully calm voice, she said, "You used to have a better bedside manner."

SARAH BETH DURST

His mouth twitched at her joke, but his eyes stayed intense. *He's serious*, she thought. He continued, "My mother, with the help of your sister, finished her examination of your blood and concluded that your illness isn't natural. It was imposed externally, presumably deliberately."

Daleina absorbed this, turned the idea over in her head, and began to laugh. She knew she shouldn't be laughing, but she couldn't stop. Her body shook, and her eyes teared.

He waited quietly until she finished.

Hiccupping, she got control of herself again. "It is grimly appropriate."

"No one knows we poisoned Queen Fara. And I don't believe in fate. I *do* believe in assassins." He knelt beside her. "Daleina, if we can find your poisoner, if we find a sample of the poison . . . my mother thinks she can manufacture a cure."

Daleina felt herself still, any hint of hysterical laugher wiped out of her. "Do you think she can?"

"She may be an amoral killer, but she's also an amoral genius. Also she's proud of her abilities. She wouldn't lie about this, not if it meant gaining my admiration. When I was a child, after she'd poison someone, she'd retell the tale over and over, expecting me to worship her for her brilliance every time. She feeds on adoration. If she saves you, she'll expect some sort of compensation—a position in the palace, she suggested; she'll want prestige and praise."

Daleina waved her hand. "If she saves me, she'll be compensated. According to my seneschal, the point of having a treasury is to bribe amoral but useful people. He's been using it to bribe the border patrol of our neighbors for years." She closed her eyes for a second as a wave of realization crashed over her. "It's not genetic. That means Arin is safe." Opening her eyes, she threw her arms around Hamon.

He held her close. She felt his breath against her neck and the tightness of his arms around her. She rested her cheek against his shoulder and let herself feel, for the first time in a long time, safe.

Remembering something else he said, she raised her head. "Did you say my sister was with your mother?"

"I'll make sure she's all right," Hamon promised. "In the meantime, we need to find the poison. Who would try to kill you?"

"No one. Anyone. I don't know." She thought of Queen Fara. The prior queen had feared the heirs, but there were no heirs to covet Daleina's crown. Due to the Coronation Massacre . . . "Maybe the families of the heirs who died? There were some of them who blamed me for surviving when their loved ones didn't. One of them could have sought revenge."

Hamon nodded slowly. "They had both motive and opportunity."

That's what she was thinking. After the coronation, she'd visited every family, joined them for a meal, comforted them as best she could . . . She thought of how they'd broken down in tears, how some had railed in anger, how some had sat as quiet as stone, as though the news had hardened them inside. Any of them could have done it. "I visited nearly fifty families," Daleina said. "Where do we start? How do we know—"

"It couldn't have been just anyone," Hamon said. "Crafting poisons, in particular creating new poisons, is a very specialized craft. This poison was designed to mimic a specific disease. Furthermore, it was designed to be undetectable by ordinary blood screens—I didn't find it on my tests. Only a few in Aratay are skilled enough for this kind of work."

"Do you know who those people are?"

He hesitated. "My mother might. But the poisoner might not be the poison maker. Most poison makers don't use what they create. The risk of being caught and imprisoned is too high."

"So we are looking for either a friend of your mother's, or someone very wealthy. At least that narrows it down. Will you speak to your mother again? Ask for a list of her poison-making friends . . ." Daleina hesitated, not sure how to phrase her next question. He seemed so tense that the wrong word could shatter him. She didn't have the time to be careful of his feelings, though. "Hamon, I hate to ask this, but . . . Is there any chance your mother could have done this?"

"Yes, of course," he answered immediately. "But I don't think she did. Her surprise at being called to the palace seemed real.

And if she'd created such a clever poison, I don't think she'd miss the chance to gloat. If I'm wrong, though . . . the guards will keep her contained."

That had to be good enough, for now. At least he was aware of the possibility. "I will send royal investigators to the heirs' families, the wealthiest first, while you talk to your mother about her friends. Hamon, we'll find who did this! I'll live!" She cradled his face as he began to cry. "I'll live."

FOLDING HER HANDS ON HER LAP, DALEINA TRIED NOT TO SHOW how much the conversation with Hamon had affected her. He'd given her hope, and it felt as powerful as the most potent wine. She'd deployed investigators, after telling them a version of the truth—that someone had tried to poison her; she didn't tell them that someone had succeeded—and now all she had to do was wait. And be queen.

She'd chosen to hold court today in the Sunrise Room. Cradled in the center of the east spire, the Sunrise Room was painted in lemons, pinks, and pale blues, with a floor inlaid with so much amber that it glowed when the sun streamed through the leaves. Her throne was in a pool of light. It was a room that felt filled with hope, and she hadn't had the energy to face its cheerfulness in days. But today it felt right to be in this room.

That said, her first meeting was less than cheerful.

She was supposed to be spared from the day-to-day minutiae of running a country—there were legions of courtiers, caretakers, and chancellors devoted to everything from trade to education to waste removal. The queen's role was first and foremost to control the spirits, and then second to be the voice of Aratay when the country needed to react in one accord. But some days, there was a lot that needed to be heard by the voice of Aratay.

For forty minutes, one of her border guards had been reporting to an audience of her and two advisers on activity to the north, at the border with the mountainous land of Semo. He'd described in minute detail the movement of guards, illustrating on a map how Semoian soldiers had been filtering into the area in small groups that added up to large numbers. "Training exercises, they call it," he said, and then fiddled with the lapel of his jacket as he talked—the caretakers had let him wear a variant of his uniform, but it clearly still had more frills than he was used to. She'd have to talk to them about that sometime. It didn't offend her to see people in ordinary clothes. It *did* offend her when they droned on for forty minutes, especially when she could be with her sister, sharing the news with her. Or with Ven. Or Alet. But her advisers had agreed it was important for her to hear this.

"Queen Merecot hasn't declared war," one of her advisers noted—Chancellor Isolek. He was a stocky man with a braided beard. The braids were tipped with jewels, and he had less patience for wasted time than Daleina did, which meant that he felt this meeting was important.

"'Training exercises' is a legitimate euphemism for mobilizing for war," the other, Chancellor Quisala, said. She was older and had been an adviser to multiple queens. Daleina trusted her opinion on foreign affairs more than any other.

"Merecot wouldn't go to war against me," Daleina said. They'd been friends at the academy. Nothing had happened to change that. Merecot—Queen Merecot of Semo—had even sent a lovely diamond statue to celebrate her coronation. "Our countries are allies."

"She may not have told her military that," Chancellor Quisala said. "Look at the positions here and here." She pointed at the map that the guard had scribbled all over.

"We signed treaties." Daleina began to feel an ache between her temples. She rubbed her forehead. This was *not* what she wanted to be doing today. She wanted to be chasing down the poisoner, but she'd already deployed the investigators. In truth, there was nothing for her to do but wait. "She can't declare war on us."

"She can't *declare* war," Chancellor Quisala said. "But she could *wage* war."

"Not Merecot. She wouldn't." She knew as she said the words that this wasn't true—Merecot's ambition was boundless—but the timing was terrible. There had to be a way to stop this before it started. Nip it in the bud.

Chancellor Isolek pushed back his chair and paced. "If we move guards into those areas, it will be seen as an act of aggression. We'll have to declare 'training exercises' as well. It will escalate."

"We have to de-escalate it," Daleina said. Her situation was too precarious for this. She needed all guards near her people, not the borders, in case of another blackout. It didn't matter whether Merecot was honoring their treaties or not. Daleina's people needed to be defended from the danger within; she couldn't worry about the danger without. "I want a message sent to Merecot, a personal message from queen to queen. Remind her of our friendship, and the treaties."

"Polite missives might not be enough," Chancellor Quisala cautioned. Leaning over the map, she pointed to various cities around Aratay. "Here are where our guards currently are. If we pull out of the cities, send them north, and leave defense to the local woodsmen until this is resolved—"

"We can't do that," Daleina said. She wished she could explain why. She knew she looked naïve and inexperienced by refusing to take their advice, but they couldn't know the truth.

"With all due respect, Your Majesty, Chancellor Quisala is correct that this requires a response," Chancellor Isolek said. "If training exercises turn into an incursion, we must have troops in place. But we need your approval."

As queen, she was the commander of all military. She had final say over deployment, though she'd never had to use that power before. Until now, the guards had functioned fine without her. *Oh, Merecot, not now!* "I won't escalate the situation, and I won't approve the repositioning of our warriors. Merecot is not our enemy, and we are not hers. Perhaps Merecot needs to be reminded who the real enemy is, but that won't be done by rattling our swords at her guards."

The border guard bowed. "Your Majesty, if she does—"

"She won't. I know Merecot, and she will listen to reason." Actually, Merecot wasn't known for listening to anyone, but Daleina didn't see much choice. Not when she could still die at any moment. Until they had a sample of poison or at least a viable heir ready, Daleina herself was the greatest threat to Aratay. Since she couldn't say that, though, she'd simply have to be firm and hope her commands at least *sounded* reasonable enough. "We try diplomacy first."

"And if that fails, Your Majesty?" Chancellor Quisala asked. "You listened to the guard's presentation. You must see the pattern."

"Diplomacy first," Daleina repeated. When they began to object, she said, "Keep me apprised of the situation, but do not leave our cities defenseless against the true enemy because of misplaced fear. You are dismissed." All of them bowed as they left the Sunrise Room, and Daleina wished she'd chosen one of the more somber receiving rooms. *Merecot, what are you doing? I don't have time for this now!* She sagged in her throne, straightening only when Alet opened the door to allow the seneschal in.

She'd inherited the seneschal from Queen Fara and had seen no reason to replace him. He was scarily efficient, carrying at least twenty lists with him at all times, and had enough knowledge of history and law to fill a library.

She wondered how he'd felt when Fara died and Daleina took the crown. She'd never thought he liked her much, but then again, it didn't seem that he disliked her either. His heart was in his job. Who wore the crown seemed to be irrelevant to him.

But what if it wasn't? He had daily access to her, and she had little choice but to trust him—he was the one who knew the day-to-day details of being queen, managed her schedule, and controlled access to her.

*Stop it,* she told herself. She couldn't begin suspecting everyone around her. If she died without an heir, the seneschal would lose his job, his purpose. She could trust his commitment to the Crown, if not to her specifically. "What's next?"

"Champion Piriandra would like your approval on her new candidate," the seneschal said, consulting his notes. "She waits outside."

"Tell Captain Alet to allow her in."

The seneschal made a note on his clipboard and then scurried to the door. Opening it, he addressed Captain Alet, and Champion Piriandra strode through. A girl followed her. She was as wiry as Piriandra and had a snarl of red hair that had been coaxed into coils. Bits of it were escaping the ribbons, and Daleina knew without asking that this was the caretakers' work again, making people "presentable." The girl barely fit in her new leather armor. She shifted uncomfortably and eyed the doors as if she wanted to bolt. She looked several years younger than Daleina. Daleina thought of Champion Ven's candidate, the woman named Naelin, who had pitied Daleina for the loss of her childhood—this girl that Piriandra had chosen looked plucked straight out of her own childhood. She was too young to be an heir and much too young to be queen.

"Your Majesty," Champion Piriandra said, inclining her head. "Allow me to present to you my newest trainee, Beilena, for your consideration as candidate."

"You had a candidate before," Daleina said.

"She died."

"My condolences." She ran through her memory, trying to recall if anyone had informed her of this. Usually updating her on the progress of candidates was a top priority. She admitted she'd been distracted lately, but a death should have registered. Daleina addressed the new candidate, "You are aware that you are embarking on a dangerous endeavor, with a shortened life expectancy. You will be in service to Aratay, and your days and wishes will not be your own. It is, however, an essential role—" She looked up at Piriandra. "Champion Piriandra, couldn't you find someone older?"

"I did," Champion Piriandra said. "Her name was Linna. You watched her die. After that, I chose a recent graduate named Ulina. The sprits killed her as well, albeit less dramatically. Beilena is a suitable next choice."

Daleina flinched and dropped her eyes. She couldn't look at the champion, not while images of her friend danced in front of her eyes: escaping the maze together on their first day at the academy, studying late at night in each other's rooms, talking and laughing and complaining at mealtimes in the dining hall, facing the trials, and then the coronation ritual . . . She'd been there, by her side, and hadn't been able to save her. One minute alive, and the next . . . She wondered if someday she'd be able to remember her friend without picturing that moment.

She had a sudden thought: What if the poisoner wasn't from the families of the heirs? What if he or she was someone closer? A champion. *No.*

These were the people she was supposed to trust beyond all others, but they were also the people who were preparing her replacements. Suspecting them was ridiculous.

Still . . .

It was no secret that most champions were displeased that she had been the one to survive. They'd considered her the least of all the heirs—in fact, it was her lack of power that had enabled her to survive. The spirits had overlooked her, considering her not a threat, until the end. She'd never told anyone that.

She'd eaten with all of the champions, spent time with them, been alone with each of them. All of them had had opportunity. *But they wouldn't risk Aratay*, she thought. Without a fully trained heir, the country was vulnerable. No champion would take that kind of risk.

Now that the suspicion was raised, though, it was hard to squash, even knowing how tremendously unlikely it was. She couldn't afford to ignore any possible avenue.

"You're approved," she managed to mumble.

Bowing, Champion Piriandra and her candidate backed out of the Sunrise Room. Alone, Daleina paced across the amber floor. Outside, the birds twittered to one another, and she felt the presence of spirits, swirling through the air, climbing through the trees, and burrowing through the earth.

At last, she raised her voice. "Captain Alet, summon Champion Ven."

## CHAPTER 18

When the summons from the queen came, Champion Ven was spearing an air spirit with a candelabra. It squawked as the iron pinned its shoulder to the wall, and then it melted into the air and flitted as wind across the room to coalesce on the balcony railing.

"Naelin, you have to stay in control of your emotions," Ven said. "You can't panic." He plucked the candelabra from the wall, scowled at the tear in the gold-leaf decoration, and then turned.

A courtier was clinging to Naelin.

"*I* didn't panic," Naelin said. "*He* did." She pried his fingers off her arm and then patted his shoulder. "You should knock next time."

The courtier bowed deeply. His eyes still looked wild, as if he wanted to bolt but his knees were shaking too hard to carry him out of the room. "Champion Ven, the queen has requested your presence with utmost haste. She is in the Sunrise Room."

"Is she—" He halted. "Of course. Naelin, please continue to practice. A *light* touch, this time. Think small thoughts."

"I'm not summoning any spirits alone."

Beside the fireplace, the wolf Bayn stretched, as if to deliberately remind them of his presence. Ven was again struck by how much the wolf understood what went on around them. "Bayn will bite anything you can't handle and howl if there's anything he can't handle. You'll be perfectly safe."

"Famous last words."

"Trust me. Or if you don't trust me, trust yourself. That's the piece you're missing. You still don't trust yourself." He crossed to her and put his hands on her shoulders, as if he could convince her through his intensity.

"I'm dangerous."

"Yes, you are—but to them too. Trust *that* to keep you safe." He could tell from her mulish expression that he wasn't getting through to her. She didn't see herself the way he saw her: strong, in every way that mattered. He'd never encountered anyone like her, someone who gave off her own kind of brilliant light, someone who made him want to be better and fight harder. But he couldn't stay and argue with her, not when Queen Daleina had summoned him. He shot a look at the wolf, and the wolf flared his nostrils as if in agreement. It wasn't a good sign when an animal understood him better than his trainee. Ven leveled a finger at Naelin. "We'll continue this later."

He then strode out of Fara's chambers. He knew the way, but the courtier insisted on scrambling after him, trying to fulfill his obligation of leading the champion, even though Ven outpaced him and was down the twisting stairs while the courtier still puffed behind him.

He tried not to think about why Daleina could need him. If she was having a blackout, she wouldn't have been able to summon him. Plus the spirits would be acting murderous. The air spirit had been irritated, but not worse than that, and he knew there were fire spirits flitting from lantern to lantern as if nothing was wrong. Maybe other symptoms had begun to manifest? But then she'd call for Hamon, not for him. *She must want to talk about her security.* He'd handed much of the responsibility over to the palace guards, but he knew Daleina felt most comfortable with him in charge.

Nodding at Captain Alet and a second guard outside the Sunrise Room, he strode inside. She wasn't on the throne. Instantly, his hand went to his sword hilt and he scanned the room, checking for threats. He saw her a moment later, in front of a mural, staring at it.

"Leave us, and close the doors," she ordered.

The guards obeyed. He heard the solid doors clank shut and noticed the room was devoid of spirits, as near as he could tell—and he considered himself to have solid instincts when it came to spirits. He might not have the power to sense them, but he was aware of the twitch of air, the vibration in the earth, and the shuddering of a flame that came with them. He and Daleina were alone.

"Do you hate me for Queen Fara's death?" Daleina asked.

The question hit like an arrow from an unseen archer. "You are my queen, and I could not hate you."

"Nice answer, but you must blame me."

He couldn't imagine where this was coming from, or why she wanted to discuss it now. "Of course I blame you. And I blame myself. But mostly I blame Fara, and the spirit who corrupted her." He corrected himself: "The spirit she allowed to corrupt her." Fara had never been an innocent in what happened. She may have been tempted, but she was the one who chose to taste that temptation. "Why are we talking about this?"

"Because of Hamon's mother." Daleina turned from the mural to face him, and he was relieved to see she looked fine. No trace of illness. Some shadows under her eyes from lack of sleep. She needed to eat more. He made a mental note to tell her sister to bake her some sweets.

"All right. I'll bite. Are you going to explain what you mean by that, or simply let that cryptic statement hang in the air? Granted, the cryptic statement is more regal, but I'm the only one here to impress."

Her mouth quirked into a smile. "Hamon's mother has determined that my case of False Death is not natural. I was poisoned."

He felt himself go very still, every muscle tense, the way he felt before an attack. He was aware of the taste of the air, the stillness and silence in the room, the warmth of sun on the amber floor, the sound of his breathing and hers. "Hamon has confirmed this?"

"He believes her, and that means I do too. It explains the early onset and the lack of other symptoms. But there's more: his mother believes she can manufacture a cure, *if* we can find a sample of the original poison. It's too diluted in my blood right now."

"Then we'll find it." He'd tear apart the palace, branch by branch. "We'll wring it out of whoever did this to you—" He cut himself off. "Who would do this? It can't be someone rational. Anyone would know that killing you without an heir would destroy Aratay. We're after a madman."

"Or someone subsumed by grief. I've sent investigators to the families of the heirs, with instructions to pry without compounding their grief. But it could also be someone who privately hates me—either with reason or without. A caretaker. A courtier. A guard. A cook."

"Then we interview everyone."

"Everyone in Aratay?"

"Everyone who has had contact with you in the past month. Your seneschal will have a list. Call them to the palace one at a time—"

"It could be a champion."

She was watching him, looking for his reaction, and so he didn't react, not at first. He considered it. His first and obvious reaction was no, impossible, and ridiculous. Champions were sworn to protect the Crown. "It couldn't."

"It could."

"We are sworn to protect the Crown."

"The Crown, not the woman who wears it."

"Sophistry."

Her eyes were still on him as he paced back and forth. He wanted to punch something—a wall, an enemy, the throne. "We killed a queen for the sake of the country," she said. "What if someone else wanted to do the same?"

He knew all the other champions. Hated a few of them. Still didn't believe any of them were guilty of regicide. But then, he'd never have expected it of Hamon and Headmistress Hanna either, nor his Daleina. "There's no heir. No champion would endanger Aratay." None of them were madmen, or so subsumed by grief as to be so irrational.

"It's a slow-acting poison," Daleina pointed out. "A champion could think he or she would have time to train a new heir. He could have realized how I'd react: that I'd push forward faster with the training and the trials. He could have known that I'd name an heir sooner."

It was nonsense. But he couldn't entirely dismiss the idea. The champions had unfettered access to Daleina and the palace. Everyone trusted them. And she was right about the choice of slow-acting poison: anyone who didn't care about consequences could have simply stabbed her. Poison was the choice of someone who wanted additional time. "It's very, very, very unlikely."

"But not impossible." Her shoulders drooped, as if she'd been hoping he would argue with her and convince her she was wrong.

He wished he could, but once the seed of doubt was planted, it took root. "Good people can do the wrong thing for the right reasons," Ven said slowly. Plenty of champions were upset when their heirs died and Daleina emerged. Many thought she was unqualified and unworthy. He'd heard rumblings . . . Nothing to suggest that anyone meant her harm, but enough to know she had few fans among the champions. They'd yet to be impressed with her. She'd been careful with her power ever since being crowned and very careful after falling ill, and while the people might have seen her as cautious, there were those who saw her as weak. "Still, these are your *champions* we're talking about. You shouldn't doubt us. *I* can. But I'm a bitter, jaded old man, and you're the fresh face of hope and light." He shook his head. Now that she'd introduced the idea, he couldn't help but cycle through each of the champions, evaluating them: Piriandra, Cabe, Ambir . . . No, it was unbelievable that he was even considering this.

"It's not a likely enough possibility for me to spare an investigator," Daleina conceded. "But I thought perhaps you could question them, if only to lay our worries to rest."

"I can't approach them in the middle of training. They'd think I was there to poach their candidate, or at least disrupt their training. You need a neutral party." Ven paced harder, his feet grinding into the amber floor. He knew the other champions. He'd never succeed in cracking through their secrets. "Not neutral. Someone who is loyal to you alone. Captain Alet."

She sank into her throne. "Yes. Of course, yes. She's perfect."

"Tell them she's there to assist, in the interest of fairness. All of them know she assisted me. Or that she's there to evaluate them, to determine if their candidates are ready for the trials. Either way, they won't suspect the truth." And if, however unlikely it was, Alet were to uncover the killer, at least she could defend herself, unlike an ordinary investigator. She was one of the few who stood a chance to survive such a discovery. She'd be able to report, even subdue the guilty party and secure the poison. He'd seen enough of her skills to know she could bring down a champion. He felt a chill, thinking of anyone taking down a champion, revealing them as a traitor and a murderer . . . "Daleina, you realize we're grasping at straws here. The poisoner is far more likely to be a disgruntled political enemy or some heartbroken citizen than a hero of the realm."

Softly, the queen said, "I know. But Ven, don't you see? There's hope now. I can't let it slip away. I have to do everything I can."

"I know," he said. "And we will."

TELLING VEN HER SUSPICIONS HADN'T BEEN SO HARD. ASKING Alet to spy on the heroes of Aratay would be harder. Daleina wasn't going to order her to do it. She wanted this to come from a friend, not a queen. She didn't know why that mattered to her, but it did. It was such a ridiculous idea that she couldn't make it a royal command.

Given that, she didn't want to talk to Alet in the Sunrise Room. She'd rather discuss it in her quarters. Coming back, she'd expected to find her sister, but Arin hadn't returned. *Just as well*, she told herself, *because this conversation isn't for her ears.* Still . . . maybe she shouldn't keep sending Arin away. She missed her. *She's safer if she's not with me*, Daleina reminded herself.

Captain Alet shut the door behind them. Daleina saw her eyes sweep over the chamber, cataloguing the points of entry and searching out any dangers. Ven did the same thing every time he entered the room—it must have been something in their training, a constant alertness. Daleina did it too, but she scanned for spirits, not humans. That may have been her mistake.

She wondered where the poisoner had caught her. Had the poison been in her food or drink? Had she been pricked by a poisoned blade, so slight that she didn't notice? Was it spread on a surface that she touched, like her pillow? It could have been dusted into her dresses. She could have breathed it in. Others could have been infected as well.

She'd ask Hamon later if his mother knew how the poison had been delivered. She'd have him look into any other cases of False Death that had been reported recently . . . That was actually a good idea. If others had been poisoned, perhaps they could find a pattern . . . The poisoner could have experimented, or simply had other targets as well.

"You're thinking," Alet said. "I know that look on your face. I will be outside if you need me."

Daleina shook her head and suddenly all the thoughts felt as if they were screaming inside her mind. She crossed the room to Alet's side. "Don't leave." In a rush, she said, "I'm not sick."

Alet's eyes widened, and her mouth parted.

Daleina suddenly realized how that sounded. "I'm still dying. But I'm not sick, not naturally. I've been poisoned."

Alet's mouth shut and then she asked, "Are you certain?"

"Experts told me it was true. And I want to believe it's true."

"You do?"

"Because poisons have antidotes." She suddenly felt herself smiling, as if the sun were beaming down through the trees. She pulled Alet across the room to the balcony into the sunlight. Only a sliver of it had beat its way through the thick canopy of leaves, but that patch was enough. "Look, it's a metaphor for hope! Feel that!"

Alet was staring at her. "I'll fetch Healer Hamon. Delusions could be a side effect—"

"Hamon told me this himself," Daleina said. "Don't you *want* to believe it's true?"

"What I want and what is true seldom have anything to do with each other," Alet said, pulling away. "It's too good to be true, especially if Hamon has the antidote. Does he?"

"Not yet. First we need to find the poisoner. Determine exactly what kind of poison was used. We don't even know yet how it was delivered. Still . . . there's hope." Daleina pointed to the ray of sunshine again, and when Alet didn't step into it, she tugged on her friend's hand again.

"I don't want you to have false hope," Alet said, not moving. "That can be even more painful."

"If it's false hope, I'll be dead," Daleina said, "and nothing will be painful anymore." She wasn't going to let go of this feeling. She was going to chase every idea she had, follow every clue, do everything she could to keep living. "So I'm going to proceed as though it's not false. And I want you to help me."

"Always, my queen."

Daleina took a deep breath. "The royal investigators are speaking with everyone who had access to me who could have had motivation . . . but there is one group they won't be approaching: the champions." She held up a hand to forestall any objections. "I know, it's ridiculous to even consider suspecting them. But I can't leave any stone unturned."

Alet merely nodded. "All right."

She blinked. "You don't want to hear my reasoning?"

"Just tell me what you want me to do," Alet said. "If it's within my power to do, I'll do it." She reached out as if she wanted to touch Daleina's hand, and then dropped back. "I don't want you to die." There was an unspoken echo: *What I want and what is true seldom have anything to do with each other.*

Daleina stepped forward and took her friend's hand. "It's going to sound traitorous. And it's almost certainly pointless. Fear and hope are twins—and I can't help but want to explore every possible avenue, no matter how remote."

"Again, all right."

"I want you to spy on the champions. Go to each of them. Tell them I plan to hold the trials soon, but that I wanted to be certain they were ready. You're there to warn them, and to assess their readiness. Get them talking, and learn what you can. Study them. Sneak around them. Determine who we can trust and who we can't. Can you do that?"

"And if I find your murderer?"

"Bring them to me. Alive."

"Alive?"

"Yes. I have questions for them." She liked that Alet didn't question that she'd be able to capture them. These were champions, the best of the best. But Alet herself was also remarkable. She'd be a match for any of them.

"Can I rough them up first?"

"That would be delightful." Daleina threw her arms around Alet's neck. "You're a true friend, you know." The captain stiffened, but Daleina knew that was just the woman's nature. She cherished what they had. A rare find. She felt as if the sunlight were spreading, even though it stayed confined to the sliver of balcony. Between the investigators and Alet, she'd find her poisoner.

She just hoped they found him or her in time.

CHAMPION PIRIANDRA THREW OPEN THE WINDOW TO THE TRAINing room—she'd commandeered one of the champion training rooms to use with her candidate. "She barely looked at you." She stomped across the room, past her candidate, to the weapons wall. Savagely, she ripped weapons off the wall and tossed them into a pile.

"She accepted me." Beilena's voice was barely more than a murmur.

"She's not worthy to be queen."

Piriandra heard Beilena gasp, but she ignored her. She pulled a heavy tarp over the pile of swords, maces, axes, and knives and then dragged crates on top of the corners of the tarp—in the next stage of training, Beilena couldn't have access to any weapons. She had to rely on her power. Piriandra wasn't convinced her student was ready, but they were perilously short on time.

"If I might ask . . ." Beilena began, "what are you doing?"

"You may have done enough to prove yourself to Queen Daleina"—she growled the word "queen"—"but you still need to prove yourself to me. An heir must be capable of handling an irate spirit by herself with only the power of her mind. No weapons. No backup."

"But I haven't yet—"

"Excuses aren't acceptable." People were always making excuses for Queen Daleina: she was so young, she witnessed a tragedy, she hadn't expected the responsibility . . . But no matter. She would be dead soon, and then another queen would take her place. Piriandra simply had to be certain that a worthy heir was ready. "This time, I won't come to your rescue. You have to rescue yourself."

Her chosen candidate had potential. Tons of potential. Piriandra wouldn't have chosen her otherwise. The girl was young—the queen hadn't been wrong about that—but all the better for molding. She didn't know her own limits, because she'd never been pushed to them. It was Piriandra's job to fix that.

Piriandra hefted a crate onto a table. It was covered in a thick cloth. "Come closer, girl."

Swallowing so hard that Piriandra could hear her, Beilena crept across the room. She was so tense that her shoulders were up around her ears. Piriandra wanted to swat her and tell her to relax, but she controlled herself. She let a note of kindness into her voice. "You have done well. So well that I believe you're ready for this."

"What's in there?" Beilena asked.

Piriandra withdrew the cloth. Underneath was a metal cage. Inside it was a spirit, asleep. It looked like a coil of silver, with crystal-like spikes that were its arms and legs. Its face was carved out of an icicle. It was no larger than her palm and looked breakable, though Piriandra knew it was hardly as fragile as it looked. She still had cuts on her leg from when she'd caught it—the thing was fast. Luckily, she was faster. "Your task is to calm it and then send it out the window."

"Sounds easy. What's the trick?"

Piriandra smiled humorlessly. At least she'd trained Beilena enough for her to realize there would be a trick. "It's going to be very, very angry at you when it wakes up."

"Why will it be very, very angry at me?"

"Because it will think you did this." Piriandra grabbed a torch from the wall and shoved it between the bars of the cage. She then stepped out of the way so that only Beilena was standing in front of it when the spirit's eyes snapped open.

Reacting to the flame, it shrieked and hurled itself at the bars of the cage. Ice spread across the metal. Beilena backed up quickly, toward the tarp-covered weapons.

"No weapons. Just your mind," Piriandra commanded.

"It's an ice spirit. I've never controlled one before!"

"You have mastery over all, don't you?"

"Y-yes, of course. But . . . but . . . they're rare."

For a second, Piriandra hesitated. It was possible that she'd never faced an ice spirit before. But surely Headmistress Hanna would not have allowed her to be chosen if she hadn't demonstrated mastery of all the spirits. "They're not rare all the time." In the worst winters, the ice spirits howled across Aratay, out of Elhim. They encased the branches in ice, froze the forest streams, and cracked the earth around the roots of the trees. "Remember: it's angry. Don't take your eyes off it."

Wide eyed, Beilena nodded. "It can't get out of the cage, though, can it?"

The spirit flitted from bar to bar, hissing angrily. The metal creaked and popped.

"Of course it can," Piriandra said, and then stepped out of the training room.

Beilena surged forward. "Wait—"

Piriandra slid the lock shut. She heard Beilena scream and for a moment she was tempted to throw the lock open, but no. It was only one spirit, and Beilena was strong enough and clever enough to handle it. She forced herself to step back from the door and walk away.

She kept walking, down to the kitchen that she'd stocked with the basics: nut bars, apples, water. She poured honey onto a nut bar and made herself sit, calm, as if her stomach didn't feel like a tight fist.

For all her training, Beilena had always had teachers around her, safety nets. She'd been in the academy, safely in the headmistress's bosom, so to speak. She had to learn she could handle things on her own, and it would defeat the purpose if Piriandra were to rush in there. *Give her space,* Piriandra told herself. *Let her learn.* If she continued to have a safety net, she'd never learn to trust herself, and that was one of the most important lessons.

Besides, it was only one spirit. An ice spirit, but still, a small one.

Piriandra ate the nut bar, making herself chew at a normal speed rather than gulp it down. Finishing, she wiped her lips with a napkin and cleaned her plate. She hadn't heard any more screams, and Beilena hadn't called for help, which was good. She wondered if she really would have the strength to stay outside if her candidate did call for her. She was a tough teacher, but she wasn't heartless. *And I've already lost one candidate.*

She pressed her ear against the door. It was silent in there. A good sign? Except if Beilena had defeated the spirit, wouldn't she have come out? "Beilena? Is it defeated?"

No answer.

If she rushed in and interrupted, then her candidate would think she didn't trust her, which would undermine everything this exercise was designed to achieve . . . "Beilena?"

Still, no answer.

Piriandra flung the door open—everything was coated in ice. She drew her sword. Wind whipped through the open window, but the cloth from the cage didn't stir. It had been frozen solid.

"Beilena?" She stepped inside.

Scanning the room, she didn't see the ice spirit, or her candidate. Everything was frosted white . . . except for the red leaking out from under the tarp. Drawing her sword, Piriandra crossed to it.

She pulled back the tarp.

In the center of the pile of weapons lay Beilena. Her eyes were open, sightless, and a drop of blood had pooled in the corner of her mouth, staining her lips. She had a collection of icicles jabbed into her throat, like a necklace.

She must have gone for the weapons but failed to reach them in time.

*It could have happened in the first moments,* Piriandra thought. *That first scream.* But the ice spirits shouldn't have been so hard to control. It was only one, and not overly bright.

A flicker at the window caught her eye, and Piriandra moved toward it, smoothly and silently, her sword raised. The ice spirit lay on the sill. It was still alive. Its arms were missing—those must have been the icicles embedded in Beilena.

Beilena must have fought back, nearly defeating the ice spirit. In the end, though, it had been too much for her.

Piriandra swore softly, then more loudly.

*I should have stayed in the room. I shouldn't have left her alone. She wasn't ready. I knew she wasn't ready. This was my fault. My fault alone.*

Piriandra scooped up the weakened spirit on the blade of her sword, carried it to the cage, and locked it inside. She covered it with a cloth. It wouldn't be punished—it had only done what it had been goaded into doing. Spirits used in training exercises were typically exempt from retribution. She'd have to take it away from the capital and release it.

She felt stiff, mechanical, as she performed the task and thought through the logistics.

The candidate's family would need to be notified, as well as Headmistress Hanna. She'd have to arrange for a burial. If she paid the caretakers extra, they would take care of the bulk of the arrangements. In the meantime, she'd have to find a new candidate, train her even faster, try not to break her. Time was short. Soon, the queen would call for the trials . . . *I am sorry, Beilena! This was not the plan!* Two candidates, dead. Not the plan at all. She felt like punching something, hard, and her eyes fell on the caged spirit.

She heard a knock behind her. Automatically, she flipped the tarp to cover Beilena's body. Standing, she turned. "Yes?"

One of the caretakers—she'd never bothered to learn his name—bowed. "A representative of the queen is here to see you. Captain Alet. She says the queen has asked her to check on your progress with your candidate."

Piriandra swore under her breath, and then sighed. "Show her in."

## CHAPTER 19

In the center of the late queen's bedroom, three water spirits circled Naelin's head. Cackling in voices that sounded like rain hitting glass, they sprayed water in her face. She flinched and put her arms in front of her, but the water hit just as she took a breath. Inhaling it, she coughed.

"Get them out of here, Naelin," Ven said.

Coughing, she seized on the one command she knew better than any other: *Leave.* She shoved it at them, and they streamed out the open balcony door, dumping water in their wake. Sloshing through the puddles, Naelin slammed the balcony doors shut and pulled the curtains. One hung limp, half torn from its curtain rod, with gashes left by an air spirit from yesterday's disaster. "This has to stop," she said, wiping the water from her face. "It's only a matter of time before I accidentally kill someone."

"You're learning control," Ven said.

He was being kind. "This is *not* control." She waved at the pool of water on the inlaid floor. "I can't control them for longer than a few minutes."

Leaning against the mantel—one of the few items in the room that her lessons hadn't destroyed, though it was singed with ash—Ven looked calm. His green leather armor was clean, while she was soaked from the water spirits. The dirt from the earth spirits had smudged into mud that ran down her arms. He looked as casual and relaxed as if he'd stopped by for a cup of bark tea. "It's not the spirits you need to control; it's yourself. Right now, your fear is controlling you, instead of the other way around."

"Please don't tell me I just need to 'calm down.' In the history of the world, telling someone to 'calm down' has never done anything but piss them off more." *Even Renet knew better than that.* She stalked across the room to a pitcher and poured herself a glass of water. After coughing up inhaled water, her throat felt as if it had been scratched. She took a sip. Her hands were shaking.

Ven laced his fingers across his stomach. He was studying her, again, clearly cataloguing her flaws. She straightened her shoulders and glared back at him.

"Do you want another pep talk?" he asked mildly. "Because I can do that, but you must have already memorized all my best speeches."

"Save it for your next candidate." She closed her eyes for a moment against his response. But he didn't launch into his usual speech. *Maybe he's as tired of it as I am.* She hated that she was disappointing him, even though she'd never wanted this. "How does Queen Daleina do it?"

"Every queen and every heir I've ever worked with has been, at their core, an optimist. Even knowing the odds were against them, they never allowed themselves to believe they'd fail. Daleina was shocked at the Coronation Massacre. She never truly believed that spirits would kill the other heirs. You, on the other hand, would have gone in there expecting it."

Every time spirits came, she was thrown back into remembering the day when her family died—how she felt huddled under the floor, the sounds and the smells. "You can't turn me into an optimist. I've seen too much death." She couldn't stop fearing the spirits, and she didn't want to. The day you stopped fearing them, the day you felt you had control, that was the day you died. Her mother didn't expect the spirits she called to overwhelm her. Neither, Naelin was certain, had the heirs who died in the grove.

He hesitated, and Naelin liked him better for that hesitation—he didn't know what to do either, and weirdly that was comforting. But then his "in-charge champion" face snapped back into position, and he was again using his voice of authority, which was probably highly effective on young candidates but less impressive to Naelin, who had used that tone herself plenty of times. "As corny as it sounds, you need to believe in yourself."

Naelin snorted. "You can't tell me the queen doesn't fear the spirits. She saw what they can do. It can't be just about cheerful confidence and a positive attitude."

"Daleina feels fear, but it doesn't cause her to retreat. She pushes back harder."

"Good for her." She buried her face in her hands. "Ugh! Why can't I do this? I sent the kraken away! These little spirits should be nothing!"

"You need that core of determination—"

"I *am* determined." How many times had Renet called her stubborn? *My pigheadedness is my defining feature.* It was why she'd stayed married to Renet for so long, even though she'd been acting more like his mother than his wife for some time. She'd been so determined to keep their marriage from dying that she hadn't wanted to admit it was already dead. "You've seen me be determined."

"With me, yes. But with the spirits? Your fear swallows your determination."

He was right, of course. Naelin knew what fear could do: it could freeze you worse than an ice spirit. She remembered when Erian was five years old, and she was terrified of climbing, which was a problem when their home was a hundred feet up in a tree and her school was even higher. *Don't look down,* Naelin had told her. But Renet had said, *Look down. It's all right to be afraid.* She'd looked down, shaking like a leaf in a stiff breeze, and didn't move. For well over an hour, she sat there, staring, and then eventually, because she was five, she got bored. And she climbed. He'd been right.

Ven was talking again, telling her how strong her power was, how she'd already proven she had the potential, how she should trust herself—and on and on.

Naelin lowered her hands. "I have a truly terrible idea."

This was enough to break through his faux relaxed pose. For

the first time since practice began, he looked interested. "I like terrible ideas."

"I want to surround myself with spirits."

"All right."

"I don't want to control them. Just acclimatize myself to them." Walking over to the balcony doors, she peered out. In the nearby area, she could sense dozens of spirits: fire spirits dancing in the candles and hearths, air spirits flitting above the canopy and playing with the flags, water spirits weighing down the clouds, earth spirits burrowing through the gardens, tree spirits, even a few ice spirits. If she opened her mind to them and invited them in . . . called them closer but didn't use them . . . "You don't think it's a terrible idea?"

"Works for me." He drew his sword.

"Last time I summoned all the spirits, a kraken nearly destroyed the academy. I can't promise that won't happen again."

"You're high above the earth. Plus Daleina knows you're training. She'll keep us from destroying the palace. Call them."

Opening the balcony doors, Naelin stepped outside. She felt wind in her face, carrying the scent of pine needles and roses. She heard the bustle of people in the city, crossing over the many bridges, beyond the thick mat of leaves. Below, guards clustered near the entrance, and a couple strolled through a pavilion. She wondered what her children were doing, if they were happy, if they were scared, if they'd eaten their lunch . . .

*Come.* She sent the word out, first to the air spirits, letting it ride on the breeze. *Come,* she whispered to the trees. *Come,* she called the fire and the water. *Come,* ice and earth.

She felt a breeze first on her face. It smelled sweet, with a hint of saltwater and overripe fruit that didn't grow within a hundred miles of the forest, and it danced around her, lifting her hair from her neck. Naelin turned to see the breeze solidify into a dancing spirit. It was joined by others, cavorting in a ring around her. Their translucent skin shimmered in the light of the fire spirits. An earth spirit climbed in over the balcony and plopped onto the floor—it was a toad with a boy's head. A tree spirit made of knobby sticks perched on the balcony. It ripped the canopy fabric with its skinny fingers. She told herself not to stop it.

More poured into the room. She felt them crawling in through the balcony window, like insects on her skin. Ven opened the door, and more crowded in—fire spirits from the lanterns, tree spirits from the walls and floors, earth spirits from the kitchen and flower gardens.

Most were tiny, the size of her palm. They zipped through the room, cackling and shrieking, chasing one another. An ice spirit decorated a wall with frost. A fire spirit landed in the hearth, set a log on fire, and tossed it to another spirit. They began to toss it back and forth, sparks flying up to the ceiling. A water spirit rained in a corner.

Naelin wanted to run out of the room screaming.

She forced herself to stand still.

She felt the spirits swirl around her, too close. An earth spirit cozied up to her ankle. A tree spirit ran along her arm. An air spirit entwined itself in her hair. She felt its tiny feet on her scalp. Sweat prickled over her skin, and Naelin wiped her palms on her skirt. Her mouth was dry, and she felt her heart beating so hard in her chest that it hurt. There wasn't enough air. The spirits were sucking away all the oxygen. She began to gasp for breath.

"Calm," Ven said.

"Doesn't help," she reminded him.

"Just breathe."

"Trying." She forced herself to take a slow breath and then exhale it. There wasn't less air. It only felt that way. The spirits pressed closer to her. She felt their claws touch her skin, dragging along the surface without breaking it. She was aware of her blood pulsing through her and how easily they could spill it.

A tree spirit breathed on her neck, its breath hot and smelling of wet moss, and it took every bit of willpower in her not to rip it away from her and fling it across the room.

"Used to them yet?" Ven asked.

"No. You?"

"No, this may have been a terrible idea."

"Told you so." She realized he'd moved next to her. His sword was in his hand, ready. His eyes were darting around them.

"How long would you like to do this?" Ven's voice was polite.

"As long as it takes." Lowering herself, she sat cross-legged on the floor. Water from a trio of water spirits pooled around her, soaking into her skirt. A fire spirit landed on the back of her hand, and she flinched. It giggled and flew off.

"And how will you know when it's done?" Still polite. It was starting to get a touch infuriating.

"Either I'll be cured of my paralyzing fear, or I'll end up so traumatized that I'll be a twitching mess on the floor." Naelin laid her hands on her knees and focused on breathing in and out, while a hundred or so of her worst nightmares spun and laughed and crawled and flew and slithered around her.

"Sounds good."

HAMON PAUSED OUTSIDE HIS MOTHER'S QUARTERS. "HAS SHE tried to leave?"

The guard on the left straightened. "Not on our shift, sir."

"Before that?" He didn't believe she hadn't tried to push the boundaries he'd set in place—she might not even have an agenda outside her quarters, but that wouldn't stop her from poking and prodding until she found any weakness. She was a caged predator.

"Prior shift reported no movement."

Since Hamon hadn't seen these particular guards before, he repeated his warning: "Don't talk to her. Don't take anything from her. Don't ever eat anything she has touched or been near or even breathed on. It's best if you don't let her touch you, or even let her close enough so she could touch you. She's a venomous snake."

The guards looked startled. The one who hadn't spoken yet said, "She's your mother."

"Precisely why you should trust me on this." He nodded toward the door. "Unlock it. And do not engage, even if she addresses you directly." The first guard nodded and undid the lock. It slid back with a solid thunk. He twisted the handle, and Hamon saw he was as tense as a spring, ready to jump away from the door. The other guard had his hand on his hilt. *Good*, Hamon thought.

Hamon stepped inside and waited while the guards shut and locked the door behind him. Only then did he step into the room. "Hello, Mother."

His mother was sprawled on the couch, her bare feet propped on a letter-writing box that had been embossed with gold and was probably worth more than his childhood home. At the long work-table, Arin was hunched over a test tube. She didn't move when Hamon entered. Concentrating, she frowned at a teaspoon of pow-der as she carefully transferred it to the glass tube.

*She shouldn't still be here!* he thought. *Why was she—*

Mother held a finger to her lips, and Hamon halted, the words he'd planned to say stuck in his throat. As Arin finished pouring the powder, her shoulders dropped and she exhaled. She stuck the teaspoon back into the jar.

"Seal it, and then drop the gloves into the basket," Mother in-structed. "You don't want to risk contamination."

Arin obeyed, adding her gloves to an already-large pile in a basket underneath the table. Hamon wondered how they'd ob-tained so many gloves if Mother hadn't spoken to the guards . . . and then he realized the answer was right in front of him. He'd given the guards no warnings about the queen's sister. She was free to come and go as she pleased. She'd most likely procured the gloves, as well as anything else Mother needed or wanted, including that pear wine and all the chocolates. *That* was why Mother hadn't pushed at the boundaries of her cage. She didn't need to. She'd found herself a loophole. "Clever," he murmured.

"Yes, I know," Mother said. Then, "To what are you referring to?"

He didn't answer. His instinct was to grab Arin and send her as far away as possible, but that wouldn't be smart, not until he knew what Mother had done to her. "What do you have her doing?"

"Practicing." Mother swung her feet off the letterbox. "No, girl, you don't cap it. You have to let it breathe. Oxygen is a key ingredient. Just be careful you don't knock it over, or you'll be spitting up blood for an hour."

"You're teaching the queen's sister to make poisons." His voice was flat. His hands curled into fists, and he forced them to relax. If she was doing this to poke at him, he wasn't going to give her the satisfaction of showing it was effective. "The queen would not approve." He kept his voice mild.

"No, Hamon, I am teaching my *assistant* to make poisons." Mother beamed at Arin. "And a wise queen would not disapprove of any knowledge fairly and freely won. Arin is an apt pupil, and she has a steady hand."

Looking at him for the first time since he'd entered, Arin flashed a smile. "It's the bakery training. You have to be precise to replicate a perfected recipe, and you need a steady hand to decorate. Ever tried to shape a flower petal out of sugar?"

"Bah, she's been wasted in bakeries," Mother said. "I have given her a true calling, and a noble purpose!" She widened her arms for effect.

"I told you to fix her," Hamon said. "This is not acceptable." This was Daleina's sister! Mother had to release her *now* before Daleina heard, before any permanent damage was done, before this became irreversible and unforgivable.

His mother smiled in that condescending Mother-knows-best smile that he hated. Sweetly, she said, "Is this truly what you came to talk to me about?"

He opened his mouth, shut it, fumed, and opened it again. He should insist she release Arin. He'd promised Daleina . . . But Mother was right—he'd come for another favor, and he knew her well enough to know he'd never convince her to help if he insisted on this.

Daleina wouldn't thank him when she learned he'd allowed his mother to enspell Arin. In fact, she might not forgive him. But as long as she was alive to hate him, that was what mattered the most. The issue of Arin could wait. Right now, she was safe enough. Mother wouldn't want to damage her new assistant, not while she was being useful.

Forcing himself to look away from Arin, he ground out the words. "We're in need of your expertise again, Mother."

Sitting up straight, Mother clapped her hands together. "Delightful! Do you have more blood for me to test? This time I'd like my assistant to try her hand—"

"We need your knowledge of people. Poison makers, to be specific. Queen Daleina requires the name of everyone with the skill to craft the False Death poison."

"Oh, Hamon, you know I cannot give you the names of my colleagues." She sounded as if she were scolding him for asking for a treat. "We work in secrecy for our own protection. My life would be in danger if the others knew I'd exposed them."

"If they're innocent, they won't be harmed."

"None of us are innocent. You know that." She smiled indulgently at Arin. "Precious few of any of us—of people—are innocent. Certainly you are not, my darling boy. Does your beloved queen know of your youthful activities?"

"She knows all." He was letting her derail the conversation. Talking with other people was never as hard as talking with Mother. He'd always been excellent at steering the conversation. Just not with her. "If you're looking to blackmail me, it won't work."

She laughed, actually laughed at that. It was a merry sound, like a tinkling of ice, and just as cold. "Darling boy, I have all the leverage I need."

*I'm sorry, Arin*, he thought. Once Daleina was safe, he'd help her. "Then garner more goodwill by doing us this favor. The queen wants names and, if possible, addresses. She wants that poison sample."

"No poison maker would admit to creating the poison that is killing the queen."

"If the poison maker didn't know the intended target, then the poison maker would be granted immunity. Absolved of all prior crimes. Free to pursue his or her profession without interference."

"That *could* interest them." She looked as if it interested her. Tapping her teeth with her fingers, she studied Hamon as if he were a three-headed mouse—she'd created one of those once, after infecting a mother mouse with one of her serums. Hamon had made it a pet, until Mother had insisted he kill it so they could study its brains. She'd had him break all three of its necks, even though one had been enough. His childhood was full of fun memories like that. He looked again at Arin and promised himself he'd find a way to extract her from Mother's influence, after Daleina was healed.

"Absolved of all past crimes, regardless of severity, in exchange for a sample of the poison," Hamon said, and wondered if he were promising more than he could deliver.

Mother smiled. "So in a way, I would be providing a potentially lucrative business transaction for my colleagues, wouldn't I? But tell me, what do I get out of this kindness? Will I be granted such immunity?"

He relished the thought of his mother in jail, with no means to create her concoctions, no ability to hurt anyone ever again, no means to intrude on his life. *A child's dream*, he thought. "Help us, and I will ensure it. With provisions."

Her eyebrows shot up. "Provisions? I don't think you're in any position to be making demands. Correct me if I'm wrong, but you need me. Therefore, I set the terms. I want this immunity, on top of the palace position we discussed."

He ignored the last part for now. "You will be forgiven for past crimes," Hamon said. "But I cannot endorse your committing future crimes." Even the first part of that pained him to say. He'd always believed that his mother's past would someday catch up with her.

"I'll accept that, so long as self-defense remains a viable option if any of my fellow chemists object to my exposing them," Mother said. "Grab yourself some paper. I am about to give you names, and if you miss any, it won't be my fault."

He scrambled for paper as she began talking.

CHAPTER 20

It had been three days, and Daleina had her first reports from her investigators, both the ones she'd sent to visit the bereaved families and the ones she'd sent to interview poison makers. Written on curled parchment, sealed with official marks, they were delivered to her on silver platters. She opened them in her throne room, with Bayn beside her and guards outside the door, and then crushed them. The brittle paper crumbled easily in her hands. Watching her, an air spirit stirred a breeze, and the fragments of parchment swirled into dust and then out the window. She let them.

No news. No suspects.

Of course, they couldn't be certain. People lie. People hide. But her people were thorough, and she was certain these reports were accurate.

The investigators would fan out into the forest. Many families were from beyond the capital, some as far as the border, and most poison makers lived in hiding. They'd need more time. She wasn't certain how much time she had. Nor did she believe they would find her poisoner.

She was losing hope, and it hurt as much as losing blood.

One of her guards opened the door. "Captain Alet, reporting as ordered."

Daleina straightened. Maybe Alet would have news. "Allow her in, of course, and then leave us." Bayn lifted his head to watch as Captain Alet marched into the throne room and then waited at attention until the other guards left. The heavy doors clanged—Daleina had picked the Amber Throne Room today. It held a seriousness that felt appropriate, with the heavy iron-crusted doors, the sconces made of old swords, and the walls sheathed in golden amber. Her throne was also coated in amber, and the armrests felt smooth under her fingers.

"Alet, please tell me you've discovered something," Daleina said.

"I am sorry, my queen, but I have not."

Daleina closed her eyes briefly, absorbing this blow, and then opened them again. "Are you at least then able to clear the champions of suspicion?"

"Again, I am sorry, but I cannot." She described how she had visited each of the champions, surprising them in the middle of training, asking them innocuous questions designed to catch them off-guard. In the cases where she could, she'd watched them covertly as they conducted their day. "Most are, I believe, truly loyal to you. But it only takes one."

Daleina felt her hands curl around the throne's arm rests. "Who?"

"I have no proof. Only suspicions," she said. "And I wouldn't qualify those suspicions as anything more firm than a hunch."

"I trust your hunches."

"I'll need to do more observation. Perhaps if I could have permission to search their quarters—"

"Granted. Do what you must, Alet. Thousands of lives are at stake—and that is not an exaggeration. But please, I must know: who do you suspect?"

"There are two whose actions merit further investigation: Champion Ambir—"

Daleina jolted forward. "No!" Her cry startled Bayn. The wolf rose to his feet. Ambir was a sweet old man, nearly broken by the loss of his candidate, Mari, during the trials. Daleina had cried with him over Mari, felt his pain. It couldn't be him!

"Again, I have no proof," Alet cautioned. "It's only that his grief runs so deep that it permeates all he does."

Daleina nodded. She tried to imagine Ambir as the poisoner, but she couldn't. He was filled with sadness, not hate . . . *But despair can turn to rage.* "And the other?" She braced herself.

"Champion Piriandra." This name, at least, wasn't as much of a surprise. Daleina exhaled as Alet continued. "She's been vocal in her disapproval of you as queen, plus she has pushed two candidates so hard in training that they have died."

Daleina had heard about the deaths and blamed herself. She'd approved Piriandra's candidate, even though she knew the girl was too young. "I told the champions to push hard. I bear responsibility as well."

"As I said, I have only suspicions. But I believe it is enough to warrant continuing the investigation. May I have your permission to do so?"

"Yes, of course," Daleina said. "You are relieved from guard duty until further notice. Alet . . . I'm asking as your friend, not your queen . . . Do you believe a champion could hate me so much?"

Alet's voice softened. "No one could hate you."

Bayn made a huffing noise, as if in agreement.

"But," she continued, "that doesn't mean they wouldn't kill you."

Captain Alet dismissed herself, and Daleina leaned back against her throne. The wolf pressed against her leg, and she ran her fingers through his fur. She wished she'd kept Arin with her. She wanted to talk to someone, be comforted by someone, but once again, she'd told her sister that she was safe enough with Bayn and her guards, and Arin hadn't lingered to argue. She'd fled as if she had somewhere else she wanted to be. *At least Arin is safe,* Daleina consoled herself, again.

Beside her, Bayn growled softly, and Daleina saw that the seneschal had entered the throne room. He was standing patiently by the door, his sheaf of papers clutched to his chest. She didn't know how long he'd been there.

"Come," she said.

He bowed and then scurried forward.

She studied him: he was a small man with mottled-brown skin and features so delicate and perfectly shaped that his face looked carved out of wood. He reminded her of a doll that Arin used to have, carved by their mother. She realized she didn't know anything about him, not even his name. "Forgive me, but what are you called?" she asked.

He bowed again. "The seneschal."

He was very good at not conveying any emotion in his perfect face. "Your name," she clarified. "I have always called you my seneschal, but you must have a name beyond that."

He hesitated for a moment, as if she'd asked a personal question and he was weighing if the social faux pas was overcome by her position. "Belsowik, Your Majesty."

"And where are you from?"

"Here, Your Majesty. Always here. My father was seneschal before me, his mother before him, back seven generations."

She blinked. "I was not aware it was a hereditary position."

"It is not. But the skills required *are* hereditary." He tapped his head with one finger. "Forgive my immodesty, but if you are looking to replace me—"

"Of course not. I simply realized I know very little about you."

He shrugged and seemed to relax minutely. "There is very little of interest to know, Your Majesty. I live to serve the Crown."

She noted he said "the Crown," not her, and wondered if that was significant. "You serve it admirably. Your predecessors would be proud."

The seneschal bowed for the third time. "Your kindness is appreciated. However, we have a schedule to keep. Chancellors Quisala and Isolek await outside. May I show them in?"

Daleina suppressed a sigh. She doubted they had good news. "Please, proceed."

He paused for one moment by the door. "You should know that Chancellor Quisala has family in the north near Birchen, by the border. Her interests in this topic are not wholly academic."

That was interesting information. She straightened. "Thank you, Seneschal."

Inclining his head, he opened the door. The two chancellors filed in. Daleina studied them—both looked as if they hadn't slept since they last spoke. Chancellor Isolek's eyes were sunken in so far that his bushy eyebrows overwhelmed them, and Chancellor Quisala looked brittle. She trembled as she walked, slightly but it was there.

"You have news?" Daleina asked.

"Yes, Your Majesty." Chancellor Isolek bowed.

"Please, be seated." Daleina gestured to the chairs. "As the seneschal either has or will inform you, I am scheduled to meet with my champions shortly, but of course I can spare a few minutes for your news." She hoped that would keep this meeting shorter than the last. She was certain that the seneschal had arranged it this way deliberately—the champions were the only ones who outranked the chancellors and therefore the only ones whose meeting could take precedence.

"There has been an incursion." Chancellor Quisala thumped her hand on the arm of her chair as she sank into it. The throne-room chairs were unpadded, to discourage long visits. Daleina's throne was cushioned with velvet.

"An accidental crossing of borders, they called it," Chancellor Isolek clarified. "One squadron of Semoian soldiers left their station at just short of midnight last night, on a night hunting expedition—"

"So they claimed," Chancellor Quisala interjected.

"So they claimed," Chancellor Isolek repeated. "During the expedition, they lost their bearings and accidentally crossed into the northeastern forests of Aratay. They were located by our border patrol three miles west of the line, near Ogdare."

"Three miles!" Chancellor Quisala cried. "Three miles is not an accident. I tell you, this was a deliberate incursion to test our border security, and they were able to penetrate three miles with a squadron before being intercepted by our patrol. They know now we are weak. We do not have enough guards to monitor the full length of border night and day, much less guard against any serious invasion."

"Queen Merecot won't invade," Daleina said. "She has given me reassurances." Prettily worded, on elegant stationery. Merecot had been shocked at the suggestion of anything that would mar their friendship. She was still fond of Daleina and treasured

her memories of their childhood together. She felt a special kin-
ship with both Daleina and, through her, the people of Aratay,
and she professed her firm desire to rekindle that friendship at
an unspecified future date . . . It had sounded nothing like anything Merecot would ever say. But the stationery had been quite
nice. "Though I cannot promise that means anything." In fact,
she was reasonably certain it didn't, knowing Merecot.

"Then you must send troops!" Chancellor Quisala said. "We
are vulnerable!"

*She's right.* Given the False Death, though . . . She wished she
could tell the chancellors the truth about why she hesitated. Closing her eyes, Daleina reached out with her senses, feeling for the
spirits in the capital. They'd been drawn into the palace again. It
was part of Candidate Naelin's training, Ven had explained. She
was trying to desensitize herself to the presence of spirits. For
the past three days, she'd drawn them into the palace. Hundreds
of them in the late Queen Fara's chambers. It was a reminder of
how many were lurking even in such an overcrowded area as the
capital. They were the real danger, not Semo.

But maybe ignoring Semo completely was a mistake.

She could spare some guards . . . a third from each city?

The door opened, and the seneschal poked his head in. "You're
needed in the Chamber of Champions, Your Majesty. Many apologies for the interruption."

She rose. "I will consider this. You will have my answer after
I return from the champions. I thank you both for your wisdom
and intelligence. Please, take a moment to rest. If an invasion is
coming, it can wait an hour."

Chancellor Quisala didn't seem willing to accept that, though.
"She is positioned to move quickly, and we are not positioned
to stop her. I ask you to remember that your people live on the
border, not merely in the cities. Everyone in Aratay is deserving
of protection, and it is your sworn duty to provide it." Her face
was flushed, and Chancellor Isolek laid a hand on her arm. She
looked at his fingers as if she were considering biting them off,
and he hastily removed his hand. She looked back at the queen.
"I beg you: send troops, with no delay."

As if her skin were being scratched by a thousand nails, Daleina felt the spirits disperse from above her. They skittered down the side of the palace and sank into the earth. They melted into the breeze and sped around it. She tasted them in the air. Ven must have called an end to Naelin's training session—he'd be making his way to the chamber now. "I have not said no. I have said I will consider it."

"Then that must suffice," Chancellor Quisala said, and Daleina felt as if she'd been scolded by the grandmother that she couldn't remember ever having. She sank back into the throne as the seneschal led the two chancellors from the throne room. As he held the door open, a fire spirit slipped into the room and lit one of the lanterns.

She watched as it buzzed like a bee around the flame, and then she forced herself to stand. She'd need to meet her champions in the chamber. *Up again.* And this time, she was dreading reaching the top more than the climb itself. She would have to look her champions in the face, with the suspicion that at least one might want her dead badly enough to endanger all of Aratay.

Climbing the stairs, Daleina was surrounded by spirits. The ermine spirit flew above her, circling, while tree spirits flitted between her feet. She stepped firmly, unwilling to let them trip her. The spirits hadn't spread far from the palace. In fact, the majority had stayed close after Naelin's training session. They felt like a weight pressing down on her. She wished she could order them to leave, just so she'd feel as if she could breathe. But she didn't dare risk hastening the next false death. She'd been lucky so far, but someday her luck would run out . . . at least until they found the poisoner and the poison.

If she found the poison sample, then she would happily move troops to the border. If she had a viable heir, the same. Without either, she couldn't leave her people defenseless from the dangers within while she prepared for the dangers without. She had to hope the champions would tell her they were ready for the trials. If they said yes, then she could meet the chancellors' requests.

She was panting by the time she reached the top of the spiral stairs. She halted, hands on her knees, and breathed in. *Illness or lack of exercise?* She hadn't been clambering around the forest the way she used to, but then she hadn't been sedentary either. She made a note to talk to Hamon. It was easy to act as if she weren't sick while she didn't feel sick, but if that changed, her plan for secrecy might have to change as well.

All of the champions were in the chamber as Queen Daleina swept into the room. Air spirits hovered around the arches, and an earth spirit had covered itself with white roses. It clung upside down on one of the pillars, blending in except for its face, which poked between the thorns and leaves. She didn't dare tell the spirits to leave.

She suddenly felt too tired for games. Sinking into her throne, she looked at the faces of her champions. Champion Ven had claimed the center chair, directly across from her. He was staring at her as if his eyes could pierce through her skin and sear away the poison inside. At least he didn't want her to die, she was sure of that much.

On his left was Champion Ambir, the eldest champion. Seeing his candidate dead had broken something inside of him, aging him several decades, until his hands shook and his eyes watered always, but still he had chosen a new candidate to train. She found it hard to believe he could be the poisoner, despite Alet's words. *She has to be wrong.* His sadness hadn't soured into anger, as far as she could tell. He still carried around a core of that grief, looking out at the world through eyes that seemed perpetually disappointed. She felt sorry for his new candidate, to train under such a cloud of misery.

Beside him was Piriandra. Could she be the assassin? She was polishing one of her knives as she waited for the meeting to begin. She bore down on one edge and did not look up at Daleina. She'd moved quickly from grief to anger after the massacre. Daleina agreed with Alet that she was high on the list of possible poisoners. Even though her candidate had died, that didn't remove her from suspicion—plans sometimes went awry. But could she truly want the queen dead, badly enough to risk destroying Aratay? Even with Alet's suspicion to fuel her own, it was hard to believe.

Next to Piriandra was Sevrin, who had never approved of Daleina. He'd made it clear from the beginning that he found her to be an unsuitable queen. He was an unlikely suspect simply because he didn't hide his distaste. But that didn't clear him entirely either.

Havtru hadn't been a champion at the time of the massacre. He'd have no reason to hate her. But she also knew little about him. He'd lost his wife during Queen Fara's rule and had ample reason to hate the former queen. Perhaps he'd transferred that hate to Daleina.

Tilden and Gura?

She ranked them in the middle—both had lost candidates in the massacre, both had kept their distance from her, both swore loyalty to the Crown and Aratay and only lastly to her. They seemed more likely than Sevrin because they hadn't been vocal in their dislike. . . .

All fifteen of her champions were here, each of them training one or more candidates in the capital. Studying them, she realized her answer to "Could it be him?" or "Could it be her?" was almost always, "It's possible. Unlikely, but possible."

She settled again on Piriandra, trying to gauge from her expression how deeply her hatred ran. *She's a champion!* Champions protected Aratay.

For an instant, Daleina imagined accusing all of them, announcing she'd been poisoned and one of them was to blame, then watching them turn on one another. Maybe the guilty one would emerge . . . Or maybe it would distract them from their primary goal, training the next heir, and the guilty party would only be warned of her suspicions. He or she could destroy whatever was left of the poison, if there was any to begin with, and she could lose her chance.

What was best: the slim chance of saving herself, or the great chance of saving Aratay?

She felt the arms of the throne under her hands, the weight of the crown on her head, the feel of the spirits hovering nearby . . . "Tell me of your progress. Are your candidates prepared for the trials?"

Sevrin exploded to his feet. "This! You called us here for merely an update?"

"Sit down, Champion Sevrin," Daleina said. "Tradition calls us here. It is the third moon of the month, or have you forgotten?"

He flushed and stammered an apology.

"You're looking for someone to be angry at," she guessed. "I respectfully request you choose someone other than me. I do not like this situation any more than you do." She moved Sevrin a few notches down on her list of suspects. He may wish her dead, but he didn't wish her dead as quickly as the poison would kill her. If he were the assassin, he'd wait until he was sure he had a trained candidate and then dispose of her. He also lacked the subtlety for poison. "Champion Jalsia"—she turned to the champion at the far left—"report, please."

She rose. "My first candidate died within a week of training, but my new candidate has shown mastery of five spirits. The sixth eludes her. She has summoned earth, but weak, inconsequential spirits only. But I am pleased with her dedication, and she will not rest until she is ready. One month, I estimate."

"Thank you, Champion Jalsia. Champion Keson?"

One by one, they reported on their progress, and she noticed a disturbing trend: candidates had been dying. At least four, including Piriandra's newest, the young redheaded girl from the academy. *The one I just met.* She'd been too young, too unready. *My fault.* The champions were pushing them too hard, per Daleina's command.

She opened her mouth to tell them they had to take more care, and blackness swam up into her eyes. Gripping the arms of the throne, she felt hundreds of spirits converging on the palace. She tried to shout a warning. But before she could, she died.

Again.

Ven saw her slump to the side, the queen's eyes blank, her arms limp, and he leapt to his feet with his sword drawn. "On your guard!" he shouted.

Only seconds behind him, the other champions sprang from their chairs. Piriandra jumped on top of her chair and then onto one of the arches—and the next instant the air was filled with the inhuman screams of spirits.

Air spirits descended on the chamber with talons like sharpened knives, flashing in the sun. Others with sharklike teeth came fast from the sides. It was as if they'd been waiting. Perhaps they had. Dozens of them, of all sizes, some smaller than Ven's fist, others twice his height, flew at the champions. And the champions fought.

Ven laid his sword into every spirit that came at him, hacking right and left, spinning and kicking. Around him, he saw the others do the same.

"Ven, down!" Piriandra shouted.

Ven dropped to the ground, and her knife sailed over his head and embedded itself in the wing of a spirit. He nodded thanks and then scrambled toward the throne, through the fighting. Champion Ambir had made it there first and thrown his body over the queen's to protect her—and died there, his throat torn.

Dropping beside the queen, Ven kept fighting with one arm and felt for a pulse in the queen's neck with his other. He felt nothing. Her flesh felt soft and warm but it did not move.

False death, or real death?

He would only know when—and if—she woke.

Until then . . . Ven somersaulted forward and then stabbed up, piercing a doll-like air spirit that had latched onto the ankle of Champion Tilden. Tilden nodded thanks and returned to methodically swatting smaller spirits out of the air with a mace.

On the edges of the chamber, Sevrin was whirling nearly as fast as the spirits themselves. He held two knives, curved blades, and was slicing so fast that the silver blurred.

The champions were trained not to kill the spirits, only hurt them enough so they fled, but these spirits didn't flee. They bled red, silver, and blue blood on the polished wood, and they kept attacking.

Ven noticed, though, that it was only air spirits attacking the champions. Where were the earth spirits, the fire, the water, the wood, the ice? *Below us*, he thought. In the palace. "Follow me!" he cried, and charged for the stairs.

"But the queen!" Champion Gura cried.

The spirits wouldn't hurt Daleina. She was already dead. But there were plenty more in the palace who weren't dead yet, and if—*when*, he corrected—Daleina woke, she'd want him to have saved as many as he could. As he ran down the spiral stairs, the air spirits attacked him from the sides, and the wood spirits reached out from the tree. They grabbed at his ankles and arms, pierced him from below and beside. He kept his blade swinging, slicing them away from him. He tried not to think what he'd find when he reached the bottom.

## CHAPTER 21

Naelin lay on the floor of the late queen's bedchambers in a puddle of muck. It was nice on the floor, without spirits around her. She breathed in and out and didn't taste the odd mix of salt and pine and moss and ash. All of the spirits were outside, flitting around the palace. They'd stayed close but they weren't right here, which was what made it nice.

*This isn't working*, she thought.

She wasn't used to them. She wasn't less afraid of them. She wasn't becoming inured to them. She was simply having more nightmares, including ones that sometimes hit when she was awake. Naelin hadn't told Ven about those—about the moments when her rib cage felt tight, her lungs felt squeezed, her skin dampened with sweat, and her vision seemed to collapse to only what was right in front of her.

The problem was she could sense them all. Every little last vicious one of them. She felt their antipathy like a sore on her skin, constantly raw. Before her training began, she'd no idea there were so many of them. They clogged the trees. They filled the air. They permeated the water, always near, always watching, always listening, always hating. Shutting down her mind, she tried not to sense them. All she wanted was a moment. Just one—

A scream broke through her thoughts.

She sat bolt upright. Outside. It was from beyond the room, the hallway, just outside. As Ven had taught her, she thrust her mind beyond herself, and she felt—a spirit? It seemed like a spirit, but one that had been torn apart or inside out. It writhed and twisted as if in pain, except it wasn't pain, it was . . . ecstasy, brutal joy that poured out of it and flooded into Naelin. She felt as if she were choking on it. *Stop!* she thought at it.

It didn't hear her. She stumbled to her feet. Preparing to broadcast the command louder, she opened her mind wider, and from every direction, she felt spirits spinning wildly, as if they were about to explode in a thousand pieces.

She couldn't see. Everything dripped red in front of her, and the world tilted. Feeling her way across the room, she hit one of the posts of the bed. She clung to it, feeling the solid wood, trying to draw her mind back from the whirlpool.

It would suck her in. It would drown her.

Clinging to the post, she tried to pull out of the rush of pain-joy-need.

Blood, the taste of blood. She tasted coppery saltiness on her tongue and realized she'd bitten through her lip.

*Stop.*

This time the command was to herself.

She was human, not spirit. She could control her emotions. Drawing in tight to herself, Naelin concentrated on her own breath, feeling it enter her lungs and fill her. She focused on her skin, the limits of where her body was—she was here in the room, not split and sprawled across the palace.

Another scream, and more. Naelin ran across the room to the balcony doors and threw them open. Outside, it was as if a storm had hit the palace. The bodies of spirits darkened the sky, blocking the sun. They were twisting and cackling.

Below, she saw people running as the spirits dove for them.

*They're attacking! Why are they attacking?*

The spirits couldn't attack here, not in the presence of the queen. The palace should be the safest place in all Aratay. "Erian. Llor." She spoke their names out loud as if that would work as a talisman, and then she ran for the door to the bedchambers. She had to reach them. She had to—

There was blood in the hallway, streaked down the wall.

A woman was huddled on the side. Her head was bent to her chest, and she was motionless. One arm was wrapped in vines that grew from the wall. The other arm had been shredded, and the bone gleamed through the red of her muscles. Blood pooled around her, seeping into the carpet. Naelin ran to her and then stopped. The woman was dead, no question.

A spirit had killed her. Here, in the palace.

*This can't be happening! This shouldn't be possible!*

And then something worse hit her:

*What did I do ... ?*

She'd summoned the spirits here. What if ...

She heard more screams ahead of her, from the stairwell. Erian and Llor were five flights down. Naelin ran toward the stairs. She thrust her mind ahead of her and felt a knot of spirits. They were caught in the same frenzied whirlwind of joy and pain. One, a water spirit, was causing water to spill through a window and cascade down the stairs in a waterfall. An ice spirit followed in its wake, freezing the water, while a tree spirit caused the ceiling of the stairwell to sprout thorns.

She plowed her mind into them. *STOP!*

For an instant, they paused, but they were vibrating, as if she were holding them steady through sheer force of will, and she was certain that if she stopped broadcasting the command, they'd break free. She wasn't going to let them. *I drew them all here; this is my fault.* She broadcast the command as she ran down the stairs and through a pack of three fire spirits. Past them, she released them and threw her mind to the next spirit.

She was too slow. Erian and Llor were too far away. And there were too many spirits between her and them. In the middle of the stairwell, a fire spirit blazed. Sparks landed on the wood and lit into fires. The spirit cackled.

Naelin didn't think about whether she could do it. She had to do it.

Opening her mind, she felt the spirits again, their wild fury. She let it wash into her, and then she grabbed it firmly, as if it were the arm of an unruly child. She held it steady and then reached farther out. She grabbed more spirits and held them.

She felt as if she were splintering, but she kept a tight grip on her thoughts of Erian and Llor. The spirits had to obey her, because she had to keep her children safe. There was no other option. *I caused this. I must fix this.*

Thrusting her hands into the water that flowed down the stairs, Naelin plunged her mind into the water, into the walls, into the fire, and into the air. Out, farther, until she'd embraced the entire palace. She felt the earth spirits in the gardens, the fire spirits raging in the stairwells, the air spirits at the top of the spire . . . *Do no harm!*

She felt as if every spirit suddenly turned its focus to her. Her heart began to pound, and she again heard her mother's screams, but she held the image of Erian and Llor firmly in her mind. She felt the spirits converging on her. Coming from every corner of the palace . . . just like she'd commanded them to come during her training, but this time, she felt their hatred. They wanted her blood. They wanted to squeeze the air from her body, to crush her bones, to burn her flesh . . .

*Do! No! Harm!*

She burned the words into them, driving them deep inside.

The spirits pressed closer, wanting, needing her pain, her blood, her death.

And she held them still.

QUEEN DALEINA FELT A WEIGHT ON HER. SHE OPENED HER EYES. Her eyelids felt stiff, as if they'd been stuck shut for hours, and she looked up at the blue sky above, framed by a circle of trees. Turning her head, she saw Champion Ambir, lying across her.

"Champion Ambir?" Her throat felt stiff, and her mouth was dry. Worse, her thoughts felt as if they were swimming in muck. She couldn't piece together why she was here, why he was here, or what had happened.

"Your Majesty!" a woman's voice cried. Looking beyond Ambir, Daleina saw Champion Piriandra leap from arch to arch around the circle of the chamber. Piriandra's knives were drawn and slick with blood. She had a cut that ran down her thigh, dripping with red raindrops. Daleina stiffened—if Alet's suspicions were right, either Piriandra or Ambir wanted her dead . . .

"Move yourself, Champion Ambir," Daleina instructed, and pushed as she sat up. The body slid onto the ground with a thump. Only then did she realize that's what it was: a body. The old champion was dead. His back had been shredded, and his throat had been pierced by a thick thorn.

She felt a *whoosh* inside her mind as her thoughts at last coalesced in a coherent order. *False Death.* Struggling to her feet, Daleina reached her mind out, feeling for the spirits. They were congregating several floors down, squeezed into a single stairwell. Why— *Why doesn't matter,* she told herself. *Champion Ambir doesn't matter. Piriandra doesn't matter.* She had to stop any more deaths. That's all that mattered.

She forced her mind at the spirits, broadcasting the core command: *Do no harm.* She felt it reverberate inside them, catching an echo and bouncing back. *Do. No. Harm.* She reached out beyond the palace, touching the spirits in the forest beyond. But the frenzy hadn't spread. It had been contained here, somehow.

She had to reach them, to see, to know why or who . . . She walked two paces and then sagged as her legs wobbled under her. She caught herself on one of the champions' chairs. Before she could regain her strength, Champion Piriandra rushed toward her. "You live!"

Daleina reached for the spirits, trying to call one to her, to defend her if necessary, but the spirits were still held tight in a ball in the stairwell. "Tell me what happened."

"You did this," Piriandra said. "Your weakness. Your failure. You brought this on yourself and on all of us."

She refused to be baited into arguing. Putting the chair between herself and the champion, she demanded, "How many died?" *Arin!* she thought. Her sister was in the palace. She should have sent her farther away. Home. Farther. Beyond Aratay into Chell or even Elhim.

A man's voice—Champion Havtru—answered, "We don't know."

"How long was I . . ."–her throat clogged on the word "dead"–
". . . gone?"

Piriandra pulled a rust-colored cloth from her pocket and wiped her blades before sliding them into sheaths. "Too long." *She won't kill me while Havtru is here,* Daleina thought wildly. *She won't want a witness.* Her poisoner had picked an unknown poison, one that mimicked a disease, rather than a blade through the ribs. It stood to reason that he or she wouldn't want to be caught. If Daleina was careful to never be alone with her . . .

"Where's Ven?" Daleina asked. He should be here, defending her. She then squashed that thought. He'd know she was safe while dead. He must have gone to defend those who weren't safe. Like Arin. "I must know what's happened. Help me."

Hurrying to her side, Havtru supported her. More slowly, Piriandra helped her on the other side. Daleina felt as if her bones had been softened into churned butter. Her knees buckled, and she leaned heavily on the two champions.

She made it three steps before she stopped. "This is too slow. Go, both of you. Find out what has happened. Help who you can. I'll regain my strength here."

Piriandra released her, and Daleina sagged half onto the floor until Havtru shifted his weight to support her against his side. "We won't leave you, Your Majesty," he said.

She hesitated for a moment. She didn't want to be alone with anyone, but Havtru was a new champion. He couldn't yet despise her, could he? He could. Any of them could want her dead. Or none of them. Or . . . She couldn't think straight. She felt as if the spirits were shrieking inside her head loud and high enough to shatter her skull. "That's an order."

"Forgive me, Your Majesty. Your safety overrides your orders," Havtru said. "Champion Ven was very clear on that, when he recruited me. You had a brush with death. We will not leave you alone until you are fully well."

"Fine. Go, Piriandra. Havtru will prove his worth." She kept her eyes on Havtru, hoping this wasn't a mistake she'd regret, hoping she hadn't misjudged him, hoping Ven hadn't. If she couldn't trust her own judgment, she thought she could trust Ven's.

Champion Piriandra sprinted for the stairs and was running down the steps without a sound. Daleina was alone with Havtru. There wasn't even a breeze. No spirits were nearby.

She went for blunt. "If you kill me when there is no heir, all of Aratay will suffer."

His eyes widened. "Your Majesty!"

Either he was an excellent actor, or he was innocent. She chose to believe the latter. Closing her eyes, she reached out her mind toward the knot in the stairs. The hostility had drained out of them, and the fire spirits spread back into the lanterns. She guided the water spirits toward the fires that had started throughout the palace. She set the earth spirits to soothing the fault lines beneath the city. She instructed the tree spirits to regrow the palace, healing the places that had been torn apart, withering the branches that had been grown where they shouldn't. She couldn't sense humans, but she could feel where the spirits had been—the damage they had caused, and she felt her stomach knot. So much damage.

*Please, don't let this cause another false death.* She had to gain control . . . but gaining it meant risking losing it again. Still, she had no choice.

After she had distributed the spirits, she opened her eyes. Havtru was watching the sky, his back was to her, and he had a staff held ready in his hands. The air spirits filled the sky again, flitting from cloud to cloud, as if they hadn't just tried to kill everyone.

She felt stronger, somewhat. "I need to see."

Putting down his staff, Havtru crossed to her and without a word scooped her up in his arms. She wanted to object, but she knew she didn't have the strength for the stairs. *And who will I impress? By now, everyone must have lost faith in me.*

He carried her down the stairs. She saw the cracks in the steps, which looked as if someone had tried to tear the staircase away from the wall of the tree. Cracks snaked up the wall, and the railing was strangled with vines. Farther down, she saw vines ran all along the outside of the palace, as if they had wanted to squeeze the walls until they split.

At the base of the stairs, she saw the first bodies: caretakers, two of them, their arms wrapped around each other as if they'd tried to comfort each other. One was young, barely a woman, and her hair was streaked red with her own blood. The man's leg was burned.

The next, farther down the hallway, was unrecognizable, a mass of blackened flesh. "Don't look, Your Majesty," Havtru said.

"I must. This was my fault."

"It was your illness. You cannot blame yourself."

She did blame herself, for not finding the poisoner, for allowing herself to be poisoned, for not pushing the champions harder to find an heir. "Take me to the east staircase."

She passed others who were still alive, but wounded and stunned. They stared at her as she passed. One leapt to his feet and kissed her hand. "You live!" he cried.

"Help them," she told Havtru, pointing to the wounded. "Wrap this around their wounds." She wormed her fingers into one of the holes of her skirt and tore the fabric. Setting her down, Havtru helped her slice off bandage-size strips.

"But your dress . . ." the caretaker sputtered.

"Wrap it tight above their wounds, as tight as you can. Stanch the flow." She remembered Hamon doing that for other wounded. "Stop the blood loss. Tell them to lift the injured limb up. Prop it up. Healers will be here soon." She hoped.

Half the eyes she passed looked at her with gratitude—she saw their relief etched into many of their faces. Their queen was alive. The spirits were subdued. But others looked at her with stares that felt like daggers. She flinched each time but forced herself to meet their eyes. They thought she'd abandoned them, that she deliberately let the spirits attack.

*I have to tell them the truth. Soon.* Speculation would be running wild. But if she told them she was dying before she had an heir, there would be panic in the city, across all of Aratay. "How ready is your candidate, Champion Havtru?" Daleina asked quietly.

"Frankly, she isn't. She can boss around one at a time very well. Have it going up, down, sideways, acrobatics, you name it.

But she can't stretch herself to command more than one. We're working on it. She'll get there. She's a good girl. Tries hard. You'll like her."

It didn't matter if Daleina liked her or not. If she couldn't command multiple spirits, she wouldn't be suited to be queen. "How many days away is she from success?"

"Don't know. Never trained a candidate before. But Esiella tells me she's been trying for a year and almost did it twice. Maybe a few months? I don't know if my candidate will be the one, Your Majesty. I wouldn't say that in front of her, of course, but I'm thinking you want honesty."

"I do. Thank you, Havtru." She hoped the others were farther along. She'd need to announce the trials soon, ideally at the same time as she announced her illness. The trials would distract the people and push the candidates to be ready. "Please push her as hard as you can. I cannot let this kind of disaster happen again."

"If I am to be honest . . ."

"Please do."

"Many of the other champions were, let's say, optimistic in their reports. I don't think any of them are ready yet. At all."

"None?" Surely he was exaggerating. They had to be close.

"Well, Yanan had one that was close, but she died. And Gura's . . . she thought hers could be ready, but she died too. The best ones keep dying off. We're pushing them too hard, I think. People have limits. *You* have limits. You should let me take you back to your quarters. The healers should tend to you."

At last, they reached the east staircase. The walls were buckled out, but there was no trace of the spirits anymore, or any hint of who or what had brought them here. This hall didn't look any more special than any other. She expected to find a slew of bodies, but there were none. Why had they congregated here if not to attack? She thought this would be the worst of it, but it was oddly empty.

"Let me take you back to your quarters," Havtru repeated.

"I have to find my sister," Daleina said. "I have to be sure she's safe."

"A guard can do that." Havtru called to one of the guards, and an uninjured woman with a streak of blood on her cheek jogged to them. "Find the queen's sister, and make sure she's in a secure location."

The guardswoman bowed and hurried away.

"Now will you rest?" Havtru asked Daleina.

She nodded and didn't ask him to let her walk. She just rested against his chest and endured the stares as they passed by more and more of her people.

As they approached her quarters, Captain Alet ran toward them. Her helmet had slipped, and her hair had unraveled. Her armor was streaked with blood and soot, and her sleeve had a jagged slit. "Queen Daleina!"

"I'm all right," she told Alet. "I'm relieved to see you in one piece." Here, at least, was one friend she hadn't lost. She thought of Linna and Revi and Mari, and how she was failing them.

As Alet checked the room for spirits, Havtru carried the queen inside.

It was pristine: perfectly made bed, beautiful sunlight through the open doors to the balcony, a slight fire in the hearth. For a moment, she was shocked, and then she realized there hadn't been anyone here to hurt. The spirits had gone after only the parts of the palace where there were people to kill. "It's my fault," she gasped. As Havtru opened his mouth to speak again, she waved away his words. "I know I didn't intend this. But Piriandra was right: I failed. I'm failing. We need the trials now."

"More candidates will die," Havtru predicted. "They aren't ready."

"Make them ready."

"You can't just will it so. Even you, Your Majesty."

She closed her eyes as he laid her gently on the bed. "I can try." Listening, she heard him close the curtains around the bed and back toward the door. She heard him and Alet talk in low voices. He'd stay and guard her, she knew, along with Alet. Ven had trained him well.

He was a good teacher. She thought of his student, the woman Naelin. He hadn't had a chance to answer on her progress before she collapsed. She hoped Naelin was as advanced as he'd expected. From the champions' reports and Havtru's statements, she had the clear impression that no one else was.

She felt a spirit arrive. The curtains shuddered, but she didn't move. Even tired, she knew she could control one spirit if she had to. But if she didn't have to, she wasn't going to expend the energy or risk another false death. The spirit perched at the foot of her bed.

At last, she opened her eyes to glare at it.

It was a tree spirit, tiny and gnarled, with leaves matted all over its body. Possibly the same spirit who had been in her bedchambers before. "Come to gloat?" she asked it.

"Yesss," it hissed.

"If you would be so kind as to gloat elsewhere, that would be delightful." She wished she could tell it to burn. She wanted to destroy every spirit that had participated in today's slaughter.

"Their blood was sweet. It flowed into our branches."

"Go," she told it, but she didn't put the force of a command behind the word.

"We watch. We wait. You will fall again, and more will be ready." It rubbed its hands together, and it sounded like leaves in the wind. "We will feast."

*It's right.* Next time, the death toll would be worse, because more spirits would be ready, waiting, watching. She couldn't let that happen. As soon as anyone was ready to be heir, she had to abdicate, whether or not the poisoner had been found.

She raised her voice. "Captain Alet! Champion Havtru!"

The two warriors burst into her bedroom, swords and knives drawn. Squealing, the spirit darted out the window. Alet shut and locked the door behind it, and Havtru stalked around the room with his sword raised.

But even with the two of them, she did not feel safe.

## CHAPTER 22

As soon as she felt the queen take control of the spirits, Naelin ran. Scrambling over the roots that bulged out of the walls, she squeezed down the stairs. There were caretakers and courtiers in every room and every hall, with healers moving between them. She saw sheets over bodies, far too many bodies. People—many who looked wounded themselves, who shouldn't even be up—were cleaning the residue from fires and hacking at tree limbs that had grown out of walls. She didn't pause.

Erian. Llor.

She burst into their room—and saw no one. "Erian! Llor! Are you here? Please answer me. Come out. It's safe now. Please be okay." She ran for the curtains that blocked the beds and threw them back. There were drops of blood on one of the sheets. Her knees began to buckle, but she didn't let herself collapse. "Erian! Llor! Come out! It's Mommy!"

She forced herself to stop and listen. She'd trained them to hide. They were sensible. As soon as they knew there was danger . . . but had they had a chance to know there was danger? They'd felt safe in the palace. Quiet, listening, she searched. Under the bed. In the wardrobe. Behind the couch. The upholstery had been shredded. Vines were wrapped around a mirror, and a crack ran down its center.

"Naelin?" Ven was in the doorway.

She ran to him. "I can't find Erian and Llor."

"It was you, wasn't it? You held the spirits."

"Help me look. Please. They would have hid, but there's blood on the bed and . . ." Her heart felt as if it was thumping in her throat. Her children were clever and quick. And small. They could squeeze into places. She scanned the room.

A wardrobe was encased in vines, sealed shut by spirits. Crossing to it, she pressed her ear against the wood. "Erian? Llor?"

She heard a voice from inside, faint, muffled by the thick wood. "Mama?" Llor!

"Llor, baby, are you okay? Is Erian with you?"

"She pushed me in! Mama, I can't get out! It's dark!" She could barely make out the words. She heard him start to cry, or continue to cry, in great heaving hiccups and she turned—but Ven was already there. He swung his sword at the vines, hacking at them.

"Search for Erian," Ven told her. "I'll free him."

"Llor, baby, stay back against the wall. Back! Understand? Champion Ven is going to get you out. I need to find Erian. Do you know where she hid?"

He was still crying, but the answer was no. Erian had pushed him into the wardrobe, told him to be quiet, and promised to get the spirits away from him. *My brave girl*, Naelin thought.

She stood still for a moment, trying to put herself in Erian's shoes. Erian must have realized something was wrong and gotten her brother to the wardrobe, but maybe there hadn't been time for her to hide too. Maybe the spirits were too close. Maybe she wanted to distract them from Llor. She must have run—she could have tried the door, but if the spirits had come in through there . . . the only other way out was the balcony.

Erian had never liked climbing, but if it was the only way, she'd do it. *My brave girl*. Naelin ran onto the balcony. "Erian? Erian!" Leaning over the railing, she looked down.

Clinging to the vines about fifteen feet below the edge was Erian.

Her eyes were squeezed shut, and she was shaking. Naelin saw blood on her arm, a smear of brilliant red against her white dress. "Hold on, Erian! We're coming! Ven! Ven, she's out there!"

Erian screamed.

The vines were retracting from the palace, as if being withdrawn.

"Don't let go!" Naelin called.

"Mama!"

The sound of her cry pierced Naelin. Before she could even call for him, Ven was at the balcony and vaulting over the side. He stabbed his knife into the wood of the tree, using it as a handhold. "I'm coming, Erian," he told her. "Hang on."

Naelin felt a solid weight thump into her thigh. Llor gripped her waist and buried his face in her stomach. "Mama!" She cradled his head but didn't move her eyes off the scene below.

*She's too far down*, Naelin thought. The vines were shrinking back into the palace. Gripping the balcony, she concentrated. She reached into the tree and touched the wood spirits who were unraveling the vines and disentangling the mess. *Stop*, she told them. *Grow.*

She guided them toward the vines that held her daughter from plummeting.

They resisted.

The queen had given them another command—she could feel it within them, an echo that reverberated: *Restore.* They were fixing the palace. They had to fix it. The queen was making them, and her strength was like iron around their brains.

Naelin chipped at that iron. She pushed, she shoved, she sawed. *Grow. Now. Grow.* And she felt them shatter inside as her command penetrated. They forced the wood out, jutting a new balcony beneath Erian's feet. As the vines vanished into the bark, she collapsed onto the new balcony.

Ven climbed down, sticking knives into the wood, until he reached her. "Grab onto me," he said gently to Erian.

Sobbing, she clung to him, and he began the climb back up, using his knives again. The process was slow, and Naelin squeezed Llor as she watched them climb up. When they were close enough, she reached over, helping pull Erian onto the balcony. She bundled Erian into her arms and held her. Erian wrapped her arms around Naelin's neck, tight.

Ven jumped onto the balcony beside them. "Is everyone all right?"

Naelin peeled away from her children to look at them. "There's blood. Who's bleeding? What hurts?" Erian and Llor dove toward her, hugging her tight again. She rocked backward but steadied herself.

Eventually, she got them calmed down, bandaged up, and tucked into bed, where they clung to each other as if they were each the other's teddy bear. She sat across the room from them and watched them as they whispered to each other and then fell asleep. Dropping her head in her hands, Naelin wished she could sleep.

She felt Ven's hand on her shoulder. "You did well," he said.

"She could have died. Both of them. I could have lost them."

"You saved them. You saved a lot of people." He crouched beside her and took her hand. She felt the warmth of his hand, the strength of his fingers, comforting her. "I knew you could. Now do you understand why you're needed?"

"No. I don't understand at all. Why did that happen? We're in the palace!" She lowered her voice. "We should be safe here, with the queen."

Ven was silent.

He still held her hand.

As the silence stretched, Naelin looked up at him. His eyes were fixed out the window but not as if he were looking at anything, as if he were thinking, and his mouth was twisted into a grimace. "What is it?"

"The queen has been poisoned. She's been given the False Death. All of the champions were in the chamber when she experienced her latest blackout—I believe the spirits were watching as well, waiting for their opportunity. Her commands have no effect while she is dead."

Naelin stared at him. She had a dozen questions: How was it possible? Who would do such a thing? Why? She settled on the most important one. "If it's a poison, is there an antidote?"

"Maybe. We don't know yet."

"How much time does she have?"

"Months, I hope. But most likely weeks. That's why we need you." He squeezed her hand lightly. "Naelin, you're the most powerful candidate that I have ever seen or heard of. You are the only one with enough raw power to be ready fast enough. I believe there is no one else who can do this."

She heard the truth in his words. He believed everything he was saying, and she had no reason to doubt it. In fact, a number of things now made more sense. Naelin had always considered herself a practical person. She wanted one thing: for Erian and Llor to be safe. If the dying queen did not have an heir, then Naelin's children were in danger. And if there truly was no one else . . . "I'll do it."

A voice from the bed: "Mommy, no!"

Erian.

She left Ven and went to them. Llor was fast asleep, curled around his pillow, but Erian's eyes were wide. Naelin wrapped her arms around her daughter and held her close.

"Please don't do it, Mommy," Erian whispered in her ear. Her breath tickled. Naelin inhaled, breathing in the scent of lilac soap, dried sweat, and little girl. Erian still fit in her arms, though her legs spilled out beyond Naelin's lap.

"I promise I will be as careful as I possibly can be. Even more careful than Llor when he climbed his first tree. Do you remember that?" She tilted her daughter's chin so Erian would see that Naelin was smiling and unafraid—or at least faking it as hard as she could.

A tiny tentative smile touched Erian's lips. "You made him wear two safety ropes, in case one broke, and wrapped him in so much padding that he looked like a sausage."

"And the helmet? Remember that?"

"It was a pot! You padded it with towels."

"And when he fell?"

Her smile wavered. "You caught him."

Naelin stroked her hair. "The queen needs me to catch Aratay. And I have to be ready to do it. Do you understand?"

"Yes, Mama."

*She's lying*, Naelin thought. But then again, so am I.

THE FUNERALS STARTED AT DAWN, WHEN THE PALE YELLOW LIGHT filtered in patches through the leaves and the birds chirped so perkily that Daleina wished she could ask her archers to shoot them all. It felt wrong that the birds were chirping, wrong that the sun was shining, wrong that the sky was blue and the wind was mild, wrong that the spirits around the palace were flittering through the roses and playing in the fountains as if they hadn't just tasted the blood of Daleina's people . . . *Calm*, she told herself. *Serene.* She kept her pace even as she processed from the palace to the burial grove, flanked by both guards and courtiers. Captain Alet was on her left, and Champion Ven marched on her right. People lined the bridges and paths, silently watching the queen pass by.

She'd buried too many people in the last year. First her friends, and now . . . These were people she was supposed to protect! People who trusted her, who relied on her, who . . . *It's not my fault. But it is someone's fault.* Someone, perhaps someone in this crowd, had poisoned her. That someone was responsible for these deaths.

He or she was what her archers should shoot. Not the birds.

Bells were ringing, sweetly, a hopeful sound. She was supposed to speak about hope and life within sorrow. She'd prepared a speech as she'd mechanically swallowed her breakfast—Hamon had stood beside her, making sure she ate every bite. She didn't taste any of it.

He was somewhere in the crowd, nearby. Her eyes fell on him, and she tried to draw strength from the calm, peaceful, measured way he walked. Looking back at her, his eyes were full of compassion.

Ahead, the grove was wreathed in flowers. The families of the fallen . . . *Fallen*, she thought. *As if they'd merely collapsed. As if they hadn't been violently torn apart. Ripped from life.* She felt their eyes on her, and she felt the accusation behind their gaze.

Beside her, a courtier drew a bell from the pocket of his robes. He rang it. Another, a caretaker, rang his bell. And another, hers. The families kept their hands clasped, in silence beside the fresh graves, as throughout the grove, bells rang together, their high tones melding into one shrill sob.

Stepping forward, Queen Daleina raised her hands, and the bells silenced. Hope. Sorrow. She knew what she was supposed to say.

She chose not to say it.

"You hate me right now," Daleina said, raising her voice to carry across the grove. Her words fell into the silence like raindrops on a still pond. "You blame me. I am alive, and your loved ones are not. You see me standing here, dressed in silks and jewels, and you think, 'If the queen is not dead, my father, mother, brother, sister, child, friend shouldn't be either.'" She'd been lucky—her sister was still alive—but so many weren't.

Listening, everyone was silent. *Not everyone*, she corrected. Flying through the leaves above, the birds cried and sang. Squirrels scurried through the branches. The spirits burrowed through the earth and slipped through the air.

She did not look at her champions or her courtiers or her caretakers. Not even at Alet or Ven or Hamon. She looked instead into the eyes of the families of the dead. "I want to say I am sorry. I am sorry that I'm standing here, not your loved ones. I'm sorry I couldn't save them. I'm sorry for the emptiness you feel." She smoothed the paper she had in her hand, the notes for her speech, and then crumpled it, and then smoothed it again as she spoke. "I could tell you that time will heal you, but I think that's a cruel thing to say, because right now you don't want time to heal you. You don't want to forget. Because forgetting means that they're really gone." She thought of her friends—Linna's smile, Mari's voice, Revi's laugh. She thought of Master Bei and of her childhood friends, the ones who died in Greytree. "I don't want you to ever forget them. But I do want you to forget *this*, the pain you feel today that feels as if it's eating your skin and consuming your soul. I want you instead to remember the joy these people brought to your lives. I want you to remember the moments they made you smile, or cry, the moments they made you feel alive. I want you to honor the ways they shaped who you are and who you will become. For they are a part of you, now and forever. And I know that it's not the same. I know that it's not enough. I also know that I cannot truly understand your pain, because your pain is not my pain. It is yours, uniquely yours, and it is all right to feel it fully and deeply for today and for as many days as you need to feel it, until you can feel joy again."

The birds kept singing. The squirrels kept scurrying.

But the spirits were listening.

And so were her people.

"Feel the pain. Feel the anger. Feel the sorrow. Feel the loss. And then when you have felt all of it, forgive them for leaving you. Forgive yourself for still being here." *Forgive me*, she wanted to say. "Forgive life for being fragile and brief. Forgive time for passing. Forgive . . ." She faltered as her eyes locked onto a child's eyes. He was tiny, maybe four or five years old, and enveloped in too-big clothes that must have been borrowed for the funeral. He was clutching the right hand of a man in caretaker garb. His hand was swallowed in the man's hand, and he was staring at Queen Daleina with red, puffy, angry eyes.

Abruptly, Daleina said, "You deserve to know why."

She heard the champions shift and murmur. One of them said, "Your Majesty . . ."

She quelled them with a look. Raising her voice so that she could be heard beyond the grove, she said, "I am sick. As a result of my illness, I was unable to contain the spirits for a period of time—during that period, your loved ones died. It may happen again, and I may or may not recover. During this time of uncertainty, I ask you all to make every effort to protect yourselves. Prepare charms. Do not travel alone. Keep away from spirits as best you can."

The crowd began to murmur. Some were crying. A few were shouting.

The queen held up both hands. "I have asked my champions to prepare their candidates. Trials for heirs will be held in ten days."

Now the champions were talking, protesting—it was too soon! They couldn't! She was asking the impossible!

"Ten days until the trials!" she said.

And the spirits, without her command, all cried together, "Ten days!"

At the sound of their voices, the people huddled together, looking up at the sky and the trees. Into the silence, Queen Daleina said, "In ten days, you will have an heir. If I am cured by then, the heir will ensure a safe future. If I am *not* cured by then, I will step down, and your new queen will protect you. Until then, be safe."

CHAPTER 23

A rin lingered by the window. She heard the bells, muffled, in the distance, hundreds of piercingly sweet bells, and she knew she should be at the funerals. "My sister needs me." She'd seen Daleina only once since the tragedy, for a few minutes to reassure each other that they were alive and unharmed, and then the champions and counsellors and courtiers had needed their queen.

Hamon's mother clucked her tongue. "I need you more, precious."

She felt a sudden warm wave of happiness crash into her—the kind of whiskey warmth that burns down your throat and shoots down your arms and legs. It hit so fast that it made her dizzy, and she turned from the window to smile at her mentor.

Lounging on a chair by the fireplace, Mistress Garnah popped a sugar-coated ball of chocolate into her mouth and chewed. She'd already eaten dozens. The lace clustered at her throat was streaked with chocolate stains. Arin had liberated the chocolates from the kitchen late last night, squirreling them away under her skirts—she'd never stolen anything before, but Mistress Garnah had wanted them and the head cook hadn't been there to ask. "What do you need?" Arin asked.

"I need your steady hands to measure six drops of tin-ease, three of goat's milk, and one tablespoon of sugar. It's the sugar that stabilizes the potion. Amateurs think it's to sweeten the

❖  229  ❖

taste, but that's not true, or not entirely true. The sugar is a vital ingredient. You can't skimp on it."

Leaving the window, Arin crossed to the long dining table that she'd convinced the guards to let her drag into the room. It was covered in test tubes, bowls, and beakers. At one end was Mistress Garnah's precious microscope, carved of heartswood and fitted with priceless glass lenses. Along the back of the table, containers of spices and powders were lined up in alphabetical order. She selected the ingredients and carefully measured them into a small bowl that used to be for appetizers—at Mistress Garnah's request, she'd relieved the kitchen of a portion of their equipment for mixing and measuring. "What does this potion do?"

"What do you think it does?"

Arin considered it. Last time she'd given a wrong answer, she'd been crushed by the disappointment in Mistress Garnah's voice. She'd spent the better part of an hour huddled under the table crying. *Thoroughly mortifying*, she thought. She couldn't believe she'd overreacted like that. It wasn't like her. She did *not* want a repeat performance. "Goat's milk soothes, but combined with tin-ease and inine pods . . . It's a sleeping potion?"

"Conks you out faster than a hit on the head," she said cheerfully. "Only flaw is that it has to be dried into a powder, which requires careful baking. That's why most people use the less-toxic-smoke-inducing tamar leaves instead, thus making their potion far less effective. But you, my dear baker, should have no problem with it."

Arin frowned at the potion. Another mixture that wouldn't help Daleina. "We're supposed to be helping my sister. How does this help?" She then felt a stab of guilt—she shouldn't be questioning Mistress Garnah! Mistress Garnah was wise and kind! Tears pricked her eyes. "I'm so sorry! I didn't mean—"

Garnah waved her hand. "Curiosity is good! It's a sign of an active mind. Now, tell me, if you were to put this potion into food, what would you cook to hide the taste of the potion? Remember it will be in powder form."

"Almond cake. I'd limit the sugar and let the potion supply that. The taste of the almond should hide the bitterness of the tin-ease." Dimly, Arin noticed that Mistress Garnah hadn't answered her question. But then that thought was replaced by another: she knew tin-ease tasted bitter. How had she known that? Lifting the powder up to her nose, she sniffed. "I've tasted this before."

"Pour the potion into a vial, and we'll start on the next."

As her hands followed Mistress Garnah's instructions, she tried to puzzle out the familiarity of the taste. She'd never cooked with it, certainly. She hadn't seen it in the palace kitchens either. She'd always been excellent at identifying flavors . . . It felt as elusive as a fish, the memory slipping away from her as she tried to grab it. "Exactly what does the tin-ease do?"

"Ah, an excellent question."

She felt a rush of pleasure.

"It activates the full power of an ingredient's essence. Alone, it has little effect. But in a potion . . . Boom! You see, that's the beauty of what we do. Single ingredients alone are nothing. It is only when they are combined that they have power. It's the interactions that produce effects. In this case, a few drops of tin-ease transform the soothing strength of goat's milk into transportation to full-out la-la-land." She fluttered her fingers in the air. "It enhances what is normally merely metaphorical."

Arin jotted a note in her notebook about the effects of tin-ease, as well as a list of ingredients for the sleeping potion. "Wouldn't the act of putting a potion in a cake change the interactions? We'd be adding more ingredients."

"Smart girl. But you always know exactly what you put in a cake, don't you?"

She did. She . . . "There was tin-ease in my cake."

Garnah popped another chocolate in her mouth. "Of course there was."

She felt a flush of warmth at Mistress Garnah's approving tone, and then she shook her head, trying to think clearly. This was *not* a good thing. She should *not* be happy. "You put a potion in my cake? Why? What potion? What did you . . ." She swallowed the words. Mistress Garnah must have had a good reason. She must have seen something in Arin that needed to be fixed or healed or . . .

"You tell me."

Closing her eyes, Arin tried to re-create the taste in her memory. Vanilla, sugar, flour, egg . . . all the usual ingredients. Had there been extra sweetness? Saltiness? She only remembered the tangy edge.

The half-eaten cake had been wheeled to a corner of the room. It was as stale as dried firewood, and the icing had hardened. Opening her eyes, Arin crossed to it. Her plate had been shoved underneath the table—Mistress Garnah had refused to allow any servants into the room, even to clean. Arin took the mostly eaten slice plus a new slice and carried both back to the table. She studied them. She smelled them. She plunged her fingers into the cake, feeling it crumble between her fingers. The icing of the cake she'd eaten felt more slippery.

She glanced back at Mistress Garnah, who was smiling placidly at her. "Did you poison me?" Arin asked, and then she felt a *whoosh* of shame for even considering . . . It couldn't be poison. She didn't feel sick. She felt much too . . . *much*. "My emotions. You affected them?"

Wiping the chocolate from her cheeks with a wad of lace, Mistress Garnah stretched herself out on the chair. She propped her feet up on a pillow. "If you can't figure out how, you aren't worthy of being my assistant."

Fear.

Excitement.

Pride.

Each emotion swept through Arin, and for the first time, she questioned if they were really hers. There were potions to make you feel strong emotions, she knew. Red pepper, mixed with sinsan root, fueled anger. Marrow from mouse bone, combined with salt and eker leaf, made fear. She flipped through her notes—she'd learned about potions to thicken the blood, to calm the heart, to ease the muscles, to soothe anger, to cause fear or despair or ecstasy . . .

She'd always felt things deeply. Pride in her sister—she'd always thought Daleina was the best and deserved the best. Passion for her work—when she chose to be a baker, she threw herself into it, worked nonstop, planned to open her own bakery. Love for Josei—when she'd fallen in love, it was no-question head-over-heels, with full-blown plans for the future. And then the despair and anger when he'd died. She thought she'd be subsumed by the pain.

She pursed her lips and examined the ingredients that were on the table. *Tin-ease enhances an ingredient's essence...* Glancing at Mistress Garnah, she lifted a cake-coated finger to her lips. First, she tasted the undoctored slice. She let it melt on her tongue, absorbing the ingredients. She knew them all—it was her cake. Eyes still on Mistress Garnah, she then tasted the tainted slice.

She let it linger in her mouth.

Extra salt. A hint of sugar. Nutmeg? No, it was sweeter than that, nearly hidden by the flavor of vanilla and sugar. She wouldn't have noticed it if she hadn't been focusing.

On instinct, she reached for ingredients. She sniffed them, and then added bits to the undoctored cake, matching it in taste. She lost track of time as she mixed, added, and sniffed. She then tossed the piece of cake and fetched another one.

She tried again.

And again.

The texture... The smell... And last, the taste.

"It's foolish to experiment on yourself," Mistress Garnah said. "Hamon once acted as you did. I cannot tell you how many times I came home to that foolish boy unconscious on the workroom floor. Eventually I brought him home a cat. He was upset when it died, but better that than him, I told him. See, I did love him. I do. He's my boy. He'll always be my boy. I don't know what I did to deserve such disdain from him."

She felt a surge inside her—an urge to comfort. Tears pricked her eyes. Arin shook her head as if that would clear away the cloud of *feelings*. "It's not a single emotion. It's all of them, targeted toward you." She looked down at her notes. None of the potions she'd learned matched, but combined? "You fed me a love potion."

Mistress Garnah made a kissy face toward her. "Aww, how sweet. And no, try again."

Scooping up a bit of tainted icing, Arin rubbed it between her fingers again. "Extra egg?"

"Yes, a special egg. A fertilized egg, the very first laid by that bird. Dehydrate it and crush it into powder, and it can have a powerful effect."

An unhatched egg. The first egg. The first child. *Tin-ease enhances what is normally merely metaphorical.* "You made me imprint on you. Like a baby duck. You made me want to follow you, please you, nearly worship you." As she said it, she felt a swirling sickness in the base of her stomach. Mistress Garnah couldn't . . . She wouldn't . . .

"Correct. I suppose in a way, it *is* a variant on a love potion." Mistress Garnah smiled, as if delighted with Arin's performance.

"I'm your cat. You experimented on me."

"I had to be certain it would work on a person before I tried it on my Hamon. Emotions are fine, but I needed to be sure they wouldn't dim a person's intelligence. Frankly, I didn't expect it to work so well."

Now she felt a rush of anger. *There it is*, she thought. Her own emotion, untouched by the tin-ease. "It worked because I wanted to believe in you. I wanted to trust you." The potion enhanced her feelings, especially the positive ones. But it didn't dictate them. It didn't force them to all be positive. This anger—it came from inside her, focused but hers. She gripped that anger as if she were in a storm and it was the strongest tree. Slowly, as she nurtured her anger, she felt the clouds lift in her mind. "It won't work on him."

Mistress Garnah's smile vanished. "Why do you say that?"

"Because he doesn't want to love you."

"And you did? You barely knew me, and surely what you knew was bad. I saw Hamon, whispering his warnings to you. Don't trust me. Don't believe me. Don't even look at me, hideous monster that I am."

"He brought you here to cure my sister," Arin said. "So yes, I wanted to believe in you. Very badly. You didn't need to use any potion on me for that." She felt clear now, at last. Her thoughts were her own again. Her emotions, her own. The anger had burned away whatever Mistress Garnah had done to her.

Mistress Garnah studied her. "Humph. I'd say the potion wasn't strong enough. You've shaken it off, haven't you? It's the anger. Self-righteous anger is a difficult emotion to smother." She sighed. "I knew you were a smart girl. That's why I wanted you for my assistant. But now I suppose you'll flee from me, like everyone does."

She should. After all, Mistress Garnah had used a potion against her. But Arin hesitated. She looked at the worktable, at the microscope, at the test tubes, at the herbs and powders.

The potion hadn't made Arin good at this. That was Arin herself. Arin had absorbed the lessons, prepared the ingredients, performed the experiments, and found the cause of her sister's illness.

If she learned more . . . perhaps she could find the cure.

"Teach me everything," Arin bargained, "and I will stay. I will be more than your assistant; I will be your apprentice."

Mistress Garnah's eyes brightened. "Oh, really?"

"Yes, *Master* Garnah."

ACROSS THE BURIAL GROVE, NAELIN WATCHED QUEEN DALEINA. The young queen held herself perfectly still, as if she were posed while an artist painted a portrait. Her shoulders were back, her chin was high, and her hands were clasped lightly together. She was the picture of regal poise. *Poor girl must be terrified,* Naelin thought.

"She doesn't look sick," Erian whispered.

"Her skin isn't sick," Llor whispered back. "It's all the stuff inside. Right, Mama?"

Leaning over, Naelin pressed her lips onto the top of Llor's head. "That's right, sweetie. Sometimes people get sick deep inside, and sometimes there's nothing anyone can do to fix it."

Around them, people were crying. Some wailed loudly. Others were silent, their shoulders shaking and their face in their hands. A few were motionless, staring at the queen as if they could unhear the words or as if they were awaiting a punch line to a morbid joke.

"Are we all going to die, Mama?" Llor asked. "I don't want to die. Ever. It makes everyone cry. And I hate itchy clothes. Why do I have to wear itchy clothes?"

"I won't let you die," Naelin told him. "And it's polite to dress nicely for a funeral."

"But you told me it's not polite to itch in public, and I'm itchy."

She wanted to laugh, but this was not the time or place. Glancing again at the queen, she saw the first hint of emotion on her lovely face: the briefest moment of panic. Around her, the champions were arguing. Some were shouting. And the crowd was growing louder ... "There's a time and a place for things," Naelin told Llor. "This is a funeral, and we must all be respectful." Guiding her children, she tried to melt backward into the crowd. She suddenly didn't want to be here, with all these people and all their emotions. It could be dangerous. This much emotion, this many people ... It didn't feel like a solemn occasion anymore; it felt like embers inside of dried tinder.

The queen's eyes landed on hers.

Naelin stopped.

*She can't fix this*, Naelin realized. She'd said what she had to say, the truth, and it was up to the people to react. *They aren't going to react well.*

Naelin staggered to the side as someone bumped hard into her. She hugged Erian and Llor tighter against her. People were shouting and beginning to shove. She saw the guards press closer around the queen, their hands on their sword hilts.

"Mama?" Erian said. "Can we go? Please?"

Naelin heard the fear in her daughter's voice. "Yes," she began to say, and then realized the crowd had pushed farther into the grove. All the exits were packed with people. Beyond them, more people. If they rioted ...

The queen spoke again. "We are here to honor the dead ..."

But a man shouted, "You killed them!"

A woman near him began shouting in his face. He raised his fist, and she slammed hers into his chin. He rocked backward, and then the knot of people around them began pushing, shoving, punching. The crowd surged, and Naelin was swept forward.

"Mama!" Llor cried.

Naelin repeated the queen's words: "We are here to honor the dead." *Honor the dead.* She pushed the thought out, hard. She felt the spirits converge, streaming in from all around. *Honor them!*

And it began to snow: white petals burst from the trees above and drifted down. Hundreds, thousands, millions, covering the people. On the ground, more flowers burst beneath people's feet. Vines wrapped around ankles and then blossomed with more white flowers.

Wind whipped through the grove—targeted wind, fast, ringing the silver bells that people held in their hands or had put in their pockets. Catching the queen's eye, Naelin mouthed one word: "*You!*"

Queen Daleina spread her arms wide and tilted her head back. Petals fell on her arms and face. It looked, to everyone else, as if she were causing this, as if she had command of the spirits. But it was Naelin who held them tightly, guiding them through the grove. *Do no harm. Honor the dead.*

The air spirits began to sing in voices full of wind. They whispered in harmony as they flew through the trees, a wordless song that was full of sorrow and hope—emotions that Naelin never thought a spirit could feel, much less turn into song.

All the people were motionless, their eyes wide, their mouths open. She saw wonder on their faces as the spirits crafted beauty around them. Water spirits flew by, leaving droplets in the air, and as the sun hit them, tiny rainbows appeared all around the grove.

"We honor our dead," Queen Daleina said. Her voice rang as clear as the bells across the grove. "We thank them for entering our lives and will remember them with joy." She then retreated— serenely and regally, but still retreated—with her guards around her.

Subdued, the crowd parted and let her pass. Taking Erian and Llor's hands, Naelin slipped out through the crowd as well, skirting the bulk of the people to reach the palace from the side. Only when they were inside the gates did she release her grip on their hands.

Behind her, the petals continued to fall for hours.

en days!

Candidate Esiella thought she might be sick. Yes, definitely. She'd held it in at the funeral grove, but she was safely back in the training room, a rented room north of the palace.

Dropping to her knees, she clutched her stomach and opened her mouth. Nothing came out. She breathed deeply a few times. Still felt sick. Still couldn't be sick.

"Aw, come on, you can do this," Champion Havtru said.

*Is he encouraging me to . . . throw up?*

*No. He's saying I can survive the trials.*

She shook her head, even as she felt his heavy, warm hand on her back. She gulped in air again, and the knot inside her felt as if it were loosening a little. Her champion was always so encouraging. He'd even been sympathetic the time she'd summoned an earth spirit and it had chomped on his leg.

"I can't do it," she said. "I can't be ready in ten days! Ten months, maybe. But ten *days*?" She raised her head to meet his gentle eyes. She knew he'd be looking at her with that mix of fondness, sympathy, pity, and belief. For some crazy reason, he believed in her, and that was extraordinary. No one had ever believed in her before. Not her mother, who used to call her worthless every time she tried to help around the house and worse than worthless if she didn't try to help. Not her father, who had informed her on her sixth birthday that she shouldn't have been born, before he walked out the door never to come back. Not her sisters, who stole her clothes whenever she didn't hide them. Not her older brother, who used to hit her but only in places it wouldn't show. Not her teacher, who'd called her a liar when she'd tried to say she felt spirits. Oh, how she'd loved the day he had been proved wrong! She'd loved the moment when it was her turn to walk out that door!

Champion Havtru had saved her.

And now she was going to let him down.

She drew a deep breath. "I'll try again."

He clapped her shoulder, and she lurched forward before catching herself. Standing, she smiled shakily at him. "Tell me what to do."

"You saw the petals fall at the funeral? How about asking the spirits to create a few of those flowers? Seems a thing that a queen is likely to have to do." He smiled encouragingly, and she thought it was a shame his wife had died before they'd had children. He would have been such a wonderful father.

"Okay." She could do this. Flowers. Closing her eyes, she reached out to touch the closest tree spirits. There were three nearby, two larger and one smaller. She selected the smaller one and focused on it. *Come.*

She felt it skittering over the branches, and then she heard it— tiny steps on a branch. She also heard Champion Havtru draw his knife, the familiar soft rattle of metal against the leather scabbard. He always held a weapon when spirits were near. It wasn't that he didn't trust her, he'd told Esiella. It was that he didn't trust *them.*

*Grow. Bloom.* She pictured the vine she wanted and then the flowers. She repeated this image, pushing it toward the little spirit. *Come on, you can do it.*

"Good," Champion Havtru murmured. "Very good."

She opened her eyes. Petals were falling inside the training room. Only a few, but still. She'd done it! If she were queen, she'd know how to commemorate the dead . . . Her stomach lurched forward, and she couldn't stop it. Dropping down, she was sick on the floor, missing the bucket entirely.

Petals fell into the mess, and the spirit skittered away.

On her hands and knees, Esiella panted. Her stomach felt empty. Her head felt light. And her sides hurt. Tears heated her eyes.

Champion Havtru patted her back, lightly this time. "It's all right. Happens to the best of us. I'll fetch you some towels to clean up. Don't worry about it. You did well!"

She heard him leave the room, his footsteps retreating then the door. Rocking back, she sat on her heels. She felt stickiness in the corners of her mouth but had nothing to wipe it with. She squeezed her eyes and let the tears fall.

If she tried to be queen, many would die. She'd be making petals fall daily over more and more fresh graves. She wasn't ready, and she couldn't be ready in time. Distantly, she heard voices: Havtru and another voice, a muffled voice that she didn't recognize. She didn't try to listen to their words. She was sure Champion Havtru was hiding her sickness, talking up how well she was doing, praising her more than she deserved—to build up her confidence, he said.

All it did was remind her of her failures.

Maybe her family and teacher had been right about her. Maybe she didn't deserve this. Champion Havtru should be spending his time with someone who didn't fall apart like she did.

Esiella heard the door creak, a tiny sound but she heard it— Champion Havtru.

He was checking on her.

She didn't turn around. She wasn't ready to face him.

*I should tell him that he's wasting his time. I'll never be good enough.* She knew what he'd say, though. He'd tell her what he always did: that he believed in her, and if she didn't believe in herself . . . well, then he'd believe enough for both of them. She had talent, he'd say. She only had to trust it. *Listen to him*, she told herself. *Not to your past.*

"I'll try harder," she said. "I won't let you down."

Esiella turned around.

It wasn't Champion Havtru.

She felt the knife slide into her body.

And her last thought was of the petals that would fall for her.

NAELIN DIDN'T KNOW WHAT IT SAID ABOUT HER LIFE LATELY that she was unsurprised when the Queen of Aratay swept into her training room. She dropped into an immediate curtsy, and the fire spirit that was dancing in the hearth hissed. Sparks jumped out onto the flagstones.

"You may rise," the queen said. She gestured to her guards, and they bowed and retreated to the door. The wolf Bayn padded inside behind the queen, and then the guards closed the door, leaving Naelin alone with Her Majesty and Bayn.

Unsure what to say, Naelin knelt to greet Bayn. He trotted up to her, tail wagging, and she scratched behind his ears. "The children have missed you," she told the wolf.

He drooped his tongue out of his mouth and managed, somehow, to look sorry.

"Don't worry. They'll forgive you if you visit soon," Naelin said. "They have the emotional memory spans of hummingbirds."

He crossed to the fireplace and growled at the spirit. The spirit darted up the chimney, and the wolf curled up on the hearth. Naelin rose and faced the queen. Inside, where shadows crisscrossed the room, the queen looked more tired than Naelin had thought. Gray-purple bruiselike shadows lined her eyes, and her cheeks were pale. Her hands were trembling slightly. Naelin wanted to guide her to a cushion-covered couch and wrap her in warm blankets, but she guessed that wouldn't be appropriate. She ventured a question. "Are you well, Your Majesty?"

Queen Daleina let out a bark that was a half laugh, half cry. "Aside from the fact that I am dying? Oh yes, I am quite well." She glided across the floor and then sat in a chair near Bayn. She perched on the edge of it, as if she didn't intend to stay. "I came to say thank you, but now that I'm here, I don't know where to begin. You saved many lives today."

"I assume Champion Ven has told you I reconsidered?" Naelin felt her face heat up. "I mean, about being heir. Trying to be heir. *Training*. Training to be heir, not . . . I wouldn't presume, that is, Your Majesty." Oh, good grief. She hadn't been this tongue-tied since she was a kid. She gave herself a mental slap. *Quit it.*

The queen gestured at the ornate couch near her. "Please, sit."

Naelin sank onto the cushions. It was low, too low, and the cushion sagged under her. She had to bend her legs to the side, but she managed it. It was amazing how a simple circle worn on a person's head could make one feel so awkward.

Queen Daleina glanced around the room, and Naelin was overly aware of the mess she'd made. The walls were scorched in spots, dirt was ground into the carpet, the mattress on the former queen's bed was gone—it had been drenched by a water spirit that Naelin had failed to control. "Queen Fara liked opulence," Queen Daleina said. "I see you have redecorated."

Naelin winced. She should have tried to clean. A hard scrub would have gotten out many of the stains . . . She surveyed the room, cataloguing all the things she could have fixed or cleaned. "I've been practicing here."

"I can see that." The queen studied Naelin. *Even when she's not on the throne, she seems like a queen*, Naelin thought. She wondered if it was an act or her natural personality, or a consequence of wearing the crown. Tapping the armrests, the queen continued to regard Naelin so intently that Naelin began to feel like an insect who had been noticed by a kitten. "You can speak freely, you know. I'm not going to have my guards chop your head off if you offend me. Besides, Captain Alet speaks highly of you."

Naelin hadn't seen Alet in days. It was nice to know that the guardswoman approved of her. She'd thought so, but she appreciated the confirmation. "You did the right thing, telling people the truth. Now they can be prepared."

"I can't predict it, so how can people prepare?" The queen stood abruptly and walked toward the balcony. She halted in the archway and looked out.

Naelin stood as well, smoothing her skirt and patting her hair. She'd changed from the brocade gown that the caretakers had provided for the funerals. She was wearing instead heavy-duty laundress clothes that would stand up to water, fire, and dirt. "Well, now that I know, *I* can be prepared. The next time—"

"I'll train you."

"Your Majesty?"

The queen spun to face her, and her sun-colored skirts flared around her. "I have precious little time, with the schedule my seneschal has set for me. There are many who want an audience after my announcement today. People need to be reassured. Champions need to be soothed. Not everyone feels that my announcement was the right decision . . . But that's not your problem. Your problem is that you have too much power. You've never learned to work small."

"I'm honored—"

"Oh, for spirits' sake, stop treating me like a queen. Come here." Queen Daleina beckoned. When Naelin joined her on the balcony, she pointed toward a tree spirit who was gnawing on an acorn several yards away. It was perched on a spire, with its hind legs planted in the bark. The tree spirit was no larger than Naelin's fist and so gnarled that it looked like an oversized walnut. Its face was a mash of wrinkles, and its spindly wood legs were pockmarked with deep, rotted-looking knots. "Tell me: what does it want?" the queen asked.

*Death*, she thought. It wanted their blood soaking into the moss, their last breath exhaled into the wind, their bodies sunk into the earth. "To kill all humans. To be free of our commands. To tear down all we've built. To rip the throats from our children and destroy our future."

"More simply. What does it want right now?"

Naelin studied the spirit. Bits of acorn flew from its teeth. "Lunch?"

"Exactly. So if you want to use the least amount of power possible to make that spirit grow a tree, choose a tree that it will *want* to grow. And then don't command. You don't want to bully the spirit—that requires more power. You want to nudge it. Encourage it. Trick it into doing what you want by making it think it's doing what it wants."

"Like getting children to help with the dishes by turning it into a game." Naelin thought of Erian and Llor. She'd turned housework into a contest—who could straighten their sheets fastest, who could wash their plates the best, who could remember to hang up their towels for the most days in a row. Here, caretakers did it all. "Mine will be so spoiled when we—" She stopped before she said "go home." She pictured home: her cozy kitchen with herbs drying upside down from the rafters, the beds piled high with down quilts she'd made, the wood floor worn from years of footsteps, and then she ruthlessly pushed the image away. *Home is gone.* Or at least so far out of reach that it might as well be. "All right, I'll try."

"Good."

Taking a deep breath, Naelin steadied herself. She cleared her mind and then sent a single thought spiraling toward the spirit: *More?*

It perked up, rising onto its hind legs and pricking its ears forward.

She pictured a nut tree. Painted an image of a belen nut, its pink shell, its chewy inside. She pushed the image toward the spirit. *Grow more, eat more.*

"Gently," Queen Daleina said. "Only suggest."

Naelin drew back her thoughts. The spirit looked around—down, up, right, left—its movements quick and jerky.

"Focus on what it wants. Encourage that."

*You're so hungry. So very hungry. You want more food.* She pictured the tree again, with its twisted limbs and wrinkled bark. She filled its branches with clusters of nuts. The spirit chittered like a squirrel, and Naelin tasted the bitter-buttery nut taste on her own tongue.

"Good," the queen said softly. "Now guide it to one of the barren patches. There's one just to the east, half a mile. Just suggest it. Don't order."

"How?"

"Picture it."

"But I've never seen it."

"The spirits have. Reach east, and look through their eyes."

"We can do that?"

The queen placed her hands on Naelin's shoulders and positioned her to face east. "Quiet your own thoughts, and *look.* Think of their eyes as your eyes."

Naelin reached out, expanding her awareness as Ven had

taught her. She brushed past the spirits around the palace. So many spirits. Burrowing, flying, sleeping, crawling . . .

"They aren't Other," the queen said. "They're you. Parts of you. See with them, through them."

She felt . . . Shaking her head, Naelin yanked away. She'd felt their hunger, their hate, and even worse, their indifference. She'd felt their oddness, their slippery, slimy . . .

"You can't hate them," Queen Daleina said, and Naelin thought she sounded sad. "That was the hardest thing, when they crowned me. They'd killed . . . Regardless, you can't hate your foot even if it hurts you. You can't hate your eyes even if they sting. In order to command them with precision, rather than bludgeon them with raw power, you need to accept them as a part of you."

Lovely sentiment, but not practical. "I hate them, and I'll always hate them."

"You can't," Queen Daleina said. "You and I . . . We don't have the luxury of hate anymore."

"I don't forgive easily." She thought of Renet. Thinking of him felt like a fist in her stomach. They were supposed to spend their future together, grow old and crotchety together, bounce grandchildren on their knees, feed each other soup when they grew too weak to chew . . . He'd taken that away from her. She could easily hate him. But not forgive. "It may be that I have personality flaws."

The queen rolled her eyes—a very unqueenly expression. "Do you believe I am flawless?"

"Of course, Your Majesty. Except for letting yourself get poisoned, and then concealing the truth from everyone so that they were caught unprepared when you collapsed." Instantly, Naelin wished she could take the words back. This was the *queen*. You didn't talk to the queen that way! If Erian or Llor had talked to anyone that way, Naelin would have sent them to sit in the corner on an uncomfortable stool.

But Daleina just sighed, looking—if anything—a bit abashed. "I was attempting to avoid panic and riots. My hope was to have an heir in place before anyone needed to know. But the champions tell me that their chosen candidates are not ready. In fact, they are so far from ready that it's laughable. Whether I hold the trials in ten days or two months, they'll die. All of them. Like the Coronation Massacre, except it truly will be my fault."

Naelin felt as if the air had thinned. "Then why—"

"You are the only one who is close," the queen said, "and if you do not quit clinging to your ego as if your hatred is some kind of child's blanket, then we are all doomed."

"You're much less diplomatic than I thought a queen would be," Naelin said.

The queen blushed slightly. "I've had a bad day."

"No, it's all right. In fact, it's good. You might be young, but you're an excellent queen. I very much hope you don't die." Naelin meant it with all her heart. She'd never truly thought of the queen as a person before, not a real flesh-and-blood one with feelings and thoughts and dreams and hopes and fears.

To Naelin's surprise, Queen Daleina smiled. "Glad we can agree." Reaching out, she took Naelin's hands. The queen's hands were tiny, with bones that felt as light as a bird's, and oddly rough—she had as many climbing calluses as Naelin did. "We're going to try this together. Be ready, though. Using my power can trigger blackouts."

"Then why risk—"

"You *must* learn. And you must learn fast. It should be safe enough, since you will be doing the bulk of the actual work. Stretch out your mind with me . . ."

Naelin reached out with her mind—and this time, she felt . . . She had no words for it, but it felt like a breeze beside her. She drifted with the breeze, touching lightly the spirits around the palace. Chasing the breeze, she followed it to see . . .

A grove.

A barren grove, but distorted, as if she were looking at it through a sheen of raindrops. She saw it from above, below, and various angles all at once, so that the barren patch was warped.

"Touch as many tree spirits as you can. *Suggest* they may be hungry."

Reaching out, Naelin pushed the thoughts out wide: *Hungry? Food? Grow?*

With a cry, the spirits flocked to the barren patch. First a few, then more, then even more until there were dozens of them diving into the earth and then rising up, pulling new trees with them: nut trees and fruit trees . . . In mere seconds, the patch was alive again and filled with ripened nuts and fruits. Naelin felt the spirits begin to feast.

The queen released her hands. "Do you feel tired?"

"No." She should feel something—that had been a lot of spirits—but she didn't. In fact, she felt amazing, as if her blood had been replaced with chocolate. She felt herself smile. "You?"

"I didn't black out, and no one died." The queen regarded Naelin for a moment, a smile creeping onto her own face. "Shall we do it again?"

This time, Naelin took the queen's hands.

rian placed the pieces of the miyan set on the board. Each piece had been carved out of a different beautiful stone: jade, quartz, and other stones she couldn't name. One had a lightning pattern of yellow. Another had pink flecks. Mama had said it cost a fortune and it wasn't for children to play with.

But breaking that rule was a lot better than letting Llor run free. It had taken him less than two hours after they'd discovered they had no guards to find the dumbwaiter that led to the kitchen, the back route to the armory, and an open window that led to the greenhouse. Erian was tired of chasing after him.

"If you don't sit still," Erian told him, "I'm going to ask Mama to tie you to a chair."

"She won't do it," Llor said. "And if you make me play, I'm going to cheat."

"If you cheat, I'll tell the palace guards."

"If you tell the guards, I'll put a frog in your bed."

"If you put a frog in my bed, I'll scream. And then the guards will come again."

Llor fidgeted in his seat. "But miyan is so *boring*."

"Not if you don't cheat."

He picked up one of the pieces and made it gallop across the board and then bash another piece. "Pow, pow, pow."

"Put that down." She finished setting out the pieces. She *thought* that was how they went, arrayed in semicircles, but she wasn't one hundred percent sure. She picked up the jade piece again and scowled at it.

"If Father was here, he'd play hide-and-seek with me."

Erian felt her throat thicken, as if she'd swallowed something gummy. "Well, he's not, and you're stuck with me. Besides, Mama hates hide-and-seek. She likes to know where we are." She blinked fast so she wouldn't cry. She'd promised herself she wouldn't cry. She had to be strong, for Mama.

He muttered so low that Erian wasn't sure she heard him correctly: "You're boring."

*He's so . . . so . . . argh!* She slammed the miyan piece onto the board, and its arm chipped off and flew across the room. Both of them watched the sliver of jade fly. It landed on the carpet by the hearth.

"Ooh," Llor said. "I didn't do it."

The door to their chambers swung open. "Didn't do what?" a woman asked.

Both Erian and Llor jumped off their chairs. "Captain Alet!" Game forgotten, they flew to the guard. Llor reached her first and hurled himself at her, hugging her neck. Erian followed behind. She wanted to hug her too but wasn't sure whether that was okay or not. Then Captain Alet held out her free arm toward Erian, and Erian threw her arms around the guardswoman. She smelled like metal and rusty copper. Erian wrinkled her nose.

"Have you been fighting spirits?" Llor asked.

"Not today, little warrior. But I have been out in the capital, taking care of a few things for the queen. Just got back and thought I'd see if my two favorite warriors were hungry."

Erian's stomach growled, as if on cue. "We had breakfast, but . . ." It had been before the funeral, and Erian hadn't felt like eating much. And then Mama had disappeared for more training, leaving them alone. *Or as alone as we can be in a palace stuffed with strangers.*

"Can I show you the secret passageway I found to the kitchen?" Llor asked, jumping from foot to foot.

"If it's secret, are you sure you should be telling me?"

He stopped jumping.

Captain Alet laughed. "I'm kidding. Yes, please show me."

"Or we could just use the stairs," Erian suggested.

But Llor was already bolting for the door and flinging it open. "The palace is really big. No, not big. That word is too small. Why is the word 'big' such a small word? It should have a super enormous number of letters."

"'Enormous' is a large word," Captain Alet said, following, "especially for a little boy."

Llor drew himself up onto his tiptoes. "I'm not little. I'm 'compact.' Mama said so."

"Of course," Captain Alet said, and then ruffled the boy's hair. Erian suppressed a sigh—Mama had spent a solid fifteen minutes trying to comb his hair this morning. On the other hand, the funerals were over, and it wasn't like anyone cared what either of them looked like. They were just two more kids in the palace. She wondered if anyone even noticed they were here. The palace was so big . . . *enormous* . . . that they could have moved in to any one of the hundreds of rooms in any of the branches and not been noticed for years. "Where is your mother?" Captain Alet asked.

"Training," Erian said.

"She trains all the time," Llor complained. "Ooh, there it is!" He scooted ahead and then dropped to his knees and crawled behind a tapestry. He stuck his head out from beneath it. "See, there's a little door! It goes straight down to the kitchen."

Bending, Captain Alet lifted up the tapestry. "You found the lift. Clever boy. The kitchen staff uses this to transport food to the upper levels. It goes straight up, all the way to the Queen's Tower, the highest point in the palace. If you pull on the rope—see, here"—she demonstrated—"it will bring up a cupboard. There's a crank in the kitchen, but you can do it manually from any level."

"Or you can just climb the rope down. Come on!"

Captain Alet laughed. "I can't fit in there."

He began scooting down. "Race you!"

*Not again!* "Do I have to follow him?" Erian still had raw red patches on her palms from the last time she'd chased Llor down the rope.

Captain Alet patted her shoulder. "We'll be civilized and walk."

They arrived at the kitchen. Captain Alet nodded to the cooks as she strode in. Erian wished she could enter a room like that— the guardswoman seemed to immediately fill a room. She hoped she could be like Captain Alet when she grew up. Her hands went to her hair, pulling it back so it would match the captain's. She glanced at herself in the reflection of a copper pot and then dropped her hands. *I look ridiculous.*

On the opposite side of the kitchen, Llor was perched on a counter. "You're slow," he proclaimed. Erian noticed one of the cooks had wrapped a white cloth around one of Llor's hands—he must have gotten rope burn. *Serves him right,* Erian thought.

At the pantry, Captain Alet helped herself to a heaping plate of pastries. She carried it over to a little table by a window and straddled a chair. "Come on. You need to refuel after such an adventure. Is this what you've been doing while your mother has been training?"

"Yes," Llor said proudly. "I'm clever."

"If she were here, she'd never let you climb through the walls like that," Erian said. "She *should* be here. Llor won't listen to me, and he's going to get himself hurt."

Captain Alet served the pastries onto napkins. "You can't blame your mother for training a lot. She only wants to keep you safe."

"She wants to be heir," Llor reported. "She told Champion Ven she'd do it." Plopping into a chair, Llor stuffed a pastry into his mouth. Erian sat next to him and selected one that looked like it had been dusted with cinnamon.

Captain Alet seemed to freeze. Her face paled, and she looked at Erian, as if for confirmation. *See, she's upset too!* Erian thought.

"Mama changed her mind and said yes," Erian said.

"And now she trains *all the time,*" Llor said, talking through a mouthful of food.

"Chew first," Erian told Llor. To Captain Alet, she said, "And when Mama's with us, she's always worried." *And I'm worried about her.* "She's been having nightmares. We hear her."

Captain Alet wasn't eating her pastry. She was mushing bits of the flakes between her fingers and looking out the window.

She looked exactly like Father did when Mama had said they were leaving. "I didn't think she'd change her mind. I was certain . . ."

Erian had a sudden idea. "Can you talk to her? Tell her why she shouldn't do it?" Surely Mama would listen to the guardswoman. They were friends.

"Yeah!" Llor chimed in. "Get her to change her mind back! She'd listen to you!"

"You know that no matter what she decides and what she does, your mother loves you very much," Captain Alet said. "You are her sun and her moon."

"Erian's not a moon," Llor objected.

"Yeah, well, you're not the sun either."

"Am too."

She was not going to argue homonyms with him. She turned back to Captain Alet. "How can we convince her not to be an heir? I don't want her to die!"

"I don't want her to either. I'll talk to her," Captain Alet promised. "But your mother is stubborn. She knows her own mind. If I can't convince her . . . You shouldn't be on your own in the palace. It's not safe. Your mother should have found someone to watch you."

"Mama thinks we are being watched," Erian said. "She thinks we've been staying in our chambers, safe and sound. She thinks we have people watching us all the time." She shot a look at Llor. "Told you you're going to get us in trouble."

"Not if she doesn't tell," Llor insisted. "You won't tell, Captain Alet, will you?"

Captain Alet sighed heavily. "No. But you need someone to look after you. Maybe we can find you a governess."

"No governess!" Llor shouted, sputtering out crumbs.

"I'm too old for a governess," Erian said.

"A guard then? I could have one assigned specifically to you," Captain Alet said.

They'd had guards in the beginning—Champion Ven had assigned them and Mama had approved them—but those guards hadn't come back after the spirits attacked, and Mama had been too preoccupied to notice. Erian thought maybe they were dead. A lot of people had died. "Can you be our guard?"

Llor hopped up and down in his seat. "Yes! Please, please, please! And the wolf too! He can have my dinners. And you can have my desserts. Half my desserts."

But Captain Alet was shaking her head. "I have responsibilities." She seemed to sag a little, as if she was even more tired than Mama, which didn't seem possible—Captain Alet wasn't supposed to ever be tired. She was the strongest person that Erian had ever met. "But I will see about finding a proper—"

"No!" Llor wailed.

"We'll be fine," Erian said. "I know someone who will watch us, if we write and ask."

Llor cut off his wail. "Who?"

But Erian didn't answer. Instead, she said, "I'll take care of it. You don't need to tell Mama anything about us. But will you please talk to her? Convince her not to be heir?"

Captain Alet nodded. "I'll try."

Erian bit into her pastry and thought about the letter she needed to write to Father.

SWORD READY, VEN WATCHED AS NAELIN DIRECTED A HALF-DOZEN tree spirits as if she were an orchestra conductor and they were her instruments. She'd kicked out the gardeners and taken over one of the palace flower gardens. Three spirits were weaving vines of roses up the palace wall. Another was forcing bushes to grow into shapes: dancers, bears, birds. Two more were devoted to cultivating a new herb garden, because Naelin insisted gardens should be practical as well as ornamental. She was humming to herself, though Ven didn't think she even knew she was. She was intent on her work.

He could watch her all day.

She gestured with one arm, and a spirit swooped up to wrap a vine around a window. Roses burst into bloom, framing the window in huge red blossoms. He watched her as she laughed at a butterfly that was startled when a bud opened beneath it. Her laugh was as warm and rich as hot chocolate. He wondered if anyone had ever told her how amazing she was, and if she'd believed it when they'd said it.

Still, as captivated as he was by her, he was trained enough to notice the sound of soft footsteps behind him. The churned dirt muffled the man's slippers, but Ven heard them, as well as the whoosh of his clothes as he moved. So yes, he knew the man was there. He just didn't care. Naelin was much more interesting to look at.

"You're supposed to be guarding her," the man—Healer Hamon—said. "I could have stabbed you by now, if I wanted to. Severed your spinal column here, and here." Ven felt Hamon's finger brush his back mid-spine and at his neck.

Spinning fast, Ven shot his foot out and swept Hamon's feet out from under him. He crashed down into the soft earth of a flowerbed. Before he could even draw a full breath, Ven was kneeling on his chest.

"Or you could have flattened me before I even drew a blade," Hamon said conversationally.

Ven released him and helped him up.

"Oof. Thanks." Hamon shook off the soil that clung to his cloak. Reaching over, Ven plucked a leaf from his shoulder. He then returned to watching Naelin. She was creating a sculpture in the center of the garden, using earth spirits to push rocks up out of the ground. It was shaped loosely like the palace tree. "She's not worried about the kraken anymore?" Hamon asked.

"She's been training with Daleina," Ven said. "She's got this." She lacked the range to protect the entire country—only a queen had that kind of power—but she had the strength to defend the palace, maybe even the capital, if Daleina blacked out again.

Spreading her arms wide, Naelin stepped back, and water spirits burst through the center of her sculpture. Water cascaded down—she'd made a fountain. It was a very nice fountain.

"And the other champions don't object? It's favoritism."

"It's practical. They know their candidates are nowhere close to ready. Daleina's last blackout scared them." They'd held a meeting. Yelled a lot. Daleina had listened to it all and then nodded and said she'd heard their concerns and hoped they felt better for expressing them, though she could not feel better no matter how much discussion they had, because she was the one dying. That shut them up. He'd been proud.

"Speaking of frightening them . . . I have a favor to ask."

Ven looked at Hamon and noticed the circles under his eyes, the sunken hollowness of his cheeks, the way his hair was uncombed and his clothes wrinkled. Hamon usually took such care with his appearance, courtesy of his former teacher's training—appearance was important to a healer. It soothed the patients. Ven guessed the search for the cure wasn't going well. "Of course. No luck yet in finding the poisoner?"

Hamon shook his head. "This is a separate matter."

"There are no separate matters. This is the only thing that matters." He made a mental note to talk to Captain Alet about her progress. With Naelin proceeding this quickly, Daleina had to be thinking harder about abdicating. He wanted to delay that moment as long as possible.

"I need you to look at a dead body. Actually, several."

That wasn't a request he heard every day.

"Can you call a guard to watch Naelin?"

Pivoting, he called, "Bayn? Guard Naelin."

Uncurling his body, the wolf stretched and then ambled over to Naelin. He drank from the fountain and then lay down at Naelin's feet. She absently scratched Bayn behind the ears before continuing to direct the spirits. Ven thought about telling her to remember to rest, but decided she wouldn't appreciate his mothering. He followed Hamon out of the gardens.

Hamon led the way to the palace morgue. Created out of stone, the morgue was tucked behind the treasure pavilion. It had been shrouded in vines so it would blend in with the trees, but the walls themselves were the kind of rock found deep within the ground. Legend said that an ancient queen had summoned it from the bowels of the earth and it had risen, a hollow chamber with a funeral bier inside, after the death of her husband. She'd housed his body inside for forty-one days, until she could lay his killer beside him. Only then did she allow him to be buried. The chamber still stank of ancient death. Ven wasn't fond of it.

Two guards nodded to them as they passed, but Hamon didn't even seem to see them. His hands were shaking as he opened the door. "Brace yourself." He handed Ven a face mask of soft cotton and strapped one on his own face.

Inside, Ven's eyes immediately watered. The chamber reeked of incense and thick, heavy flowery smells that were trying—and failing—to cover the smell of decaying flesh and old, sour blood. This wasn't ancient death; this was new.

On the tables were bodies. All were uncovered. All were young women—girls, in truth—in varying states of decay. Ven carefully shoved all his emotions away and ignored the part of him that wanted to march out the door and seal it behind him. "You have been digging up corpses," he said evenly.

"It was my mother's idea." Hamon held up a hand to forestall any response. "I know I shouldn't listen to her ideas, but in this case . . . She thought there was a possibility that the poisoner experimented on other victims before attempting to kill the queen. Other victims whose deaths could easily be attributed to another cause. If the poisoner killed before, there might be a clue to his or her identity . . . or a clue to the poison itself."

"Did you find any such clues?" Ven asked.

"Unfortunately no. And in the process of looking at these recent deaths, I discovered something unsettling."

Ven thought that everything about examining dead bodies was unsettling. There were six total. Most had been ripped open—a rib cage exposed, a leg that looked as if it had been savaged, flesh peeled back . . . "These weren't killed by poison. They were killed by spirits." He'd seen this kind of damage far too often to doubt it.

"Yes, I know. Except . . . not." Hamon moved between the bodies. "This one, she died of blunt trauma to the head. And this, her throat was slit. Here, three wounds beneath her rib cage. Another, the back." He beckoned to Ven to come closer to one, one of the freshest.

Ven glanced at her face and then wished he hadn't—he knew this one, the redheaded girl he'd considered at the academy, the one whom Piriandra had chosen. Beilena. He swore and then looked at the other faces. He recognized another—Esiella, Havtru's candidate.

"Are they all candidates?" Ven asked.

"Forget what you're thinking, who they were, what could have or should have happened. Just look here, at this wound. Look at the precision of it, the cleanness of the slice . . . And if you look inside"—pulling on gloves, Hamon spread open Beilena's wound, to show the sliced muscles and bone—"see how it's cut, with a twist? And the depth of it? It nicked the bone. See that?"

Ven was not a doctor. He had seen—and caused—his share of violence. But Hamon casually peeling back the skin of dead girls . . . "So if I were to be sick . . . ?"

"Bucket is under the table. Don't think of them as people. Think of them as puzzles. And tell me: ignoring the circumstances in which they were found, ignoring what you know of who they were and what they were doing, what made this cut?"

"Knife," he said instantly.

"How are you sure?"

He pointed. "The slice on the bone."

"Could have been a claw. Or a tooth."

"It's not a bite," Ven said. "It's only one slice."

"Single claw? Single talon?" Hamon was watching him intently. Ven felt as if he were taking an exam. He bent over the body, trying to focus only on the wound, not on the girl's face, not on the thought of how young she was or how scared she must have been. *I know wounds like this*, Ven thought. *I've made wounds like this.*

"Every spirit I have ever seen attacks to rip apart, not stab—that's their instinct, to destroy," Ven said. "They use claws and teeth. There should be multiple wounds, not a single slice. There's no question this was a knife." And the spirits don't use knives. Ven looked up at Hamon. "You think . . ."

"This is the wound that killed her. All the other wounds, including the icicles that supposedly stabbed her throat, were inflicted *after* death."

"She was stabbed and then . . ." Left for the spirits? Given to them? Mutilated to look as if it were spirits? He straightened and looked at the other bodies. "What about the others?"

"Some were clearly killed by spirits. But not all." He led Ven around the morgue, pointing out the injuries. In the worst, the candidate had her extremities frozen—an ice spirit—but it was again a knife thrust that had killed her. It was hard to see, Hamon explained, but once he'd known what to look for . . . He showed Ven her wounds, as well as the wounds on three other girls. Finishing, they left the morgue and stripped off their face masks.

Ven sucked in the sweet outside air. He walked away from the morgue toward the treasure pavilion, not looking back.

"Am I right?" Hamon asked.

"Yes," Ven said. "Someone is murdering candidates." *And I have left Naelin alone.* He broke into a run. His feet pounded over the paths, crushing the delicate flowers that grew between them. He vaulted over one of the tree roots and scrambled up another, running along it, leaping over the decorative statues and vines.

He reached the garden—

The wolf rose and trotted over to him. He was wagging his tail. Naelin was standing on top of her new fountain, and the water spirits were swirling around her, casting rain on all the flower beds but nowhere else. Naelin's eyes were closed, and she was smiling, just slightly, only the corners of her lips turned up.

"You guard her," Ven told Bayn. "Every second that I'm not near her, you are." Kneeling down, he looked the wolf directly in the eyes. "Can you understand me?"

The wolf regarded him evenly and then—clearly, deliberately—nodded.

"Thank you," Ven said gravely. Someday he would need to ask Daleina what she knew of the wolf—where he'd come from, why he was so intelligent—but later, once she was well. For now, it was enough that Bayn would do as he asked.

Rising, Ven crossed to Naelin.

She wouldn't be like one of those girls in the morgue. She was powerful and intelligent and fierce . . . As he reached her, she opened her eyes. Seeing him, she smiled. "Aren't I doing well?" she asked. "And yes, I'm fishing for praise. So go ahead, tell me I'm amazing, and I'll blush and deny it, but inwardly I'll agree, because this . . . I never thought I could do this."

He wanted to take her in his arms and tell her she truly was amazing.

But she wasn't finished. "Galling to admit that Renet might have been right. I suppose this means I owe him an apology."

"He still endangered you and your children," Ven pointed out. Her former husband was unworthy of her. But that wasn't the conversation he intended to have. "I need you to be careful—"

"You think I'm not careful enough?"

Out of the corner of his eye, he saw the spirits disperse. Earth spirits dove into the soil, air spirits spiraled up toward the clouds, tree spirits skittered along the branches. He put his hands on her shoulders. "Hear me out, before you decide to be furious at me. You're already careful with spirits. I need you to be careful of humans." And he told her what Hamon had showed him, what he'd seen, leaving out the details. As he talked, he felt her sag.

And then she straightened and looked him in the eye. "All right then. Spirits want to kill me. People want to kill me. Anything else?"

He wanted to kiss her.

But he didn't. Instead, he pulled out one of his knives, the short dagger he kept tucked in his boot, and said, "I'm going to teach you how to survive this."

## CHAPTER 26

For three days, Naelin trained. She worked with Queen Daleina as often as the queen could manage, and with Ven every other waking hour. She learned to stretch her mind to control multiple spirits at once, and she learned to push her body to react to an attack.

"You don't need to know how to kill," Ven had told her. "You need to know how to not be killed. Slight but important distinction." He made her repeat the same maneuvers over and over: how to break a hold, how to dodge a knife thrust, how to twist so that a knife would only hit something nonvital. "Your mind doesn't need to memorize this; your body does." And so she practiced, because he'd described the murdered girls in enough detail that she didn't need to hear any more.

He also insisted she allow the wolf Bayn to come with her everywhere at all times, which was fine, albeit a little awkward in the bathroom. He usually politely faced the wall. But it was a plus when she had a free moment to visit her children. Llor would forgive any absence in exchange for the chance to play with the "doggie," and even Erian couldn't stay angry when Bayn licked her cheek.

So on the night of the third day, when Ven told her she was done, she looked around Queen Fara's old chambers for Bayn. He was sitting by the hearth, chewing on the thigh bone of a deer. "Ready to have a small child get sticky fingers in your fur?"

He thumped his tail and then trotted over to her side.

"I'll walk you there as well," Ven said.

She didn't bother to argue that she was safe in the palace, with all the guards who milled through every corridor and a very large wolf by her side. A little paranoia was a fine thing. Admirable, even. She shot him a look as they walked down the spiral stairs in the center of the palace tree. He was scowling beneath his beard, with his forehead crinkled and eyes fierce. "You look under stress," she said, even though it was an understatement. "Are you getting enough sleep?"

He quit scowling. "Are you trying to mother me?"

"The proper word is 'nag.' I am trying to nag you into taking care of yourself, not just taking care of me. I'm fine." In truth, she felt as if she'd been rolled down a set of stairs and then stomped on, but that didn't bear mentioning. She also had a headache that pounded as if she had tiny drummers trapped inside her skull.

"I can handle it."

"Of course you can. Until you collapse from exhaustion and malnourishment. Look at it this way: I only nag because I care."

He stopped for a moment midstep and looked as if he wanted to say something, but then he continued down the stairs without speaking. She thought about asking him if there had been any progress in investigating the murders, or any progress in the search for the poisoner, but if there had been, he wouldn't look so intense. She wasn't sure she'd ever had anyone care for her well-being so much. She had to remind herself it was only because he wanted her to be the heir. He valued her for what she could do, not who she was. Not unlike Renet.

She was still thinking about her former husband when she walked through the door to her and her children's chambers—and he was there.

Renet.

Sitting on a couch, with Erian and Llor on either side of him.

Looking recently washed, with wet tousled hair, velvet clothes that weren't his, and a sheepish expression that was one hundred percent his.

Naelin stopped so abruptly in the doorway that Bayn's snout

bumped against the back of her thighs. The wolf poked his head around her.

"Doggie!" Llor cried, and shot off the couch.

She felt Ven's hand on her shoulder and his breath on her neck as he murmured in her ear, "Do you want me to stay or go?"

She liked that he asked. "Stay, please," she murmured back, and stepped inside.

Bayn pushed past her and bounded over to Llor. Llor threw his arms around the wolf's neck. "Don't do that, Llor," Erian said. "He's been eating. You'll get blood on your shirt, and Mama doesn't have time to wash it out."

"I'll take care of it, Erian," Renet said. "I can clean stains. Contrary to popular opinion, I'm not useless." He smiled to soften the words, as if he could charm his way back into her life.

Naelin felt as if her head were swimming. She wished she could force her headache away. She did *not* have the energy left to deal with this. "The palace has its own laundry. You know that, Erian. And Renet, you've never scrubbed a stain out in your life. But that is far less relevant than the question: *What are you doing here?*"

Llor's eyes went wide. "Uh-oh, Mama's mad."

*Yes*, she wanted to say. *I am.* She was about a half second away from screaming, or collapsing into a pile and weeping. She did *not* need this. She did *not* want this. She did *not* deserve this. Clenching and unclenching her hands, she tried to calm her breathing, to speak calmly, to not burst into tears or throw things or walk out the door or scream. "Renet, answer please."

"You need me here," Renet said. "The children need me. They said so."

"Father came fast!" Llor said. "Isn't that great, Mama?" His face was shining, as if he could convince her this was a wonderful thing if only he said it cheerfully enough. Or maybe he was simply happy about it. His father was here. Hooray.

"Truthfully I was halfway here already," he said, using his sheepish expression again.

"Llor, Erian . . ." She was about to tell them to go into the other room, so she could talk to Renet without them, but she caught the look on Erian's face. Erian was digging her toe into the wood floor and looking everywhere but at Naelin. "Erian?"

"Captain Alet said we needed someone to watch us while you're training," Erian said in a rush, "and I'm too old for a governess, and we didn't want some guard that we don't know. Father said he missed us and he's really, really sorry."

Renet rose, and she knew that look on his face: the penitent puppy-dog look that he'd perfected years ago. It used to make her laugh and forgive whatever ridiculous thing he'd done. He'd swear never to do it again, and she'd kiss him and he'd remember to come home when he said he would instead of lingering out in the woods, or take the rotten food far from the house instead of dumping it at the base of the tree, or fetch Llor from school at the correct time . . . *I shouldn't have had to tell him any of that,* she thought. She thought of how she used to nag him, as if she were his mother, as if she had three children instead of two. She thought of how she used to see his absentmindedness, his wild ideas, his enthusiasm for ridiculous risks as charming or even exciting. But she couldn't see it that way anymore.

He hadn't changed.

She'd changed.

"Mama, can he stay?" Erian asked.

"I am truly sorry," Renet said. "I– Can we talk alone?" He bowed to Champion Ven. "Forgive me, great sir, but my wife–"

"Former wife," Ven corrected. "She left you, spoken and witnessed."

"I am hoping she will reconsider that," Renet said.

Erian moved to Renet's side and took his hand. "We want to be a family again, Mama."

Naelin felt as if she'd been stabbed by one of Ven's knives. All three of them were looking at her with eager eyes: Erian, Llor, and Renet. It would be so very easy to say yes. She closed her eyes. She'd been fighting spirits all day, fighting her own body, fighting fate. She didn't want to fight her family too. "Renet . . ."

"I swear I will never endanger the children again," Renet said. "I know what I did was wrong. I was wrong. I didn't think about consequences. Or at least not about bad consequences. I knew you'd protect them. I thought they'd be fine. I'm an optimist—you know that. I believed everything would work out, if I could just make you see how incredible you are—"

"Stop. Just stop." The ache in her head pounded harder. She squeezed her eyes and tried to make it recede so she could think and react in a reasonable way. She felt Ven's hand, still on her shoulder, and she felt Bayn press against her side, his warm, furry body holding her up, if she needed it to.

"They're my children too," Renet said, "and I love them."

If she opened her eyes, she knew what she'd see: Renet, with his arms around Erian and Llor, the picture of the perfect father. And he *was* a good father to them, mostly. He loved them. Even if he was occasionally scatterbrained and reckless, he did love them. And they adored him. She knew if she opened her eyes, she'd see hope burning bright in her children's eyes. They were waiting for her to say she forgave him, as she always did.

"I'll be the perfect husband," Renet said. "Give me a chance, Naelin. Please. See, look at me, begging in front of the Queen's Champion, sacrificing my pride. I will dote on you, adore you, worship you, just give me another chance. I swear I'll listen to you. I'll respect your wishes. I'll do anything you want me to do."

She didn't answer. Couldn't answer. Couldn't think. "I didn't want you to come. I told you not to, and you came anyway. How is that respecting my wishes?"

"The children needed me." He sounded wounded, and her instinct was to heal, to soothe, to fix, as she always did.

She opened her eyes, and the picture was exactly as she'd imagined: Renet with his arms around the children, Erian with tears on her cheeks, Llor with a hopeful smile. And then Erian broke away from Renet and ran to her. Naelin instinctively dropped down on one knee, and Erian launched herself into Naelin's arms. She buried her face in her mother's neck. Naelin inhaled the sweet smell of her hair, the faint hint of honeysuckle and lavender. Erian still fit so neatly into her arms. Naelin wondered how much longer that would be true. Erian grew more every year, and soon she wouldn't want her mother's comfort like this. "I wrote him," Erian said in her ear. "I'm sorry, Mama. I asked him to come."

Naelin hugged Erian tighter. *This* she could forgive, easily. "It's all right, baby. I understand." She'd been leaving them alone while she trained. They had to be lonely and scared. She hadn't known how to fix that, so Erian had found her own solution. In a way, it was clever. Pulling back, Naelin forced herself to smile. "Just because things have changed between your father and me, it does not mean they've changed between you and me or between your father and you. I love you, and he loves you, and that will never change."

"Naelin?" Renet's voice was hesitant. "What are you saying?"

"You know what I'm saying, Renet." Naelin stood, her arm still around her daughter. "You may stay. Be father to our children. I will ask the palace caretakers to find you quarters nearby." Or maybe not so nearby. Another level. Another tree. Another country.

"But not here, with you?"

"That's right," she said.

Renet's face darkened. "Is it because of him?" He pointed at Ven.

Naelin felt her jaw drop open. Did he mean . . . He was accusing . . . She shook her head as if to knock his reaction into something that made sense. Ven had nothing to do with her and Renet's failed marriage—their love had died years before the champion ever heard of East Everdale. "It's because of you and me, and if you can't see that . . ." She trailed off before she said something she'd regret in front of the children. He was still their father. She didn't have the right to tear him apart in front of them, though she wanted to. She had the urge to send him to the corner, to think about what he'd said, like he was a five-year-old. Instead, she turned and crossed to the bell pull. She yanked on it, harder than necessary.

Thankfully, she didn't have to wait long for a caretaker to come. "This man has had a long journey and is almost certainly hungry. Could you please take him to the kitchens and then arrange for a bedchamber to be prepared for him"—she almost said near theirs but then changed her mind—"in the main tower? Just above the kitchens?"

"Of course." The caretaker bowed.

To Renet, she said, "I begin training at dawn. You may return then to spend time with the children."

"Naelin, this is ridiculous," Renet said. "You're my wife, and they're my children. And I don't need your permission to spend time with—"

Ven cut in. "Candidate Naelin is here by express invitation of the Crown. You are not. If your presence here distracts Candidate Naelin from her training in any way, you will be asked to leave."

Llor began to cry.

Naelin closed her eyes again. She wanted to sag into a heap on the floor. But she didn't. She held herself upright and her expression firm until Renet left with the caretaker. Even then she didn't allow herself to collapse. She gathered her children into her arms as the door clanged shut behind him. "Everything will be all right," she promised them.

"You don't know that," Erian said, pulling away from her. "At least this way we won't be alone when you're killed." She ran into the bedchamber and slammed the door behind her.

Llor sobbed louder.

Hugging him, Naelin tried to scoop him up, but her muscles were tired and shaking, and he was a solid six-year-old boy. Coming around her, Ven picked him up and carried him with her into the bathroom. There, Ven helped her dry Llor's tears and prepare him for bed, washing him, brushing his teeth, dressing him in a nightshirt. Together, they tucked him in, and Naelin kissed his forehead. "Don't die, Mama," Llor begged sleepily.

"I won't," she said, and hoped she wasn't lying.

Trotting in, the wolf licked the tip of Llor's nose, and Llor giggled. He then closed his eyelids. Naelin watched him for a moment longer until he was breathing evenly. She then went into her bedchamber, where Erian had thrown herself on Naelin's bed.

"You're mad at me," Erian said, "but I'm not sorry."

"I *am* sorry," Naelin said, and kissed Erian's forehead. "And I'm not mad at you. I'm mad at the situation. I'm mad that I have to be apart from you for even a second. I'm mad that things change.

But I'm *not* mad at you. And even if I were, you know what? I'd still love you."

"But you don't love Father anymore."

Naelin sighed. "People change."

"What if *I* change, and you decide you don't love me anymore?"

She did *not* want to have this conversation right now. She silently cursed Renet for forcing her to. "How about I promise?"

"You married Father. Didn't you promise him then?"

She had a point. Naelin was supposed to always love him. They'd built a life together. They'd had a home. They'd raised children. They were supposed to grow old together. If she could just forgive him for this one mistake . . . Except it wasn't one mistake. It was the culmination of every mistake. It was the fact that he'd never grown up, never taken responsibility, never . . . But Erian was waiting for her answer. "That's different."

"Why?"

"Because he also made promises to me . . . and he didn't keep them. I loved him, and he thought that meant that he had no responsibilities, that I would mother him and you, that I'd fix his problems, correct his mistakes, and keep us all safe no matter what whim struck him . . . and that almost cost me you and Llor. And I won't let that happen. I *promise*."

Erian relaxed. She padded to the room where she and Llor slept, and let Naelin tuck her in and kiss her forehead. She even smiled at Ven and gave Bayn a pat on the head. Tiptoeing out with Ven and Bayn, Naelin shut the door on the children.

"Are you all right?" Ven asked her.

"I owe you an apology for all the family drama," Naelin said. "I know it's not the role of a champion." She tried to summon up a smile, but it required too much energy. She sank onto the couch.

"But it *is* the role of a friend." He sat beside her.

"Aw, that's sweet. You know, you look deadly, but you are a sweet kitten inside." Without thinking about it, Naelin leaned against him, resting her cheek on his shoulder. After a moment, he put his arm around her shoulders, and she was suddenly conscious of how close they were. They'd been close before, during training, especially when he was teaching her how to break holds and dodge knives, but that was entirely different, when Renet's accusation still hung in the air. She felt his chest rise and fall with each breath, and she breathed in the smell of him: a mix of leather and sweat and pine needles. She could move away. Stand up, say good night, fall asleep in her own bed. But this . . . was nice.

She fell asleep like that, head resting on his shoulder, his arm around her—safe.

Two more days of training.

Naelin spent the mornings with Queen Daleina and the afternoons with Ven. Throughout, the wolf Bayn stuck with her. She took to requesting raw meat with every meal, so that she could feed him too. "You should be out hunting," she told him. "You're a wolf. It's the wolfly thing to do."

He merely looked at her with his yellow wolf eyes and then lay down in the hearth in the late Queen Fara's chambers.

"He likes you," Ven said.

"He likes the meat."

"That too." Coming up behind her, Ven put one hand on Naelin's wrist. "Now, what do you do if I grab you, spin you, and try to stab you?" He pulled her around, and she spun to face him. His other hand was formed into a fist, as if he held a knife. She felt his fist against her stomach. If it had been a real knife, she'd already be dead.

It wasn't a knife, though, and she was aware of how close he was, holding her pressed against him. It was damn distracting. She twisted away and jabbed upward with her elbow. She hit hard enough that he loosened his grip.

"Faster. You won't have time to think about your reactions. It has to be instinctual." This time, when he spun her, she twisted and jabbed at the same time. "Good. Again."

They repeated the maneuver over and over, until she was sweating and hungry and thoroughly done with it. As he spun her for the hundredth time, she called an air spirit—a small one—

with her mind. She twisted—and the air spirit swept his feet out from under him.

He thudded down backward.

The air spirit perched on the arm of the couch and giggled. It was a tiny spirit, comprised of mainly white and brown feathers. Its giggle was shrill, like the sound of glass breaking.

Naelin sent the spirit away and grinned at Ven. "Got you."

"Clever." He held out his hand. She took it and pulled. He sprang up. He wasn't winded at all, damn him. He looked like he could keep doing this for hours.

"I need to rest," she told him.

"An attack could come at any time." He spun her again. But this time, she didn't move. She let him hold her, close against him. Tilting her head, she studied his face. It was the beard that made him look so stern. You couldn't see the gentleness in his lips. His eyes weren't stern. He looked worried, and she knew for a fact that he spent most of his waking hours worrying about either her or Daleina.

"It's a shame you aren't a father," she said.

"Sorry?"

"You'd love your children with all your heart."

"I'm not cut out for parenthood. It doesn't suit my lifestyle. And why are we talking about this? Are you delaying so you don't have to practice anymore?"

"Yes. I'm tired. I told you, I need to rest."

"Then rest." He released her, and she felt suddenly cold as a breeze sliced between them. The windows to the balcony were open. He crossed to them and shut them, as if he'd seen her shiver. He probably had. He watched her closely, she knew. *Because he's evaluating me*, she reminded herself. *Nothing more.* She knew Queen Daleina was relying on him to say when Naelin was ready for the trials.

"What would you be if you weren't a champion?" she asked.

"You keep trying to get to know me, as if I were complicated. But I'm not. I knew at a young age that it was my responsibility to carry on the family tradition. That was my goal. I never wavered."

"You never wanted an ordinary life? A house, a wife, a family?"

"That was never my destiny."

She snorted. She didn't believe in destiny. She believed in random chance that you pushed and pulled at to give you a life you could live with. "You never fell in love?"

He looked away. "Once."

"What happened?" As soon as she asked, she thought maybe she shouldn't push. "You don't need to answer that. We can train more." Naelin stepped back closer to him. She'd jab and twist, or whatever she needed to do.

"She changed. And then she died."

Naelin laid a hand on his arm. "I'm sorry."

"That too is the destiny of champions: to love people who die."

She wanted to say something sympathetic. She knew that was what the situation called for, but he was sounding ridiculously melodramatic. "At the risk of sounding insensitive, everyone dies, so by definition, everyone loves people who die. The fact that your love died doesn't make you a brooding hero out of a tale. Actually, the fact that you're both brooding and a hero is what makes you one, but that's not what I'm trying to say. I mean . . . I don't know what I mean. Except that you don't need to be so afraid. I'm not planning on dying."

"Good," he said.

And this time, when he spun her around, she again didn't twist away. Instead, this time, she kissed him. He kissed her back.

## CHAPTER 27

Daleina leaned back against her throne and rubbed her temples. She'd already discarded her crown—it wasn't as if anyone was likely to forget she was queen—but her head still ached. Lack of sleep, Hamon had told her. Also stress. *It's not as if I can prevent that.* "You are dancing around something, and I don't like it," she informed her chancellors.

Chancellor Isolek fidgeted uncomfortably in his high-back chair. "It is only that we take no pleasure in bringing you this news."

"You don't want to say 'I told you so'?" Daleina guessed.

"Precisely," Chancellor Quisala said. She looked smaller, as if she'd shrunk during the past few weeks. Her wrinkles had folded in on themselves until her skin looked more like tree bark. Leaning across the table, she placed markers on the map of Aratay. Chancellor Isolek jumped forward and took the markers for her, positioning them along the border with Semo, clustered in the northeast. Chancellor Quisala sagged back into her chair for a moment and then fixed her posture—Daleina thought about ordering the woman to sleep more, but that was as likely to be effective as Hamon telling Daleina to rest. Both of them had better things to do.

"Over the last few days, we've seen significant movement here"—Isolek pointed at the map—"and here, in the northeast. Each marker denotes a squadron. That puts three squadrons just

over the border in Nimoc, with another positioned due north of
Ogdare and another northeast of North Garat, leaving only one
behind north of Birchen."

"It's undeniable," Quisala said. "This is no training exercise."

*Oh, Merecot, why are you doing this?* Daleina thought. "We
can send more envoys—"

"Your Majesty . . ." Isolek's voice was gentle. "We believe the
time has come to admit that diplomacy has failed."

"Queen Merecot is invading," Quisala said, thumping her
frail fist on the table, "and we must respond. It may be too late
already. She will sweep across the northern border—the guards
there are not plentiful enough to repel an army of this size. She
could reach Mittriel quickly."

"Here is where we disagree, Your Majesty," Isolek said. "She
won't come from the north; she'll come from the northeast. She
does not have enough soldiers to take Mittriel, even if she passes
the border towns successfully."

"Which she will," Quisala put in, bitterness thick in her voice.
"We left those woefully undefended." She then shot a glance at
Daleina. "For a reason. I understand that now."

Daleina nodded to show she was not angered, at least not at
her advisers.

"She may be positioned to attack the capital, but not with a
large enough army to claim it," Isolek said. "Our spies have not
reported any increase in troops to the north. We believe there is
an alternate explanation—that she may be trying to bite off a corner of Aratay, absorb it into Semo and expand her borders, rather
than attempting a full-scale invasion. Look at the mass of troops
near Ogdare and North Garat!" Isolek tapped the map. "We must
make a choice as to where to send our soldiers: to the northeast to
prevent an incursion there, or north to defend Mittriel. Frankly,
I think the choice is clear: northeast. It's the only place she has
enough soldiers to form a true threat."

"But that risks leaving Mittriel exposed!" Quisala said. "And
the border towns will surely be overrun if you are wrong. Birchen
will be destroyed."

"Look at the numbers, Quisala!" Isolek jabbed at the map so

hard that he dented it. "She has no hope of capturing Mittriel. Clearly the threat is in the northeast. That's where we send soldiers . . . assuming that we can spare them at all. Your Majesty . . ."

With Candidate Naelin in the palace, Daleina was less worried about the spirits attacking the capital if and when she had another blackout. She *was* worried about that squadron north of Mittriel. Yes, it was only one squadron, but Chancellor Quisala was correct: if Daleina sent all the guards to the northeast, it exposed the capital, and if Daleina fell in battle before an heir was named and Merecot were able to take Mittriel . . . she could take it all. "It depends on whether she wants to annex a small portion of Aratay or wants the entire country," she mused.

"Your Majesty, you know her best," Quisala said, spreading her hands.

*She wants it all*, Daleina thought. Merecot was nothing if not ambitious. Leaning over the map, Daleina studied it again. A lot of forest lay between the capital and the northern border, but Daleina knew the shape of the land. She'd felt it as she sank herself into the spirits. She'd been with them as they soared over. The birches due north were easy to travel through, a direct line to Mittriel. "Northeast is a decoy. She wants us to send troops there to leave Mittriel exposed. It's a trap."

Quisala slapped the table. "Exactly as I said!"

"But she doesn't have enough troops to take Mittriel," Isolek protested. "There's plenty of forest between the border and the capital and plenty of people who will rise to defend their homes. With one squadron, she can't do it."

Daleina closed her eyes, not wanting to say it but knowing it needed to be said. "She'll use spirits."

Both Quisala and Isolek protested. No queen would *ever* use spirits against humans. It was not done. It violated everything a queen was sworn to do.

Daleina knew for a fact that didn't stop all queens—Queen Fara hadn't hesitated to use spirits against humans.

Daleina thought of Sata and of Mari, who had been crushed by six tree spirits on the late queen's orders. When they'd poisoned the queen, Fara had been bargaining with a spirit to exchange the lives of villagers for more power and control. Merecot might not be doing the same, but she wouldn't hesitate to order the spirits to do whatever she felt had to be done.

"Send the troops north. We protect Mittriel." If Queen Merecot took the capital before an heir was ready, she could claim all of Aratay. They had to keep Merecot's people out of Mittriel, away from the throne.

"But the northeast . . . it will be overrun."

"Can we protect both?"

Isolek studied the map. "No. You have to choose. If you're wrong, all of our troops will be out of position, twiddling their thumbs while Queen Merecot's army bites off the northeast."

"And if I'm right?"

"All of our troops will be in the right position, fighting spirits, while Queen Merecot's army still takes the northeast." Chancellor Isolek slumped back in his chair. "You paint a grim picture, Your Majesty. A choice that is no choice."

How ambitious was Merecot? Would she really use spirits to attack the capital?

Very. And yes.

There had to be a way to protect all her people. She tapped the table. If she weren't afraid of another false death, she could use spirits to defend the capital. Except she'd never been as strong as Merecot. Nowhere near.

But Naelin was. Or she would be, if she were queen.

All Daleina had to do was abdicate and let Naelin take the crown. She could then send the troops to the northeast to fight the army, and Naelin could defend Mittriel from Merecot's spirits.

Question was: was Naelin ready to be queen?

And was Daleina ready to die?

THE DRUMS HAD ANNOUNCED IT: THE TRIALS WOULD BE HELD AT dawn.

Naelin ate dinner with Erian and Llor (without Renet) in their chambers. Or at least she pushed food around her plate with her fork. She couldn't manage to swallow more than a few bites. While the children were engrossed in their own meals, Naelin sneaked a slab of steak from her plate and fed it to Bayn under the table.

"I beat Erian in miyan today," Llor announced.

"That's wonderful," Naelin told him.

Erian whispered in Naelin's ear. "I let him win."

Naelin patted Erian on the shoulder to say that of course she did, it was the right thing, and don't say that where Llor could overhear.

"You did *not* let me win," Llor said.

"You weren't meant to hear that. I was whispering!"

"I won fair and square, because I'm smart," Llor said.

Erian scowled at him. "If you're so smart, how come you dumped your socks into pickle juice? I had to tell the cooks that you'd ruined their batch."

He shrugged. "I was experimenting. When I grow up, I'm going to be a scientist like Healer Hamon. But not with people, because people's inside stuff is icky. And you have to work with a lot of poop."

"Llor!"

"Healer Hamon said so. It was part of his training. He had to learn all about how bodies work, and that includes—"

"Don't say 'poop' again," Erian warned.

"*You* just said it."

Naelin smiled at both of them. It wasn't even a forced smile. She loved them both so much that she felt as if her heart were going to burst out of her chest. Tears pricked her eyes.

"Mama has a big day tomorrow," Erian said. "You should be on extra-good behavior."

"It's all right." Reaching across the table, Naelin took both their hands. "Be on whatever behavior you want. Be yourselves. Who you are is wonderful, exactly as you are. Always remember that." She squeezed their hands.

Now Erian looked on the verge of crying.

"Don't worry about me," Naelin told her. "I've been trained by the best champion Aratay has ever had *and* by the queen herself. Everything is going to be fine." *I even almost believe that,* she thought.

After dinner, she tucked them in to her bed—after she was done making sure everything was ready, she planned to crawl in with them. But she couldn't sleep just yet. Her mind was buzzing too loudly to fall asleep. She'd exercise, tire herself out, and then sleep.

Clearing the furniture to the side, she began a few of the stretches that Ven had taught her. She was stronger than she used to be—physically stronger, not just mentally. She had muscles on her arms that hadn't been there before, and she could fold herself in half to touch her toes without any problem.

Not that the spirits would be impressed by that.

She heard a thump from the balcony. *Odd,* she thought. Stretching her mind, she felt for nearby spirits. There were a few tree spirits above her, clinging to the outside of the palace tree, and a few fire spirits in the hallway, dancing in the lanterns, but none were on the balcony.

She went to check—and saw her friend. "Captain Alet!"

Captain Alet was crouched on the balcony, as if she'd dropped there from above. As she straightened, she said, "Sorry to drop in on you so literally. Champion Ven wanted me to check on you. Tomorrow's an important day, and you know how paranoid he is. Since there are already guards in the hallway, I thought I'd secure this exit."

Going out onto the balcony, Naelin looked down. There were a few flagpoles that jutted out from the outer wall, plus windows, but they were all far apart. The night wind whipped around them, fluttering Naelin's skirts. "You climbed up?"

"Down, actually." Alet pointed up toward another balcony.

"You could have broken your legs. Or neck."

"I've had plenty of practice," Alet said. She shifted, and Naelin thought she seemed nervous . . . *Tomorrow is important to everyone in Aratay,* Naelin thought. "You're not the only one who trains all the time. Speaking of which . . . are you ready for tomorrow?"

That was the key question. "I'd like another few days. Or years. Or a lifetime. But yes, I suppose I am ready. Ven thinks I am, or else he's just saying that to keep me calm." She didn't think he could, or would, lie to her, but she also knew he desperately wanted her to be ready. *He might be seeing only what he wants to see*, she thought.

"You can still refuse," Alet said. "There's no dishonor in that. Plenty of the other candidates have already refused. They know they aren't ready, and Queen Daleina was happy to approve their decision. She wants to have some potential heirs in waiting. You could easily sit out these trials, let someone else be heir, and wait until you're needed."

She wished she could. But from what Ven had told her, there was no one else. None of the other candidates were close to ready, though several planned to try. "I'm needed now. Apparently, Renet was right: I'm powerful. You know, Erian told me you were going to come talk to me days ago. I'd expected you before now."

"I had other things to take care of. And . . . well, I was hoping I wouldn't have to have this conversation. I was hoping you'd come to the right decision on your own."

Naelin was confused. "What?"

"Naelin, please walk away from this. You can still have everything you want: your family safe. I can help you. I'll get you out of the palace. Right now! You can run away, with Erian and Llor. Ven won't even know. You can go far, far away. Even leave Aratay. You can start a new life, in the mountains of Semo. You'd be safe."

Naelin shook her head, even more confused. "And what would happen to Aratay if I left?"

"It will fall to Semo. Queen Merecot will take care of the people like they're her own. You don't have to do this. It doesn't need to be your responsibility. There's another choice."

Naelin couldn't believe Alet was saying this—abandon Aratay!

"You think if you refuse, then the spirits will kill everyone, but it won't happen that way. Merecot won't let it. She's poised to save Aratay. As soon as Queen Daleina falls—"

"You mean dies." She didn't want to hear this. It was crazy. "How can you say that?"

"She is going to die no matter what I say or what I feel or what

I want," Alet said. "Either she abdicates and the spirits kill her, or she stays queen and the False Death kills her. I'm telling you that the second option won't be the disaster that you think it will."

"But . . . You're talking about a war. An invasion!" She couldn't believe Alet was saying this. Alet was a royal guardswoman! Sworn to the Crown!

"It won't be a war if no one fights back," Alet said. *She's serious*, Naelin thought. "Please, Naelin. You could flee with your children. Keep them safe, while knowing that the people of Aratay will be cared for. It's everything you ever wanted. You've trained enough to keep your family safe from spirits. Take that knowledge and run."

Naelin shook her head. She pictured Ven and the young queen. "If I become queen, I can protect Daleina. I can keep the spirits from hurting her until a cure can be found. She might not have to die. And Ven . . . If I leave and if Semo invades, he'll fight. You know he will. You'll have to fight too." Unless Alet planned to run too. *No, she wouldn't. And I don't want to talk about this anymore.* Naelin turned to go back inside. "I can't be having this conversation right now."

From within the chambers, Bayn howled.

She felt Alet grab her arm and spin her—

—and Naelin reacted instinctively, as she'd been trained: she twisted and jabbed upward. Deflected, the knife slid into Naelin's side, slicing her skin but missing her organs. Even as she did, the wolf leaped through the archway and slammed into Alet.

Stumbling backward and clutching her side, Naelin called for the spirits.

They swarmed the balcony. Tree spirits skittered over the palace wall. Fire spirits burst through the chimney and out. Water spirits swept toward them in a wave of rain. Shrieking, they converged on Alet. The guardswoman screamed.

*Stop!* Naelin ordered. *Hold her!*

The tree spirits bound her wrists and her ankles with vines. Bark closed over her stomach, securing her to the balcony. *Go,* she ordered them. She pushed them back with her mind but kept them close.

She saw Alet's face. It had been burned, badly. The fire spirits had seared her cheek. One eye was sealed shut. Her hair smoked. Naelin had been slow to stop the spirits—too slow. She smelled the stench of burnt flesh.

"Mama?" she heard behind her. Erian.

"Go back to my room," she ordered. "Now. Lock the door. Lock the windows."

Erian hesitated. "Captain—"

"Now!" And Erian retreated. She heard the lock click, and turned her attention back to Alet. Bayn stood over the captain. His teeth were bared. Naelin noticed that Alet was bleeding around the bark that pinned her down. Red leaked onto the balcony, spreading into a pool. *She's hurt beyond the burn*, Naelin thought.

*Get Hamon*, she ordered the air spirits. *And bring Ven. Now!*

She knelt next to the woman she'd thought was her friend and waited.

## CHAPTER 28

Ven left Daleina's throne room feeling as if he wanted to punch something. He hated Daleina's plan and had expressed his views clearly, logically, and with minimal shouting. Her plan *might* save the northeast and Mittriel, or it might kill both Daleina and Naelin and not save anyone. She was trying to do it all and be the hero, but there was no good option here.

He stalked through the corridors of the palace.

She'd told him she planned to cancel the trials. At dawn, she'd announce that she was declaring Naelin her heir. There were no other candidates who were remotely ready, and Daleina claimed Naelin had been tested enough with what she'd endured already. Instead of facing the trials, Naelin would face the Queen's Grove and the coronation ceremony, alone.

And Her Royal Majesty had left it to Ven to inform Naelin.

Bad, bad idea.

All of it.

Naelin was going to hate this. *He* hated this. She should have the trials so she could test herself before she faced the minds of every spirit in Aratay. She shouldn't have to bear this responsibility so soon. And Daleina shouldn't give up so fast. Hamon and his mother were still working to find a cure! Investigators were still searching for the poisoner! According to Daleina, Alet hadn't yet cleared all the champions. In the meantime, three more candidates had died—killed by spirits, they'd told the public, but

Hamon and Ven were convinced it was an assassin. They'd had no progress on that investigation front either.

They needed more time!

He heard a whoosh of wind and had a sword out before he was finished turning around. Three air spirits were diving for them. *Daleina!* She'd lost control! She'd—

But there was no screaming.

He tipped the sword up at the last moment, and the air spirits flew beneath him, sweeping him off his feet. He braced, expecting to feel their teeth and claws . . . but the spirits cradled him, flying him fast—faster than he could run, as fast as the wind, up the stairs, out the window, and then straight up the side of the palace tree. He kept a grip on his sword.

They dumped him onto a balcony.

He absorbed the scene: Naelin, slumped against the balcony railing, holding her side. Blood stained her fingers. Alet, pinned to the ground by roots and vines. Half her face was burnt, and a pool of blood lay beneath her.

He felt his heart lurch. He clamped it down fast.

Sword ready, he scanned the area, looking for their attacker.

A half second later, the air spirits deposited Hamon next to Ven. The healer hurried to Naelin's side. Naelin—brave, selfless Naelin—shook her head. "No, see to Alet."

"You're the one who must live," Hamon said.

"Deflected it. Just a scratch."

"I'll decide that." Hamon forced her to lift her hand, and he applied pressure. Kneeling beside him, Ven saw she was right: it was a shallow cut. A knife cut. *She'll live,* he thought—and the relief hit him like a tidal wave. "Hold the gauze," Hamon ordered, then turned to Captain Alet.

"What happened?" Ven demanded. He noticed Bayn was standing over Captain Alet, guarding her—*no, guarding Naelin,* he corrected. "Did you lose control?" He wanted that to be the answer. But she'd sent the air spirits to fetch him and Hamon. That wasn't the act of someone who had lost control. And the cut was a single slice, straight as if from a blade, not claws . . . All the clues were there in front of him. He didn't want to add them together.

"Don't be dense," Alet croaked. She coughed and blood spattered. "I tried to kill her. But you . . . you trained her well, when I . . . wasn't looking. You should be . . . proud."

"Don't try to talk," Hamon told her. "You may have a pierced lung. I'll need these roots cleared so I can see to work." He glanced at Naelin, who nodded. Tree spirits began to unwrap the wood.

Ven leveled a sword at Alet's throat. "Move, and you die."

"Dying anyway," Alet whispered.

"Why?" Naelin asked. Her voice was so raw that Ven felt her pain like nails against his skin. He wanted to comfort her. Or skewer Alet. Or both. "I thought . . . You're my friend. I trusted you."

Ven had trusted her too. He'd trusted her with Daleina's life, as well as Naelin's. She'd journeyed with him through the forest, helped him find Naelin, watched Daleina when he couldn't. He'd thought he knew her! He'd considered himself good at knowing when someone was hiding a secret—he remembered he'd even bragged to her about it once, yet he'd never suspected this.

*I should have guessed, somehow*, he thought. He was supposed to be observant, alert to all threats. He'd failed, and Naelin had nearly died.

"I'm sorry, Naelin." Alet tried to turn her head to face Naelin. He saw her wince, and he heard Hamon suck in air as the wood retreated, revealing her wound. It was, to put it bluntly, bad. She'd been torn apart. *Those are spirit wounds.* Naelin must have called on the spirits to defend herself, after she'd deflected the blade. He wanted to tell her he was proud of her.

"Stop!" Hamon cried. "Put the wood back! It's holding her together."

Naelin's lips moved, and the wood began to reknit itself. The spirits chittered to one another. Bark sealed over Alet's torso. Alet coughed again. Her breath sounded like a rattle. Ven knew that sound—he'd heard it too many times to mistake. Alet was dying.

Ven placed a hand on Hamon's shoulder.

Hamon backed away. Squatting by Naelin, he pulled more supplies out of his healer's robe and began to work on Naelin's injury.

Naelin batted at his hand. "Healer Hamon, see to Alet. She's hurt worse . . ."

"Hush," he told her. "I can't help her; I *can* help you."

Ven knelt beside Alet. "Why did you do it?"

"Because she didn't walk away," Alet said. Her voice was a broken whisper. "She could have refused. I thought she'd refuse. I thought I wouldn't have to . . . but then . . ." To Naelin, she said, "If you had said no, I could have left you alone. But you didn't, so I couldn't . . ."

"Ask your questions quickly," Hamon advised Ven as he worked on Naelin.

"Did you kill the other candidates?" Ven asked. The knife thrust. He remembered the bodies—he'd wondered how the killer could have gotten so close.

"Yes."

"Why?" He tried to keep his voice even. He would *not* kill her. She was already dying.

But he sorely wanted to.

He didn't expect her to answer, but she did. She pushed her cracking voice louder, as if she wanted to be sure he heard her, as if she needed him to understand. "So there would be no one strong left when Queen Daleina dies. Merecot . . . needed it done. It will be a peaceful takeover. She will take care of our people."

Ven tried to keep his anger in check. He squeezed the hilt of his sword. He hadn't sheathed it, even though there was no longer any danger. Not from Alet. Never again from her. "Murder is not 'peaceful.'"

"I killed a few to save the many." Alet closed her eyes. "Merecot needs Aratay. In Semo . . . there are too many spirits and not enough land. She must . . . Semo needs . . . She has a plan. Good plan. She won't be stopped. Aratay and Semo, united. There will be peace."

"There *was* peace, before you started murdering people," Ven said. He couldn't keep the harshness from his voice. Didn't want to. "You're a royal guard, Alet! Trusted by your queen!" A dark thought came to him. "Did you try to kill her too? Did you poison Daleina?"

Hamon froze. "Ask her what poison she used. Ask her if she has any left."

Alet's eyes fluttered.

"Keep her alive," Ven ordered.

But Hamon was already at her side. "I can't work miracles. I can extend her life for only a few minutes. Maybe less." He was pulling herbs out of pockets. He found one and, hands shaking, poured it into his hand. He then funneled it into her mouth. "Taste it. There. That's it."

"Helps," Alet said. Her eyelids fluttered again.

Ven knelt closer so he could hear her. He'd failed to suspect Alet. But he wouldn't fail now. "The poison. Where is it?"

"Too late," Alet said. "I am sorry. Tell Daleina . . . I'm sorry."

"Why is it 'too late'?" Hamon asked. "What is the poison?"

Alet didn't answer. She just breathed, shallowly, with a horrible rattle that made Ven want to scream. This woman had all the answers they needed, and she was slipping away.

"Tell us!" Ven demanded. He couldn't threaten her. He had no leverage. And she had no reason to tell him anything—

"Merecot, my sister," Alet whispered. He could barely hear the words. "Naelin, you understand . . . what you do . . . for family. Did it for my sister. Tell Daleina . . . I'm sorry. So very sorry. It was for the best. Greater good . . . You must understand: for the greater good. I am a hero."

*You're a murderer*, Ven wanted to say. He didn't. "Alet, where is the poison?"

"Medicine good. No pain. Thank you. Kindness . . . I didn't expect. You will understand, when Merecot comes. You will forgive. I did what was necessary, for the future of our people."

"Why is it 'too late'?" Hamon asked again. His voice was calm, soothing, as if he were merely tucking Alet into bed. "Tell us, Alet, why is it 'too late'?"

"Because I already told her. About the trials. She will begin at dawn."

"Who's 'she'?" Ven demanded. "Queen Merecot? Begin what?" But he thought he knew the answer. "She's beginning the invasion?"

"Tell my sister: I died a hero."

She didn't speak again.

## CHAPTER 29

*H*ope.
That's what the dead woman was, Hamon thought. As soon as he'd stitched Candidate Naelin's wound—which would heal; she'd managed to keep the blade away from anything vital—he dropped to his knees beside the assassin.

He'd need to search her and search her possessions. She may not have told him what the poison was or if she'd had any remaining, but at least he at last had somewhere to look! He refused to think about the possibility that she had tossed the rest or that there was none left.

"Keep my queen alive," he told Ven. His eyes were only on the body. He began to check her pockets, outer first. "All I need is time."

"Time is one thing we may not have," Ven told him.

"Make time. Find a way to delay." Nothing in the outer pockets. Inner? "Tell her I'm close to a cure. Just give me time!"

"I won't give her false hope," Ven said.

"It's not false! I *will* find her cure. And when I do, she has to be alive to take it. Don't let her be a martyr." He jumped to his feet and grabbed the front of Ven's armor, curling the leather in his fist. "You're her champion. Be it."

Ven's expression didn't change. "Work fast."

"I will." He strode to the door and flung it open. "You and you"—he pointed to two startled guards—"will carry a body and come with me." He wouldn't be working alone. He'd bring the dead woman and all her belongings to his mother. Together, they'd save Daleina.

*OW, OW, OW.* NAELIN PRESSED HER HAND TO HER SIDE. SHE'D been stitched up, but it still hurt like . . . like . . . well, like she'd had a knife stuck in her. Standing, she leaned against the balcony railing while a guard and two caretakers helped Healer Hamon with the body.

The body.

Alet.

*Oh, Alet.*

*If only . . .*

But there wasn't time for thoughts like that. There wasn't time for anything. "I have to get Erian and Llor to safety." She wouldn't be able to watch them. Neither would Ven. Or Alet. *Poor Alet. Her sister . . .* Naelin knew she should feel angry. *Later, maybe.* Later, she could feel whatever she wanted. Anger. Sympathy. Sorrow. Guilt. "Renet has to watch them." She hated saying it, hated that she had to rely on him, hated that he was right in any way.

She began to walk toward the bedroom when Ven stopped her. "Wash first. You'll scare them."

She loved that he thought of that, of how her children would feel. Veering, she hurried to the washbasin in the corner of the room. She scrubbed her hands, trying not to think about how this was her blood, how it had felt when the knife had slid into her . . . that moment before it started to hurt, when she knew it would hurt. And then it did. Ven produced a robe from somewhere, and she wrapped it around herself to hide her bloodstained clothes. It wasn't perfect. But it was better. She noticed Ven had pulled the curtains over the entrance to the balcony, a mercy.

Knocking on the door, she called, "Erian? Llor? It's okay. You can unlock now."

She heard the lock click, and then Erian and Llor both tumbled out, squeezing together through the doorway to throw themselves into her arms.

"There were scary sounds, Mama!" Llor cried. He was clutching his stuffed squirrel, the one his sister had made him from old bedsheets. Both button eyes had fallen off.

"I know, baby." Naelin stroked his hair. "And now I need you to hurry. You two are going to stay with your father tonight. The queen needs me, and I need to know you're safe and with someone who loves you. Now, be good, and come with me."

The five of them—Naelin, Ven, Erian, Llor, and Bayn—hurried out of the chambers and through the corridors. As they went, Naelin reached out with her mind and touched the spirits around the palace and then farther out, in the capital. She couldn't sense any invasion, but then she couldn't reach much beyond the city. She wondered what Daleina could feel. As queen, she could sense every spirit within her borders. She should be able to sense when the queen of Semo's spirits crossed into Aratay.

At Renet's door, Naelin knocked.

No answer.

She knocked harder.

From inside, she heard shuffled footsteps. A muffled *oof*. And then the door opened. Renet stood in the doorway—bare chested, with a towel around his neck. His hair was wet and sticking out at all angles. She would have combed it for him if they'd been home.

Home felt very far away.

She herded Erian and Llor forward. "Keep a close watch on them, Renet."

"Of course." He opened his mouth to ask more questions, but she didn't give him time. She bent down and hugged both Erian and Llor.

"Listen to your father," she told them. "Unless he proposes something unsafe, in which case ignore him. I'm counting on you both to be smart and very grown-up until I'm back."

"You're going somewhere?" Renet asked.

*To war*, she thought. But she didn't say it. "Keep them safe."

She saw his eyes shift to Ven, and she couldn't help glancing at Ven too. He was scowling at Renet, and she thought Renet was going to insult him or argue with him. But all Renet said was "Keep her safe too."

"I will," Ven said.

Then it was time to visit the queen and tell her things she wouldn't want to hear.

QUEEN DALEINA LISTENED TO THE SOUNDS OF THE CITY. FROM her balcony, she could hear the hum of voices—too far to hear any individual words—but she heard the soft murmur of intertwined voices from the bridges and paths closest to the palace. She heard birds flying back to their trees, and the spirits rustling through the leaves as they skittered along the branches. Somewhere, far in the distance, someone was singing. And she heard bells, perhaps at the academy. She wondered if she could hear that far away.

The night sounds were soothing, and she needed soothing. This day had been—

Her door slammed open. "Queen Daleina?" Ven strode in. Behind him came Candidate Naelin and the wolf Bayn. *Looks like this day isn't over yet*, Daleina thought.

"Your Majesty, they insisted—" her guard began.

She waved the guard away. "You're covered in blood," she noted. Stains had seeped through Naelin's robe. She forced down the immediate panic: *I need her whole!* "Yours? Have you been to a healer?"

"Healer Hamon," Naelin said with a nod. "Your Majesty . . ." She hesitated.

"Your Majesty, Healer Hamon believes he has a clue to finding a cure," Ven said. "I won't lie to you—it is still a long shot, but . . . there's hope. We know who the poisoner was. *If* he finds the poison among her belongings, he *may* be able to create an antidote."

Daleina's breath caught in her throat. A cure!

He held up his hand. "That is the good news. There is also bad news. Plenty of it. The assassin was Captain Alet, working on behalf of the woman she said was her sister: Queen Merecot. The queen of Semo plans to conquer Aratay. Alet told us before she died that Semo is overrun with spirits, and Queen Merecot needs to expand her lands. The murders were her attempt to do so with minimal bloodshed. Without a queen or viable heir, Aratay would be easy to take. She plans to begin the invasion at dawn, while we are distracted by the trials."

Naelin was staring at him. "You are terrible at delivering news. Are you *trying* to cause a relapse?" Naelin crossed to Daleina and took her hands.

Daleina realized that she had been, in fact, clutching her heart, but that was only because it was beating so hard that it felt like it was going to leap out of her body. She let Naelin guide her to a chair. Picking up a pitcher, Naelin poured the queen a glass of water. Daleina took the glass and held it in her hands without drinking. "Alet?" Daleina said. "And Merecot?" She didn't look at Naelin. Her eyes were glued to Ven. He wouldn't lie to her.

"Yes."

That *yes* hurt. Like a knife to her gut. But she couldn't let it distract her, not now. She had to stay in control—feeling the pain could wait, but the invasion couldn't. Balling up her thoughts and emotions, she ruthlessly shoved them deep down.

She set the glass down, and then she thrust her mind out—beyond the palace, beyond the capital, through the woods, toward the northern border . . . and she felt them, spirits, other spirits, whose minds she couldn't sink into. They felt slippery, like wet moss, between her fingers. She felt the mass of them, whirling between her spirits.

"You said dawn?"

"Yes."

"They aren't waiting for dawn." Daleina touched her spirits, felt their anger and fear. "They've already crossed." She felt her earth spirits scrambling—the rocks were heaving around them, and they weren't causing it. Jumping to her feet, she crossed to the door. Throwing it open, she ordered the guards. "One of you, find Chancellors Isolek and Quisala. Bring them here." She stopped, considering it. "No, bring them to the Queen's Tower. It has both privacy and a view of the north. I also want Headmistress Hanna from Northeast Academy and Champion Piriandra." She shut the door as they hurried to comply.

Naelin and Ven were watching her.

She paced the length of the room, her gown brushing the edges of the furniture. The carpets absorbed her steps. She felt the spirits around her, in the palace—none of them were alarmed. Yet. The foreign spirits were still too far away.

She had time.

If she was willing to sacrifice the border.

"I'd hoped for more time, to get into position, to move our soldiers, to prepare you, Naelin." Daleina took a deep breath. "This is the choice: option one, I use my power to control the spirits near the northern border. Fight off the invasion. But if I do that, I risk losing control in a false death—the spirits will turn on our people the instant they feel my control disappear. At the border, the spirits are too far away for you, Naelin, to control. Many would die."

"Option one is bad," Ven said. "Got that."

"Option two, I abdicate right now. You become queen—go to the Queen's Grove right now and take control. You control the spirits to fight off the invasion at the border."

"Also bad," Ven said. "While Naelin is repelling the invasion, she may not be able to defend you. The spirits will kill you."

"But they won't kill our people." She didn't like that option either, especially if Hamon was close to a cure . . . How close? How much time did she need to buy? Alet might not even have more of the poison in her possession. "Option three is the most selfish option, but it's also the one most likely to work. We let the invasion happen. We don't stop them at the border. We wait until the invaders reach the capital, and then once they're here, within Naelin's range, Naelin uses our spirits to fight Merecot's spirits, while our soldiers repel Merecot's soldiers. Once Hamon has the cure, I fight with her. Together, we drive them away."

Naelin was frowning. "What happens to Aratay between the border and the capital?"

"We evacuate it, as best we can." Their best, though, wouldn't mean much. There wouldn't be time. She knew that. Merecot wouldn't be hampered by the speed of soldiers; she'd move at the speed of spirits, carrying her soldiers with her. Daleina turned to Naelin. "Merecot is powerful. And she's had training. She's also a queen, with all the extra strength that comes with it. What I'm asking—"

"I'll do it," Naelin said. "There's no one else. I know that. I'll stand between the queen of Semo and Aratay, between her and my children, for as long as you need me."

As the wolf leaned against her as if in agreement, Daleina felt a little tendril of hope. She didn't *like* this plan. She'd have to sit and wait while Merecot's spirits tore apart her land. She'd have to leave her people undefended. But it was the best way to save the most lives . . . maybe even her own.

## CHAPTER 30

Perhaps Captain Alet would be buried with honor at a later date, or at least dignity, but for now her body was laid on a kitchen cart that had last held a cake. Hamon had spread all of her belongings, lugged over from her quarters, across the floor of his mother's living quarters. He, his mother, and Daleina's sister, Arin, were pawing through them.

"Not the way I expected to spend tonight," Mother commented. "Did you have to bring the corpse? It has an odor."

"All death has an odor," Hamon said without looking up. "You should know that by now. You've caused enough of it."

"Now, is that the way to talk to someone who is letting you use her carpet?" Mother chided. She picked up a canister of cosmetics, opened it, sniffed it, closed it, and tossed it over her shoulder. It clattered to the ground, burst open, and sprayed rouge powder over the side of a couch.

"Technically, it is Queen Daleina's carpet, and have you found anything?" Hamon knew he shouldn't let his frustration show, or any emotion at all. Any emotion was a toy for his mother to play with. He'd theorized it was because she didn't have any of her own. Except curiosity. That she had in abundance. It was a shame it wasn't tempered by a shred of morality. Nodding at Arin, he said to his mother, "She shouldn't be here."

"*She* chose to be here," Arin said without looking up from Captain Alet's belongings.

"It's true," Mother said smugly. "Of her own free will. Not everyone thinks I'm evil."

Hamon turned to Arin. "Arin, she used one of her potions on you—"

"I know. It wore off. I know what I'm doing, Hamon."

He shook his head. She couldn't possibly understand. Even if she had shaken off the effects of whatever potion, his mother was still a terrible influence. "Oh? What are you doing?"

"I'm saving my sister." Arin lifted a black box out of a pile of clothing. Sitting back, she placed it on her lap. "I think I found it."

All three of them crowded around as she opened the box. Rows of glass vials were packed between black silk. Reaching over, Hamon's mother plucked one out. She held it up to the candlelight and shook it lightly. Amber liquid sloshed. "Interesting. Very interesting. And not part of an ordinary guard's med kit." She put it back into the box.

Hamon selected the next one. It held white crystals with gold flecks.

"Worth a fortune," Mother commented. "You know what that is?"

"Dirthium." It loosened muscles, lowered inhibitions, and caused blissful happiness, unless you took too much and then it resulted in painful death that shredded your internal organs at the same time as it messed up your sensory input. He put it back in the box.

"Your friend had a wealthy benefactor," Mother said.

"Her sister," Hamon said curtly. The dirthium was strong evidence that Alet had been telling the truth—*But where's the poison?*

After examining them all, they had three vials with unknown substances in them. Mother clapped her hands like a child. "Exciting! Now if we only had someone to test these on—"

"No," Hamon said. "We test them with equipment."

"Poo. You're no fun at all."

"At least one of these is deadly," he pointed out.

Mother held one of the vials up. "Ooh, or maybe all of them!" Humming happily to herself, she carried the first one to her makeshift workbench. "Just a drop, my dear," she said to Arin. "Once we've identified the compound, we'll need more to synthesize an antidote, and then more to test it. Since my son refuses to be practical..."

"No murder," Hamon said. "We're here to prevent death, not cause it." That was a sentence that really shouldn't need to be said out loud. Hovering, he watched his mother and the queen's sister. Mother had set herself up well, using a combination of kitchen and medical supplies to create a decent laboratory. But it was Arin who took command of it.

Arin was the one who handled the poisons.

Arin was the one who set up the experiments.

Arin was the one who stayed calm, steady, and serious while Hamon hovered over her and Mother issued directions from the comfort of the pillow-laden couch.

And it was Arin who identified the poison: a mix of heartease, soldier grass, and six other compounds that no one should have ever thought to mix together. Crowding around the workbench, the three of them stared at the innocent-looking amber liquid.

"Now," Mother said, "we get to work."

HEADMISTRESS HANNA FELT EVERY BONE CREAK AS SHE CLIMBED the palace stairs. She hadn't been in the Queen's Tower for years, and she didn't miss it. Her own office was high enough, thank you very much, but one didn't ignore a summons from the queen just because it was inconvenient or uncomfortable—which this most certainly was. She was puffing by the time she reached the top.

Several others were already squeezed into the tiny space: Queen Daleina, Champion Ven, Champion Piriandra, the palace seneschal, and two chancellors, who were both folded into wooden chairs and looked unhappy either because of the situation or their seating arrangements. Or perhaps they were unhappy because of the large wolf curled at their feet.

And most surprising of all: Candidate Naelin.

Hanna was certainly not expecting her. Still, she hadn't gotten to where she was in life without having a little patience. Hanna knew all—or at least, most—would be explained.

"Are you well?" Ven asked the headmistress.

"Old age," she replied. "Nothing that a bit of death won't cure."

One of the chancellors, a man with a full beard—*Chancellor Isolek*, her memory supplied—sprang to his feet and offered her his chair. Hanna motioned for him to sit back down. If Hanna sat down, she knew her muscles would clench and it would be that much harder to stand again.

"Thank you for coming," Queen Daleina said to all of them. "Rumors will start flying soon, as news trickles in from the north. Until then, this is the most private place in Aratay. Naelin will be keeping away any spirits while we talk." Hanna noticed that Naelin was focused out the window. Her fists were clenched, and her eyes were scanning the night sky and the dark forest canopy below. Hanna knew she wasn't looking with only her eyes, which meant she had advanced much since they had last met.

It was a crisp night, and the wind blew through the open windows of the tower. The flames in the lanterns wavered, and shadows crossed the queen's face. *She looks tired*, Hanna thought. *So do we all.* She doubted many in the kingdom had slept much since the queen had announced her illness.

Champion Piriandra was scowling. "Why are we here?"

"To the point, then . . . we are being invaded. It has already begun." As Hanna gasped, Daleina smiled sadly at the two chancellors. "I was correct: they are coming from the north, straight to Mittriel."

"I know you take no joy in that," Chancellor Quisala said stiffly.

"They sense weakness," Piriandra said, and Hanna wanted to scold her for the hostile tone of her voice. Young or not, inexperienced or not, powerful or not, Daleina was queen.

"Here is what we know," Ven said, stepping in before she could say anything. "Queen Merecot arranged for Queen Daleina to be poisoned, using a slow-acting concoction that masqueraded as a natural illness."

"Presumably she guessed that I would react exactly the way I did: keeping our soldiers in Mittriel to protect my people in case I lost control, rather than sending them to the borders," Daleina said. Hanna had the sense she'd pace if she could, but the tower was too cramped. Instead she fidgeted, twisting the sleeves of her gown and fiddling with the pearl embellishments. "I do not regret this decision, though it nearly proved disastrous—Merecot effectively silenced whatever minimal border guard we have. We received no warning through them when the invasion began."

"Then how did you know?" Piriandra asked again.

"I can feel them," Daleina said simply.

Ven spoke again. "We believe Queen Merecot used this poison in order to buy herself time to gather Semo's soldiers *and* spirits at our border."

"We will send our troops north to intercept," Chancellor Isolek said, rising. "If we begin immediately, they can be in Birchen by—"

"No," Daleina said. "We make our stand in Mittriel. I want every soldier, every champion, and every candidate positioned at the northern edge of the city."

Chancellor Quisala gasped. "But the border towns! You can't—"

Daleina cut her off. "We must. Naelin, how far can you reach?"

Naelin didn't move from the window. "No more than two miles from the northern border of the city. Keep them within that line, and I can do it."

"Who's she?" Champion Piriandra demanded. "I don't take orders from a candidate."

"She's my heir," Daleina said.

Champion Piriandra began shouting, as did Chancellor Isolek and Quisala. It wasn't done! The trials had to be held! She couldn't—she wouldn't—she didn't—

When they finally took a breath, Headmistress Hanna spoke. "She has proven herself to you?"

"She has," Daleina said.

"Then that is sufficient for me." Hanna quelled the others with a look. After all, she had decades of experience training and evaluating potential heirs. She surmised that this was why Daleina had requested her presence, to lend credibility to the queen's decision. "This is not a time to be without an heir. A trial now would be both a luxury and a foolish risk, and there are no other suitable candidates. It is Naelin or no one."

The others fell silent. Piriandra visibly swallowed back whatever she planned to say. "Champion Piriandra"—Daleina turned to her—"I appoint you to lead the champions and their candidates. You are one of our most experienced champions."

Straightening her shoulders, Champion Piriandra said stiffly, "With all due respect, Your Majesty, I may not be your best choice. My misjudgment has cost two candidates their lives."

"I can't speak to the first candidate's fate, but as to the second . . ."

Hanna saw the queen hesitate.

Ven spoke for her. "She was murdered, Piriandra. We believe your candidate Beilena was killed by an agent of Semo, on orders from Queen Merecot."

"Her death was not your fault," Daleina said.

All the color drained out of the champion's face. Her hand drifted to her sword hilt. Headmistress Hanna laid her own hand on Piriandra's shoulder. "Revenge will come later," Hanna told her quietly.

"No revenge," Daleina said. "I need you focused on protecting our soldiers. Can you do this? Lead the champions with their candidates? Protect our soldiers from whatever spirits Merecot sends against them?"

"Of course." Piriandra bowed.

"Chancellors, you will focus the troops on the human enemy. It's a single squadron. You should be able to hold them. Chancellor Quisala, you will command the soldiers in the northeast of the city, and Chancellor Isolek, the northwest. We cannot let Merecot take the capital."

"But the spirits—" Isolek protested.

"We will protect you from them," Champion Piriandra promised.

"Only those that attack the troops directly," Daleina told the champion. "Let the others pass you. Do you understand? Keeping Merecot and her soldiers out of Mittriel is your sole goal."

Piriandra objected. "If the spirits—"

"Heir Naelin will handle the spirits that target the city. Your duty is to the soldiers. Do not let them take the capital. Headmistress Hanna"—Daleina turned—"you must protect the academy. I believe that Merecot will send forces to attack you and your students directly. Her strategy has been to remove anyone with power. The academies will be among her prime targets. Inform your colleagues, and then prepare your students."

Hanna suppressed a shudder. Surely Merecot wouldn't attack students. They were children! Then again, she wouldn't have thought Merecot would attack her homeland either. So yes, if she did, then Hanna would guard them—with her life, if necessary. "We will be ready," Hanna promised. Her teachers would all make the same promise, she knew.

Daleina turned to the seneschal. "Refugees will be coming from the north and northeast. People will be frightened. They'll flee to the palace."

He bowed. "We will keep them out."

She shook her head. "I want you to let them in. Open the storerooms. Distribute supplies. Set up cots in the throne room and halls. Use the palace however you see fit to house as many as you can."

The seneschal looked pleased. "It will be so."

"Your Majesty," Chancellor Isolek protested, "won't Queen Merecot target the palace?"

"She will, but as a prize. She won't destroy it," Daleina said. "She wants it for herself. And we will not let her take it. She will not rule here."

Hanna had never been more proud of her than she was in that moment. Daleina looked every inch a queen. There would be many more tales written about her, many more songs sung, beginning with the story of this moment.

*Assuming anyone lives to tell it*, Hanna thought.

CHAPTER 31

Daleina gripped the tower window. Wind whipped against her. Leaves swirled over the city, and the trees swayed. She could feel them: the foreign spirits. They were flowing across the forest like a wave, sweeping away everything in their path.

Merecot's earth spirits were tearing through the land, causing bedrock to tilt and pierce through the surface. The land shifted, and the trees toppled. Daleina felt her own spirits howl in rage. But Naelin was holding them back, within two miles of the city.

The enemy wasn't close enough.

It was sound logic: if Daleina controlled them and blacked out, they'd feel her death and turn on her people. If that happened outside of Naelin's range, there would be no stopping them. So it was better to wait and let Naelin control them from the start. Avoid the risk altogether.

Daleina dug her fingers into the wood and wished she dared command them. North of the city, people were fleeing from the destruction. Their homes were crumbling around them. The very earth was betraying them. *She* was betraying them. She'd sworn to protect them, and here she was, seemingly doing nothing while they lost their homes, possibly even their lives.

*I could abdicate*, she thought. She could let Naelin take the crown now. Naelin could then command the spirits throughout Aratay... unless she couldn't. Unless the coronation failed. There had never been a coronation ceremony with only a single heir, and there was no guarantee the spirits would accept Naelin. Plus she'd need to take the crown without the traditional seven-day grace period. Daleina had no proof that the spirits would even accept a new queen without those seven days. They might, if the new queen were powerful enough—the seven days could be mere tradition—but she didn't know for certain. No, it was too great a risk. She'd hold out and wait, until the spirits reached the capital, until Hamon had her cure. He *had* to find it.

Alet . . .

*No, I can't think about her right now. Not yet.* She'd lost so many friends, to death and now betrayal. Every loss felt like another bit of her soul was sliced away. She wasn't certain how much more she could take, but she wasn't ready to give up. Abdicating felt like failure. "Am I being selfish, Ven?" she asked softly.

He was beside her, close enough to hear. Naelin was on his other side—she gave no sign that she'd heard Daleina, and Daleina hoped she hadn't. "You must be. Aratay needs you."

"Naelin could do it."

"I'm not burying another queen," Ven said.

So she held her power in check and kept the spirits close.

The chancellors had issued orders to her soldiers. She knew they waited as well, as the refugees poured into the capital. Her seneschal was welcoming as many as he could. He'd had tents set up in the gardens. The palace cooks were distributing food, and the caretakers were handing out blankets and other supplies. She'd received word from Hamon that her sister was with him— Arin was safe, at least for now, and if they could keep the invaders out of Mittriel, she'd stay safe.

"I hate waiting," Ven said.

Daleina nearly laughed. He sounded like a grumpy child. A choked giggle burst out of her lips. She swallowed it back in.

From near one of the tower windows, Naelin snorted. "You should like waiting. When the waiting ends, the killing and dying begins. I'd rather wait an eternity."

"You don't feel it? The taste of the air, the beat of your heart— there must be a part of you that wants to release all your coiled energy. Strike out. Let loose your anger and your fear."

"Mostly fear," Naelin said. "How am I supposed to defeat a queen?"

"You just have to hold her and her spirits back until Hamon finds the cure," Ven told her. "You don't need to defeat her; you just need to buy time. Until Daleina can fight too."

*Except Merecot was always stronger than me,* Daleina thought, but she didn't say it out loud. It was the best and only plan they had. Daleina's advantage was that she was defending her home. Her people. Her sister. She hoped that would be enough.

Daleina leaned out the window and looked across the canopy, across Aratay. The enemy was close enough to see: a thickness in the air, like a fog that hung heavily over the forest. It was a wall that advanced toward them. She wanted to strike at it.

"There's a new mountain." Daleina pointed. A peak, or the shadow of one, rose out of the swirling swarm. *Merecot's changing our land. My land.*

"We'll fix it," Naelin said. Her voice was kind—she must have seen, or guessed, at Daleina's feelings. "After the killing and the dying will come the cleaning and the recovering."

"You can't be looking forward to that part?" Ven looked incredulous, like Naelin had just told him that she didn't like his beard. Daleina wondered if he felt fear, underneath all his casual bravery. He must. She wondered if he was hiding it for her sake or his own.

"You can stop trying to glorify battle," Naelin told him. "I won't like it, no matter how exhilarating you claim it is. It's better to avoid a fight than win one. Even Queen Merecot doesn't want a fight. That's why she used Alet."

Daleina widened her eyes. "You're right," she gasped. Queen Merecot didn't want to destroy Aratay; she wanted to rule it. Daleina had realized that when she'd looked at the map with the chancellors. She'd known it when she'd invited the refugees into the palace. But she hadn't fully followed the thought to its logical conclusion. Merecot wanted to become Queen of Aratay as well as Semo. To do that, she needed to claim both the capital and the spirits. "You need to go to the grove. Now."

Both Naelin and Ven stared at her.

"What?" Naelin said.

"We aren't leaving you," Ven said simultaneously.

Naelin nodded. "Your Majesty, we're here to defend you."

"The attack. The grand entrance. Why is she doing this?" Daleina didn't wait for them to answer her. Up until today, Daleina had assumed that Merecot didn't know about her illness—all her strategy had been based on that assumption—but of course Merecot knew about it. She'd caused it. Merecot had always been stronger—in a head-to-head battle, it would take all of Daleina's strength and cleverness to keep her out of the city, which Merecot knew. She was trying to force Daleina to use all her power to defend her capital—she was trying to trigger a false death. And she'd had Alet kill off any candidates who could take the crown. *Oh, Alet, how could you? Sister or not, queen or not, you should have refused her!* "It's brilliant. She didn't bring her spirits and soldiers to conquer the city. She brought them to *protect* it."

Ven pointed out the window at the approaching storm of spirits. "That's an invasion."

"Yes, *now*. But when I fall . . . She plans to use the invasion to force me to trigger a false death, and in the midst of the chaos, she will walk into the Queen's Grove. She'll try to crown herself, *during* the invasion, not after! And the people will support her because, in the meantime, her spirits will be saving them. She wins the power, the land, the spirits, the people—everything she ever wanted—all at once." Which meant there was one way to outsmart her. One way to win. Daleina fixed both of them with the fiercest expression she could. "She doesn't know Alet failed to kill you. You have to stop her. Go to the grove. Now."

"What will you do?" Naelin said.

"I will be queen, for as long as I can."

Naelin hated to use the air spirits for travel, but she saw little choice. Reaching out, she beckoned to one. *Fly with us.* She didn't make it a command. As Daleina had taught her, she tempted instead—she picked a restless spirit, one that didn't like being held at the border, and reeled it in like a fish on a line. It came eagerly. Climbing onto the window ledge, she held her hand out to Ven. "You'll like this part," she told him.

He raised his eyebrows. "We jump?"

"Yes," she said, and leaped from the window, yanking him with her. For one terrifying, exhilarating minute, she plummeted, and then the air spirit was there. She thudded onto its back. Ven landed diagonal with her and quickly righted himself. He helped her sit upright and wrapped his arms around her stomach.

"See, I think you secretly crave adventure," Ven said, "but you think you shouldn't." She could hear the forced lightness in his voice—inside, she knew he was twisted with worry. They were leaving their queen.

She forced lightness into her voice too. "Oh? You know me so well now?"

"Yes." His voice was warm in her ear. "Right now, you are trying to decide whether it would be worth the risk of my falling if you were to elbow me for being obnoxious."

Naelin couldn't help herself: she laughed. "You're just trying to distract me from being afraid." She twisted to look at him. Seated on the air spirit behind her, he was very close, less than an inch away. "Thank you," she said, and then she kissed him.

He cupped her face in his hands as he kissed her back, deeply, sweetly. The wind raced around them, and she felt the air spirit skim the tops of the trees. The first rays of sunrise spread across the leaves, lighting them in green and gold.

Pulling back, she directed the spirit, *Lower. Don't be seen.*

The spirit dropped. They raced through the trees. She saw them in a blur: a smear of green, a flash of brown. As they flew faster and faster, the colors ran together as if the forest were melting around her. A twig hit her ankle, and it stung as it broke the skin.

Behind her, she felt the foreign spirits cross into her range. They felt like oil poured into water. They slid through her awareness like a shiver through her body.

"Are you ready?" Ven asked.

Her answer surprised even her. "Yes."

Ahead was the grove.

CHAMPION PIRIANDRA HEARD THE SEMOIAN SPIRITS BEFORE SHE
saw them. They sounded like a storm, the kind that snapped
sturdy oaks in half, the kind that ripped houses out of their
branches, the kind that flattened plants that had withstood a
hundred rains. She attached a clip to the wire path and pushed
off, sailing between the trees. "Be ready!" she shouted to the soldiers below. To the candidates, she called, "Hold them still! Our
spirits are your arrows; you are the taut bow! On my mark!"

Ahead the wire ended. Still flying through the air, Piriandra
reached up and unclipped. She fell, and then landed on a platform below in a crouch. Drawing her sword, she faced the coming storm. "Keep your line! Hold steady!"

Through the trees, she glimpsed the largest earth spirit she'd
ever seen: a hulking mass of mud and rocks. On its back rode a
woman with black hair and a crown of crystal spikes.

Queen Merecot of Semo.

She was positioned behind the foreign spirits and invading
soldiers, out of reach of any arrows. Riding back and forth behind her troops, she was shouting—

"Be ready!" Piriandra shouted to the other champions.

And then the foreign spirits attacked.

Earth spirits tore through the soil. She saw beasts with razor-
backs and spikes and claws, and others that looked like mounds
of rocks with boulders for arms. Air spirits whipped through the
sky, blotting out the faint light of the dawn. In a mass, their translucent bodies blended into gray streaks. The wind hit the front
lines like a punch, and the ground exploded at their feet.

Dropping, Piriandra clung to the platform as it swayed beneath her. "Come on," she muttered. "Pass us by." If Queen Daleina was wrong, if the bulk of the spirits did not stream toward
the city, if instead they stayed and fought, if they were more
interested in slaughter than conquest . . . Queen Daleina was
young, weak, sick, and inexperienced, and Heir Naelin was just
an untested, barely trained woodswoman. *We're all going to die
out here*, Piriandra thought. They'd be ripped apart before they
even got a chance to fight. The candidates were too few to fight
back—*But I am not weak. I will fight.*

Raising her voice, Piriandra shouted, "Now!" She jabbed her sword into the air.

The soldiers charged forward.

And the spirits flew above them and around them—exactly like Queen Daleina had predicted—heading for the heart of the city. *Well, well, what do you know?* Now Piriandra had to hope the queen's prediction about her heir was equally accurate.

"Shield our soldiers," Piriandra ordered the candidates. "Don't engage the spirits *unless* they attack our troops. Do you understand?" She'd given them this order before, but it bore repeating. As the foreign spirits streamed around them, she had to fight with herself not to slice at them with her sword. Their job was to stop the human army. Just that. Don't let the soldiers take the capital. Don't let the foreign queen set foot in their city. "Only defend our soldiers. Let the other spirits go."

*Queen Daleina,* she thought, *you had better know what you're doing.*

And then she had no more time for thinking. Leaping onto the forest floor, she landed between two soldiers, and she began hacking at an earth spirit that was trying to rip them apart.

HEADMISTRESS HANNA HAD WRAPPED THE ACADEMY IN AIR spirits. They swirled around in a controlled tornado. She had the other teachers stationed throughout the academy. Master Chirra had instructed earth spirits to dig a trench around the roots of the academy trees, and Master Sondriane had had water spirits flood the trench to create a moat. The spirits lurked within the moat, ready to pull any enemies under.

Master Sondriane had reported they liked that idea very much.

The students were clustered in the training circle. Hanna wished they could be tucked in bed, sealed inside their rooms, but she remembered how good Merecot had been with tree spirits—she could easily crush the students with their own walls, if she were so inclined. Master Klii, who specialized in fire spirits, had the students within a ring of fire. Triple layers of protection. The headmistress couldn't do any better than that. No one had ever protected an academy so thoroughly.

She hoped it was enough.

In her office at the top of the tree, she watched the foreign spirits pour across the city border. She heard the crack and crash of trees as they fell beneath the onslaught. And she both saw and felt Queen Daleina send Aratay's spirits out to crash against the incoming storm.

She was ready when a few spirits broke away from the battle and flew toward the academy. Tightening her control, she prepared the air spirits. She'd meet them in midair–

The earth spirits came from below.

They tunneled through the roots. Master Klii directed the fire spirits at them, but their rock bodies didn't burn. Master Sondriane sent the water, pouring down, washing the earth back. But the rock creatures crawled out of the mud and muck.

The children were screaming.

And the window by Hanna's desk shattered as the air spirits slammed into it. She turned and ran out the office door and to the stairs–and then she leaped. She called air spirits to her as she fell, and three flew to her, breaking her fall. She flew down toward the children. As the foreign spirits pressed closer, the headmistress and the teachers drew a shell around them: wood, earth, fire, water, wind, and ice. They layered it and clung to one another within, as the enemy burned, rained, froze, and tore, trying to reach them.

*She's too strong*, the headmistress thought. Her former student had only grown in power. Heir Naelin wouldn't be enough. Only a queen could hope to defeat a queen. *Fight her, Daleina. Fight with everything you have.*

## CHAPTER 32

Alone except for a wolf, Queen Daleina stood atop the Queen's Tower and watched as the spirits of Semo rolled over the border of the city. She wished she'd had a chance to say goodbye to her sister. *Keep her safe, Hamon*, she thought. "Are you ready?" she asked the wolf.

In answer, he lifted his head and howled.

She spread her arms as she released her mind. *Fight!*

The order flew through the air. She felt it release her spirits, and she felt them rise to meet the invaders. She felt their swirling fury, their defiance, and their sheer joy. It flooded her body and filled her throat until all she could see, all she could feel, all she could breathe were the spirits. Their howl was her howl. Their rage was her rage. She felt herself with them, as they plunged into the gray mass of air spirits and plowed into the phalanx of earth spirits.

Air spirits sliced through water spirits, breaking them into thousands of droplets. Water spirits embraced fire spirits, and around them wood and rock exploded as they crashed, fighting, on the forest floor. Her earth spirits were trampled beneath the feet of the giant mountain earth spirits, and so she sent ice spirits to stiffen the enemy's joints and water spirits to weaken the ground beneath them.

She fought the way she thought: cleverly. She couldn't out-power Merecot, but she could outwit her. She sent her spirits behind the invaders, striking from directions they wouldn't expect. She slipped ice spirits into the ranks of Merecot's soldiers, forcing her to use fire spirits to protect them. As soon as the fire spirits were close enough, Daleina caught them with earth spirits, burying them in soil, or trapped them with branches that her water spirits doused with water.

The forest burned.

But the city did not.

*I can do this*, she thought. *You will not take Aratay. You cannot win.*

But she couldn't win either. She was stalling them, keeping them within Naelin's range, keeping them from killing more of her people, but she wasn't winning. Merecot was fueling her spirits with her strength—and she was very, very strong.

Reaching out, Daleina directed several spirits to the academy. They peeled the enemy spirits away from the walls, plucked them out of the practice ring, buried them in the earth, flooded them. She had her spirits sweep through the streets—her people were hiding, and her spirits kept them safe, harrying away any spirits that attempted to pry off doors and break through windows. She sent others to the palace, defending the refugees.

She tried to pull the spirits out the second she felt the blackness rising. She tried to send them out of the city, away from her people, toward the grove. She pushed them as far as she could and hoped she'd given Naelin enough time.

"Now, Bayn," she told the wolf. "Find him."

She heard him run from the tower as she collapsed.

ARIN BIT HER LIP SO HARD SHE TASTED BLOOD. SHE COULD DO this. All she had to do was focus and keep her hand steady. So far, they'd tried twelve possible antidotes, and all had failed when they encountered a drop of the poison dissolved in a drop of Arin's blood. She was on their thirteenth try.

Behind her, Hamon and his mother were arguing. Again.

The poison was a chameleon, changing whenever it was close to human blood, cleaving to the cells. It hides in the blood, Garnah had said. Disguises itself. She admired the poison, Arin could tell. "Such a clever beauty," Garnah would murmur, which would lead to Hamon yelling. Luckily, Arin didn't need either of them to do this part.

Squatting so that she was even with the jar, Arin squeezed one drop of distilled water. It plopped into the drops of her blood—they'd started with samples of Daleina's blood but had switched to Arin's when it ran out. There wasn't time to go bleed her sister, and anyway, she was busy, Hamon had said.

"What could be more important than discovery?" Garnah asked.

Arin felt the same way. Daleina should be here. This was her life they were trying to save. *She's probably off somewhere being noble.* Of course, she was certain that Master Garnah was interested in results for entirely different reasons—she loved the poisons themselves, not the people.

Adjusting the microscope, Arin positioned a slide under it and peered in. She watched the cells constrict and then expand as they were invaded by the poison.

Behind her, Hamon was saying, "Yes, I do. I love her! Is that what you wanted to hear? Are you going to murder her now, to see how I react? Or to make me need you? Because it won't work. You'll only drive me further away."

"My boy, I'm trying to save her!" Garnah captured the tone of wounded innocence perfectly. Arin assumed that Hamon could see right through it. He had much more experience with his mother than she did.

"Master Garnah," Arin interrupted, "what would happen if we added feather-moss extract?" She knew why you never baked with feather-moss extract—if it hit sugar, it reacted badly.

"Ooh, interesting, but no. Not unless you want to make your queen vomit for a week."

"So long as she lives," Hamon said.

"Sadly, that would not be a side effect," Garnah said. "But what if you add red lichen—" Coming to Arin's side, Garnah picked up one of her vials and twirled it. "Perhaps we're coming at this wrong. Perhaps instead of attacking the poison, we could redirect it. Give it a new target."

The palace shuddered, and the workbench rocked to the side. Arin hugged the microscope so it wouldn't fall as the tubes and jars rattled together. Outside, she heard screaming. Hamon rushed to the window.

"That is not good," he said grimly.

"*That* is not our problem," Garnah said. "You really must learn to focus. That was always what prevented you from excelling. Instead of focusing on the problem at hand, you get distracted by irrelevancies."

"Other people's lives are not irrelevancies."

Arin wanted to tell him to stop trying to change her. In a way, Garnah was right: he was focusing on the wrong problem—his mother—instead of the right one: the poison. Yes, people outside were screaming, probably dying. Like Josei had died. But that only made their task more important, not less. For those who hadn't yet lost the loves of their lives. "Tell me what to do," Arin said to Garnah.

"Bleed more," Garnah said. Before Arin could react, she pressed a blade to Arin's arm and then caught the drops of blood on a slide. "All right, begin a new batch. Start with the red lichen. . . ."

Muttering to himself, Hamon applied a bandage to Arin's cut while she mixed the ingredients and ignored the sting of her arm. He kept glancing at the window.

"Hamon, if you're not going to focus, you might as well go to her," Garnah said.

"I'll go when I have the antidote to give her," Hamon said.

The palace shook again, but this time Arin was braced for it. The chandelier swung side to side, and a fiery log rolled out of the fireplace. Flames leapt onto the carpet. Hamon stomped the flames out and shoved the log into the fire. He tossed a bucket of sand over the fire. It died. Quickly, he sealed the fireplace. He then checked the locks on the windows and pulled the curtains.

From the corridor outside the room, Arin heard screaming.

That was close. Much too close.

The enemy spirits couldn't have reached the palace tree already. She'd been told they were held at the city border. They shouldn't have reached the palace at all. She worried about Daleina. "Hamon . . ." Arin began.

"Something's wrong," Hamon said. "I'm going to her."

He crossed to the door and pulled it open.

A spirit flew at him, claws out, teeth aimed at his neck. Arin screamed. Garnah lunged forward, grabbing one of the vials. Arin caught her arm. "No, you'll hurt Hamon!"

Hamon kicked at the spirit, but it bore down on him. And then a massive gray shape launched itself through the door and slammed into the spirit. It knocked the spirit against the wall, and Arin saw it was a wolf—Bayn!

The spirit fled.

Baring his bloody teeth, the wolf turned to look at Hamon and then he grabbed the healer's robe in his teeth and tugged. "Daleina?" Hamon said.

"Go," Arin told him.

"Go to her," Garnah said, a sigh in her voice.

He ran out of the room with the wolf at his side.

Garnah barred the door behind him. "Perhaps we can get some work done now." She crossed toward Arin, and the window shattered open. An air spirit howled as it flew inside, and before Arin could even scream, Garnah threw the vial she was holding into its face.

It screamed and clawed at its face, then it fled.

"And *now* we can get some work done."

"What was that?" She'd never seen a spirit flee like that—a charm could repel them, but the spirit had acted like—

Garnah rapped on the table. "Focus, my apprentice. We have a task to do."

Side by side, they bent over the workbench. Arin measured and mixed. Garnah peered through the microscope. They tested. They failed.

And then . . . And then . . . they did *not* fail.

Garnah looked up from the microscope. "Arin? Use your young eyes and tell me if you see what I see."

She looked, and her breath caught in her throat. "I see what you see." Her heart was pounding fast. She wiped her hands on her skirt and tried to keep herself calm. "Will this work?"

"We won't know until we try it," Garnah said.

"But if she—"

"We don't need to try it on the queen." Garnah nodded toward the locked door. "But there are others in the palace, much closer by."

Arin wanted to believe that Garnah wasn't suggesting what she thought she was. "There's no one out there except Daleina who has this illness."

"Well, no one yet, but . . ." She gestured at the door that led to the hallway. "We should be able to find a spare guard or a caretaker or someone."

Arin shook her head so hard that it made her dizzy. "No."

"It needs to be tested. Working under a microscope is not the same as working in a human body. You must know that. You taste your cakes, right? You don't simply hope your flavor combinations will taste right simply because you've followed the recipe right. All we do is infect a guard and then heal him—he'll never know the difference."

"Absolutely not. Daleina wouldn't want this."

"Your sister wants to live," Garnah said. "Also, she doesn't need to know."

Outside the window, she heard a mighty crash. She ran to the window and peeled the curtain back. Jumping back, she clapped her hands over her mouth to stop a scream. Spirits! Everywhere! And people . . . Trees were falling. Massive trees, tilted against one another, and the gardens below had been ripped apart. Arin began to shake. She'd seen this before . . . when the old queen had died, when Josei had died, when everything was nearly destroyed, but now, here, in the palace . . .

"Pull yourself together, girl," Garnah said.

"She's lost control," Arin said. "That's why Bayn came for Hamon. She's dead. False death. Not real death." She couldn't be really dead. Not Daleina. Not now, when they were so close! Arin ran for the antidote. "We have to do it."

"Her body is weak, and the potion is potent. If it's not right, it will most likely kill her permanently. You will only get one shot at this."

"Then test it on me." Pivoting toward the workbench, Arin grabbed the poison. Distantly, she noticed that Garnah wasn't stopping her. In fact, Hamon's mother was watching eagerly, her hands clasped as if she were about to receive the best present ever.

Arin tipped the test tube and poured the poison onto her tongue.

It tasted, she thought, like blackberries. And sugar.

She swallowed.

"Good," Garnah said. She pressed the vial of antidote into Arin's hand, and Arin drank it. "Very good." She then handed a knife to Arin. "Now, bleed."

Arin pressed the blade against her arm. Red welled up in a line. She held her arm over a plate of glass on the microscope. And she bled once more, for her sister.

## CHAPTER 33

The Queen's Grove.

Naelin had never expected to see this place. She'd never wanted to. Horrors had happened here. Directing the air spirit to set her down, she climbed off, along with Ven.

"You can do this," Ven said.

She glanced at him. He was staring up at the trees as if they would crush him. He'd been here, she knew. He must have seen Queen Daleina walk out of the grove, after the massacre. He may have gone in and seen the bodies. "*You* can do this," she told him.

His eyes widened for a second, and then he nodded.

At the edge of the trees, Ven hopped onto one of the broad roots and began to climb. "I'll watch for Queen Merecot. Do you sense any spirits?"

She reached—inside it felt empty. Peaceful. Climbing over the roots, she squeezed between two tree trunks. In seconds, she was within the grove. Looking around, she was shocked at how beautiful it was. And serene. Morning light filtered through the leaves and spread across the mossy floor. An orange butterfly spiraled lazily over a flower. She walked forward, and her steps were muffled. She couldn't hear any of the sounds from the city—the screams, the crashing, the cries, all of it faded.

Naelin reached out to touch the spirits. All of them were focused outward, facing the army from the north. They seethed like a storm. She couldn't hear the queen's orders, but she could feel the spirits' reaction. Queen Daleina was using the spirits to attack from below, behind, above: water against fire, earth against ice, air against earth . . . She wasn't attacking head-on; she was undermining the foreign spirits. "I think the queen is winning, or at least holding her own." So far, she hadn't triggered a false death. *I hope I truly am ready*, Naelin thought. She was slightly farther from the city border now than she had been, but the spirits were still within range. She could reach them, if and when she needed to.

Shielding her eyes, Naelin looked up at the trees. Ven had climbed high and was partially hidden within the branches. He'd taken a small telescope from his pocket and was looking north.

"Anything?" she called.

He lowered the telescope. "I feel as though I have run away from battle."

"We were *ordered* away from it." Within the circle of trees, sheltered from the rest of the forest, Naelin felt as if she'd been tucked away in a closet, like a family heirloom, for safekeeping. Here, the blue sky and the gentle wind that caressed the leaves seemed far removed from the chaos and destruction they'd left behind. "I think Queen Daleina lied to us, or else we misunderstood. Queen Merecot is focused on the capital—she's not coming here, not until she's conquered the capital."

"Daleina knows Merecot. If she thinks—"

"I don't think Queen Daleina sent us here to fight her. I think she sent us here to keep me safe." Naelin could feel the battle like pinpricks on her skin. So far away. Yet close enough that she could still sense the spirits and, if she tried, still reach out and command them. "I am her backup plan." If Queen Daleina continued to repel the invaders, it was likely that Queen Merecot and her army would never make it as far south as the grove. If not, if Queen Daleina suffered another false death . . . then Naelin would repel them from the safety of the grove. It was clever. The Semoians wouldn't know who they were fighting if she was hidden here.

"It's possible," Ven conceded. "But she could—"

Apparently she couldn't.

Naelin felt the moment that Daleina lost control. It felt like a glass vase rupturing, and her head filled with screams. Distantly, she heard Ven calling to her. She felt the wild glee/rage/hunger surge through her—

*Do no harm!* she projected. She sent the thought as far and broadly as she could. She hammered it into the spirits. But there were so many! So many more than just in the palace. The queen must have drawn them from the forest beyond.

Already caught up in bloodlust, they didn't listen to her. She'd never pull them back to peace. She had to redirect them. *Yes. You can do this.* As Queen Daleina had taught her, Naelin pushed the spirits, refocusing them on the enemy. She made them reshape the bedrock that the foreign spirits had unearthed, regrow the trees that had been felled—but they fought her.

They wanted blood.

They wanted death.

Human blood. Human death. Naelin squeezed her head between her hands. They wanted it so badly that it hurt. She dropped forward, crashing onto her knees in the soft ground. She felt the earth kraken moving beneath the city, rocking the palace. *Erian and Llor!* Seizing the kraken, she redirected him away from the city.

But there were too many. She couldn't control them. At best, she could hold them, limit their destruction, but she couldn't do it indefinitely, and the enemy was rolling over the capital. She couldn't repel Semo's spirits while she contained Aratay's—

"She's coming!" Ven called. He climbed higher into the tree.

"I can't fight her!" Naelin could barely hold the spirits. She wasn't going to be able to keep them from destroying the city *and* face down a queen at the height of her power.

"Naelin . . . You were right, but not for the reasons you think," Ven said. "She didn't send you here to fight; she sent you to avoid a fight!"

Naelin didn't understand what he meant.

And then suddenly she *did* understand.

CHAMPION PIRIANDRA PLUNGED HER SWORD INTO THE SIDE OF AN earth spirit. It kept marching forward. As it swung its massive arm, she ducked beneath it. Gravel rained on her head. She yanked the sword out and swung again.

Beneath her, the forest floor buckled like waves. Aratay was predominantly tree spirits, but Semo had mostly earth spirits. She hadn't realized until now how difficult they were to fight. Climbing up onto one of the trees, Piriandra clung to a branch as it swayed. She surveyed the enemy soldiers—it was hard to see them through the flood of spirits—but she could pinpoint the location of . . . *Where is she?* "Can anyone see Queen Merecot?" she called. "Eyes on the enemy! Can you see her?"

The queen of Semo had been in the back behind the soldiers, directing the spirits. She'd been clever enough to stay out of range of any arrows, but she'd been ever-present, riding back and forth. Now Piriandra couldn't see her. She didn't know what that meant, but her gut said it wasn't good.

Still, she had little time to consider it. Two earth spirits were trying to break through the line of guards by pulling the soldiers hip-deep into the earth. Running along the roots, Piriandra helped lift soldiers up into the trees. They scrambled up the trunks, like ants, as one of the spirits of Aratay caused a spring to erupt in the path of the earth spirits. It swept them backward. *Good*, Piriandra thought. If they could focus on keeping the soldiers out of Mittriel—*You can't conquer a place you can't reach.* She'd feel better if she knew where Queen Merecot was, but—

One of the soldiers screamed. Piriandra swung up toward him. He was prone on a branch, and a tree spirit had pinned him down. It was gnawing on his leg. Jumping onto the branch, Piriandra kicked the spirit hard in the chest. It sailed backward, crashing against the trunk. And then spirits were all around her.

*Their* spirits. The spirits of Aratay. "They've gone rogue!" she shouted. "Defend yourselves!" She brought her sword up and then leaped onto the next vine, swinging low and slashing with her sword as air and tree spirits turned on their people.

The cry began to spread through the ranks. "The queen! The queen is dead! Queen Daleina is dead!" As Piriandra fought, she saw the soldiers begin to fall, caught beneath the claws and teeth.

"She will wake!" Piriandra shouted. "Fight, you idiots! Buy her time!"

She joined the other champions, circled around the candidates. Sword held in her sweating hand, she backed up shoulder to shoulder with Champion Havtru and Champion Keson. They fought, defending the remaining candidates, but there were too many.

All around, people were dying.

Soldiers. Candidates. Champions.

She knew in the city people must be dying.

Mothers, fathers, brothers, sisters, children.

And suddenly, she knew they couldn't wait. If they waited for Queen Daleina to wake, they'd all be dead. She'd rule an empty forest.

"Stop them!" she shouted to the candidates. "Make them freeze!"

"You mean—"

"Yes!"

"But Queen Daleina will wake!" Havtru cried.

"If we wait, she'll wake to our deaths!" To the candidates, she yelled, "Do it!"

As one, they began to cry, *Choose! Choose!* Piriandra felt the command, even though she had no power of her own. It swept like wind through the forest.

And the spirits drifted away.

All the spirits of Aratay simply retreated, slowly, distractedly— the air spirits floated into the air, the earth spirits sank into the earth, the tree spirits wandered vaguely away from the bodies they'd been savaging.

Unblocked, the spirits of Semo renewed their attack.

Leaping in front of one of the candidates, Piriandra blocked an air spirit, and then felt a sharp pain in her side. She looked down. An earth spirit had risen through the muck beside her and pierced her side. She felt another sharp pain in her arm. She swung her sword and kept fighting even as the blood flowed from her.

With only the swords of the champions and the spears and

swords of the soldiers to stop them, the army of Semo swept past the border and into the city of Mittriel.

As they rushed by Piriandra, she dropped to her knees. Her sword slipped from her fingers, and she spread her hands over the gash in her side. *I failed*, she thought.

The last thing she heard was screaming.

It could have been her own.

NAELIN FELT THE COMMAND SWEEP THROUGH THE SPIRITS: *Choose!*

*No!* she thought. *Queen Daleina will wake! Wait for her to wake!* But the spirits were already caught in the ancient command. She felt them detach and then drift. Their emotions fragmented. They'd drift until the next coronation ceremony.

"She's coming," Ven shouted. "And she's bringing her spirits!"

Naelin grasped for the spirits. *Help me! Fight!* But they only milled listlessly around her. She had no defenses, only Ven's sword. And if she had no defenses . . . neither did the city. Neither did the palace. Neither did Erian and Llor.

Queen Merecot was coming to the Queen's Grove.

And Naelin knew what she had to do, what Queen Daleina wanted her to do.

She reached out to the spirits, touching them with her mind as far as she could. She brushed against them and focused her thoughts. *Choose me.*

*Make me queen.*

## CHAPTER 34

Erian crouched under the table with her arms wrapped around Llor. Their father was huddled beside them. "If we're quiet, they won't know we're here," Father whispered. He flinched as something heavy crashed against the door. There was screaming out in the hall. Lots of crashes and the tinkle of shattering glass.

"I want Mama," Llor whimpered.

"Shh," Erian told him.

"Your mama is out there, helping keep us safe," Father said.

"She's doing it wrong," Llor said. "She should be in here, keeping us safe. You shouldn't have made her so mad. Then we'd all be together. It's your fault!" His voice was rising with each word.

Erian clapped her hand over Llor's mouth. "Shh! Spirits will hear you!"

He bit her hand.

"I'm going to find Mama!" He dove forward, out from under the table, and both Father and Erian scrambled after him. He was as quick as a squirrel, darting across the room, over the couch and under a table to the door. Throwing back the lock, he threw it open just as Father reached him—and a young woman rushed inside.

She slammed the door shut and locked it. Then she sank down, hugging a glass bottle to her chest. Her hair was singed and dirt streaked her cheek, and she looked a little familiar.

"Are you all right?" Father asked her.

"It worked," the woman said. Girl, really. She looked maybe fourteen. Older than Erian, but not as old as Mama and Father. "I'm not dead. Not temporarily. Not permanently. It worked, and I have to get it to her." Her voice became more and more shrill.

"Slow down," Father said. "It's not safe to go anywhere. There are spirits out there. You can hide with us." Father saying "hide"— that scared Erian more than all the screaming. He was the one who waltzed out of the house forgetting his ax. He was the one who forgot to stuff charms in their school bags. He was the one who said everything would work out fine, as long as they were cheerful and positive. Mother used to get so angry when he'd say that.

The older girl shook her head. "Can't. Got to get to the queen. I can do it. I can cure her. But the spirits came. They—I don't know if Master Garnah's alive or dead. I don't know if everyone's dead. I took it, and I ran." Tears leaked down her cheeks.

"You aren't making sense," Llor told her.

"Shh," Erian said. "She's upset." But she agreed with Llor. She didn't know what the scared girl was talking about, let alone who Master Garnah was.

"The queen is in the tower," the girl babbled to Father, "the tallest one. The Queen's Tower. So she could see the battle. I have to get there, but there are spirits everywhere. . . . You have to help me!" She showed them the bottle she'd been hugging: a vial filled with ruby-red liquid. "This will heal the queen."

Erian stared at it. Heal the queen!

If the queen was better . . . then Mama wouldn't have to be an heir anymore. Then she wouldn't have to be away, she wouldn't have to train, they wouldn't have to be here, she'd forgive Father, and they could all go home! *If the queen gets better, then Mama won't die.*

Father was shaking his head. "I promised my wife I would take care of our children. No risks. I have to prove she can trust me—"

"We'll help you," Erian interrupted. She then turned to her little brother. "Llor, we have to be sneaky to get past the spirits."

His grin lit up his face. "I'm the sneakiest." Dropping to the floor, he stuck his face against the tiny space at the bottom of the door. "Looks messy out there," he reported. "But nothing's moving. We could go now!"

"Llor, Erian, you aren't going anywhere," Father said firmly. "I told your mother–"

"Mama would do it," Erian argued. "She'd want to help the queen. She's helping her right now." She unlocked the door and peered out.

Father reached over and pushed it shut. "I know I've made mistakes. But ever since you were born, ever since I looked in your faces, I've wanted to give you everything. I never wanted to say no. I never wanted to make you cry. So I let your mother say no. I let her be the parent. I wanted to be the friend, the one who could make you happy. I thought if your mother came here, if she became an heir, that we'd have everything we needed–no more worries about anything. You could have all the toys and books you wanted, all the food we could ever eat, the biggest house . . . It was stupid. I know that now. I wasn't thinking it would be dangerous. Your mother . . . nothing has ever stopped her or scared her. I didn't think . . . Anyway, I am here now. And I am going to keep you safe and make the smart choices, even if it means saying no. So no, you cannot leave this room. We are going to hide here, safe and sound, until it's all over."

The older girl reached into a pocket of her skirt, pulled out a handful of dust, and blew it into Father's face. He crumpled onto the floor.

"You killed Father!" Llor cried. Balling up his fists, he ran at her. Erian intercepted him, catching him around his waist. Father didn't look dead or even hurt.

A second later, Father began to snore.

"He'll wake," the girl said.

"Wow!" Llor said. Erian let go of him–in an instant, he seemed to have forgotten his desire to beat her up. "How did you do that?"

The older girl didn't answer. "You two stay here. Keep yourselves hidden. Out there is no place for children. The spirits have gone rogue."

"But you said you need help!" Erian said. "I want to help." Especially if the queen was sick again. That meant that Mama was out there, fighting the spirits all by herself. *I have to help!*

"You aren't much older than us," Llor put in. And then his eyes went wide as if a sudden thought had occurred to him. "Erian"—he pulled her closer to whisper—"we can't go with her! Mama said never go anywhere with a stranger!"

He was right. But if they could help Mama . . . "What's your name?" Erian demanded.

"Arin," the girl said. "I'm the queen's sister." She cracked open the door and poked her head out. Erian noticed that it was quiet outside: no crashing. Peeking out around Arin, she didn't see any spirits. She did see a mess: half the roof was caved in.

"I've seen you!" Erian remembered seeing her in the garden— the queen had pointed her out, when they first met her. "It's okay. She's not a stranger," she told Llor.

"I'm going," Arin said. "Stay here, and stay hidden."

"We're coming with you," Erian insisted.

"I don't have time to argue—" Arin began.

Erian cut her off. "Then don't."

"Wait!" Llor said, and then he tucked his stuffed squirrel under Father's arm. Father mumbled in his sleep but then continued to snore softly.

They all slipped into the hallway. Llor grabbed Erian's hand as the door closed behind them. Shadows were everywhere, and it was strangely silent. They tiptoed through the hall, stepping over broken chandeliers. Scorch marks ran across the wood walls. Vines crisscrossed over them, as if they were bandages over the burns.

Arin hurried forward. "She's up—"

She halted.

Llor bumped into her. "Hey!"

"Shh," Erian said. "What is it?" She tried to see around Arin.

"The stairs are gone." Arin stepped aside, and Erian and Llor pressed forward. The stairs down were fine, but the stairway up had collapsed, folded together, as if the walls had been squeezed by a giant hand. "I don't know another way up."

Llor grabbed both their hands. "I know all the ways!" He pulled them away from the stairs, and they hurried back through the hallway.

He led them through the maze of corridors, to another set of stairs and up, but this one was blocked before the next level with branches that had woven together into a thick barrier.

"No!" Arin cried.

"Follow me," Llor insisted. "There's one more stairs."

They hurried through another corridor—and then stopped again. Here, the wall had been ripped off the building. Erian caught Llor's arm before he barreled forward. Outside were trees and sky, and the stairs dangled into emptiness.

In the city, spirits drifted aimlessly among broken trees. Several treetops hung upside down, split in the middle, and she saw black smoke staining the sky.

This time, Llor didn't race away. He stood staring at the open sky as if someone had stolen his favorite toy. They stood side by side.

"Llor," Erian asked, "are there any other stairs?" She knew the answer. She just hoped she was wrong.

He gulped. "No."

Arin clutched the vial of medicine. "I can't fail! She needs me. Don't you see? She never needed me before. She was always the one who was going to protect me. Protect everyone. But now I have a chance to save her . . ."

A sudden thought struck Erian so hard that she took a step backward. "The secret passageway! Llor, didn't Captain Alet say it went all the way up?" She knelt in front of her brother, forcing him to look at her and not at the swirling spirits and smoke outside. "All the way up to the *Queen's Tower*?"

"Yes!" Excited, he pulled them until they were running back through the corridor.

"It's not really a secret. It's a dumbwaiter, a lift," Erian told Arin as they ran. "The kitchen staff uses it to send food up, so they don't have to climb all the stairs."

"Yeah, you could ride in it! Like you're food!" Llor said.

"It's controlled by a crank in the kitchen," Erian explained.

Arin was nodding. "I've used it before, to send a cake. But how—"

This could work! It really could! "We could go turn the crank for you, and you could ride it up." The two of them together should be able to turn the crank—it hadn't looked that hard.

And behind her, she heard a crackle.

Glancing back, she saw ice spread across the wall. It looked like a many-figured hand reaching to grip the palace. "Ice spirit! Run faster!"

Wind whipped around them, hurling shards of ice in every direction. One hit her cheek. She felt it sting and then felt wetness and knew she was bleeding, but she kept running, stumbling over her feet but running faster.

Behind them, in a nearby corridor, the spirit shrieked.

"Faster!" Llor shouted.

Turning a corner, they reached the dumbwaiter, and Erian, with Arin and Llor, lifted the door. "Hurry, hurry, hurry!" Erian cried. She could hear the spirit in the corridor behind them—she didn't know if it had seen them or not. Maybe it had gone another way. Her fingers felt so cold that it hurt to move, and the wind continued to howl. It was close but not here yet.

Arin pulled on the rope, raising up the lift. She engaged the lock that kept it from plummeting when she released the rope. "Run, both of you! Get to the kitchen! Before the spirit finds you!" Without looking back to see if they'd obeyed, Arin tried to climb in—and Erian saw at once she was too tall. Inside, the cupboard itself was large, but the opening was narrow. She couldn't fold her legs enough to fit through. She tried to shove herself in, grunting and wincing. "Can't do it," she panted.

Llor hopped from foot to foot. "I'm little! I can fit!"

Arin was shaking her head. "It's too dangerous! If anything goes wrong, if a spirit finds you, you'll be trapped. I can't let you go. I have to find another way."

"But I can do it!" Llor cried.

Erian said to Llor, "You aren't going." If a spirit found him inside the shaft, he'd be trapped with nowhere to run. Plus anything could be up there. More spirits. A dead queen. "I am." She climbed into the lift and held out her hand for the medicine. "You have to promise to take care of Llor. Hide him from the spirits. And Llor, you have to promise to take care of Father when he wakes." Her heart was thudding. She didn't want to leave Llor, but bringing him wasn't the responsible—

The ice spirit screamed again, closer. *It's coming!*

Llor climbed in with her, his elbows and knees bumping against her as he squeezed in with her inside the lift. "I'm just as safe in here as out there. Safer! Please don't leave me!"

It was the "please" that convinced her. Llor *never* said please. And what if the spirit turned down this corridor? How could she leave not knowing if he'd have time to hide? "Okay." She held out her hand to Arin. "Medicine?"

Arin hesitated and then handed Erian the vial. "The queen's my sister. Not just a queen. She's family. Please . . ."

"We can do it," Erian promised. "Can you turn the crank in the kitchen? I don't think I'm strong enough to pull us all the way up." *I know I'm not.* It was a long way up.

"I can," Arin said. "I will."

Erian tucked the vial into her pocket and kicked the lock to release the dumbwaiter. It jerked down, but she and Llor held on to the rope at the back of the lift. Together, they pulled the rope. The dumbwaiter lurched upward.

Soon, they were in darkness.

Below them, they heard Arin scream.

## CHAPTER 35

*A*rin slammed the door to the dumbwaiter shut as the ice spirit swept around the corner. She saw it—too close—with its eyes like white stones and its body covered in icy spikes. Opening its mouth, it screeched and flew toward her.

She screamed once.

And then she ran.

Right, left, right again, then down a set of stairs. She didn't think. Just ran. Behind her, she heard shards of ice shatter against the walls. The steps beneath her feet were slick with ice, and she grabbed onto the railing as she half fell forward. She didn't look back.

Cold pricked her neck, and wind howled in her ears. Ahead, she saw the hallway writhing—the walls were undulating with ripples as if the wood were water. Vines were snaking across the floor.

*Tree spirit!*

She looked back.

The ice spirit was on the ceiling of the stairwell. It had jabbed its spiked fingers into the wood and was studying her as if she were delicious meat. *It's toying with me,* she realized. It could kill her at any time. "Daleina!" Arin screamed. "Daleina, help me!"

She knew her sister couldn't hear her. She was near the base of the palace tree, and Daleina was at the very top. For all she knew, Daleina wasn't even alive to hear her. *Don't think that.* Daleina had to be alive, and soon she'd wake and take control again . . .

But she wouldn't be cured until that little girl and boy reached the top, which they couldn't do without her.

Arin kept moving, knowing that if the ice spirit didn't catch her, she'd run into the tree spirit. Tears were rolling down her cheeks. *I don't want to die. Please, I don't want—*

Behind her, the ice spirit screeched again, and she clapped her hands over her ears and ran faster. The vines tangled around her feet. She fell onto her knees, and the vines closed over her ankles. "No!" She tried to push them off. Jamming her fingernails into the soft wood, she tore at it.

And the tree spirit scurried toward her. It looked like a twisted knot of brambles but with stones for eyes and thorns for hands. It launched itself at her shoulder. Pain shot through her as it dug into her arm, and she screamed and yanked at it.

"Cover your face!" she heard.

She buried her face in her hands and then felt a splash of water—her skin began to burn. She screamed again as every bit of flesh touched by the liquid felt as if it were on fire. But the wood spirit was yelling louder.

"Get free, girl!"

Arin forced her fingers to shove at the vines—they were loose—and she scrambled to her feet. She wiped with her sleeves at her face, neck, and arms, wiping the liquid off.

A blast of icy air slammed into her back and knocked her forward.

"Down! Crawl!"

She obeyed, even though she couldn't see who was shouting the orders. Looking up, she saw Master Garnah step around a corner and hurl a vial above Arin's head. It shattered, and flames licked through the corridor.

"Now! Follow me!" Master Garnah ordered.

Arin scrambled to her feet and ran. She glanced back once and saw the ice spirit wreathed in flame. The creature's body was contorted and blackened, but it was still alive, still screaming. "How did you do that? What was in that vial?"

"Lesson later; live now."

"You came for me?" Arin stared at Master Garnah. The older

woman had blood on her cheek and her left arm. Her skirt was torn, and soot and dirt stained it in streaks. "You're alive?"

"Obviously. Now we need to–"

"I have to get to the kitchen. Please, help me!"

To her surprise, Master Garnah didn't ask why. "I want full freedom of the palace. Full pardon for anything I have done or may do. You swear to convince your sister of this, and I'll get you wherever you want."

"You'll have it." If the antidote saved Daleina, she knew her sister would agree.

Master Garnah held up a hand. She wasn't done yet. Arin wanted to scream–they didn't have time to make bargains! "And I want full access to the queen, whenever I need it."

"Fine," Arin said. "So long as you promise not to harm her. *And* you teach me how to make whatever was in that vial." She'd never heard of a potion that could hurt spirits.

"Easily promised. I want my son back, and the only way to him is through the queen. Win her over, and I'll win him. You have the antidote?"

Arin didn't know if Master Garnah was telling the truth or not, but this wasn't the time or place to worry about it. "I have a way to get it to her, but we need to be in the kitchen *now*. I have to turn the crank to the lift–the antidote is inside. Only way to reach her." She'd drop to her knees and beg, if that was what it took. But she didn't need to. Master Garnah didn't ask any more questions or make any more demands. She shoved an unmarked brown bottle into Arin's hands and then propelled her forward.

"Wash away the fire liquid," she commanded. "You don't want it to scar you."

As they hurried down more stairs, Arin doused her skin everywhere it stung. The new liquid cooled her. She stoppered the bottle and tucked it into a pocket–and then Master Garnah stopped. She put a finger to her lips.

They crept forward, down the stairs. Arin wondered how many more stairs until they reached the kitchen, and how many more spirits were between here and there.

More steps.

And more.

And then: the kitchen!

Arin caught a glimpse through the doorway of the ovens and—Master Garnah shoved her back and flattened against the wall.

"Spirits?" Arin mouthed silently. "How many?"

Master Garnah nodded for her to look.

Leaning forward, Arin peeked around the corner of the stairs into the kitchen. And saw a nightmare. Three spirits . . . no, four . . . no, there was another! An air spirit was feasting on the body of a dead cook. An earth spirit was tearing the ground open. Three tree spirits had wrapped a half-dozen other cooks in vines. Some were clearly dead. Others . . . Arin hoped they were dead. The floor and walls were spattered in blood, and there were . . . parts. Human parts.

She felt herself begin to gag. Clamping her hands over her mouth, she retreated back to Master Garnah. She squeezed her eyes shut, trying to erase what she'd seen, but all she saw was red. She could smell it now too, sickly sweet and coppery. Like licking a coin. The smell coated the back of her throat. "Too many," Arin whispered.

"Exactly how many and where?"

"Five." She described where they were: by the wall, by the hearth, under a table. She didn't describe the bodies. Didn't want to think about them. She wanted to pretend they weren't real, that this was all some dream, some hideous nightmare.

Master Garnah reached for her belt and began to unstring pouches. She pressed five vials into Arin's hands and then tied the other pouches around Arin's waist. "Throw them, into the mouths if possible, and then run for the crank. It won't kill them. It should slow them." She kept a few for herself. "If you succeed, remember your promise."

Arin nodded, even though her thoughts were screaming. *Don't do it! There are spirits! They'll kill you!* But Daleina had to be cured. She was the only one who could stop all of it. And Arin and Master Garnah were the only ones who could help her.

"Good luck," Master Garnah said. "And try not to die. You're the best apprentice I've ever had—barring my son, of course."

"Wait—you aren't coming?"

"The queen is your sister, not mine," Master Garnah said. "Don't look at me like that. I never pretended to be altruistic, and I haven't survived this long by taking foolish risks."

"If I die, I can't keep my promise."

"Throw the vials, and try not to miss." She patted Arin's shoulder. It was *not* comforting. "Survive, and I'll teach you how to make these."

Arin swallowed hard once, then again. Her mouth felt so dry that she couldn't remember ever having saliva. Her heart was thumping so fast and hard that she felt it throughout her body. She clutched the vials in her sweaty hands.

*Throw the vials,* she told herself. *Just throw them and turn the crank. And that's it.*

Stepping forward, she walked down the final steps into the kitchen. At the bottom, she froze, staring at the spirits and the bodies and the blood and . . .

A tree spirit saw her. It shrieked and flew toward her.

*Throw!*

A half second later, her arm obeyed, and she flung a vial.

Her aim was off. It hit a table, shattered, and the liquid oozed out, sizzling the stone. The tree spirit opened its jaws and reached, and Arin threw a second vial.

It hit the tree spirit in the teeth.

The glass shattered, and the liquid sprayed into the spirit's mouth. The spirit jerked backward as if she'd stabbed it. And then all the spirits were coming for her, and she was throwing vials in every direction, one after another.

The air was filled with inhuman screams, and she was screaming too.

And then suddenly, the air was empty. The spirits were all alive, screaming and writhing on the floor, but they weren't attacking. Arin ran toward the crank. She slipped in a puddle of blood, fell, and then scrambled to her feet.

At the crank, she turned it. Harder and harder, faster and faster.

Behind her, she heard the spirits growing louder. She risked a glance back. They were beginning to shake off the effects of the vials. She reached for her belt. She had more.

As the earth spirit raised its head, she threw another vial. As the tree spirit crawled toward her, another. She turned the crank more, pausing to throw vials.

And then she was out of vials.

The lift was not at the top.

"Run, girl!" Master Garnah shouted as she flung a powder into the kitchen.

Arin ran through the powder toward the stairs. A tree spirit clawed at her leg. She felt its thorns rip her skin, but she didn't stop. She raced past them and to the stairs.

Master Garnah grabbed her arm, and together they ran up, away from the kitchen.

Arin hoped she'd done enough, that the children were high enough, that they could make it the rest of the way on their own, that they weren't already dead, that her sister wasn't already gone.

The spirits in the kitchen howled, and there was no more time to worry. There was only time to run.

IT WAS QUIET INSIDE THE SHAFT. THE ONLY SOUNDS WERE THE squeak of the rope and the grunt of their breaths as they pulled, pulled, and pulled. It jerked up at first and then it began to rise more smoothly as they fell into a pattern.

"It's a good thing I'm not scared of the dark," Llor said.

"Yes, it is," Erian agreed. She wasn't crazy about the dark. She tried not to imagine spirits coming into the shaft with them. They wouldn't be able to run. They'd only be able to fall. Very, very far. She found herself listening extra hard.

"I'm not scared of anything."

"Then you don't have a very good imagination," Erian said.

Llor thought about that for a few minutes. She could almost hear his brain chewing over that idea. "I am a little scared of fire spirits. If they set the rope on fire, we'd fall down. And I'm a little scared of tree spirits. If they grew the walls in, we'd be squeezed. And ice spirits—"

"Llor, please shut up."

He shut up.

Erian's arms began to ache. She didn't know if she could pull much longer. She wondered if Arin had made it to the kitchen. She could have encountered spirits. She could be dead.

*Don't think that*, she told herself.

Leaning against the rope, she panted. "I have to rest." She hooked the rope so it wouldn't fall farther. Her arm muscles felt as if they'd been twisted and stretched like taffy.

Llor curled beside her. "What do we do?"

"We wait. Arin will turn the crank. She just needs to get to the kitchen." If she could. If there weren't too many spirits in the way. If she wasn't already dead.

They waited together, in the darkness.

Minutes stretched.

When she felt like she could, Erian pulled on the rope again. This time, she only managed a few pulls before her arms felt like they were on fire. She had to rest again. *I can't do it. I'm not strong enough.*

The top of the tower was so impossibly high above them. Inconceivably high. Erian's eyes felt hot, and she dashed away tears with the back of her hand.

"Are you crying?" Llor asked in the dark.

"No."

"Yes, you are."

"Am not." Then she added, "I don't want to."

"Mama says it's okay to cry if you're really hurt. Are you hurt, Erian? My foot feels uncomfortable. Prickly. Do your feet ever do that? It helps if you shake them." The lift began to wobble–Llor was shaking his foot. "Do you think we're going to die in here? If no one ever knows we're in here, do you think we'll starve? What do you think it's like to starve?"

"We won't starve," she told him. "Don't talk like that."

"What if I have to pee?" he asked.

"Don't."

"But if I really have to?"

She heard a creak from above them, and she froze. Beside her, Llor fell silent without even needing to be told. She listened, trying to hear what it was. She heard a scrabbling sound, like a chipmunk running across dried leaves.

"What is it?" Llor whispered. "Is it a spirit?"

It could be. Very, very much could be. She wrapped her arms around Llor. If it was, there was no place to run. No place to hide, except where they were. Nothing to do, except wait.

So they waited, in the darkness, listening to the spirit crawling around in the shaft.

Time passed. She didn't know how much time. It could have been hours or just minutes. It felt like forever. She wondered if she'd ever see outside this lift again, if she'd ever see sunlight, if she'd ever see Mama or Father. She started crying for real this time, and her tears fell onto Llor, but he didn't say anything. He just squeezed her tighter.

The lift lurched upward.

"Erian, what's happening?" Llor whispered, his voice high and scared. "Is it Arin?"

They rose faster, up and up. "Yes, I think so." Hope blossomed inside her, and she looked upward, as if she could see anything in the darkness, as if there were anything to see besides the roof of the box.

"She made it," Erian breathed. "We're going to make it."

The lift jerked to a stop.

Silence.

And then the skritting sound, closer this time. Llor squeezed against her, and she held him tight. It sounded just above them. *Definitely a spirit.*

They rose again.

Higher.

A thump on the roof.

"It's above us," Llor whispered, directly into her ear.

She said nothing. There was nothing to say. If the spirit realized they were inside . . . She heard it growl, that familiar and awful rumble of a tree spirit, just above them, riding the lift with them.

And then the lift halted again.

They waited.

It didn't start.

Slowly, quietly, Erian unwound herself from Llor. Her muscles had had a chance to rest. She could do it, raise them up a little more. She grabbed the rope and began to pull.

The spirit on the roof moved—they heard its paws as it paced—but Erian didn't stop. She kept going, even when her arms began to ache again.

They rose higher and higher, until at last—at long last—their heads bumped into a ceiling, and the rope jerked to a stop. They were here. The top of the tallest tower. The Queen's Tower. Together, they locked the lift into position.

Bending, Erian opened the little door. She heard a voice, muffled, male, human. She hoped it was someone friendly. She squeezed out and then held her finger to her lips to signal Llor to be quiet. He jumped out next to her. Together, they crept up the final steps to the tower platform.

Erian peeked and saw a man in healer robes, bent over a pile of silk and lace and—*the queen!* She hurried forward, pulling the vial from her pocket.

At the sound of her steps, the healer spun—he had a knife in his hand. Erian halted, and then she heard a half whine, half bark. Llor cried, "Doggie!" He ran toward Bayn.

But Bayn lunged past him. Jaws wide, the wolf jumped onto the tree spirit who was climbing out of the dumbwaiter. Bayn pinned the spirit down—it was a small one, chipmunk-size, with thorny claws. Howling, it struck at Bayn's face, but Bayn tore into it.

Right before them, the wolf ripped the spirit to pieces. Erian stared, unable to match the sweet wolf she knew with the savage beast she saw. The spirit was like a limp, lifeless doll. Growling between his teeth, he shook its body in his jaws and then dropped it.

"Erian, the queen!" Llor shouted, tugging on her sleeve.

Erian held out the vial to the healer. "The queen's sister gave this to us."

Llor nodded vigorously. "She said it will make the queen better."

The spirit lay silent, in a pool of brown saplike blood. Erian tried not to look at it. Bayn trotted over to them, and Llor threw his arms around the wolf's neck.

With a trembling hand, the healer took the vial. Erian, Llor, and Bayn crowded into the tower and watched as the healer tilted the queen's head back, gently parted her lips, and poured the liquid into her mouth.

HAMON'S HAND SHOOK AS HE POURED THE ANTIDOTE INTO Daleina's mouth. He stroked her throat, willing her to swallow, even though her body felt dead—was dead—beneath his hands. She had the unmistakable cool stillness that typified the False Death. Or real death. He didn't know if this was the one, the False Death that became true death, the one she wouldn't wake up from. He prayed she'd wake. He prayed the antidote would work.

He kept her head tilted so that the liquid would flow down her throat. Beside him, the two children and the wolf waited quietly. All of them watched the queen, as if staring would cause her lungs to suddenly expand, her heart to beat, her eyes to open. Lifting her hand to his lips, he kissed her fingers. "Wake, Daleina."

She didn't wake.

"What if it doesn't work?" the girl asked, her voice anxious.

"It'll work," the boy said. "It's medicine. Medicine fixes you."

*Not always*, Hamon thought. He knew that far too well. Beyond the tower, he could hear the sounds of battle—the border had been breached, and the enemy spirits were within the city, close to the palace. And their own spirits were out there too, killing, burning, destroying.

"Mama gives me medicine when I'm sick," the boy said. "It tastes bad. Maybe the queen doesn't like the taste, and maybe that's why she's not waking up. I wish Mama was here."

"She'll come back for us," the girl said.

"She'll be mad we left Father," the boy said.

"No. She won't."

Hamon forced himself to look at them. They really were young. The boy couldn't have been more than six. "What are your names?"

"I'm Llor." The boy stuck his thumb toward himself. "My sister is Erian."

"Where are your parents?"

"Father's asleep," Llor said. "The queen's sister blew some dust in his face, and he fell asleep. And Mama's off fighting the monsters."

"Do you think Father will wake?" Erian asked. "Arin said he would."

"If he doesn't wake on his own, I can wake him," Hamon promised. It was the least he could do, given the risks these children had taken to bring the antidote. Even if it didn't work.

"Don't see how," Llor said. "You're stuck in this tower. All the stairs are broken, and you're too big to fit in the lift."

Hamon glanced at the boy's sister, who nodded seriously. She flinched as a tree cracked close to the palace. The sky was dark with spirits, and he couldn't tell if they were from Aratay or Semo. At this point, he wasn't sure it mattered. People were dying, either way. He should be out there, helping the wounded. Instead, he was here, unwilling to admit that the antidote had failed, unwilling to admit that Daleina was gone, unwilling to admit it was true death and she wasn't going to—

The wolf leaned forward and licked the queen's cheek.

Daleina spasmed.

She sucked in air, and her body jerked and arched. Hamon caught her body, cradling her. "Breathe, Daleina. Come on, breathe." He felt warmth flood through her limbs. He felt her lungs expand again as she took a second breath, and then a third. "Daleina?"

She opened her eyes.

He felt tears fill his own eyes. "Daleina."

She spoke. Her voice was rough and broken. "My sister?"

The little girl, Erian, spoke. "She helped us reach you. She's in the kitchen—she's fine. She wouldn't have been able to turn the crank if she wasn't fine."

"She is well," Hamon reassured her. "As are you."

Daleina drew another breath. "No, I'm not.

"There is another queen."

## CHAPTER 36

Naelin felt as though she were soaring through a rainstorm. Her mind was shrouded with grayness and pummeled with the thoughts-feelings-awareness of thousands of spirits. They swallowed her, and she felt as if she were fracturing within the storm.

She latched onto her own thoughts, to who she was, to her memories. *Erian. Llor.* She clung to them, to her images of them. They were her anchor, and she used them to pull herself back through the mass of minds into her own body.

And then she found it: herself. She felt her own breath. She felt the roughness of the bark of the roots beneath her. Opening her eyes, she saw the patch of blue sky above her.

"I can feel them all," she whispered.

Every spirit, in all of Aratay.

"Naelin, she's here!" Ven called to her. "Control the spirits! Use them!"

Plunging her mind into the earth, she sent her will out. *Come to me,* she told the earth kraken. It moved eagerly and quickly beneath the surface, racing toward the grove. To the other spirits, she ordered, *Hold the enemy.*

Don't destroy. Just hold. Stop them.

Stop their advance, stop their destruction, hold them where they were.

Until Naelin could talk to Merecot.

Queen to queen.

She rose and felt as if her body were somehow larger than it was. She felt as if she were connected to the trees, the earth, the air, in a way that went beyond the metaphorical. Her breath was the sky. Her blood was the sap in the trees. Her heart was within the earth, deep down. She *was* Aratay. And Queen Merecot was an interloper. For all her spirits, she did not belong here. But Naelin did. She was the trees, the rocks, the air, the streams. She was mother to this earth.

Walking forward, Naelin felt as if she were gliding. Raising her hands, she called tree spirits to her, and they parted the trees to open the grove.

Standing on the backs of two air spirits, the queen of Semo flew into the grove. Three fire spirits flew behind her, sparks landing on the grasses and moss. Naelin sent her own spirits, only a few, to douse the flames.

Queen Merecot was young, as young as Queen Daleina, with black hair that flowed in the wind and a dress that shone like the sun. One white streak of hair gleamed beneath her crown. Like the streak in Alet's hair. Clasping her hands in front of her, Naelin waited for her to be close enough and then she said, "Welcome to Aratay."

Her words were echoed by spirits. *Welcome, welcome, welcome.*

She added, "And now I must ask you to leave."

*Leave, leave, leave.*

Queen Merecot's face twisted in a flash of anger and then smoothed into a peaceful smile. She was beautiful, the kind of beautiful that comes from complete confidence. She radiated strength and youth and conviction. "Please, step aside."

"I cannot." Naelin almost felt sorry for her. She looked like a woman who had never heard no, who had never failed, who had never met anyone stronger than she was. Until today.

"I don't want to hurt you." Sincerity dripped from her tongue, but Naelin didn't believe her. The spirits whispered, *Lies, lies, lies.* "I do not want to hurt anyone. I never did."

"Then don't," Naelin said reasonably. "Stop this war."

"I *must* have Aratay," Queen Merecot said. "My people need this land."

"And what of my people?" *She's only a child*, Naelin thought. A child who wanted more toys than she had. She shook her head. "You may try. You will fail. You're on my land, facing the spirits who belong here. You cannot win." She could feel all the spirits, swirling inside her head, tingling on her skin. She'd never imagined it would feel so exhilarating, or so wonderful.

"Queen Daleina would understand what I have done and what I must do. I have responsibilities, to my people and to my land. I have sworn to protect them and nurture them, and this is the only way." She sounded as if she thought what she said was reasonable, as if she thought she could talk Naelin into surrendering Aratay. "We will not survive as we are. There are too many spirits in Semo. The mountains—they rise and they fall. We *must* expand, or my people will die. It's nothing personal; it never was. Daleina's my dearest friend, but my people need this land. They'll die without it."

"You cannot have Aratay," Naelin said. "It's not yours. It's *mine*." Mine to protect. Mine to love. Like Erian and Llor. She'd claimed all the people, the spirits, the rocks and trees and streams as her children.

Queen Merecot narrowed her eyes, but Naelin was ready. When her spirits flew at her, she had her own fly to meet them. Air met air. Fire met fire. Wood met wood. And beneath the earth, the kraken reached the grove. Its hands burst through the rock and seized the earth spirits that were creeping behind Naelin.

*Hold them*, Naelin ordered. *Do not kill.*

Queen Merecot didn't deserve to have her land's spirits killed. Her people certainly didn't deserve that. She would—

"Attack!" Queen Merecot ordered.

Lightning slammed into the ground, and fire swept in a circle around Naelin. The earth buckled and split, and Naelin screamed as she plummeted into a crevasse. She reached out with her mind, and three air spirits swept under her, catching her, but Merecot's air spirits dove into them, wrestling them away. Naelin was knocked against the side of the crevasse.

Hands made out of dirt reached from the soil and clamped onto Naelin's wrists. She felt a tree root snake around her throat and begin to tighten. She reached for her own spirits—but they felt so distant, like whispers.

*She's too strong*, Naelin realized.

*I'm going to die.*

As the root squeezed her neck, she thought of her children. She'd sworn to protect them, yet here she was, miles away from them, trapped.

Black spots swam in front of her eyes.

She called to the earth kraken and felt him move within the earth, felt him grapple with the spirits of Semo, felt him try to reject them from his land. She called to the water spirits to loosen the soil around the tree. She called to her tree spirits to force the root to release her. But Merecot's command of her spirits was absolute.

*I'm sorry, Erian. I'm sorry, Llor. I love you.* She wished they could hear her, that she could see them one more time. Darkness rose like a shadow over her eyes. This wasn't how she wanted to end. She thought of Ven and how he'd believed in her . . . *I'm sorry.*

And then darkness.

Black nothingness.

Emptiness.

She floated through silence, her thoughts fragmenting, her self unraveling. She was a cloud dispersing in the sky. Water evaporating in the sun. Snow melting in the spring. Death was here to embrace her.

Naelin heard—no, she *felt* a voice. Distant. Soft. Sweet. Like the first touch of sunrise. *"There is another queen,"* the voice whispered. She suddenly felt as if she were split, and she was looking out at a tower, at the face of a healer, at . . . *Erian and Llor!* They were there, peering down at her. No, not her. At . . . Queen Daleina? Was she . . .

The root around her neck loosened.

Only a little, but it was enough.

Air rushed down her throat. Pain blossomed in her head, and

she was back in her body, awake, alive. She pushed again toward her spirits. *Free me!*

The air spirits dove for her, and earth spirits gnawed at the root around her. She fell into the feathery arms of a spirit and was lifted up out of the chasm.

The grove was on fire. Flames roared through the trees, and smoke choked the air. Merecot had ringed herself with Semoian spirits and was calling more to her. Naelin saw the air around the other queen was clear, and she called her own air spirits to her, blowing fresh air through the smoke. She breathed, air rushing painfully down her throat.

Queen Merecot was facing away from Naelin, toward the capital, toward the palace, toward Naelin's children. "Leave them alone!" Naelin cried. "You fight me!" She wasn't as well trained as Merecot, but she was strong, and this time she was ready—she could buy Daleina time, enough time to protect Erian and Llor, perhaps enough to save Aratay.

*That* would be worth dying for.

Merecot's air spirits were holding back Naelin's water spirits, keeping them from the flames, so Naelin called to her earth kraken again. She called the earth to rise up and swallow the flames in dirt and rock.

As the fire died, Merecot's attention shifted back to Naelin. Raising her arms, Queen Merecot directed her spirits directly at Naelin—

And then Merecot collapsed.

## CHAPTER 37

N aelin stared at Merecot's unconscious body, sprawled across the roots, and then she looked up at Ven, who stood behind Queen Merecot with his sword raised. He'd hit her with the hilt of his sword.

She felt a smile, unbidden, bend her lips. The queen of Semo had been so focused on her own power, on the power of queens, that she hadn't watched for a straightforward attack—well, as straightforward as it could be, coming from behind. "Thank you, Ven," Naelin said. She put every bit of emotion into those three words: everything she felt for Aratay, for her children, for herself, for him.

"You're welcome. Thank *you* for distracting her." He smiled back at her, and it felt like the sun coming out from behind the clouds. She felt as though she should hear singing. She suddenly and inexplicably wanted to laugh.

She sent her spirits to disperse the smoke and squelch the remnants of the fire. The spirits of Semo rustled at the edges of the grove—hemmed in by the spirits of Aratay. She felt the spirits of Aratay holding the spirits of Semo throughout the city.

Closing her eyes, she reached out—she felt/saw Daleina rise and summon air spirits. All of them climbed on: Daleina, Hamon, Erian, Llor, and the wolf Bayn, and they flew. *Come*, Naelin sent the thought to them. *To the Queen's Grove.*

*We come*, Daleina answered back. The words reverberated

through the spirits. Naelin couldn't see into Daleina's mind, but she could hear her *through* the spirits. She could hear her because the spirits could.

"The queen . . . she's not dead," Naelin said. Her throat hurt as she spoke, but she said the words anyway. "Erian and Llor . . . they're alive. We're alive." In two steps, she reached Ven. He wrapped his arms around her, tight, and she wound hers around him.

They were kissing when the air spirits arrived.

QUEEN DALEINA HAD TREE SPIRITS WRAP MERECOT IN VINES. She was still unconscious, but Hamon said she would wake soon. *Bind her tight*, Daleina thought.

Bayn sat next to Merecot, his heavy paws on the queen's stomach, holding her down. When the spirits finished, she nodded her thanks to them and the wolf, and then looked up at the others. Ven stood beside Naelin—he'd been displaced by her children but still hovered close to her. "You're alive and using your power," Ven said to Daleina. "Does this mean . . . Are you . . ."

"She's healed," Hamon confirmed. "My mother made that antidote. She doesn't make mistakes. I will test the queen's blood as soon as this is all over, but I have no doubt." His voice was filled with all his old confidence.

Sagging, Ven exhaled. Relief was etched on his face, and Daleina noticed how tired he looked. He looked far older than he was, as if the last few hours had squeezed him like a dishrag. She felt the same way, but she refused to show it.

This wasn't over yet.

"Your Majesty," Naelin said. "I never intended to take your crown." She tried to curtsy but couldn't. Her children were clinging to her, draped around her neck like heavy necklaces. She looked battered from the battle she'd faced in the grove, but whole.

"You did not take it," Daleina said. "The spirits still acknowledge me. They have embraced us both as their queen." She managed a smile, despite the fact that her old friend lay bound at her feet, despite the fact that another friend had betrayed her and died for it.

"No country has ever had two queens. I'll abdicate immediately."

"No," Ven said. "You'll be killed."

Her children began to wail. Daleina couldn't remember their names, but she knew that sound. She'd heard it in her palace, in the city, as she'd woken from the False Death. She would hear it in her dreams. Consoling her children, Naelin said, "She can use her power again. She can keep me safe."

"Until someone tries to kill her again," Ven said.

Daleina saw Naelin hesitate—uncertainty was written clearly on her face. Her arms were tight around her children's shoulders. Both children had quieted and were still clinging, whimpering softly, to their mother.

"Don't abdicate. Not yet," Daleina said. "Aratay may still need you."

"You mean because of her." Naelin nodded at Merecot.

Lying there, she looked so much like the friend Daleina remembered. A few years older. But her face was the same. Not the face of a killer. *Oh, Merecot.* "She had me poisoned." Daleina tried to understand how she could have done it, how anyone could kill a friend. "She'd always been ambitious, but I never thought . . . I never suspected . . ."

"You could eliminate the threat," Hamon said softly. "Now and forever. It could be painless. She'd never need to wake."

"If you kill her, her people will suffer," Naelin warned.

That was true. The spirits of Semo would go rogue, and then everyone would suffer. "I'm not going to kill her," Daleina said. *I don't kill friends.* "Her spirits are in our land. I don't want them going rogue here, and I don't want her crown." It was hard enough to be responsible for all of Aratay. The last thing she wanted was more lives on her conscience.

"You could take it," Ven said to Naelin. "Give up Aratay and take control of Semo. I could kill her for you. Daleina, you would not have to watch." There was a look in his eyes that belied his words. He looked as if his words were poison on his tongue. *He doesn't want to kill her,* Daleina thought. But he would, if his queens asked.

The little boy gasped. "Killing's wrong!"

"Shh," the little girl said. And then she hugged her brother.

Daleina looked down at Merecot, who was beginning to stir. Her head rocked to the side, and she groaned. She'd caused so much damage, both through her sister, Alet, and with her army. Daleina knew she should be angry. But she only felt sad. "The boy's right."

"Daleina, she tried to kill you," Hamon said. His voice was still soft, but she heard the anger in it. Anger and fear. "She *did* kill others. She could kill again."

"A healer advocating death?" Daleina fixed her eyes on him and noticed how worn he looked, as if he hadn't slept in weeks, as if he'd spent every waking moment worrying and working . . . *He had,* she thought. *For me.* "That's your mother talking." She said it gently but firmly.

He blanched and fell silent.

"No," Daleina said, decided. "I won't kill another queen. We will find a different way." She raised her eyes to look at Naelin. Queen Naelin. *It suits her,* Daleina thought. *Mother of Aratay.* "There's been enough death."

Naelin was silent for a moment—Daleina felt as if she was being evaluated, all her flaws tallied up and slated for correction, all her strengths recognized and catalogued—before Naelin said, "Yes."

At Daleina's feet, Merecot groaned and tried to roll to the side, but the vines held her firm. The tree spirits chittered and tugged tighter on the vines. Bayn growled. Daleina knelt beside her old friend. Merecot's eyes fluttered open, and Daleina felt a pang—sorrow? Anger? She didn't know. Pity, maybe.

"You're alive," Merecot said.

"Yes."

Merecot struggled once against the tree spirits and then lay still. "I heard you were ill. I knew Aratay would need a new queen. I came to help—"

"Don't lie to me, Merecot," Daleina said. "I know what you did, and I am sorry to inform you that your sister, Alet, is dead. And that it's your fault." The words felt like broken glass in her throat. It hurt to say them. Daleina thought of her own sister. The spirits had confirmed she was alive and well. Safe again, for now.

"Alet . . ." Merecot's eyes filled with tears.

Daleina couldn't tell if the tears were real or not. She hoped they were, for Alet's sake.

Naelin spoke from behind Daleina. "Tell your spirits to stop fighting. Or ours will tear them apart, and Semo will be destroyed. Your mountains won't survive the death of your spirits." Her tone brooked no argument. *Mother of the world*, Daleina thought.

Merecot stared first at Naelin and then at Daleina. "You're both . . . Oh, how very clever. And complicated. I don't believe it's ever been done before. However will you rule with two queens?"

"That's not your concern," Daleina told her.

"But Semo *is* my concern," Merecot said, straining to sit upright. Even prone and tied, she commanded attention as if she were on a throne. She was born to be a queen. "We cannot survive as we are. We are overrun with spirits. There simply isn't enough land to support them all. They'll tear my land apart. Leave my people homeless. Helpless."

"Then why didn't you ask for help?" Daleina asked. "Why do this?"

Merecot snorted. "What would you have done if I'd come to you? Given me your country if only I'd said please?"

Merecot was every bit as infuriating as Daleina remembered. She wanted to shake her. Or scream. Or cry. All of this could have been avoided! If only Merecot had trusted her, tried to work together, done anything but this! "I don't know! But we could have found a better solution, together."

Kneeling next to Daleina, Naelin addressed Merecot. "We still can. It's not too late. You're going to go back home, with your spirits, and you're going to send emissaries, in good faith. We will find an equitable solution through diplomacy that suits both our lands."

"A solution that doesn't involve murder," Daleina said. "Merecot, how could you? Attempting to assassinate one of your only friends? And using your sister to do it?" She knew she was shouting but didn't care.

Shackled by tree spirits, Merecot was a strange mix of haughty and pathetic, with her dress stained with dirt and blood and her crown askew on her head. Her black hair had slithered out of its elaborate braids. "I had no choice."

"There's always a choice," Naelin said, and Daleina heard her hesitate before she added, "Granted, sometimes the only choices are bad."

Merecot nodded as if she'd found an ally. "I faced a terrible choice: I could either be a good friend or a good queen, but I couldn't be both. I was trying to save my people! You have to see that."

"You can't trust her," Hamon said quietly.

"I *don't* trust her," Daleina told him. "But I do know her." Merecot wanted to keep her throne. She wanted Semo strong and safe. She could be trusted to act in her own best interest.

"Daleina, please believe that I am sorry," Merecot said. "I didn't want—"

Daleina cut her off. "Here's what is going to happen: you are going to take your spirits and go north. You are going to repair as much damage as you can on the way, and then you are going to cross the border and stay there. When you're done licking your wounds, you are going to send emissaries, exactly as Queen Naelin said, and we are going to discuss Semo's problem like civilized people." She leaned forward. "And Merecot? Don't confuse mercy for forgiveness."

She ordered the tree spirits to release her, even as ideas started whirling in her head about what to do in Semo.

Linked through the spirits, Queen Daleina and Queen Naelin watched Queen Merecot as she flew on the backs of air spirits, instructing her spirits to restore the earth. Streams flowed again. Trees grew. And Aratay began to heal.

Naelin—Queen Naelin—positioned her son on her lap and her daughter next to her, tucked up against her, as she leaned against the trunk of one of the trees in the Queen's Grove. Erian was breathing evenly, already asleep, and Llor was close to sleep. Naelin could feel Daleina guiding the spirits northward. Stretching her thoughts out, Naelin scooted them along as well, ordering them to assist in the cleanup. It wouldn't be perfect. New trees could be grown, but old ones couldn't be restored. Lost lives couldn't be returned. But at least it felt good to be fixing things.

"This could be a mistake," Ven said quietly. He was sitting at her back, on a root. She felt the warmth of his breath on her neck.

"It could be," Naelin agreed. Merecot could simply try again. Send more assassins. Invade again. She could feel desperate now that her plan had failed. Or maybe she'd be smart and realize they could help. Together, they could find a better, less bloody solution. There had to be one.

"You don't think it is." It wasn't a question. "If Daleina had decided to kill her . . . If *I* had agreed . . ." He sounded as if he already knew her answer before he even formed the words.

"Yes, I would have stopped you." Leaning over her daughter, she pressed her lips to her sleeping daughter's hair. It smelled a bit like smoke and a lot like dust. Erian's hands and arms were streaked with dirt, and her palms were red. So were Llor's. Later, she'd ask them all about what they'd seen and heard and did. For now, it was enough that they were together. A sudden thought occurred to her. "But you knew that. You knew that when you offered to kill her, didn't you?" Twisting around as far as she could without disturbing her children, she met Ven's eyes.

He caressed her cheek. "Yes."

She smiled. "I'm that predictable?"

"You're that *good*. You will be a good queen."

Naelin looked across the grove toward Daleina. The queen of Aratay was standing beside her healer, and all her attention was focused northward. She hadn't collapsed again, despite how much she was using her power. "Aratay already has a good queen."

"And now it has two," Ven said. "Doubly lucky. Like I am, for having found you." He moved closer, leaning against her.

Llor shifted in her lap. "And me," he said sleepily.

Ven laughed softly, a rumble that she felt through her back. "Triply lucky, for having found you, Erian, and Llor."

"And the nice doggie too," Llor said.

"Yes, Bayn too."

The wolf raised his head and regarded them with his yellow eyes. He then scooted closer and lay his head across Naelin's feet, as if he agreed with Ven and Llor.

Naelin hadn't thought of it as luck, and she'd certainly never considered it *good* luck. Fate maybe? Or simply the convergence of many people's choices, bringing them all to this grove, together.

Maybe it didn't matter what they called it, chance or choice, as long as they were together.

She pulled Erian and Llor closer, feeling their warmth. She felt Ven behind her and Bayn at her feet—all of them, cocooning her, believing in her. And despite everything, she felt, for the first time in a long while, safe.

## CHAPTER 38

White blossoms fell on fresh graves so often that the sweet smell wafted across Mittriel with the evening breeze, becoming as familiar as the scent of bread from the bakeries and sweat from the workers who were repairing the city.

Two days after Queen Merecot's retreat to Semo, Queen Daleina presided over the funerals for Champion Piriandra and the other champions and candidates who had fallen. She spoke of their dedication and bravery and sacrifice, and she called to the spirits to cover the earth and fill the air with white flowers. A day later, she attended the funerals for the city and palace guards, as well as the caretakers and courtiers who had been killed by spirits. Again, more flowers. Then at the ruins of Northeast Academy, where Headmistress Hanna, who'd lost the use of her legs while defending her students, led a ceremony for the fallen students, teachers, and staff. After that, there was the memorial for the men, women, and children of Aratay—each family had their own private funeral, but Daleina wanted to honor her people and all their losses. At this, the petals were as plentiful as snow in a winter storm.

By the end of it, she was sick of death, sick of pain, and sick of tears. Grief and guilt felt like rain that had permeated every inch of her skin. She could not escape it. And still there was one more to be buried: Captain Alet.

No one wanted a funeral for Alet.

Except Daleina. And, to her surprise, Naelin. The other queen joined Daleina while she was arguing with a knot of chancellors in the Amber Throne Room.

All the chancellors bowed when Queen Naelin entered. She was followed closely by the seneschal, and Daleina was certain he had brought her here—he was intent on doing his duty to both queens. He was the one who had insisted that a second throne be set up on the dais. Borrowed from the Sunrise Room, its pastels were jarring in the somber, rich gold of the Amber Throne Room.

But then, everything about having two queens was jarring.

Naelin had yet to sit on her throne.

"Your Majesty . . ." one of the chancellors began, and then stopped as if uncertain how to continue—it was Chancellor Xanon, who had been pushing the most strenuously for Alet's body to be shipped back to Semo in an unmarked crate.

"You were discussing the funeral for Captain Alet," Naelin said. She had the skill of making a simple statement sound like a rebuke. Daleina admired that.

Chancellor Xanon looked, for an instant, like a toddler who had been caught with chocolate smeared on his face; then he composed himself. "She committed high treason. Surely such a criminal cannot be honored, nor mourned. Her death is a victory, not a tragedy."

"Every death is a tragedy, Chancellor . . ." She let the name dangle.

"Xanon," the chancellor supplied with another bow.

"She was our friend and our enemy, Chancellor Xanon," Naelin said. "We will mourn our friend who was killed by our enemy. Surely you understand that a life is more complex than a label. We can love who she was while we hate what she's done."

"Well said," Daleina murmured. She'd been searching for words like that for the better part of the last hour. She wondered briefly if Naelin was a better queen than she was. *It doesn't matter if she is*, she thought. *The spirits chose us both.*

"But . . . but the people . . ." Chancellor Xanon stammered.

It was time to end this argument, as queens together. Daleina caught Naelin's eye, then deliberately looked at the two thrones. Together, they both swept past the chancellors, climbed up to the dais, and sat side by side.

"The people can feel what they want to feel," Daleina declared. "We will bury our friend."

There were no more arguments.

THAT SAID, THE FUNERAL FOR CAPTAIN ALET WAS SMALL.

Only Daleina, Naelin, Ven, and Hamon, plus Naelin's children and the wolf, Bayn. Arin had offered to come, but Daleina had told her she didn't have to—Arin had accepted the reprieve with relief. She was ready to move on from all the final farewells and go back to living.

Daleina couldn't let go just yet though.

Alet's body was wrapped in white linens and lay in a red cedar coffin. She wouldn't be buried in the forests of Aratay—she would be returned to her sister in Semo to rest in the mountains.

Daleina wasn't certain how she felt about that. After all, it was Merecot's fault that Alet had killed and therefore her fault that she'd died.

She could forgive Alet.

She couldn't forgive Merecot. Not yet. Maybe not ever.

But Alet deserved to find whatever peace she could, amongst the remains of her own people. Even Daleina's anger couldn't refuse her that.

Each of them took turns speaking, sharing a memory of Alet. Even the children. Erian spoke about how Alet had taught her to punch, and Llor said he'd heard her laugh once and it was a nice laugh. Ven spoke of her skill and her confidence. Naelin told of the regret in Alet's eyes and all the conversations with the oblique warnings that only now made sense.

Daleina went last. There was so much they hadn't known about Alet, including the fact that Merecot was her sister, or that Merecot even had a sister. But today that paled in importance next to what they did know: who they thought she was. "Captain Alet was more than my guard. She was the one who filled the hole left behind when the heirs died, when I lost my friends. She was the friend I talked to, relied on, trusted, and loved, as a new queen who felt so alone."

Hamon took her hand in his. "You were never alone, Daleina."

"And you're not alone now," Naelin said. She took Daleina's other hand, and Erian took hers, then Llor hers, then Ven his, until they were all in a circle around Alet's body, holding hands.

The petals began to fall. And Daleina felt at peace.

# Epilogue

Queen Merecot of Semo stood in front of her window and watched her spirits rip apart a mountain. Two earth spirits, each a hundred feet tall, hurled chunks of rock at each other. Air spirits caught the rocks and propelled them higher and higher, then dropped them so they impacted like meteors on the soft dirt below. Fire spirits blackened the earth, and water spirits loosened the soil until the face of the mountain slid away in mudslides that thundered toward the valley below.

Concentrating, she diverted the rushing mud from the village in the valley by using tiny earth spirits, and she steered the falling rocks away from her people with blasts of freezing wind from ice spirits.

She could keep her people safe.

For now.

But for how much longer? There were too many spirits in Semo, and it was only a matter of time before they tore her country to shreds. And then, how long before the rest of Renthia suffered the same fate? Everything they'd built, all that their people had created, would be destroyed. Their cities would fall. Their lives would be extinguished. Renthia would become worse than the untamed lands.

Damn Daleina. And damn that woman Naelin.

And damn herself too.

"I failed," Merecot said.

"You did," the old woman behind her said. "You allowed your emotions to cloud your judgment. When I was queen, there was no softness in me. I showed no mercy."

Merecot clenched her fists, then unclenched them as she commandeered an air spirit to deflect a boulder away from the castle. It crashed into one of the giant earth spirits. "My sister is *dead*. I have been the opposite of soft and weak. Indeed, I have sacrificed too much."

"How much is too much when the world is at stake?" The old queen rose and tottered to join Merecot at the window. She smelled of dried apples, and her face was as shriveled as rotten fruit. "You have a chance to do what I could not do: make all of this right. Make this stop. Yes, you have had a setback, but you must let it harden you in your purpose."

"The price is too high." She thought of Alet—so very brave. Alet had always been that way, the younger sister watching out for the older, reckless one. When they were little kids, it was a five-year-old Alet who scared away a tree spirit that a six-year-old Merecot had summoned to play with. It was Alet who had taught herself to swim and then insisted Merecot learn. Alet who had stayed behind when their father was dying, who was strong enough to feed him and bathe him and wipe away his tears and his vomit and his filth while Merecot fled first to the academy and then to Semo. And it was Alet whom Merecot had turned to when she realized she'd become queen of a doomed country.

The old queen snorted. "No price is too high. You must be the hero that Renthia doesn't know it needs. You alone have the power, so you alone bear the responsibility. You must embrace your destiny."

"Quit talking like you're some kind of wise old prophet," Merecot said. The former queen of Semo was neither wise nor a prophet; she was merely old. And she was becoming increasingly more annoying. It would do her well to remember she lived only because of Merecot's protection. "You could have done it—you had the power once—but you failed far worse than I. Instead, you allowed *this* to happen." She waved her hand at the window, at the spirits whose rage could be slaked only by destruction.

The old queen was quiet for a moment. When she spoke again, her voice was softer and kinder. "You're right–I am not wise. But I do have the benefit of hindsight that you, in your youth, do not. I see in you a chance to right old wrongs, to undo past mistakes, not only those done by me, but those done by every queen of Renthia that has come before. You can make the world a better place, if you dare."

Outside, lightning struck, and a field caught fire. Merecot instantly forced the water spirits to make it rain, extinguishing the flames. She then flung yet another boulder back at the earth spirits. *We can't survive like this. If I can fix the world . . . then I must.* "I dare."

The old queen patted Merecot's arm in approval, and Merecot felt a rush of warmth. Her own mother had never quite approved of her. It was nice to have someone notice that Merecot made the right choices, the difficult choices.

Her resolve strengthened, Merecot reached out with her will and forced the warring spirits to turn away from one another. They'd had enough playtime for one day. It was time to let the frightened people come out of their homes and live their lives. She'd let the spirits spend more of their rage tomorrow. "So that's it then? I try again, but this time to remove *two* queens of Aratay?"

The old queen smiled. "It will not be difficult now. The spirits will not stand for two queens of the same land. Soon they will see. All you must do is remove the queens' protector."

She was startled. She hadn't thought Champion Ven was that much of a threat. He had surprised her in the grove, of course, but now that she knew to watch for him, he would not be a threat twice. "You mean the champion?"

The old queen laughed. "Oh, my sweet, innocent child, no."

"Then who?"

"I should think it obvious. You must kill the wolf."

In the heart of Aratay, within the palace, the wolf called Bayn padded into Queen Naelin's bedchamber. She was sleeping soundly, with her children tucked on either side of her. The boy had dropped his stuffed squirrel toy on the floor. It lay in a pool of moonlight.

Gently, Bayn picked up the toy in his jaws and placed it next to the boy. He then circled the bed and nudged the girl's arm back onto the mattress. She murmured in her sleep and curled up tighter against her mother.

There were more of the soft, strange humans to protect now, but that was good. It was better to have a pack. Before this, he had been alone too long.

In truth, his memory of what came "before" was fuzzy. He was aware that he wasn't like other wolves. In fact, he wasn't certain he'd always been a wolf, but that didn't bother him. He knew his purpose now:

Keep them safe. At all costs.

# Acknowledgments

A couple years ago, I was at a writing retreat in the woods, and I was marveling at how the light hit the tangle of trees . . . and I tripped over my own feet, fell on my face, and cut my lip. In that moment, Renthia, with all its bloodthirsty nature spirits, was born. Trees + blood = this book.

So I'd like to thank those trees for the somewhat painful inspiration.

I'd also like to thank my magnificent agent Andrea Somberg, who has believed in me from the start, my amazing editor David Pomerico, and my fantastic publicist Caroline Perny, as well as Jennifer Brehl, Priyanka Krishnan, Pam Jaffee, Angela Craft, Shawn Nicholls, Amanda Rountree, Virginia Stanley, Chris Connolly, and all the other wonderful people at HarperCollins who helped bring Renthia to life.

And thank you with all my heart to my husband, my children, and all my family and friends. You are all magic, and I love you so much.

# About the Author

S arah Beth Durst is the author of thirteen fantasy books for adults, teens, and children, including *The Queen of Blood, Drink Slay Love*, and *Journey Across the Hidden Islands*. She won an ALA Alex Award and a Mythopoeic Fantasy Award, and has been a finalist for SFWA's Andre Norton Award three times. A graduate of Princeton University, she lives in Stony Brook, New York, with her husband, her children, and her ill-mannered cat. Visit her at www.sarahbethdurst.com.